THE WATCHERS

by Carol Van Drie

Arlington, Tennessee 38002

For my grandchildren
Kaylee, Mark and Rebecca
who are a continuous source of joy as well
as a constant living, breathing reminder of
God's perfect love.

VATICAN CITY - Believing that the universe may contain alien life does not contradict a faith in God, the Vatican's chief astronomer said in an interview published Tuesday. The Rev. Jose Gabriel Funes, the Jesuit director of the Vatican Observatory, was quoted as saying the vastness of the universe means it is possible there could be other forms of life outside Earth, even intelligent ones.

Associated Press: updated 10/25/2007 5:56:17 PM ET

Most Americans Believe Alien Life is Possible, Study Shows

by Tariq Malik, Staff Writer

Date: 31 May 2005 Time: 04:12 PM ET

While most depictions of extraterrestrials are confined to science fiction, nearly two-thirds of Americans believe that some form of alien life exists somewhere in the universe, according to a new survey.

The telephone poll, which questioned 1,000 Americans, found that 60 percent of those surveyed believe extraterrestrial life exists on other planets.

Of those who believed, most agreed that they would be "excited and hopeful" upon learning of the discovery of extraterrestrial life while 90 percent of them said Earth should reply to any message from another planet, the poll reported. At least two-thirds of those polled who said they did not believe in extraterrestrial life also stated that Earth should respond to an alien signal if the situation arose, the survey reported.

Conducted by the Center for Survey and Research Analysis at the University of Connecticut, the telephone poll surveyed 523 women and 477 men above the age of 18 between April 20 and May 2. The survey was commissioned by the National Geographic Channel, which debuted its television special 'Extraterrestrial' on

May 30, in association with the Search for Extraterrestrial Intelligence (SETI) Institute.

"It is quite likely that there is life elsewhere in our galaxy, and there's a real possibility that we will find evidence of intelligent extraterrestrial life by the year 2025," said Seth Shostak, senior astronomer for SETI, who appeared in 'Extraterrestrial.'

*   *   *

80 Million Americans Believe in UFOs

If you believe in UFOs, you may be in better company than you think.

Thirty-six percent of Americans, about 80 million people, believe UFOs exist, and a tenth believe they have spotted one, a new National Geographic poll shows.

Seventeen percent said they did not believe in UFOs, or Unidentified Flying Objects, and nearly half of those surveyed said they were unsure. Perhaps reflective of today's political climate, there appears to be near-universal skepticism of government — nearly four-fifths of respondents said they believe the government has concealed information about UFOs from the public.

The first angel sounded, and there followed hail and fire mingled with blood, and they were cast upon the earth: and the third part of trees was burnt up, and all the green grass was burnt up.

And the second angel sounded, and as it were a great mountain burning with fire was cast into the sea: and the third part of the sea became blood;

And the third part of the creatures which were in the sea, and had life, died; and the third part of the ships were destroyed.

Revelation 8:7-9

Prologue

"At long last, after watching the human race for generations, allowing them glimpses of our brilliant space crafts, creating crop circles, giant stone structures and the pyramids, the time has arrived. Select abductions that have been flawlessly carried out have grown awareness. Now we can go forth and execute the rest of our mission."

The enormous eyes of those present were all focused intently on the speaker. Shoulder to shoulder, the beings would have covered five football fields.

The leader continued, "Through the ages we have followed the earthborn carefully, watching and waiting. Now my chosen followers, come with me, come with me home."

Sometime in the future…

CHAPTER 1

Bianca Giovanna thrilled at the sound of her own voice; her untrained, natural soprano nearly matching Kiri Te Kanawa's note for note. As she plunged her hands into the dishwater she imagined them reaching out to the operatic audience. *I'm nuts, I've really gone nuts.*

A glance out the window revealed her real world and it had turned threatening.

"Dominic, honey, you better mow the lawn before this storm hits. It looks like we're in for a big one."

She watched through the window as her dog Toby sniffed a crazy figure eight in the grass searching for just the right spot. When she glanced back at the sky, charcoal and black clouds roiled above the trees. She picked up the remote for her kitchen TV and switched to the weather channel. Odd, the graphic at the bottom of the screen didn't indicate anything unusual about local weather conditions. The cheerful forecaster was pointing to the symbol for scattered showers over Salt Lake City. Not much information there. It would be ten minutes before the local weather information was broadcast.

Dominic yelled down from the upstairs office, "I'll just wait for it to blow over and mow after I do the bills!"

Bianca rolled her eyes. *Typical—just let the grass grow longer than everyone else's on the block.*

She sighed and tried to focus on finishing the breakfast dishes, but could not take her eyes off the ominous sky. Suddenly a warning alarm screamed raucously from the TV, startling her. She turned to the broadcast, the weather news crawling along the bottom of the screen. *High winds... tornado watch... severe thunderstorms expected for all Leavenworth county...* Bianca told herself this was just normal for Kansas in August, but her throat tightened and her stomach lurched uneasily.

An image of tree limbs hurtling through the air and landing on her tiny dog drove her to rush out to the backyard deck. "Toby!" she yelled, but a sudden jet-engine roar of wind drowned out her voice. Sweeping away the long black hair whipping into her eyes, she called out again. "Toby!" A lawn chair smacked the back of her legs and tumbled out of sight. Frantic, she scanned the yard but saw nothing. *Oh, Lord please... please...* "Toby! Toby!" Again, the wind sucked away her words as swiftly as they left her mouth.

Shivering, she wrapped her arms around herself. The short-sleeved polo shirt and white shorts that were comfortable just moments ago felt strangely inadequate now. Day turned into night as if a huge theatrical switch had been flipped, making it difficult for her eyes to adjust to the sudden darkness. Solar yard lamps gave off an eerie glow as she stumbled across the yard. "Toby! Toby!" Her pulse pounded wildly in her temples and her mouth was stone dry. It was like a dream—a nightmare in which her movements seemed oddly disconnected from reality. At last she spotted silky tan and black fur vibrating in a corner, butt up. Toby was intent on digging under the fence, oblivious to the storm. A golf ball-sized hailstone skipped off Bianca's shoulder. A moment later, hail rained down furiously.

Hurriedly making her way to Toby, she shielded her forehead in a futile attempt to protect her face. She flinched as the thin layer of ice bit into her bare feet. Although it could not have taken more than a few moments, it seemed an eternity before she was finally able to reach the dog. Just as she bent to sweep him into her arms, a huge ball of ice smashed into his little body. With a strangled yelp Toby went down, all four legs splayed out from underneath him. "Toby! My little baby!" Numb to the pounding ice, she quickly scooped him up, cradling his limp body under her shirt and turned toward the safety of the house. A sharp crack of thunder reverberated inside her skull and she glanced back to see a bloodied hail stone roll into the garden. "Don't worry, that didn't really hurt," she crooned to Toby. Her legs turned to water. Trying to hold on to Toby she watched the ground tilt away from her as she toppled over face first, her eyes focusing on the smashed flowers of her garden a few yards away.

Chilled by a bed of bloody ice, Bianca felt Toby's warm little body still snugged up against her. Her vision narrowed to a deep and dark tunnel as thoughts were jumbled into bits and pieces. From a vast hollow distance, she heard Dominic calling her name between strains of LaBoheme. Then sight and sound faded to black.

CHAPTER 2

Alana was startled awake by the ringtone of her phone. Her law office had just issued new tablet/phone devices and she was still trying to figure out how to use the thing. At least she had transferred her contacts correctly... or so she hoped. Her caller ID showed her sister's smiling face as the low battery signal beeped. *How could the battery be so low? It was plugged into the charger; was the electricity out? And why is Bianca calling me so early on a Saturday morning? She knows I have a huge court case to prepare for on Monday.*

She fumbled with the touch screen answer-on button and feared she disconnected it.

"Bianca, what do you want, you nut?"

She heard an unfamiliar voice. "Hel—hello? Is this

Bianca's sister Alana?"

She rechecked the phone. Bianca's number and photo icon stared back at her, so who *was* this? "Yes, this is Bianca's sister." Alana's face instantly flushed hot.

"There's been an accident." The woman sounded out of breath, distraught. "Your sister—"

Alana bolted upright in bed, her heart slamming like a jackhammer against her chest, her free hand clutching the comforter. Dread flooded her gut like acid. "What? What's happened to Bianca?"

"I'm so sorry, your sister—she's—she died. Her husband as well."

Dead? Bianca dead? "Wha—who *is* this? What do you mean Bianca and Dom are dead?"

"I'm sorry, Alana. My name is June Blythe. I live across the street from your sister. There was this freak hailstorm. The destruction was enormous. My husband and I ran over as soon as we could when we heard the screaming. When we found them… Dominic was on top of Bianca. It looked as if he tried to protect her. Even their little dog was killed. I am so sorry."

Alana moved a hand to cover her mouth as the room became a swirling mix of pastel images. Bile rose in her throat as the woman went on.

"I—I called an ambulance, but the whole town, I guess the whole state is a mess! We don't have electricity and getting a GPS signal was close to impossible. All communication systems must be overloaded. I tried through the night to reach you. We've heard the governor has already declared a state of emergency. The paramedics took close to an hour to get to your sister's house, but Bianca and Dominic were already gone. They said there was nothing they could have done."

Dropping her phone on the bed, Alana ran for the bathroom, barely making it to the toilet before she retched. After pulling herself upright, she stumbled back to her bed on shaky legs, blindly groping for the phone through scattered legal briefs scattered on the bed. "Are you still there?"

"Yes, dear, I'm still here. Are you all right?"

"No! I'm not all right! Oh Lord, Lord, Lord..." Rocking on the bed Alana couldn't stop the tears as shock and grief constricted her ribcage, strangling every intake of breath.

"Alana, can you get here? What can I do? I'll do anything I can to help."

"I'm on my way. Just keep her cell—"Alana stopped mid-sentence when it dawned on her what she'd just said. She was telling someone to use her sister's phone, a phone Bianca would never use again. Her stomach felt like it was in a blender. "I'll call or text that number if I need to contact you. Give me your cell number just in case." Alana rummaged around and found a pen to take down June's number. When they finally disconnected, she realized she'd forgotten to thank her.

Grabbing a suitcase from her closet, Alana forced herself to concentrate on packing. Her colorfully decorated room, always a soothing haven, seemed cold and foreign to her now.

She quickly showered, but when she tried to use the blow dryer, she realized the electricity was out. She was so distracted cramming for her court case she hardly noticed the sounds of a storm that hit in the night. It must have knocked out the power after she'd gone to sleep.

She dragged a comb through her wet hair and squeezed off a few pumps of hairspray. Throwing on a pair of Calvin Klein jeans and a white button-down blouse, she tossed a navy scarf around her neck. Grabbing a long cardigan sweater-coat, she pulled up the telescopic handle of her suitcase.

Wheeling the heavy bag down the hall, Alana dialed the airlines with her free hand. She knew there was a direct flight from Albany to Kansas City, but every call produced discordant tones followed by *all circuits are busy, please try your call again.*

A sob crowded its way up her throat. She gripped her neck trying to stop its progression. *I can't cry now. I have to get to Kansas. This is no time to fall apart.*

Once in the garage, she threw her suitcase in the trunk of the car. She'd given up trying to reach the airlines so she'd just have to take her chances. She hit the garage door opener out of habit, but it didn't move, obviously.

Jumping out of the car, she yanked the manual rope pull-release and grabbed the garage door handle at the bottom, heaving it upwards. She almost lost her grip when she saw what she couldn't believe. Was that snow?

The world before her was slush and ice covered despite it being the dog days of summer. The scene was so surreal her head swam. Stranded vehicles littered the street.

A hailstorm in upstate New York in mid-August that leaves this much ice on the ground? How could that possibly be? Get a hold of yourself, Alana. Focus.

Her resolve to stop biting her nails vanished as she gnawed on a fingernail down to the quick. Another surge of grief threatened her fragile hold on her composure as she pulled her cell phone out and dialed again. All local airports were closed. With herculean effort, she stopped herself from pitching her phone in utter frustration. A shiver ran through her body from head to toe as a chilling breeze swept through the garage.

Think Alana, think. She couldn't drive in that mess with her electric-powered Chrysler sedan even if it did have all wheel drive. There probably wasn't a place to recharge it anyway. Maybe she could borrow her neighbors SUV.

As she looked out, the sky seethed and churned with angry pewter clouds. She quickly grabbed a pair of boots in the garage and pulled them on. Climbing back in the car, she navigated her way out of the garage onto the apron. As she jumped out to close the garage door, she slipped on the ice, but managed to right herself with a jolt. She headed to the last house on the block, the car fishtailing all the way.

Her once familiar neighborhood took on a weird disaster movie staging. Trees and debris besieged the street in every direction. Nothing was familiar, nothing looked real. She winced at the acrid odor of smoke.

How could this possibly have happened? How could there be ice and snow in August?

Alana ran up to her neighbor's door and pounded hard enough to feel a jagged pain in her hand. As the door slowly opened a crack, she stammered breathlessly, "Seth, M—Mindy, it's Alana. I—I—need your help." Seth opened the door wide while gripping a shotgun with his wife standing tentatively behind him. He set the gun aside and pulled her into the foyer.

"What are you doing out there? I don't think it's safe."

"I can't worry about that now," her words came out in a rush. "I need to trade cars. Here are the keys to mine. It's electric—brand new—barely three months old. My—my sister Bianca and her husband were killed," she blurted through the tears. "They live in Kansas—I have to get there but the airports are closed. I don't know if my car would make it with all the power outages."

Seth told Mindy to get their car keys. "Is there anything else we can do?"

"Not right now. Thank you—I have to get to Bianca to—" She let the rest of her sentence trail away. Alana told them she had no idea exactly what had happened, but it definitely had something to do with a storm.

Seth's shock registered on his face, "You mean there was a storm in Kansas too?"

Of course. Two storms. In her shock, Alana hadn't considered this... *two devastating storms in two different locations.* The reality of it churned in her stomach. "Yes, I guess so," she barely whispered.

Amid protests about her leaving them her new, luxury sedan, Alana threw her things into the back of their Jeep and thanked them both. She punched her sister's address into the GPS and headed toward Route 7.

Once she maneuvered onto Route 7, she saw the beginnings of a cleanup effort, but the going was still erratic. Sometimes she was able to go the speed limit, but often she had to sit in traffic or devise alternate routes due to accidents, downed power lines or other mishaps that blocked the roads. The disjointed *recalculating* blared so often from the GPS that she eventually shut the audio off altogether.

While the Jeep sat unmoving in what had turned into a highway parking lot, Alana decided to send a text to Patti, one of her co-workers at the law firm, but instead of answering the text, Patti phoned. As Alana explained her absence, Patti interrupted, "Alana, Alana, don't worry about a thing. You just take care of family matters. Probably no one will be in the office even on Monday, it's such a disaster. I'll tell everyone for you—and Alana, I'm so sorry about your sister and brother-in-law."

This small gesture almost caused Alana to have a total melt down, but she was able to end the call before she dissolved into a nonfunctioning puddle of grief.

She turned on the satellite radio only to hear the stunning news that the freak storms had occurred nationwide. Damage to U.S. crops, forests and other vegetation was immeasurable. Fires had devastated tens of millions of acres due to lightning strikes, and power outages were affecting enormous swaths of the populace. It was estimated that the death toll could be in the millions.

With slow deep breaths, Alana tried to calm herself. The 1300-mile drive ahead of her could be hazardous and she needed to stay focused. With detached calm, the announcer reported that the President would be holding a news conference shortly, most likely to declare martial law. This newest revelation brought Alana to the edge. Her fingers ached from gripping the steering wheel and fear shot tiny shards of ice through her veins as her thoughts raced.

How treacherous will the roads be? What if I can't get to Kansas at all? Could this mean the end of the world? She suddenly recalled the Book of Revelation describing such events, but she had never given much credence to it before. Now she wished she had. Digging deep to find the courage to make it through, she called out to God. "I need you Lord, I need your strength now. Jehovah the Lord is my strength and he maketh my feet like hinds feet and will make me to walk in high places."

Even before she finished the prayer, she felt a steady calm deep in her very core. It gave her renewed strength to hold herself together.

After a deep cleansing sigh, she pressed on. With no idea what to expect along the way, she was resolute in her determination to take care of her family's remains. She had to. There was no one else.

CHAPTER 3

Alana had driven almost five hundred miles, but it felt like a million. Her hands were sore from clenching the steering wheel and her back stiff from the uncomfortable seat. Her hair was limp and flyaway, prompting her to finally pull it up into a messy bun. Her eyelids felt like lead was weighing them down with each blink. The night had become oppressive, like a dark tarp thrown over her world. It was time for a break. Although she was still east of Indianapolis, she knew she had to stop for the night. Voice command gave her some options for nearby hotels and she took the next exit, only to find it dark with a makeshift sign that read, CLOSED DUE TO POWER OUTAGE. She sat in the parking lot and dialed other hotels in the area. Still nothing.

She merged back on to the interstate in hopes of finding

a place with power. The Jeep back-up battery needed charging and the sounds of her stomach grumbling reminded her it was time to stop, though the idea of food didn't appeal to her in the least. A few minutes down the road, her headlights picked up a gas/charging station with a sign that read GENERATOR IN USE. She sighed as she turned into the overcrowded parking lot. Eyeing the long lines for gas and recharging, she figured she could park the Jeep while she went inside to eat. She squinted in the glare of the cold, lifeless fluorescent lighting as she passed through the doors of the store. Business was booming, with animated chatter coming from the many patrons.

A short, dark-skinned man enthusiastically greeted new customers, repeatedly reminding them he was the owner. He assured everyone who entered the bell-clanging double glass doors that he was grateful for their patience and that every cash register was open.

Two hours later the hybrid gas/electric Jeep charged and gassed up, she left the station. Fighting fatigue, she drove for another hour searching for a hotel with a vacancy. Eventually, she gave up and pulled off at a rest stop. There were no lights on inside the small building containing the restrooms, but she could see a cardboard sign secured to the front window that said they were working.

Streetlights illuminated the tractor-trailer filled parking lot with a creepy greenish hue that clung to everything like a thin layer of ghostly goo. She parked directly under one of them, figuring ghostly goo was safer than total darkness.

With the engine off, Alana almost immediately felt a chill as she dug around the back of the SUV for her cardigan. She was greatly relieved to find that Seth and Mindy kept a stash of emergency gear that included rain slickers, several reflective blankets, rechargeable flashlights, and other camping essentials. She silently thanked God that Seth and Mindy were avid campers and hikers.

Drained, she struggled to improvise a sleeping place in the back of the Jeep. Finishing up outside, with the back hatch open and flashlight in hand, she made a makeshift bed—then, crawling into the back, she closed the hatch behind her. Now, without any distractions, her thoughts ran wild.

One million were dead with predictions going as high as two million or more. Remembering the loss of Bianca gave her a fresh punch in the stomach. The emptiness the future held was too daunting to face as new grief welled up inside her with an intensity that made breathing a struggle. She didn't know how she'd ever stand the pain.

Why God? Why did you take her away from me? Tears flowed with an ease that alarmed her as she surrendered to a grief that encased her body like a shroud. Eventually, she wept herself dry and wilted into a dreamless sleep.

Alana awakened to the sound of rapping on the back glass. Disoriented, she sat up and tried to collect herself when she saw a figure at the driver's side window. Reality returned in a bitter rush as she glanced at her cell phone. It was 3:15 a.m.

Green fluorescence framed the silhouette of a man as the knocking persisted. Through the fogged windows she couldn't see his face. Heart thudding in her ears, she crawled toward the front seat as her internal alarms went off. Or was she was being paranoid? Maybe he just needed help. She squeezed up through the center console and into the driver's seat. "Yes?" she shouted through the closed window.

"Yeah, hi! Ah, I was wondering if maybe you had anything to drink? I ran out and thought—" His sentence trailed off.

Her fight-or-flight radar kicked in and she made two decisions instantly. There was no way she would open her window or door and the second he left, she was going to drive out of there.

"Gee, I hope you understand, but I'm just not going to open the window. I'm really sorry, but I'm not comfortable with that. Maybe one of the truckers could help you."

Her heart continued pounding inside her head like muffled kettledrums. Hands became ice. *How did he take the rebuff?* she wondered.

He turned his head slightly away from her. Wiping some of the condensation off the window, she could see he had a goatee and long side-burns. His greasy, slicked-back hair that curled over the back of his neck was framed by a halogen halo. He wore a faded, Bon Jovi T-shirt, a leather jacket and soiled jeans. There was something about his body language that made her gut turn to soup.

Keeping his gaze turned away he said, "I see… I guess I understand. Oh well–can't blame a guy for tryin.'" He turned toward the back of the Jeep.

Alana realized she didn't have her keys. As she started to crawl back to get them, she heard knocking on the window again. This time the *tap tap tap* had a distinct metallic sound.

She turned back around to face the barrel of a gun pointing directly at her head.

CHAPTER 4

Heart hammering wildly, Alana slowly pushed opened the Jeep's door. Her thoughts scattered, refusing to coalesce into anything resembling a plan of escape.

"That's it, nice and easy and don't try anything stupid or I'll blow your pretty little head off without even blinkin'—got it?"

Sliding off the seat, Alana nodded mutely as she put her feet on the ground. Grabbing her arm with one hand and twisting it behind her, he used the other to jam the gun into the small of her back.

"You just come with me real quiet and you won't get hurt. I'm gonna put you in your place you worthless whore. You think you're so high and mighty, you—" He finished with a string of filthy epithets.

Although he was taller than her five foot eight frame and definitely outweighed her 130 pounds, he wasn't a huge man. Nevertheless, judging by the way he was able to lift her off her feet with one arm, she was no match for him even *without* a gun. Alana realized her only option was to talk, to try to reason with him. Her mind raced, trying to come up with anything remotely conciliatory when she suddenly realized something he'd just said didn't make any sense. He acted as if he *knew* her. If she did, she had no memory. None at all.

"You didn't see me back there at the gas station. Your nose was stuck too high up in the air. You ain't so high now, are ya? Are ya?" He jabbed the gun roughly into her back.

She answered in uneven gasps, "Li—listen—I wasn't being rude to you or anyone. I'm heading to my sister's. I just found out she was killed. I was upset. You mistook my grief for being rude. Look, I'm a defense attorney. I don't look down my nose at anyone."

He hesitated for a beat. *Have I gotten through to him? Oh Lord, let him believe me.*

She didn't have to wait for her answer. He grabbed a fistful of hair, jerking her head back so forcefully she cried out. Leaning close he hissed in her ear, "I said be quiet, you lyin' whore! Figures you'd have some stupid excuse. Women like you are all alike. Waitin' for some Brad Pitt kinda guy and sticking your noses up in the air at the rest of us. Well, your high and mighty days are over! Now keep walkin' and shut up!"

With her peripheral vision, Alana could see the vapor from his rank breath. He smelled like an ashtray and sweat. Tears slipped down her cheeks. As they approached his rig, one thought overrode all others: *If he takes me in there, I'll never come out alive.*

The gun poking into her spine made any thought of escaping impossible. She prayed silently, *Father, please protect me. I'm so frightened. Please give me your strength.*

Shoving her in front of the rig's door, he ordered, "Open it!" She grasped the door lever and struggled to pull it out when finally it gave way and the door opened. Scooping his free arm under her legs, he heaved her into the cab. Alana couldn't help but think of the rig as her coffin.

He told her to open the door in the back of the cab between the driver and passenger's seats. Again, she obeyed and was immediately assaulted by the putrid smell of rotting food, sweat, and stale cigarette smoke.

Powerful hands thrust her through the opening and she found herself face down on a grimy mattress. She could hear him fumbling with something and then dim lights lit the interior. Before she could get her bearings, he yanked her head back by the hair and put a knife to her throat.

"Now you're gonna do just exactly what I say and I might not slit your throat. But if you make a peep, I'm gonna carve you a new windpipe. Now turn around and face me, real slow."

As she turned, the razor sharp blade bit into her skin and Alana felt a trickle of blood run hot and slow down her neck. His breathing became rapid, as he seemed to take pleasure in seeing her bleed. When she was flat on her back facing him, he proceeded to methodically slice open her shirt, one button at a time, his eyes never wavering from hers.

Terrified but grimly accepting her fate, Alana readied herself to meet her Creator, praying softly, "I love you Jesus, I love you Jesus, I love you Jesus."

Ebony eyes blazing with fury widened to twice their size. "STOP IT! STOP THAT!" he screamed.

Alana repeated the incantation over and over until he backhanded her, splitting her lip and sending her head into the side of the cab wall. She willed her mind away from the pain and prayed louder. *I love you Jesus. I love you Jesus.*

"I SAID STOP THAT!"

He backhanded her again with a force that made the cab shudder, but she continued to pray. *I love you Jesus.*

Suddenly, she felt like a third party to what was happening, like she was looking down at them both as he hit her repeatedly. His enraged demands that she cease praying seemed to come from far away. She watched herself calmly put up an arm up to fend off a blow. Then, staring boldly straight into his eyes with calm conviction, she annunciated every word, "I. Love. You. Jesus!"

Abruptly, he stopped, his hand poised above her

for another strike. His face registered shock, uncertainty. And then, terror filled his black eyes. "Get out! Get out!" Cursing, he grabbed her by the front of what was left of her blouse, pulled her upright and started pushing her roughly through the opening. Alana opened the cab door and fell out, hitting the ground hard, scraping her hands and her knees tearing the fabric of her jeans. Scrambling to her feet she ran to the Jeep, pumping her legs harder than she'd ever done before. Once inside the Jeep, she grabbed her keys from the pillow and jammed them into the ignition. Pebbles from the asphalt grinding into her palms, Alana took hold of the steering wheel, threw the Jeep into drive and screeched tires out of the rest area.

CHAPTER 5

In the tiny fishing village of Qoliquoli in the Philippines, Semisi Rialon brushed back the wisp of short black hair that fell onto his forehead, trying unsuccessfully to avoid getting fish slime on his face as he did so. Brilliant sunlight whitewashed the colors of his surroundings like an overexposed photograph. From under a battered straw hat sweat trickled down his brow and spilled to the ground. Earlier, a chance encounter with a pitted fragment of mirror hanging from a vendor's pole in the market place startled him as he walked through town. He was surprised to see such an old man in the fractured reflection. The deep creases at the corners of his eyes made him look as if he were perpetually squinting and his skin resembled worn, brown leather. For some reason, observing these things made the ache in his back much more pronounced.

Semisi fished every day to keep his family fed, often from sunrise until well past sunset. He was constantly exhausted, as he was this morning. As he was every morning. He supported his wife, her mother, her sister and his three children with what he caught and sold at market.

Every day he made his trek along the shores of Suva City where beaches were littered with trash. He walked past homes that were mere shanties, makeshift structures that were clones of his own. Bent over and weary, he made his way to his boat barely conscious of each footfall.

Today was Semisi's birthday. He wondered if this was the cause of his foul mood and concluded it probably was—a reminder he was another day closer to the time when he would be unable to support his family.

He yelled at a stray dog to *scat!* Many mangy mongrels with protruding ribs constantly followed him in search of food, and he considered them nothing more than large, furry parasites. He hated them as much as he did the stench of dead fish and the rotting garbage that were endemic to his home, his life, his entire being.

Semisi was almost at his boat, impatient to head out. The sooner he was out in deep water, the sooner he'd be able to start fishing. The day before, even though he'd placed his nets carefully before sunrise, the size of the catch was disappointingly far from sufficient. He must do better today.

A swirling flock of seagulls circled and squawked in the air above him scavenging for a meal, perhaps some bait or fish scraps. Nearby, a great-billed Heron eyed him warily.

With efficient movements born of repetition, Semisi prepared his boat. His gnarled arthritic hands lifted the starter lever, then tugged hard at the motor's pull. The old engine sputtered. Semisi shook his head in disgust. He lived in fear of the day it would no longer start at all.

After tinkering with it for a few minutes, he coaxed the motor to life. Fishing gear safely stowed, he removed the hat that provided him his only protection from the relentless sun and swung the boat around toward the open sea. Long ago he'd had the misfortune of losing a hat to the wind; he wasn't about to repeat it.

Hours later, he was fishing in waters he knew were too far from the beach for his small boat, the shoreline now a mere scratch in the distance. He hoped this time when he brought up his net he'd have something worthwhile... maybe even an octopus. That would fetch a good price at market. Yes an octopus.

A sudden roar from the west made Semisi turn. To his horror, he saw a giant wall of blue-gray water twenty stories high and a hundred times as wide coming toward him. Semisi gasped in terror. His little boat tipped, took on water as the sea beneath him churned. A deafening howl filled his ears as the colossal wave arced above him. The last cogent thought he had was how curiously fine the mist was that gently filtered down from the giant wall of water that swallowed him whole.

CHAPTER 6

His own snoring jarred Mitch Abbott awake. He was mildly surprised to find that he was not in his bed, but fully dressed in his *La-Z-Boy*. *I must have passed out last night.* Gingerly he sat up, assessing the damage. When he ran his tongue around his mouth it was cotton dry and disgusting. The underside of his eyelids felt like a cat had used them for scratching posts.

Raking his hand through his hair he could swear a small man with a sledgehammer was thumping the inside of his skull. A little hair of the dog could help solve that problem along with a few dozen aspirin. He needed to silence the brain piercing sirens and he needed a drink. He reached for the bottle of *Jim Beam* and simultaneously slammed the window shut. He brought the bottle to his lips and took the last swig.

Sitting in a rumpled dress shirt and trousers, Mitch decided his current condition required a few things, namely a shower, aspirin and more booze. Easing himself off the recliner, he tested his legs. A little wobbly, but they would hold him up. Shivering; he looked around for his jacket and checked his smartphone for the time. Not quite nine-thirty a.m. He tried to switch on the table lamp, but it wasn't working. A string of curses rolled across his tongue. He remembered hearing thunder in the middle of the night— or was it this morning? Maybe the electricity was out. He stumbled over to the TV to grab the remote. No sound, no picture, no electricity.

He tossed the remote and let loose more profanity, placing his palms on his temples. *Okay, next thing on the agenda: get some aspirin or a chainsaw to remove this head, anything to stop the relentless throbbing.*

As he searched for relief, tormented memories snaked their way into his head. "No, no, NO! Not now! Great now I'm talking to myself," he announced to his empty house.

He forced himself to block the thoughts as he gave up on aspirin and searched the kitchen for another bottle of whiskey. Nothing. All he found in the refrigerator was a molded piece of cheddar cheese, a bottle of soda and some water. He grabbed the jug of water and gulped it down too quickly. Nausea swept over him, his head was killing him and he offended himself with the smell of his own body odor. *Note to self—aspirin and then a shower.*

He bumped his way down the hall toward the bathroom. *Gotta pee like a racehorse—*

After he relieved himself, he found a bottle of aspirin and poured a fistful into his palm then chased them down with more water. It seemed that no matter how much alcohol he consumed, those thoughts—those haunting terrible memories were constantly crouching in wait, ready to spring into action.

He glanced at his hands and noticed they were shaking as if he had palsy.

I need another drink. He ditched the water and frantically began searching. Pay dirt! Under the sink was a pint he hadn't opened. After three huge gulps, a hiss escaped between clenched teeth.

He felt almost human again following a quick shower and change of clothes. Wiping away the fog on the mirror, he took stock of his face. Absently rubbing his chin, he tried to examine his image in the medicine cabinet's mirror but it was so dim he could barely see his reflection. Odd it should still be so dark out. Focusing back on his image, he tried to convince himself that his twenty-something face didn't look vastly beyond its years. Boiled reddened eyes with chocolate irises sported puffy bags underneath, but surely they'd be gone by lunchtime. A quick pull of his fingers through his short hair and an attempt to spike it into a semblance of some sort of style lasted only seconds. *Enough of this. I need food and booze, and not necessarily in that order.*

He started down the hallway toward the front door. Why were those sirens still going? *That must be one monster of a fire.* He tripped over a shoe that never made it back to the closet. His place would be nice if he wasn't such a slob. *Another note to self: hire housekeeper.*

Overlooking the mess, he knew the house had good "bones" as people like him in the real estate business would say. That was the benefit of being an agent. You got first dibs on hidden treasures. So why did he feel like King Loser of the World?

As he stood in the middle of his open living room area, he paused for a second and inspected his surroundings. Everything he surveyed spoke of success. His designer black and white leather furniture staged by a professional decorator was top of the line. Shortly after buying the house, he installed high-end upgrades, imported hardwood floors, commercial grade appliances and granite countertops in the kitchen as well as each bathroom. He spared no money on a sound system piped into every room that totally rocked. All of this—his place, his expensive suits and luxury vehicle, screamed success. Yet every day he woke, he was more depressed than the day before.

Since that thought brought him too close to introspection a physical shake of his head symbolically halted his mental trek down that path. He tried to focus on the matters at hand as he continued preparations to go to the office. Before any of that though, he had to stock up on more Jim Beam and grab a fast food breakfast.

Then something dawned on him, *I wonder if the office has electricity?* He stood still with his keys in his hand. *So what? I have to go in and get my media card anyway.*

Minutes later, he opened the front door and froze. The entire horizon glowed against a menacing sky no matter what direction he looked. Fire trucks and emergency vehicle sirens were sounding non-stop. It reminded him of the old classic scene from *Gone with the Wind* when Atlanta burned down. Only this was no movie set.

CHAPTER 7

Daniel Kelsey sat hunched over his tablet PC at the University of West Florida in Fort Walton Beach. Empty candy wrappers and chip bags littered the desk and floor around him, a testament to his version of the USDA's diet pyramid: salt balanced with sweet, balanced with lots of greasy foods. His fingers flew effortlessly around the virtual hologram keyboard hunt-and-peck style, but produced few results. He was stumped. His glasses slid down his sweaty nose for the umpteenth time and he pushed them up thoughtlessly. Tipping his head back, he wracked his brain for alternate ways to pose the same question. *What was the probability of several catastrophic weather events happening simultaneously? What was going on, strictly meteorologically speaking, was huge.* Why wasn't he finding anything on it?

One entire eastern wall of windows to Daniel's left allowed the relentless Floridian sun to steam up the 24x14 lab room. The tinted windows were useless against the direct Florida sunlight, no less in a room with the air-conditioning on the fritz.

Blacktopped lab tables with natural stained wood legs were lined up behind him eight deep. The lab table Daniel worked on was strewn with evidence of his day's work.

Three different e-readers propped up on stands displayed respectively an almanac, an encyclopedia, and an meteorological reference book. As a student pursuing his Masters in Marine biology, studying global weather patterns was essential to his research and although he didn't consider himself an expert, his knowledge concerning climate activity was extensive. He pulled up several radar and satellite weather maps and checked the tropical intra-seasonal oscillation data, but what he saw made no sense. It looked like this event simply couldn't have happened. Even studying shifting weather patterns didn't offer up any clues.

As he labored in the sweltering room, he tried to get his head around the idea that a hailstorm could have such magnitude that it could dump trillions upon trillions of gallons of water in the form of hailstones back on the earth. *There simply isn't enough moisture in the atmosphere for it to occur,* he reasoned.

Wondering vacantly how long it would take to get the electricity back on, he marveled that his tablet device was able to pick up a GPS signal. Wireless Internet-Anywhere Service or *WIAGPS* was the most important thing to him. The signal came from the satellite directly to any device. No need for power. As long as the satellite was cranking, you got a signal. The signal was always strong even miles out from shore on one of his lab analyses. This gave him the ability to type in the data on sea or land. Gadgets, computers, WIAGPS and long battery life were the features that rocked his world, and he appreciated these modern miracles, especially on a day with no electricity.

The University's network was down for an undetermined time frame and waiting for it to get back on-line was proving to be futile. His stomach growled in protest, forcing him to glance at his watch. Almost four-thirty and he hadn't had any breakfast or lunch. Stuffing candy bars throughout the day wasn't cutting it anymore. It was time to get some real food. He glanced down at his belly and gave it a pregnant mommy rub.

Pushing his glasses back up his nose for the tenth time in as many minutes he tried to finish up. His wild, white man's Afro was in its usual style, parted in the middle and billowing out on both sides to his shoulders. Feeling perspiration trickle down the back of his neck, he grabbed a rubber band to tame his fuzzy mane. He packed his tablet into his backpack along with his other electronics and set out on his search. He'd just have to get off campus and see what he could find—fast food, 7/11, anything that was open.

As he entered the hallway, he heard a small group of students talking excitedly. He managed to catch a few words. Earthquakes. Tsunamis. Lava.

"What's going on?" he asked.

Beth, a fellow geek adjusted her glasses and said, "Well, we heard that catastrophic earthquakes are occurring all over the planet as well as random volcanic eruptions accompanied by seismic activity." She stopped and glanced at a printout from AP. According to the Associated Press, a massive tsunami hit the Philippines and Hawaii altering their geography. The island of Kauai has become one third it's former size due to an earthquake and tidal wave hitting soon thereafter. Major volcanos all over the world have erupted including Mauna Loa in Hawaii, Mt. Vesuvius in Italy, Ruapehu in New Zealand and Sakuri-jima in Japan. When she finished she wilted as if the information had drained her of all energy.

Under any other circumstances, Daniel might consider this studious geeky young woman the girl of his dreams, but other pressing matters came to mind. "Dude..." He trailed off deep in thought. He remembered talking to his dad on his landline just yesterday morning and everything seemed fine—but this was scary. "I better get home and make sure my dad's all right."

Beth began reaching for something in her back jeans pocket, "Yeah, I think I should too. I better call my mom and dad and tell them I'm out of here and heading home. Where are you from?"

"Leavenworth, Kansas. You?"

"Atlanta," her concentration already was shifting to rapidly texting.

"Well, thanks Beth. Have a safe trip—I'm at least a day's drive away, so I better jet—later!"

He rushed back to his tiny apartment to throw some things together. His one-room living area, decorated à la dorm-décor, was stuffy even when the electricity and air conditioning were on. Now it was like a hot box.

Trying to pack wasn't easy going. He lived in typical bachelor fashion in compact efficiency with the chaos and mess to match. He put his microscope and other equipment in their cases to take with him along with a few other necessities. No sense stopping his thesis work just because the sky was falling. He packed everything into his VW bug parked just outside. First priority: food.

As he drove through town he could see the palm trees dotting the roadside were missing branches and limbs. One mighty palm he passed was bent over, as if someone had tried to chop it in half and didn't finish. The area looked more like the aftermath of a hurricane than a hailstorm. He finally spotted a small bistro that was open and bought two sandwiches and some chips. He figured he had enough juice in his solar car battery to make it at least 325 or more miles before he'd need to recharge. That is, if there were any operational charging/fuel stations. He punched coordinates into his GPS and programmed it to check for charging stations along the way. There were plenty. Pointing the car toward US 98 West, he flipped open his phone to call his father. On the fifth try, he finally got through only to get voicemail. He just talked to him a little while ago, why wasn't he answering?

Daniel ate the two sandwiches so fast he felt queasy. After an enormous belch, his thoughts quickly turned back to his father. He tried to call him again but still no answer.

He drove onto Interstate 10 going west with few problems. The hail had long since melted, and despite the damage done from the downed trees and other debris, he knew the area so well that he was able to make detours off the interstate and avoid tie-ups.

Emergency crews were everywhere, but weren't even making a dent in the destruction around them. He wondered what it would be like the rest of the trip. More importantly, why wasn't his dad answering the phone? Finally his tablet phone rang, and the caller ID revealed his father's number. He touched the screen where the green phone icon was flashing to answer. "Dad! You gave me a heart attack! I've been trying to call you, why haven't you answered your phone?"

The only sounds coming from his father's end were some muffled indiscernible noises.

"Dad? Dad? Can you hear me?" Alarmed, he looked at the phone's screen and saw a strong signal. "Dad? Dad, talk to me! Dad!"

The only answer he received was silence.

CHAPTER 8

Daniel blitzed straight through to Leavenworth, taking only short power naps along the way. To his relief, numerous rest stops either had electricity or were running on generators. Finding service stations with gas was a bit more troublesome, but he didn't need them too often given the large solar battery that powered the VW.

The brilliant golden-white afternoon sunlight seemed oddly out of place as he pulled up to his father's house. He was relieved to see his father's familiar old gas-guzzler Cadillac parked in the driveway. Given its pristine condition, Daniel noted that it must have been in the garage during the hailstorm.

He parked his car and ran up to the front door. Trembling as he attempted the key-lock code, he had to try again before the bolt slid free. Cautiously opening the door, he called out to his father. A foul odor instantly assaulted his nose and he heard the droning buzz of flies. Dread pumped thickly through his veins. Almost gagging, he covered his nose and mouth with a bent arm. He told himself the odor was garbage his father had merely forgotten to take out.

From the crook of his arm came his muffled cry, "Dad?"

No answer. He scanned the living room and the adjoining kitchen. His heart was on a treadmill, sweat poured down his temples. "Dad! Where are you?" He ran down the hallway to his father's bedroom, glancing quickly into every room along the way.

He found him on his back on the bedroom floor, his phone lying next to him. Daniel's eyes saw what his mind couldn't comprehend. He was looking down upon his father's dead body.

"Dad!" Daniel dropped to his knees next to his father. His father's skin was cool to the touch. He grabbed his smartphone to call 911 but couldn't get a signal. Reluctantly he left the room and ran to the kitchen for the landline, wildly hoping a call would bring help on time. Picking up the handset, he heard a dial tone and the disembodied voice of the dispatcher. He somehow managed to relay the necessary information and hung up. He ran back to his father's side, picked up his cold stiff hand and wept.

CHAPTER 9

Mitch sullenly slumped into his well-chafed leather recliner. He had been there so long he wondered if the chair was beginning to adhere to his bottom. He flipped the switch to his satellite radio. All the news was grim. Worldwide calamities had caused extensive damage to the oceanic ecosystem. This in turn had a direct, catastrophic impact on marine life. Ocean going vessels were capsized by the thousands due to tsunamis and other seismic activities. The calm announcer's voice serenely reported that one-third or more of all maritime ships had been destroyed. This was really freaking Mitch out. What next?

Almost a full week had passed and still no electricity. Mitch felt a little stir crazy. Most businesses in Leavenworth were closed, including the real estate office he worked in.

Fort Leavenworth, the Army post nearby, had remained accessible for local civilian residents in need of emergency rations. The most excitement he had experienced all week was going on the Army base to pick up some staples. Too bad what the Army considered a "staple" didn't include bottles of Jim Beam.

He had even resorted to surfing the web, but his tablet battery had run down and there was no way to recharge it. He never was much of an Internet aficionado anyway. He wasn't a book reader either. Other than drinking, his days were uneventful and bleak. No TV and no work—which meant no paycheck, or at least a delayed one—was a combination that made him want to climb the walls. He was relieved to discover that one local liquor store and a 7/11 had stayed open, otherwise he would have gone into withdrawal. Even though he had stocked up with cases of Jim Beam and six packs of beer, at the rate he was pounding them down, it wouldn't be long before his supply ran out.

In a few hours, a town hall meeting was scheduled at a large church downtown. Maybe the meeting would shed some light on what had happened and why. Would there be some good news for a change? Or better still, maybe he'd find someone who'd go to an open bar with him afterwards.

Mitch finished the lukewarm beer, closing in on a baker's dozen. He heaved a huge sigh. He had no family to speak of and fewer friends. From his perspective, they had abandoned him. His so-called friends had staged an intervention to tell him he was self-medicating. So what? He didn't smoke or gamble. He had plenty of money to buy all the booze he needed and wasn't one penny in debt. No one really *got* him anyway. They couldn't possibly comprehend what he'd been through. Who were they to judge?

As he opened yet another brew and brought it to his lips, he grimly hoped there would be enough alcohol to numb him through the rest of the day.

CHAPTER 10

Aidan McCafferty pinched his tear ducts. He was exhausted and his vision was starting to swim because he had been staring at the four monitors in front of him for hours. It was almost 1:30 a.m. and even though he had been working hard for weeks on his postgraduate analysis, it seemed as if the work ahead of him would have no end.

He now regretted his resolve to finish this part of his project thesis on a Saturday. It was unusually quiet at the Armagh Observatory because everyone else was at the local pub celebrating the upcoming nuptials of another student. Everyone except him. He was cursed in a way, cursed by his academic tenacity.

Something in his peripheral vision caught his attention. He scooted the office chair, wheeling himself in front of the farthest screen on his right.

"Holy—" he said to the empty room. He opened up a calculator on another monitor and, in another window next to the calculator, began making a mathematical equation.

He stared at the screen in shocked awe. He blinked, his mouth gaping.

Suddenly, he started fumbling around his desk in a panic looking for his smartphone. He frantically patted down his shirt pockets, then shot to his feet and started on his jeans. He grabbed a landline phone before realizing he needed his contacts on his phone to find any of the numbers he wanted to dial.

Whipping his head back and forth between the screens, he grabbed a scratch pad, copied some information, tore off the sheet, stuffed it into his back jeans pocket, and snatched his leather jacket off the back of his office chair.

It occurred to him to check his jacket pockets. "Yes!" He pulled out his phone. He decided to call Doctor Mac Dara—this was important enough for Aidan to risk interrupting him at the party.

He commanded the phone, "Call Doc Mac."

A digital voice repeated, "Did you say 'Call Doc Mac?'"

"Yes!"

He cursed when the number dialed went directly to voice mail. He disconnected.

Instead of voice dialing, Aiden manually selected the number for his friend Sean and hit send.

Sean picked up after the fourth ring. "Yeah, Sean, is Doc Mac with you? I called his cell, but he didn't answer." Aidan glanced at the monitor again.

"Tell him he needs to get back to the observatory and see this—I know—I know, but he needs to see what—I—I've spotted a... I think it's a massive NEO." He had to shout because Sean could barely hear him over the din in the pub. "I said I've seen a Near Earth Object! I'm pretty sure it's an asteroid that's going to hit, and when it does, it's going to make the one that wiped out the dinosaurs look like a skipping stone!"

People began filing into the large Baptist Church a few hours earlier than the five o'clock scheduled meeting time. The newer building was chosen because it could seat up to two thousand, and the mayor was expecting a huge crowd. Other than the rumors going around, most residents hadn't gotten any news in over a week. The sanctuary quickly filled to capacity with every space in each pew taken. Along the walls, people were standing two and three deep.

John Culver, Leavenworth fire chief, sat in the third row with his eleven-year old daughter Lizzy and his father John Sr. He was silently praying about the meeting. He finished and glanced around the church. As the local fire chief, he realized the sanctuary was probably busting the fire code and noted that at least one of the exits was blocked. However, this wasn't the time to assert his authority. He had gotten only a few hours of sleep over the past seven days, leaving him bleary eyed with exhaustion. The challenge of extinguishing all the concurrent fires had been tremendous, but finally, all of them were out.

The mayor walked a few steps up to the altar and stood behind the podium. Suddenly the murmur of nervous chatter faded and all eyes were on Mayor Jeffrey Leigh.

He cleared his throat and began with authority. "Citizens of Leavenworth, thank you for coming. I have many announcements, but I will try to be brief. Before we close, I'll take your questions so please, hold all of them until then."

Aside from a few fussy babies, no one made a sound.

Leigh continued, "I have been told by Governor Thomas that our electricity outage was caused by numerous lightning strikes across the nation. Hail storms downed over 60 percent of the power plants throughout the U.S. This created a ripple effect much like the August 2003 outage that struck the U.S. and Canada. What we're talking about today is on a much larger scale—"

The crowd shifted uneasily in their seats.

"Teams are working around the clock to restore our power. Some of the surrounding areas have their lights back on. No promises but everyone's electricity should be back on soon. However, some of the outlying areas will have a longer wait. This is much the same case for landlines. We have teams of telephone repair workers on twelve-hour shifts, twenty-four hours a day. We are also aware, of course, that some of the wireless towers were damaged, but we've been advised that two towers are already back to about eighty to ninety percent working capacity with minimal outages and interruptions in service."

The mayor then informed them that the natural catastrophes that had been happening globally might cause a contamination of much of the world's fresh water supply.

This was met with more audible murmurs and some gasps.

Mayor Leigh went on, "I assure all of you, that everything possible is being done to prevent a future water shortage. Studies are being conducted to identify the organism that's been found in several bodies of water, and the results should be forthcoming. Apparently a species of algae that's blood red in color is the contaminant. Preliminary testing revealed the organism is poisoning not only the oceans, but is seeping into the fresh water supplies. I strongly urge everyone to begin collecting as much drinking water as possible and storing it as a precaution. The Missouri River normally would be a good source of water in an emergency, but if it turns red with the algae, even boiling won't make it safe for consumption, so proceed with great caution."

The murmurings became a din of alarmed chatter.

Surveying the audience, Mayor Leigh took a deep breath and continued, "Ladies and gentleman, I do have some other news and it would appear that it, too, is not good."

The sanctuary instantly became quiet as a tomb.

"Just before meeting with you, I received an email indicating that there is an object... that is very large and it's headed toward Earth."

He raised his voice over the commotion. "The assessment from NASA is that this object is probably an asteroid. It is heading toward Earth and is expected to hit somewhere in the southern part of the Indian Ocean, off the coast of Madagascar, Africa. The predicted time of impact is approximately thirteen and a half months from now, around mid-October."

The church erupted into chaos and many shouted questions.

With a hand raised, palm out, the mayor yelled, "One at a time, please!"

As a member of his staff handed each person a microphone, the mayor took questions. The greatest concern of the townspeople seemed to be the lack of information about the object that was on a collision course with Earth.

"Due to widespread power outages, not all of NASA's equipment is working properly, and information from them is spotty at best," The mayor explained. "But I assure you that when any updated information is received, I will make certain the town hears it as soon as possible."

Mayor Leigh answered the remaining questions patiently, as each person took his turn at the mike. After an hour's worth of addressing the seemingly endless concerns of the crowd, he attempted to wrap things up. He assured the listeners that as long as the power outage continued, he would meet with them every day at the same time and place with more updates about the object in space. Then he called for final questions.

The mike was handed to a young man in the back of the church with his hands jammed in his front pockets. He had very pale skin, long frizzy dark hair parted in the middle and a paunch. His black T-shirt and cargo pants were wrinkled. The five o'clock shadow he sported was patchy. He appeared excruciatingly uncomfortable as he cleared his throat before speaking, nervously shoving his horn-rimmed glasses up the bridge of his nose with a shaky finger "My name is—I'm Daniel Kelsey. My Dad lives down the street—ah—*lived* down the street." He paused a moment. From the third row, John Culver thought he noticed him choking back tears. Daniel continued. "I was told all the funeral homes are full and my Dad's—ah—remains are being held—in some kind of airline hangar. I know this may be a strange thing to bring up now, but I've also been told I need to bury him myself and I need to do it fast. I don't have a clue how to do this. I was going to ask if anyone would be willing to help me... ah... bury my father?"

61

Others jumped to their feet saying they too were faced with the same situation. The mayor suggested that the individuals standing remain standing, and perhaps those seated with the means and ability to help them would offer to do so.

John felt he should lend a hand to Daniel and leaned down to tell his father so. His Dad nodded approval. As John walked toward the back of the church, he saw a young woman also moving toward Daniel coming from the opposite direction. She had a split lower lip; her right eye had a shiner and a greenish-black bruised right cheek. The top of a large gash on her neck was poorly covered with a white bandage. He wondered if she had been in an accident.

Regardless, her body moved with confidence despite her obvious wounds. Long thick curled locks of blond hair moved independently as she walked... bouncing, shimmering, dancing on her shoulders. But what struck him most, even amid all the chaos around them, was her eyes. She must have been wearing colored contacts. No one's eyes could be so green.

Alana got to Daniel first and was already talking when John walked up. He overheard her saying that she had to take care of her family's remains.

John interrupted. "Excuse me, but maybe I can help." They both turned in unison as John extended his hand, "Hi, my name's John Culver. I'm here with my daughter and father. I have a huge flat bed truck you can use if you'd like."

"Hi, I'm Alana." Her hand was diminutive and smooth in John's large grip. "Daniel and I know each other because he's a neighbor—his dad was a neighbor of my sister's. My sister and her husband were killed during the storm and I need to bury them as well." She was unable to hold his gaze, but John caught the depth of her grief in the instant before she looked away. Compassion grabbed his heart.

"Please accept my sympathies for both of your losses. I know what it's like to lose someone you love. I lost my wife to cancer just after my daughter was born. I'm Leavenworth's fire chief. I'm sure with the resources I have access to, along with my family's own resources, we'll be able to give your family members a proper burial. Why don't you both come over here and meet my dad and daughter?"

John led them to the pew where Lizzy and his father sat. Introductions were made when John Sr. added, "Did my son tell you he's fire chief for these parts?"

Both Alana and Daniel nodded.

"Well—if anyone can help you two, he can. I'm an old man—but I'm sure I'll be able to lend some kind of helping hand! What do you think, Lizzy?" He winked at his granddaughter.

Lizzy turned adoring eyes to her grandfather, "Sure Grandpa—you can do anything!"

"Mr. Culver…" Alana began.

"Everyone calls me Parson."

"Well—Parson—I just wanted to say this is exceptionally kind of you and your son. I've been feeling pretty lost lately…"

Parson's face warmed with concern. "Forgive my interrupting, but may I ask how your pretty face got all torn up little lady?"

Tears welled up in Alana's eyes. "I was attacked at a rest stop a few weeks ago."

Parson took Alana by the arm and gently helped her sit down next to him, "What happened? What did they do to you?"

"It was only one guy, he hit me a number of times… I managed to get away."

"Well thank the Lord for that!" Parson exclaimed.

"Have you gotten medical attention, Alana?" John asked.

"Actually I did, I'm all right. I'll be fine. Thank you."

Lizzy scooted over next to her and said, "Miss Alana, those black and blues will go away and your face will be as pretty as it ever was. You look just like my Barbie doll!"

John had to agree with his daughter.

CHAPTER 11

Lizzy's touching encouragement brought another rush of tears to Alana's eyes. She struggled to regain control as Daniel fished in his backpack for a tissue. He found one and offered it to her.

"You're safe now, Alana." John said gently. For some odd reason, she believed him. As she looked into his cobalt blue eyes and examined this nice stranger, she tried to figure out why. He was tall and broad shouldered. She liked the Harry Connick Jr. swept-back thing he had going on with his dark blond hair, especially the few stray wisps that fell casually on his forehead. But the rest of him was decidedly Daniel Craig/007—all testosterone and authority. His strong hands hung easily at his sides giving him an air of confidence, but not arrogance. Inexplicably he exuded an aura of strength. John's voice broke her study.

"Would you mind if I prayed for you and Daniel right here?"

And a Christian too. Yet she was still surprised by the feeling of trust and familiarity that she seemed to immediately associate with this man who was a virtual stranger.

John had them stand in the aisle and hold hands in a circle as he bowed his head in prayer. The others followed by bowing their heads as well. "Father, we come to you with battered bodies and battered hearts today. We ask that you comfort Alana and Daniel in their grief over the loss of their loved ones. Be with them, Lord, as they go through this trial. Help us to help them give their family a proper burial. Let us be a safe haven for them both. We pray this in the name of your son, Jesus Christ, A—"

John didn't get to say the full Amen. The entire building trembled as if a freight train was running over the roof, rattling the stained glass windows around them.

John leapt into action, yelling, "Everyone, get away from the windows! Get into the pews and on the floor!"

Everybody ran to the nearest pew to duck underneath. Some were crying and screaming. Using his body as a shield, John tried to position himself over Alana, Daniel, his father and Lizzy as they huddled under the pew.

A cacophony of sounds filled the sanctuary. Steel grinding on steel made strange hollow screeching and clanging noises. The clamor reached an eardrum-splitting decibel. Screams and frightened cries came from scattered areas of the sanctuary. Lizzy called out, "Daddy! What is it?"

"I don't know, honey. Keep your head down!" John squeezed his daughter tighter.

The grating sounds continued to rock the church. Finally, a tremendous shudder heaved through the entire building, passing under their feet, around and above them, the intensity of it raining pieces of plaster down around them. Then everything went still. Dust clouded the air. No one moved for several seconds. Those closest to a window stared. Gasps were heard throughout the sanctuary. Others cried out to no one in particular.

With Lizzy in his arms, John ran to the closest window. Daniel, Parson and Alana crowded around him.

Someone cried out, "Is that what I think it is?"

Another said, "What in the world?"

Parson said, "That's just the thing—it would appear it's *not* of this world!"

The hair on the back of John's neck stood up.

He had to blink as the sun flashed off something metallic and momentarily blinded him. When his eyes adjusted, he saw a gigantic structure next to the playground that looked like an enormous silver and gold-segmented missile, so tall it towered out of sight.

Could it possibly be a spaceship gleaming in the Kansas sunset?

CHAPTER 12

"It's a bomb!" someone screamed, Startled, Alana jumped, nearly losing her balance.

Chaos erupted inside the sanctuary as Alana tried to cover her ears with her hands. Mayor Leigh rushed to the altar and grabbed the microphone.

"Everyone, everyone wait just a moment, please! I don't think it's a bomb! The sheriff, who is a retired Army First Sergeant, believes it must be some type of space shuttle or aircraft. Perhaps some sort of secret military project. Remember, we are next to Fort Leavenworth. This could have been a test flight that went wrong!"

Gradually everyone began to calm down.

Mayor Leigh continued, "Let Sheriff Jackson and I go out to see what this is all about. Finding Mr. Culver in the crowd, he added, "John, would you please go with us?"

John nodded.

"The rest, please stay here inside the church," the sheriff ordered.

At least a third didn't listen and went out the side exits. Some of the crowd made their way to the front of the altar and huddled together uneasily.

Alana, Daniel, Parson and Lizzy surreptitiously shadowed John as he and Mayor Leigh, Sheriff Alistair Jackson and several deputies went through the large wooden double doors at the front of the church. Sheriff Jackson, with both hands cradling the pistol grip, aimed his gun straight ahead as they exited the church. His deputies followed.

Outside, standing on tiptoes, Alana craned her neck to try to get an unobstructed view of the craft. What appeared to be smoke, steam, or both came from somewhere out of sight on the opposite side of the craft but there was no other movement or sound.

The top of the ship, which Alana estimated was at least five hundred feet high, disappeared into the turquoise Kansas sky; its metal box-like segments seemed to push through the clouds. Through the dust stirred up from the landing, Alana could see each edifice upon the other was in perfect symmetry.

"You know what this looks like?" Daniel piped up. "It looks like that skyscraper in Dubai, Burj Khalifa, just on a smaller scale!"

"Sir, for your own safety, please step back into the church," the Sheriff said.

Daniel and the others did what the Sheriff said, stepping back in unison.

From the far side of the craft a metal door opened with a whoosh. Alana instinctively grabbed for Daniel's arm. A massive headdress emerged around the side of the aircraft. Another followed and another as more of these beings poured out and afforded the people of Leavenworth their first glimpse of life forms from another world.

Each one of the tall beings held a scepter or staff ornamented with what seemed to be precious jewels. When they moved, Alana thought they were gliding as they made their way majestically toward the sheriff, Mayor and John. As they approached and their faces came into clearer focus, Alana could swear she was looking at character models for a Steven Spielberg movie with aliens or some other artist's renderings of aliens. While very human looking, with elongated necks and high foreheads, their eyes lacked irises giving them a distinct inhuman appearance. Almond shaped dark orbs framed by thickly lashed lids blinked at them. Their noses weren't noses at all, just tiny bumps with two tiny round holes at the base. Their mouths had no lips, they were simply openings containing rows of human-like teeth with the exception of double length incisors on the top and bottom rows, making them appear almost vampire-like. Alana shuddered.

As if rehearsed, the aliens lined up in perfect formation twelve across and four deep facing the front doors of the church. Alana stared in utter disbelief, completely unnerved by the magnificence of these beings and the bizarre events unfolding before her. She studied the others around her. While all of their new guests were smiling, the townspeople were cowering in the church doorway, their faces displaying only shock and terror.

Parson Culver exclaimed in wonder, "Bless my soul and body, it would appear they are all at least nine feet tall!"

CHAPTER 13

A number of people in the church burst through those who were crowded at the door, nearly knocking Mitch Abbott down. They scattered in all directions—some dragged frightened children, others tried to hide behind anything they could find and many just ran. Shouting and screaming filled the air as several men and women who had pushed their way to the front brandished handguns and rifles. Mitch wanted to run, but remained rooted to his spot at the center of the church entrance.

Sheriff Jackson holstered his gun and stood facing the crowd. "Now everyone put down your weapons. Stay calm. We have no idea what kind of weapons they have against ours. Don't go off half-cocked and get us all killed. Everyone, lower your weapons now!"

Reluctantly they all lowered their pistols and

shotguns. "That's better. Let's just hold on here a minute and hear what they have to say."

"What if they get us with a... a... death ray or something Sheriff? I'm not gonna stand here and just let 'em do it!"

"Now Bill Starling, if they *did* want to use one of those weapons you're worried about, I'm betting your old Winchester wouldn't do much good anyway. Just hold on to your britches, and like I said, let's see what they have to say. They don't seem too aggressive to me." Sheriff Jackson's face didn't reflect the confidence of his voice, but it seemed to appease the crowd temporarily. For a moment, the only sounds were the gentle breezes that filtered through the black hickory trees and the "chip, chip, cheriee" song of a Great Crested Flycatcher seemingly oblivious to the fuss.

The alien in front with the tallest headdress bowed deeply and, using the hand not holding the bejeweled staff, gestured openly with a wide sweep of his arm. Mitch noticed some type of symbol on the top of his headdress also matched something on the door of the spaceship.

Straightening from his bow, he spoke, "I assure you, we mean no harm. We are here in peace. We come from another star system. It is the one you call M104—or The Hat Galaxy, I believe, is the translation."

With this, one of the other majestically clothed beings walked up to him. This second one too had the same symbol on his clothing as they all had. He whispered in the ear of the one speaking which produced a broad smile and laugh.

"It would seem my translation of your language needs more practice. Your Hubble Telescope has published images of our galaxy. The name your scientists have given it is 'The Sombrero Galaxy.' Please excuse the error."

The aliens chuckled, but the townspeople remained stone faced. Mitch's eyes darted to those around him. He suddenly realized his mouth was gaping open. Snapping it shut, he cringed when his teeth clicked audibly.

The speaker continued. "One of our main ships will remain in your planet's orbit. Please don't be frightened. We truly mean you no harm. We've been watching events unfold and have come to earth due to the signs of the times."

The alien's voice was deep, rich and resonated as if he were speaking into a microphone. His diction and accent were as perfect as an Oxford professor's. And despite the fact that all the aliens appeared to be men and Mitch was a very hetero kind of guy, he still couldn't help but note their incredible beauty. Aside from their amazing costumes or robes or whatever they wore, Mitch could see they were movie-star stunning, each in his own way. He rubbed his eyes and blinked several times. This had to be some bizarre dream.

The same being spoke again. His black eyes blinking rapidly, with long dark lashes fluttering, before he spoke. "This must be unsettling to all of you. Please, let me repeat, in no way do we wish you any harm. The one you call 'the Messiah' has come to your planet in your earth's historical times. You see we have the Bible too. What we call it would translate into 'The Great Books of the Creator.' Our people are also familiar with the book of Revelation, and it would appear that the events the Apostle John wrote down as the Morning Star dictated he must do, are now coming to pass. We collectively decided to come to earth to await the Messiah's return." When he spoke, the alien's long slender hands gestured, as would a guest speaker standing behind a lectern.

Mayor Leigh slowly walked up to the speaker. "My name is Jeffrey Leigh, and I—I'm what we call mayor of this town. May I… ask who you are?"

"I'm sorry, forgive me. We should introduce ourselves. My name in your language is Abijah. I am an Elder and represent our group here. This is Lael." He stepped back and gestured to his right. The one who whispered the correction, bowed. If possible, Lael looked more African with wider nostrils and flawless deep chocolate skin. His large well-spaced eyes were so dark they looked almost black, yet they were also somehow inviting.

Abijah introduced them all one by one, each giving a deep bow when he called their names.

They all looked physically similar, tall and thin with attenuated fingers and graceful swan-like necks. Their skin was smooth, without blemish or wrinkles. Some looked Caucasian, others had skin as dark as an African, some the color of café au lait. Yet while their skin color varied, their facial features were similar. Their eyes were all a blackish brown or just black, large and cat-like with thick long lashes and what seemed to be tattooed black eyeliner framing the shape of the eye. Their noses were elegant narrow strips running down the center of their faces, ending with a tiny upturned bump. Some were bald under their headdress; others had long, silken hair braided in the back or down either side of their head. No redheads that Mitch could see. He was surprised at how closely they resembled all the depictions of aliens he had ever seen in the movies, yet they were fundamentally different, their appearance human but at the same time, not human at all.

Man this is totally creeping me out; I need a drink like yesterday. Mitch wondered how much longer until he could bolt.

Mayor Leigh said, "Well, I'm guessing nothing like this has ever happened before, I'm not sure how we proceed. Do you have somewhere to sleep? Ah... *do* you sleep?"

Abijah chuckled. "Yes. We in fact are physiologically much like you humans in almost every way. Except, of course, our stature." With this he smiled broadly, showing two rows of straight, small white teeth and the double Dracula-fangs that unnerved Mitch each time they flashed.

"So where will you spend the night? Do you—will you need accommodations?" Mayor Leigh asked.

"For now, since this must be quite unsettling for your town, we'll just spend the night in our craft. We have all the amenities we need: food, lodging—we are completely situated with all the necessities. We just ask if it would be possible to meet here at the church tomorrow evening? Until then, your security detail and you, Mayor, are more than welcome to accompany us to our ship."

The mayor and Sheriff Jackson exchanged a glance

before the mayor said, "Please do not take offense. Perhaps tomorrow we can explore your ship, but not today—thank you."

Mitch was glad there were no other takers because he didn't want to watch anyone go on that exploratory expedition. The idea of the town's police force going into an alien space ship made his head swim.

"That sounds like a wonderful idea, Mayor Leigh. Thank you so much. We'd be delighted to meet you here tomorrow evening. For now, we bid you and the people of Leavenworth a good night."

With that, the aliens all bowed as one and slowly turned back to their ship.

Mitch found it odd they didn't talk amongst themselves as they departed.

Sheriff Jackson's forehead creased into furrows, "Mayor, I don't want you going into their space craft. We need to call the state police and I'm guessing the FBI. Holy cow, I can't believe I'm not dreaming here."

Mitch looked at his phone for a signal. "You can use my satellite phone, Sheriff, if yours doesn't have a signal."

As the Sheriff took him up on his offer, Mitch instantly regretted the gesture. *What was I thinking? Now I just might be standing here the rest of the night letting them use my phone when I could be heading to find an open bar. If I have to, I'll leave the stinkin' phone and get that drink.*

CHAPTER 14

People dispersed and headed to their cars or homes chattering excitedly. Some stood around the space ship staring upward, gesturing. Others just stared in silence at the structure, clinging to each other. The entire scene was at odds with the quiet serenity of the emerging twilight sky and the community spirit of safety and peaceful living. John had a sense that from this hour forward nothing would ever be the same.

John turned to Lizzy and his father. "Pop, what do you think?"

"Well son I have to tell you, it's all bizarre, I'll give you that." A shadow briefly flit across Parson's face. "I honestly don't know what to make of it, but I will say this—everything here tonight, what the mayor said, these... beings, it's all deeply troubling."

"That's how I'm feeling Pop. I'd feel safer if I brought Lizzy to the lake. What do you say?" John raked his fingers through his hair and left them there. "I was going to take a leave of absence so you and I could get the resort started up again like we planned. That wasn't until next month though."

"Maybe you should still go next month, John, if you think your absence will cause problems at work."

"What I'll do is call Jim Stanton. He was going to be my replacement next month. If he is willing to take over for me earlier, then we'll be all set. If he can't, what I can do is go up now, get the place ready, and then just come back until Jim is able to step into the Fire Chief position. I can join you all again once he's set. I'd better call him right away."

Lizzy interrupted, "Daddy, you said you'd help Miss Alana and Mr. Daniel."

John put his hand on top of his daughter's head and smiled down at her, "I haven't forgotten, honey." He turned to Alana and Daniel who were standing behind Parson. "If you'd like, Dad and I want to invite you to our resort in northern Michigan called Sleeping Bear. We've had it closed down for two seasons, only going up there ourselves. Dad couldn't keep it up, and my new duties as Fire Chief didn't allow me to head north to help him. But it would be easy to get it up and running again. If you'd like to join us, pack some things. Make it for a long stay. If you have cold weather clothing, you'd better pack that too. Tomorrow, at seven a.m., why don't we plan to meet at Bart's Diner. Do you know where that is?"

Alana said, "No, I don't think I do."

Daniel offered, "I do. You can follow me, Alana."

"Good, we'll meet there first thing in the morning, then go to the hangar you mentioned. Alana, the remains of your sister and her husband are there, too, right?"

Alana nodded. John realized she was a little shell-shocked by the bluntness of his question. His voice softened, "Are you going to be all right?"

Alana smiled sadly, "Yes, yes, I'll be fine."

"Good, then we'll pick up your relatives, place them in the back of my truck and take them with us. I have a plan." He turned to his father and said, "Dad, you with me on this? You get where I'm going?"

"I'm with you all the way, son."

"Good. This is what I think we should do. We'll all drive up to Sleeping Bear. It's on Little Lake Chippewa near the Manistee, Michigan National Forest. It's close to Lake Michigan as well. We have a little over twenty acres and two-dozen small, but completely equipped cabins plus the main lodge. We also have boats and fishing equipment. The property has its own well and small water tower. We also have a number of large generators." John paused to hug Lizzy. "So it's a good place to hole up for awhile until we can figure out what is really going on here. Anyway—my feeling is—let's just go somewhere far away from this right now, somewhere a little secluded and wait this out. We can bury your family members on our property, if that would be all right with you both."

Alana and Daniel nodded.

John flipped his mobile phone open, looked at his screen. "Does everyone have a phone that's getting a signal?"

Alana's worked and so did Daniel's, but the signal was weak. They exchanged numbers and agreed to meet just as John had suggested. John asked if Daniel would make certain Alana made it safely to her car and Daniel assured him he would.

John and Parson walked with Lizzy to their truck. As they did, John had the distinct, unsettling feeling that someone—or something—was watching them.

CHAPTER 15

Alana and Daniel sat in Bart's Diner discussing what each of them planned for funeral services once they got up north. Somehow, the cozy atmosphere of the 1960's inspired décor of apple red booths, red and white calico curtains and miniature jukeboxes at each table made Alana feel safe. Given the current circumstances, the cheery setting was comforting.

"What do you think, are we doing the right thing?"

Daniel gave her a crooked smile. "Yes, it's right. I can't be sure, but it feels right." He paused and his smile broadened to a grin. "You know, you talk really fast, but I'm catching on."

Alana blushed, "Oh—it's a habit, sorry."

"No, it's okay. I'm just not all that swift this hour in the morning... takes a little more concentration, that's all."

"Daniel, you will go with me, right?"

"Well—if you think you can fit all of my gear."

"We'll make it fit Daniel, trust me!" She was amazed at how quickly she had bonded with this nerdy, sweet guy. She figured this connection was probably due to their sharing a loss, but she felt somehow there was a little more to it than that. Maybe it was his shyness. She wondered if he knew the Lord yet and felt an impulse to share what God had done in her own life.

"So, what do you think about the 'men' from Mars?" she asked.

"I really don't know. I stayed up half the night, and I don't have any more answers now than I did before going to bed. It's way creepy on the one hand, but on the other, it's fascinating what they could potentially offer civilization."

At that moment, John walked into the diner and Alana could again see why he was Leavenworth's fire chief. He held a newspaper in one hand with a headline that said "Freak Storm—Death Toll Rises." Parson and Lizzy followed him in. Lizzy was yawning, but when she saw Alana, her whole face brightened. "There she is, Daddy!"

Alana smiled and was a little unprepared for Lizzy throwing her arms around her in a big neck-hug. *What a sweetheart.*

She wasn't particularly good with children. Kids were all right, but it was definitely better when they belonged to someone else. This little girl was special. Alana found herself brushing a soft brown curl out of Lizzy's eyes and wondering what it would feel like to be a mother.

CHAPTER 16

John entered the diner and automatically took charge. "All right—I think we should eat a good breakfast and then head to the hangar. Sound good?"

Since there were no protests, he went on, "Hey Cathy, what have you got for us today? Is the griddle up and running?"

Cathy, Bart's wife, answered, "Great to see you Chief! We have everything. The generator is keeping us going at least through today. We're hoping the electricity will come back on soon. We don't know just how long the generator will keep us juiced, so get it while you can! I'll bring over some menus. We're a bit limited on selections, but give me just a second here and I'll tell you what we do have. Coffee, right?"

"You know it!" John called back.

Just as John slid into the booth, someone sitting alone at the other end of the diner caught his attention. He sensed he wasn't supposed to just ignore this stranger.

"What is it John?"

"I'm not really sure, Dad."

John sat down and bowed his head in silent prayer, *Lord, please guide me according to your will and not my own. Show me what it is you wish me to do in this and all things.* Then the words came clearly to John's mind, words he felt rather than heard:

Ask him to go with you.

John hesitated, then slowly got out of the booth and walked toward the young man. The closer he came, the more he could tell that the guy was high, drunk, hung-over, or all three. *Okay Lord, I guess you know what you're doing, because I sure don't.*

The young man had black stubble on his face, and his thick sable hair was unkempt. John took a deep breath as an unpleasant mixture of alcohol and body odor assaulted his senses. He forced a smile. "Hi, my name's John Culver."

Gradually, the man looked up through hooded eyes so bloodshot the whites weren't white any longer, only shades of pink and red. "Hmmm?" He struggled to focus his eyes on John. He was nursing a mug of steaming coffee with both hands, cradling it as if it was capable of keeping him upright in the booth. John felt the stirrings of compassion for him.

"I said my name is John Culver. I'm the fire chief for Leavenworth. I noticed you sitting alone. I thought maybe you might like to join us for breakfast."

Raking his hand through his messy hair, he tried again to bring John into focus, then answered, "Uh... sure, I'll join you. I'm Mitch... Mitch Abbot." He stuck out his hand and John took it in a firm, but warm grip.

"Good to know you, Mitch. I'll show you where we're sitting."

John was a little concerned his daughter might have a problem with this man joining them, especially given his current state.

"Pop, Lizzy, this is Mitch. He's going to join us for breakfast this morning."

"Good morning Mr. Mitch. I guess you don't like mornings either. Neither do I, do I Daddy?" Lizzy suddenly scrunched her nose and just as John thought he had better whisper something to her, to her credit and kind heart, she averted her gaze and began coloring the placemat in front of her.

"Hi, Mitch, please call me Parson." John's father was partially standing in the booth, his hand extended.

John said, "Alana and Daniel, I'd like you to meet Mitch Abbot."

Mitch's brow furrowed as he studied Alana's face. It seemed as if he was waiting for an explanation.

"I was attacked at a rest stop," she finally admitted.

John wondered if the alcohol was responsible for Mitch rudely staring at her, or if boorish behavior was his usual manner.

Mitch blinked rapidly. "Oh, wow—I'm sorry.

Glad to know you're going to be all right." With some embarrassment he began to study his place setting.

John glanced away as he began to wonder if it had been such a good idea to ask this guy to join them.

After they ordered, the two main topics of discussion were the aliens and the asteroid.

In the midst of the lively conversation, John could see Mitch had eaten little of what he'd ordered. When the bill came, Parson quickly pulled the check toward his plate as Mitch began to protest.

"This one's on me, Mitch."

Mitch looked decidedly uncomfortable as he thanked him.

As his father got up to pay the bill, John realized he should ask the others about Mitch accompanying them to the lake. To his relief, Mitch excused himself to go to the men's room.

When Mitch was out of earshot John said, "I believe I should ask Mitch to go with us. Are there any objections?"

Daniel acted a little surprised, but said, "It's your resort John, you can ask the Tooth Fairy if you want."

Mitch came back from the rest room. Clearly he had taken a comb to his hair. He caught Alana's eye and winked. She ducked her head and looked down at her hands. Witnessing this, John felt a twinge of something he couldn't identify, but quickly ignored whatever it was to focus on the matter at hand. "Mitch, we hoped you might want to go with us to our resort in northern Michigan." He went on to describe all the resort had to offer. "Do you have any family you'd like to include?"

Mitch let out a long sigh, "Ahhh—no—I don't have any family—just me. I uh—"

"You're more than welcome to come with us, and if you agree to help around the resort, that will more than pay for your room and board. That's all we ask in return."

Alana offered, "I'll be driving a Jeep and Daniel has his VW Bug."

"Unfortunately, we can't give you too much time to think about this," John said. "We're heading out in about an hour, hour-and-half from now. Do you think you can make up your mind that fast?"

Mitch held his gaze for a moment as if confused, then replied, "Sure, but can I pack a few things? And I'd really rather take my Solar SUV—don't you think that would be a better vehicle than a VW Bug? It can pack more, go over rough terrain and hold more passengers if need be. No offense." He was looking at Daniel.

"None taken, man," Daniel said with a smile.

John explained to Mitch that before heading out they'd be stopping at the hangar to pick up the remains of Daniel's and Alana's families, and it was decided that while they did that, Mitch would go home and pack. They agreed to meet in the parking lot in a few hours.

As they all made their way to their vehicles, somewhere deep inside his core, John re-examined his impulse to invite Mitch. He believed he was being obedient to the Holy Spirit when he invited him, but he had serious reservations.

I'm stepping out in faith, Lord, and I feel as if I'm not on solid ground here, even though I believe this is what you would have me do. I pray that you will continue to guide my steps in this.

John glanced at the sky, as if seeking guidance. It wasn't that he doubted the Lord, but he definitely doubted himself.

CHAPTER 17

Fresh out of the shower, shaved, hair spiked with gel, Mitch considered imaginative ways to hide the stash of alcohol he was bringing. In every shirt, he rolled a pint of whiskey or bottle of beer. He even put a quart between his underwear and socks. He tried not to feel dirty about his little secret. He slipped a pint into his faded jeans back pocket and draped his Hawaiian shirt over it. There had better be stores near this resort so he could restock. Until then, he'd just have to cut down to make it last longer.

He wasn't sure why he was going, other than getting a chance to be near that hottie Alana, banged up face or not. If he *really* thought about it, he knew he *wanted* to go on this adventure, and not just because of that hot girl. He kept to himself at work and didn't pal around with anyone there. He had no hobbies, unless drinking and watching TV counted. And since his company was going to remain closed until further notice, his only chance of human contact would dry up. Not that it mattered, but it did provide *some* interaction. Still, he wasn't able to put his finger on exactly why he was doing something so impulsive.

"What could a week or so in northern Michigan hurt?" He voiced. "Nothing at all, my friend!" The sound of his voice as he talked to himself out loud emphasized how lonely he actually felt and this depressed him.

Grabbing the unwieldy duffle bag and slinging it over his shoulder, he picked up a suitcase and headed toward the front door.

Mitch was standing outside the door and turning the lock when his phone rang. He skipped saying hello. "I'm on my way. I was just—" He froze. Something was terribly wrong. He sensed someone on the other end but the feeling was eerie. Goose flesh broke out up and down his arms and the skin around his temples tightened. He felt an evil presence in the air around him, coming through the phone itself. He was just about to disconnect when he heard a voice, profoundly dark and menacing. "We are watching you, Mitch. Do not make foolish choices."

His hand shook. This wasn't the I-need-a-drink kind of tremor; this was the real McCoy. The only time he ever heard a voice even remotely like it was in a horror movie. Hands down, this was the most bone chilling experience he'd ever had and he was clueless as to who it was, but he knew he didn't want to meet him. Working around a suddenly dry mouth he managed, "W—who is this? How do you know my name?"

His question elicited a deep, raspy chuckle. Then a low beep sounded and the connection was gone.

His mobile startled him by ringing again, almost making him drop it. Holding it at a distance for a second, he answered with a tentative, "H—hello?"

"Mitch, it's John. You ready?"

"A—yeah, John. I w—was just on my way out the door. I'll be there in a few."

"Sounds good. We're here at the diner now. We'll be waiting."

Mitch disconnected. He was still trembling and wanted out of there fast. He locked the door and walked as fast as possible toward his SUV in the driveway, his suitcase banging him in the calf all the way. Eyes darting around, he quickly stashed his bags in the back.

While he slipped into the front seat, fear pressed down on him like a weighted vest. He felt like he was being watched, just as the voice had said. In his panic he couldn't make sense of the dashboard and was doing things by rote. He pushed the ignition button and forgot to look behind his vehicle. Squealing tires reminded Mitch that he was, in fact, driving, and he made a conscious effort to slow down, even though he badly wanted to put the pedal to the metal. A golden orange morning sun reflected off the children playing in the street, giving them an ethereal glow. As he drove past them, their laughter—like musical notes—contrasted starkly with the threatening atmosphere enveloping his car.

The oppressive feeling began to fade the more he drove. The memory of it was like a steamy Kansas summer day—nothing he could see, but it hung heavily in the air. Groping inside his glove box, he retrieved a bottle of whiskey. Trying to uncap it with one hand, he swerved and narrowly missed a fire hydrant.

Finally the cap was off and, putting it to his grateful lips, he took three large pulls.

This time he was pretty sure that no amount of alcohol would dim the sound of that voice looping over and over in his head.

CHAPTER 18

They all gathered in the diner parking lot as scheduled at nine am. John suggested they go caravan style and gave the riding arrangements. He would take the lead in his truck; Alana, Lizzy and Parson next, with Daniel and Mitch taking up the rear. The trip would be about 730 miles and as agreed, if all drivers could, they'd try to make it in one day. John handed Alana and Daniel each a two-way digital pager and gave instructions on how to synchronize their GPS tracking apparatus. He also instructed them how to program it to track the vehicles in front and behind. They programmed their GPS systems, and then piled into their assigned vehicles.

Mitch took Daniel aside, "Hey—I was wondering if you'd mind driving?"

"Sure, I always wanted to drive an SUV like yours.

Dude, you must have sold a mother lode of houses. This ride is pimp! You did say you were a real estate agent, right?"

"Yeah, I've been lucky I guess." Mitch thought he sounded unconvincing even to himself.

As they settled in and snapped their seat belts, Mitch showed Daniel the sound system. "We can get satellite radio during the drive so we'll always have something to listen to even when we get to the boonies, which is apparently where we're heading."

"Yeah, I've heard northern Michigan is big on trees and lakes and small on population," Daniel said. "I've never been there myself."

Their caravan headed out, John in front with his truck, Alana in the Jeep next, with Daniel bringing up the rear. Mitch found a station broadcasting news and switched it on in the middle of a bulletin.

"...*The specific force and velocity is not being made public at this time, but as we receive more information, we will keep you informed. We are still waiting for more data from the federal government's Star Wars One Project or SWOP. Once again—scientists report an asteroid is heading toward earth and is expected to hit somewhere in the southern Indian Ocean off the coast of Madagascar in approximately thirteen months. Estimates vary as to the size of the asteroid, but it is believed to be 20.8 miles wide and if it doesn't break up when it hits earth's atmosphere, it is expected to cause cataclysmic damage. We will keep you updated as soon as more information is provided."*

Daniel's voice trembled, "Get the others on the two-way and see if they've heard this."

Mitch called Alana and asked if she was listening to the radio. He told her what he heard. She said she'd call John and disconnected.

Neither of them said anything for several minutes until Daniel broke the silence. "Do you think the aliens are doing all of this?"

Mitch's gaze remained fixed straight ahead. He absently reached for his satchel, and fished around for a bottle. He took a swig, replaced the cap and said, "I have no idea. None of this makes any sense to me either. I really don't have any answers for you." He wiped his mouth with the back of his hand, his gaze never shifting.

He took another gulp and said, "If I tell you something, will you promise not to tell the others? They'll think I'm nuts, and I'm not." He turned to study Daniel's face and saw Daniel's surprised expression.

"Sure Mitch, your secret's safe with me. I mean—we hardly know each other, but I'm good with a confidence. What is it?"

Mitch told him about the phone call before meeting in the diner parking lot.

"Sheesh, Dude, I have no idea what to tell you. Do you have any enemies? I mean, it could be some guy has it out for you and used one of those voice scramblers or something."

"No, I really don't think that was it."

The SUV was silent except for the sound of the radio broadcast. Then Daniel added, "Man, this whole thing just gives me the creeps. Everything. The world is coming apart at the seams—whacko storms, giants dropping out of the sky, mountains exploding, tsunamis. Now we've got a doomsday rock hurtling toward Earth. I mean, what's next for crying out loud?"

Mitch answered by taking another swig from his bottle. He offered Daniel some, but he waved him away. "No thanks. Not when I'm driving, man."

"Oh yeah, sorry." Mitch said sheepishly.

"Hey, no sweat. Do you always drink this early in the morning?"

Mitch felt his cheeks flush hot. "Uh—"

Daniel interrupted "Now I should apologize. It's none of my business. You don't have to answer that, but I would feel better if I did the driving on this trip."

"Sure, sure. Have at it. No apology needed. I like to party, no question about it. And uh—this helps the morning… uh, after a night at the bars—which lately have been my living room—" Mitch trailed off realizing too late how disturbing that sounded.

"No sweat, man!" Daniel tried to be overly cheerful.

They drove nearly five hours, easing into a comfortable banter as they went. Eventually, Mitch found himself dozing until more breaking news erupted from the radio. Mitch stirred.

This just in from the Jet Propulsion Laboratory in Pasadena, California. An asteroid will collide with the earth in twelve and a half months. The JPL's updated information on the trajectory of the asteroid indicates the impact will be in the Indian Ocean, somewhere off the coast of Madagascar,

Africa. The asteroid rates a ten, the highest rating on the Torino Scale, a Richter-like measure for potentially threatening space rocks. Again, the newly discovered asteroid is expected to impact within thirteen months. We will bring you more information as soon as we receive it."

Mitch shook himself fully awake when Daniel said, "These things could go sixty or seventy thousand miles an hour. The impact would be beyond our comprehension. It was probably something like this that wiped out the dinosaurs!"

Mitch switched the channel as another broadcast interrupted. He grabbed for his bottle with shaky hands.

The average estimate is between 375 and 400 landings by what experts are calling 'life forms from another solar system.' Africa, Europe, Asia, Australia, New Zealand, and North and South America have all reported landings. The majority of ships appear to have landed in the United States and Canada with at least fifty sightings of spacecraft landings in the U.S. and close to that number reported in Canada. All official reports deny rumored aggressive behavior on the part of these alien beings. Communications indicate that they have come here on some type of religious pilgrimage due to the 'signs of the times' as they say they are waiting for the so-called Christian Messiah to return.

In other news, numerous townships and cities throughout the U.S. are still experiencing blackouts, fires, and burst water mains. These areas are also experiencing widespread looting. Police are stretched to the limit and in many states the governors are calling for the National Guard to assist with restoring order.

Mitch felt light headed. The whiskey spread it's

warmth through his limbs and rushed to his face. He caught a sideways glance at Daniel as the two-way digital device blared. "Are you guys listening to the news?"

"Yeah, man. Aliens land and tell us it's a 'sign of the times' or whatever it is they said. What's up with that?"

"Hang in there Mitch. Can I talk to Daniel?"

Daniel answered unsteadily. "I'm all right. How remote is this resort? I don't think anything is gonna be remote enough to make me feel safe at this point."

John said, "I think I have an idea of what is going on, but it's only a theory. We'll talk about it when we get to the lake. For now, let's just concentrate on getting to the resort. Roger?"

"Yeah."

Wide-eyed Mitch practically squeaked. "How can you be so calm? Are you trying to tell me you actually understand all this?"

"Now isn't the time to get into a discussion Mitch. We can talk about all of this later."

"Okay, I guess," but Mitch wasn't feeling okay at all.

Hours later, Alana's Jeep followed a bend ahead of them and disappeared from sight. Mitch noticed Daniel let up on the accelerator as they rounded the curve. For a split second, Mitch saw something that made him focus on what he knew he couldn't possibly be seeing. Directly in the middle of the road, an alien stood, his blood-red robe billowing in the wind. The color of it contrasted starkly against the backdrop of the asphalt and plush greens of the jack pine trees.

Daniel slammed on the brakes as he swerved to avoid it. Mitch hollered incoherently and instinctively braced himself against the dash. As the Navigator fishtailed, it swapped ends, sweeping past the creature and missing it by mere inches. Despite this near hit, the alien didn't flinch.

For a brief suspended moment, Mitch could see the face of the extraterrestrial clearly. Like a scene in a Stephen King movie, black orbs replaced the creature's eyes, its face tight and incomprehensibly blank. Its mouth opened revealing pointy needle-teeth as if it wanted to take a bit out of the car. The SUV came out of the skid only to flip end over end several times before coming to a clattering halt upside down. But Mitch's consuming fear was not about his survival. His fear was in the horror of those soulless eyes.

CHAPTER 19

John glanced at his GPS and noticed that Mitch's car was off the road and stopped. A glance in his rearview mirror verified it. He punched in Alana's number. "Alana, do you see Mitch?"

"No, they're not behind me."

"I'll pull over and wait until it's safe to turn around, then we'll go see what's happened. They aren't answering," John said.

They both pulled over on a paved meridian road and made a U-turn back onto the highway. As they retraced their route, John feared the worst. He prayed under his breath. Only moments passed before the overturned SUV came into view, but it seemed much longer.

John quickly pulled over and as he and Alana got out of their vehicles, he yelled, "Lizzy, stay with Grandpa."

Parson held Lizzy's hand as John and Alana made their way to the crash.

John was already peering into the SUV windows, gripping a first aid satchel he kept in the truck. "They're both still strapped in. And the air bags deployed. I can't believe the top of the SUV wasn't crushed." John reached in on the driver's side to open his door locks. Daniel was conscious but dazed. Mitch was unconscious.

"Daniel, wait a second!" John cautioned as he opened the door. "Don't move yet, don't unlock your seat belt until I check Mitch. Try to check yourself out first. "

Both Alana and John made it to the other side of the SUV and tried to open the door but it could only open a small crack. Mitch's limp arms and legs were in front of him like a seated sleepwalker.

"John, we have to get Mitch out of here, he's almost hanging himself!"

John checked for Mitch's pulse. "He's got a pulse, but it's weak. Mitch, can you hear me? Mitch?"

No response.

"I've got to force this door open, stand back a second." John dropped his bag and grabbed the top of the door. With a mighty heave, and a loud protest from the door, he opened it wide enough to reach for Mitch.

"From what I can tell, he doesn't seem to have any broken bones. I'm not certain about his spine though, but I'll try to keep him as stable as possible. Let's get him out of here. Alana, when I say go—unlatch his seatbelt."

Alana fumbled around trying to find it. "Got it!"

"Ready, go!"

Alana unlatched the seatbelt and Mitch fell into John's arms. "Good thing they had their belts on, I just hope there aren't any internal injuries."

Keeping Mitch's back and neck as straight as possible, he brought him from the car, set him carefully down on the ground and gave another quick check of his pulse.

John rushed back to Alana where she was already standing at Daniel's side of the SUV.

John said, "Daniel, I want you to tell me if you feel any numbness.

Daniel took a moment to carefully move his feet, legs, neck and arms, "No—no I think I'm all right. Just really sore across my ribs and neck."

"That'll be the seat belt burn from the impact. You might have a broken rib though, so let me just get a hold of you first and then you can unhook your seat belt."

John put his arm under Daniel and his other arm behind his back.

"I've got you now. Unhook your belt."

After following John's instructions, Daniel fell into John's arms. He brought Daniel out to the median and laid him down next to Mitch. "I was a paramedic before I was a fireman," he assured Daniel.

Mitch woke up and uttered a profanity. "What happened?"

"Take it easy there Mitch, you've just been in a pretty nasty car accident."

For the first time, the smell of Mitch's alcohol-laden

breath wafted through the air. It seemed to come from his pores.

"Yeah—did you get the license plate of the guy who hit me?" Mitch's attempt to be glib fell flat. "Hey, wait a minute, what about Daniel?"

"He seems just fine." John took a pen light he always kept on his keychain and used it to check Mitch's pupils. "I think you've suffered a concussion. Are you feeling dizzy or nauseated?"

"No, I don't think so."

Parson and Lizzy came closer. "Are they all right Daddy?"

John was checking Mitch's vital signs when he answered, "I think so honey, you just stay there with Grandpa."

John gently manipulated Mitch's arms and legs then checked his abdomen.

"Everything seems to be in working order for now Mitch. You good?"

Mitch was trying to check himself. "Yeah, I guess so."

John asked, "What about you, Daniel?"

Daniel attempted to get up. "I'm fine I guess, just banged up a bit."

Alana tried not to laugh when she noticed Daniel's cockeyed glasses perched crooked on his nose. "Ah—I think your spectacles have seen better days though."

"Yeah, and I'm going to have one mother of a bruise too." He lifted his shirt to expose a wide red welt that was forming across his chest.

John helped Mitch to his feet and called to the others, "Let's load up everything in the other cars."

"What about my car?" Mitch's voice was almost a whine.

"Well, Mitch my friend, there's probably little we can do about that right now. I think we need to get to the resort as soon as possible. We can always come back and get the Lincoln later. Right now, if there are any hospitals or clinics open on the route, I'd like to get you to one. If there aren't any with electricity, you'll still need a safe place to rest and recover. You shouldn't fool around with a concussion. In fact, I'm thinking we should call 911 and see if we can't get you to a hospital right now."

John tried to dial 911 on his smartphone. "I'm not getting a signal Alana, what about your phone?"

"I'm not getting a signal either."

"Dad? How about you?"

"No, son, I checked as soon as we got out of the car. It's pretty remote out here, so that's not surprising."

Mitch fumbled around checking his pockets, "I have a GPS phone, at least I did when we started the trip." He pulled a cracked phone out of his front pocket. "I must have crushed it on impact, it's dead."

John put his phone into his back pocket, "I guess that means we go to plan B. Alana and Daniel, you're back together. Lizzy and Dad, keep a close eye on him for me. Mitch, you're coming with me."

John gathered up his emergency bag and supported

Mitch as they began walking toward the cars. Mitch stopped. "What about all my stuff?"

"Don't worry, I'll get everything, but I need to get you to my car first."

Once Mitch and Daniel were situated, John and Alana went back to the SUV. Pungent fumes like the aftermath of a frat party greeted them. "Wow, did he bring a whole liquor store with him?" Alana asked.

John waved a hand in front of his face and let out a cough. "You know, I didn't notice it in the rush to get them out."

"Me either... Phew!"

John said, "Let me get inside and grab their things. I'll hand you what I can."

One of the first bags John was able to reach was Mitch's. Many of the bottles were smashed, but some remained intact. John took the duffle and handed it to Alana. "Be careful, this one's full of broken glass and it's soaked through."

Alana grabbed the bag and carefully removed the unbroken bottles. Working together, they emptied the car of all personal belongings.

"Throw those bottles into here," John said, pointing to the bottles Alana had lined up while he held open another satchel.

"Aren't we sort of enabling him?"

John pulled his fingers through his hair. "Well—I see it this way. I think Mitch may have a problem. He might even have a serious problem. I certainly don't want him drinking at the resort—not to excess. However, he also just suffered a concussion. Forcing him to stop cold turkey could literally put his life in danger if he is as addicted as I suspect he is. I think he's pretty well past the 'social drinker' stage. So we probably should take along what is left, for the time being. I've been praying about it since we met him in the diner. I'm not sure where this all fits into what we're trying to do, but I believe Mitch is a part of it."

Alana tilted her head to one side. The topaz blue of the cloudless sky framed and enhanced the emerald green of her eyes. John paused, unable to look away. He had never seen anyone with eyes that color, like new grass on a sun soaked spring day.

"So you're saying you believe the Lord has placed this burden on your heart to include Mitch in our little exodus here?"

John stopped what he was doing. "You're a Christian?"

Alana continued placing things on the ground when John resumed handing them to her. "I became a Christian as a little girl; Bianca brought me up to have a solid respect for the Lord." Pausing for a moment, she moved a few wisps of hair from her face. "She raised me after our parents were killed… in an accident similar to this as a matter of fact." She paused again, staring at nothing for a few thoughtful seconds, then went on. "Bianca was the greatest influence in my life."

John watched her carefully. She was fighting tears. "Bianca taught me how to read the Bible. She was a wonderful example to me."

"I'm sorry about your sister and parents. How old were you when that happened?"

"I was seven years old. I don't know how she did it, but Bianca just took over."

John's heart went out to her. She was so young to have all this tragedy in her life.

"You must have loved her very much."

Alana brusquely wiped away tears that had crept out at the corners of her eyes and said, "Yes, I did indeed." Then as a way of trying to compose herself, she seemed to switch gears. "Were you brought up Christian?"

"Pop is a retired preacher," he said with pride in his voice. "He was a pastor for over thirty years. He lost Mom a few years ago, not too long after I lost Kate, my wife." John abruptly became aware that other than with his father, he hadn't spoken this openly to anyone in years. He put both hands on his hips, not certain he should go on.

"I too am sorry for your loss. If you feel you can go on, I'm listening."

His hesitation vaporized. How easy it felt to talk to her. He kept spilling. "Well, between raising Lizzy, becoming fire chief, and running the resort in the summers, I had plenty to keep my mind occupied. It did help being so busy with—just with life."

"And that resort must be where we're headed to, right? You and your father have been amazingly generous to invite us all."

John felt his face flush. He dropped his eyes from her steady gaze. He was quite taken by her maturity and poise even though there must be at least fifteen to sixteen years age difference between them. "My father inherited it from his parents who made quite a lot of money with several resorts they owned around Michigan. When he inherited it, he vowed to use it for the Lord's work. So it's the least we can do for you and Daniel considering what you two have been up against. It's really nothing at all. Actually, it's our pleasure." He stole a glance and wondered what it was about her that made him feel as if he could talk all day. He usually wasn't this open around women, to say nothing of one so stunning. The breeze picked up some stray blond tendrils and slowly wrapped them around her slender neck.

They finished transferring everything over and were chatting like old friends. When they headed back to the others, Lizzy called out, "Daddy, he didn't go to sleep once. I sang songs to him to make sure he stayed awake!"

"You sure are my best girl!" John picked her up and kissed her forehead.

"She's a regular Celine Dion; I didn't have the slightest desire to doze off—" Mitch's tone dripped with sarcasm, but he smiled as he rubbed his head.

"Well, it isn't considered necessary to keep someone with a concussion awake these days, but I just wanted to see if you could remain alert and clear." John took another quick look into Mitch's eyes before saying, "Now honey, you get back to Miss Alana's car, Mitch and I are going to ride together."

Everyone got into the two vehicles as John assigned them. John snapped his seat belt and Mitch asked, "Uh— did you get all my stuff?"

"You lost most of the bottles in that duffle, but some survived. However, I'm going to strongly advise that you not drink at all. Not a drop. Do you understand what I'm saying?"

"W—why not?"

"Mitch, I told you, you've had a concussion; this is nothing to fool around with. It's something serious and should be taken seriously. You shouldn't have any alcohol."

Mitch sat sullenly, petulantly crossing his arms as John pulled his truck back onto the road. Mitch's body language screamed that he had no intention of following John's advice whatsoever.

CHAPTER 20

As it turned out, taking Mitch to a hospital was not an option. Some hospitals had generators or were on their own emergency back-up power, but the few that were actually functioning weren't admitting anyone unless there was an actual life or death emergency. Just south of Grand Rapids they stopped at a hospital where a couple in the waiting room said they'd been waiting almost 24 hours for the man's broken arm to be set. That was all Mitch needed to hear and they moved on.

John was concerned. "Mitch, your pupils are dilated. At that last stop you drank some alcohol didn't you?"

Mitch mumbled something unintelligible.

"Well, it doesn't really matter right now, but you've got to stop for your own good—please."

John was surprised that for the rest of the ride he

and Mitch talked easily. Although he tried to draw him out about himself, Mitch was adept at steering the conversation in other directions. During any break in the conversation, John prayed silently.

It turned out they didn't need to make an overnight stop, arriving without any further incident just after midnight. Lizzy remained sound asleep in the back seat of the Jeep while the rest slowly emerged from their vehicles and stretched.

"Welcome to Sleeping Bear everyone" John announced.

John noticed that Alana was focused on the body bags in the back of his truck. This was where he had secured the bodies of her sister and brother-in-law and Daniel's father after retrieving them from Leavenworth Armory. He walked over to her and leaning close to her ear said quietly, "Alana, we'll bury your family and Daniel's father tomorrow morning. We have a large walk-in freezer and refrigeration unit. It's in one of the near-by pole barns. I'll take them there for the night. Why don't you go in the main house with Dad and he'll get you situated?" John was mildly startled at how being so close to her unsettled him. She had a lovely clean, light, floral scent that lingered with him even after he left her side and began unloading the vehicles.

A second later he looked over to see Alana taking in the property. He hoped she approved. He hoped they would all approve. He took pride in this place; grateful the Lord had blessed his father and him with such a beautiful retreat.

To the west of the lodge, John heard Little Lake Manistee lapping against the shore. His eyes came back to the main lodge, a majestic log chalet equal to those featured in architectural or travel magazines. No matter how many times he came here, the peaceful and natural surroundings always managed to surprise him anew.

As Parson approached the door with a large flashlight John recalled how he and his father had planned the unique entranceway during the extensive renovations they made on the place. They wanted it to be impressive, and judging from the reaction of visitors, they had achieved their goal. The forest green awning was held up by two, custom made, enormous rough-hewn log supports. Beyond those were the massive entrance doors. These were also made of logs, each one as thick as a telephone pole, and each intricately carved with pines, bears and wildlife indigenous to the Manistee National Forest. The door handles, hammered hand-forged black iron, were designed so when closed, they formed the Celtic Trinity symbol.

"Wow, this place is wonderful," Alana said, her voice soft and breathless.

"Glad you like it, Alana. I hope this will be home to you for awhile." John leaned into the Jeep to scoop up a still sleeping Lizzy. Alana asked Daniel if he needed any help as he gathered his bags.

Parson drew forth a large key chain and opened two locks on the main doors, swinging them inward in a wide arc to reveal a spacious entranceway. "I don't know if we have electricity, John."

"Not sure, Dad, but I'll check the breaker box. If not,

I'll switch on the emergency generators."

Lizzy, waking at John's voice, lifted her groggy head from his shoulder and said, "I'm not a baby anymore Daddy, you don't have to carry me!" He set her on the ground and grabbed another flashlight out of the truck. "You're right, how could I forget what a big girl you are?" With a quick tousle of her hair, he headed toward the woods. He went down the path to the outbuilding nestled in the mature pine trees.

◊ ◊ ◊

After an initial flicker in the power surge, the lodge lit up. Lamps and wall sconces revealed the splendor of her surroundings. Alana had always loved log cabins, but this was no cabin. An outside covered porch, decked with rustic willow and twig rocking chairs, seemed to stretch for miles. Blanketed by shadows, Alana could make out numerous smaller cottages and other buildings below her.

Above the awning to a peaked roof, the lodge had a magnificent triangular-shaped glass window that spanned the entire entranceway. Etched in the glass was a quote from the Bible:

> *AS FOR ME AND MY HOUSE, WE WILL*
> *SERVE THE LORD.* Joshua 24:15

As Alana stood looking up at the window, the words were backlit by a warm amber light.

The comforting sounds of the lake murmuring in the

distance seemed to surround her like an embrace. The air was so crisp and clean it was as if the invigorating scent of pine could clear the sinuses with one deep breath. Alana filled her lungs as she continued to soak in the beauty of the place. Even in the false glare of electric lighting, she could see this was a paradise tucked away in the evergreens. Nestled in the forest, it was as if the lodge had organically risen from it. Down the incline in front of the lodge was a large all-sports lake accessed by a sandy beach and two docks. Alana smiled at the joy of being near the water while secreted away in a splendid forest. For the first time in many days, she felt a glimmer of hope. She spoke aloud to no one in particular, "I really believe Bianca and Dom would have loved it here. Even little Toby would have had a blast running around this place. It's so beautiful."

John smiled broadly coming back up a path, ducking under some branches. "Glad to hear it, Alana."

Mitch was unsteadily walking up the porch steps between Parson and Lizzy, who were doing their best to be inconspicuous about helping. Alana forced herself to leave her serene thoughts and noticed Daniel struggling as he tried to grab his things. She rushed over to help him. "I'm fine," he snapped, but it was obvious from his expression that he wasn't.

Daniel's dark, haunted eyes bothered her and immediately put a damper on the pleasant atmosphere. "You're scaring me. What is it Daniel?

He turned his face away from her, "I just need some sleep, that's all." Alana wanted to persist, but decided she'd back off and try to talk to him later. He seemed so frightened, but why?

As she and Daniel shuffled into the entranceway weighed down with their luggage, John announced, "For now—everyone can sleep in the main house. Tomorrow we can start getting all the cabins ready, but tonight there's plenty of room for you to stay here. We'll show everyone to their rooms."

Parson offered, "I'll show Alana and Daniel where they'll sleep, John. Why don't you take Mitch?"

"I know where to go!" Lizzy cried out, fully awake and excited now.

The handcrafted log check-in counter directly in front of everyone had a small night light on the wall behind it, casting a warm glow. On either side of the counter were hallways. Parson explained the two closed doors directly behind the counter: one led to an office and the other to a private hallway leading to John and Parson's living quarters. Lizzy went through the door on the right.

Suddenly, the cozy atmosphere made Alana aware of how tired she was. She was grateful Parson was already showing them where they'd be staying.

Parson brought Daniel through a sitting room to a smaller room anchored by a king sized four-poster log bed. On the floor was a soft wool carpet resembling a plaid blanket that complemented hunter green curtains. Lamps with burnished brass bases and bear cutouts on the lampshades sat on both nightstands. Alana could see inside the entrance to the room's bath where a three-foot high black bear carved out of wood whimsically held a toilet paper roll.

As Parson led her down the hallway, Alana found herself smiling as she noticed all the little touches John and his father had incorporated to make their guests feel welcome and at ease. Parson unlocked the door to a room almost identical to Daniel's but with an opposite layout. "This is your suite, little lady. Will this suit you?"

"Oh yes, Parson, it certainly will. Thank you so much." She walked through the sitting room to the bedroom and tried to decide if she had enough energy to unpack a few things for the night.

Parson started to leave. "I'll just get to my room, unless there's something you need."

Alana assured him she was fine. Then Parson was gone.

Unfortunately, it was then she realized she was famished. She was rooting around her bag for her pajamas and toiletries when she heard a soft knock on the door. "Miss Alana?"

"Yes, Lizzy, come in!"

"Miss Alana, Daddy told me to tell everyone to meet in the kitchen if you're hungry. He said he's brought some things in from the freezer and there's lots of canned stuff and crackers."

"Oh wonderful, Lizzy. I was just thinking how hungry I am. How do I get to the kitchen?"

Lizzy's face beamed. "I can show you."

"Sounds like a plan." Lizzy and Alana walked back into the hall when Lizzy stopped. "Oh! I have to go tell Mr.

Daniel first."

"Sure, that's a good idea." Alana was once again caught off-guard by her growing affection for this little girl.

Daniel, Lizzy and Alana came into the kitchen and saw John, Parson and Mitch watching Fox News on a large flat screen T.V. on the far wall. Greta Van Susteren's broadcast was a repeat of an earlier airing explaining the latest news about the asteroid. There was no doubt that it was heading to Earth. The reports maintained it would land somewhere in the Indian Ocean and according to experts, the impact would definitely have catastrophic results. Some were predicting the end of civilization if something drastic wasn't done to stop it.

THE WATCHERS

CHAPTER 21

The weary travelers clustered around a crescent shaped granite topped island. Mitch was eating a sandwich even though he didn't feel much like solid food. They were discussing the latest news, with several different conversations going on at once.

Daniel pushed his glasses up his nose. "Do you think we'll be safe here at Sleeping Bear?"

Alana chewed on a thumbnail, looking anxiously from Daniel to John.

John said. "Well so far as I can tell, probably. But it won't hurt to begin acting like survivalists as soon as possible."

Mitch felt exhausted and sore and he was getting a

headache. Still, out of habit, he glanced around the kitchen they were standing in.

An open floor plan with a cathedral ceiling created an airy openness. The kitchen cabinets were naturalized log, a building material utilized throughout. A slate floor gave the room a sense of solidity and provided more of a rustic touch. He figured with the recessed lighting and professional-grade stainless steel appliances, the place would fetch quite a lot on the market. Mitch always viewed property through the eyes of a prospective buyer or seller, and rarely just as a casual observer.

He especially liked a light fixture made of antlers hanging directly over where they stood now. He studied it a bit trying to figure out if it was made of real antlers or if it was a clever reproduction made of resin. The rest of the room comprised a slightly more formal dining area with a large log table and a much grander antler chandelier. A stone fireplace that rose to the rafters graced the center far end of the room and could be enjoyed from any angle. Built of large natural stone, it was sculpted in the shape of a tree trunk with stone branches reaching to the ceiling. Mitch had never seen anything like it. Even though the room was long and spacious, it still managed to feel cozy and inviting.

Mitch turned his gaze to Parson who was trying to start a fire with a small pile of kindling and a few logs that had been stacked neatly on the fireplace ledge. He knew he could make a killing on this property given the right economic conditions.

As warm as the ambience was and as genial as the company, Mitch didn't want to be around anyone any longer. Besides, he needed a drink and he needed it yesterday.

He excused himself and as soon as he did, John said, "Mitch, now that I think of it, how about you and I bunk together tonight? I'd like to keep my eye on you. Mind if I take your vitals again and give you a quick check before you head to bed?"

Mitch stood there holding his wrist, trying to tame the sudden tremble of his hands. "Bunk together? Ah—I don't know John, I haven't slept with anyone since I was a little boy. A sleepover is really taking me out of my comfort zone."

John chuckled. "I don't mean we have to share a sleeping bag Mitch, just stay in close proximity. I have a suite that doubles as our home when Dad and I stay here. It has four bedrooms. They're not big, but they'll be fine, especially for tonight. You can have one of those rooms. Each room has its own bath—you'll have your privacy. I just want to be able to check on you if I have to."

Mitch reluctantly agreed to the arrangement, and just as reluctantly allowed John to examine him again. John said he was pleased that Mitch's pupils were finally reacting normally and everything else seemed normal as well.

Daniel quietly interjected, "Mitch, I'll walk with you to your room."

"We'll be there in a bit. Do you two think you can

find it, or do we need to drop breadcrumbs?" John laughed.

"Yeah, we'll find it." Mitch could feel his temper sliding quickly from cordial to short-tempered. He craved a drink and some sleep.

After they left the kitchen, Daniel lowered his voice to a whisper. "Hey, Dude, do you remember what happened just before the accident?"

"What do you mean?"

"What do I mean? Seriously, Mitch?"

"Yeah, that's exactly what I said, *what do you mean?* The last thing I remember is—ah—" He swore under his breath and raked his fingers wearily through his hair. "I really don't know what I remember anymore."

Daniel agitatedly pushed his glasses up his nose twice. "Do you mean to tell me you don't remember that alien standing right there in the middle of the highway?"

Mitch had a vague recollection of something that had completely unnerved him, but it was like having something on the tip of your tongue that's almost within reach before it slips away. "Well sort of, but why don't you go ahead and tell me what happened?"

Daniel looked at him with anger and disbelief. "Dude! I just told you! I can't believe you don't remember that... that *thing* in the road. That... alien thing! He was right there, standing in the middle of the road like he owned the place! I had to swerve to avoid him and that's what caused the accident! How can you not remember that?"

Mitch could pull up some fuzzy images in his mind, but it still was far from clear. "No man, I'm—I can't remember. Maybe it's because my head got clunked. What I do know is I have a dull headache that's starting not to feel so dull. Sorry, Danny boy—nothing's making sense to me right now."

They had come to the door of the room where Mitch would be staying, but he hesitated at the threshold. He avoided Daniel's eyes. "Ah—hold on a sec, I left some things in the room I thought I was going to stay in. Let me go grab them."

"Sure, Mitch, I'll wait here."

Mitch moved quickly down the corridor to the guest room where he had left his bags earlier. The room had two upholstered easy chairs in green plaid on either side of an oval pine coffee table. Sitting in a chair, he picked up his bag and placed it on his lap. He opened the satchel and was impatiently rummaging through it when he felt a change in the room's atmosphere. The hairs on the back of his neck and head began to prickle. He stopped looking for the bottle. He looked around the room as if someone might materialize on the pine four-poster bed, and plant himself right in the middle of the oversized downy white comforter. If it didn't seem patently paranoid, Mitch would have moved the numerous decorative pillows aside to make sure nothing was behind them.

A flash of red glided silently past the door, gone before he could actually register what he'd seen.

The air in the room felt heavy. The lamps with the little black bears on the lampshades threw insufficient light to dispel Mitch's fear—he was definitely spooked.

Mitch stood and softly approached the partially opened door, edging his face out the crack to check the dimly lit hallway. No one. But at one end of the hall, the shadows seemed to shift. He quickly ducked back into the room, closed and locked the door, then grabbed for his satchel.

He found what he was looking for this time and hurriedly unscrewed the cap. In his haste, as he brought the bottle to his lips, he missed his mouth. He didn't bother wiping his chin. He swore and greedily gulped almost one-third of the pint. Letting out a long wet hiss between clenched teeth, he slipped the slim bottle into his back pants pocket, replacing the pint he had finished a while ago. This felt much better. He always liked the feel of a bottle there: his pacifier, his comfort, his friend. He grabbed a few more of his things and started out the door.

When Mitch arrived at his room in John's suite, Daniel stood up from the overstuffed black leather chair he had been lounging in. Mitch again avoided his eyes, staring instead at the specks in the Berber carpet.

"Mitch, maybe we both need some sleep. It's almost two in the morning. How about we talk about this after the funeral?"

Mitch noticed Daniel's nose was wrinkled. *He couldn't smell the whiskey, could he?* Out loud he said, "Oh, yeah, gee man, I almost forgot. Sorry about that whole thing with your dad, really. Man, that's gotta stink."

"Sure, thanks Mitch. Look, get a good night's sleep. I'll see you tomorrow—I mean, later today."

When Daniel left, he almost bumped into John and Lizzy. "Hey thanks, John, for inviting me here. It's a really great place."

"It's our pleasure Daniel. Glad to have you." John handed Daniel a large flashlight with a rubberized handle. "Here, I've been passing out flashlights just in case the generators don't automatically kick in if we lose the electricity. I'll see you at daylight."

Mitch said his good nights and went down a short hallway past a full bath to one of the empty bedrooms in the suite. It was decorated almost identical to the one he had just left. He didn't bother brushing his teeth or changing his clothes. Stripping down to his boxers, he dropped onto the bed and was asleep almost as soon as his head hit the pillow.

CHAPTER 22

Before his eyes snapped open, Mitch felt an incapacitating terror, a malevolent presence in the room. The deliberate tick, tick, ticking of a clock somewhere in the room sounded peculiarly loud and ominous. Struggling against the panic pinning him to the sheets, he pushed himself into a sitting position and tried to focus his eyes in the blackened room. He couldn't see a thing. Sweat covered his body in a moist sheen. He shivered. He kept blinking, trying to see something in the inky darkness that would explain his crashing heart and heightened alertness. Nothing. He had a childish impulse to check under the bed or lie back down motionless or get up and flee all at the same time. He started to lie back down when he heard the sound.

Directly above the bed, floating just below the ceiling was a scarlet-robed alien. In a flash of instant recall, he knew this was the alien he and Daniel had seen just before the accident.

"Ah, excellent. So you remember me, Mitch." The alien smiled unctuously.

Mitch felt the unspoken menace behind the words as the room turned inexplicably cold—it was as if someone had opened the door to a winter blizzard. His trembling became uncontrollable.

One moment the creature was hugging the ceiling, the next he was hovering just a few feet above Mitch, arms outstretched, robe fluttering as if a strong wind held him aloft. For a second, the eyes of the alien were no longer eyes—they burned an empty, ghostly white, then reverted into eyes again.

"Mitch, we watch. Always. We are concerned for you and your well-being. We are concerned for all humanity, but you are a special one to us. We know you Mitch, and we know what is best for you. If you do the right thing, all of it will go so much easier for you. Trust me. We have your best interests in mind." The alien's voice was solicitous in a strangely effeminate way.

Why were these ordinary, almost kind words striking terror in him all the way to his core? Every muscle in his body was tensed to the point of solidifying—he wanted to run for his life, but he couldn't move.

"Do the smart thing, Mitch. Get away from these people and come along with us. We need someone with your intelligence. We can make you a very powerful man."

Mitch managed to squeak from a parched mouth. "Who are you? How do you know my name? Why did you almost kill me?

"I am called Ranulf. And you must be referring to that incident in the road. An unfortunate accident Mitch, but frankly, Daniel was at fault. He overreacted but I made certain the car landed gently enough. You merely received a bump on the head, however you are perfectly fine now. We can always protect you, just as I did when the car flipped and spun onto the median. Yes, Mitch. If not for us, you could have died. We can do this and so much more. We can safeguard you from all global disasters. You must realize these people can't offer you anything like that."

Words that should have brought relief to Mitch had the opposite effect.

"I—I don't know..."

"I'll give you some time to think this over." Ranulf drifted down to within inches of Mitch and smiled. A rank odor like raw sewage emanated from the orifice of his mouth, filling the room. Mitch wanted to cringe, but thought better of offending the alien.

"You asked how I knew your name. I told you. We have been watching you, Mitch. You are a unique and strong personality. We wish to include you in our plans.

And our plans would comprise an endless supply of all the Jim Beam you can consume. No limits. We need people like you. With our guidance, you could help the entire human race. We have the power to arrange it all. You could become an important world leader. Very important, indeed."

Ranulf was still smiling widely when he suddenly metamorphosed into a hideous leather-faced monster. The transformation of his body sounded like a balloon being stretched beyond capacity. His height and girth grew so massively he bent in half to accommodate the constriction of ceiling and walls. His gruesome face now filled Mitch's entire field of vision. Skin covered in grotesque bumps and pustules erupted from every inch of him and glistened with putrid secretions. Enormous ram's horns protruded from blackened flesh-covered bases on each side of his forehead. His mouth contained yellow-stained, crooked spikes so large he was unable to close his black lips. Drool dripped down and pooled on Mitch's chest. Its misshapen pig snout moved rapidly with nostrils flared as if sniffing out prey. Mitch tried not to breathe in the stomach roiling smell while staring into eyes that changed from an eerie luminescent white to red.

The magnitude of his terror and revulsion finally broke Mitch's paralysis. He scrambled backwards crablike, screaming at the top of his lungs.

"Mitch, Mitch, it's a nightmare, wake up!" John had both his shoulders and was shaking him briskly.

Sweat was pouring off him to the extent that, for

a moment, he thought he had wet the bed. He looked at John, bewildered and confused. "What the—" He was still in the grip of what he had seen, unable to clear his mind or shake off the fear. "I, I—need—a—a…"

"Drink, Mitch?" John finished the sentence for him.

Remembering the bottle in his pocket, Mitch got unsteadily to his feet, reaching for the pants he'd thrown over a chair.

"Mitch, when are you going to face that monkey on your back?"

Mitch ignored the question. "Listen man, you don't know the nightmare I just had. And I'm not talkin' just a nightmare. It was—*real*, or at least it felt way too real to me. Anybody would need a drink after what I just saw!

With that, Mitch finished off the rest of the pint, then dropped the empty bottle on the floor.

"I'm sorry, I didn't mean to do that." Mitch bent to pick up the bottle, but felt the floor tilt at a crazy angle as he did.

"Whoa, hold on there, buddy!" John bent down and retrieved the bottle for him. "Mitch, listen to me–you've had a concussion, I've already told you a number of times that alcohol consumption is a bad idea when you've had a head injury. Try to listen to me—I'm not asking you to stop cold turkey—I'm asking you to work with me and let me monitor your use."

John bent over Mitch, a palm on either side of him.

The concern in his eyes was obvious. *Why do I feel I can trust him?*

"Look John, you've been really nice to ask me here to your place. Thank you. But frankly, I don't think I can promise you that." Mitch was ashamed by the admission and peeved he had to say it. "I mean—I'll give it a try, but can we talk about this later?"

"Sure, no problem. Why don't you try to get some more sleep?" John glanced at his watch. "It's about 4:00 a.m. We've got a while before daylight. You take as much time as you need. You're not expected to come to the funerals." He headed to the door.

Mitch heard what John said but it didn't register. The alcohol was already coursing through his blood, numbing his neck, his face and his mind. His limbs went slack and his lids began to feel heavy. He mumbled something in reply as he started to drift off. Still, at the edge of his consciousness, he worried that as soon as he closed his eyes, he'd see that hideous face.

CHAPTER 23

Mitch joined the group gathered around three mounds. The service was already underway. He felt guilty he was arriving late, but in his own personal attempt to show respect, he didn't take a drink before coming. He had showered and gotten dressed in a shirt and tie, not sure why he packed them in the first place. He bowed his head with hands folded in front of him, and tried to listen to what was being said. For the most part, the informal service droned.

They were standing in an oval clearing of the forest, about a football field's distance behind the main lodge. There wasn't a wisp of a cloud in the luminescent topaz-blue morning sky. Gentle breezes swayed the tops of the pine trees that surrounded them like perfect soldiers. A small John Deere tractor stood poised and empty nearby the plywood coffins.

Parson was speaking, "As we pay tribute to Dominic and his wife Bianca Giovanna and Thomas Kelsey, we ask you Lord for your strength and comfort for their loved ones Alana Engels and Daniel Kelsey. Reading from your Word, we take a passage from Revelation chapter 21."

Parson read from the old, worn leather Bible he was holding.

"'Then I saw a new heaven and a new earth; for the first heaven and the first earth had passed away, and the sea was no more. And I saw the holy city, New Jerusalem, coming down out of heaven from God, prepared as a bride adorned for her husband; and I heard a loud voice from the throne saying, Behold, the dwelling of God is with men.'" Parson paused to turn the page, then continued.

"'He will dwell with them, and they shall be his people, and God himself will be with them; he will wipe away every tear from their eyes, and death shall be no more, neither shall there be mourning nor crying nor pain any more, for the former things have passed away.'"

To Mitch's astonishment, this passage moved him but he immediately stuffed the reaction. Alana wasn't attempting any such acts of bravery. Neither was Daniel. Both wiped away tears.

Parson continued. "Father, we commit these dear ones to you, in the name of the Father, the Son and the Holy Spirit. Amen."

Everyone except Mitch repeated, "Amen."

Mitch had rarely ever stepped inside a church and was not practiced in the tradition of ending a prayer with "Amen." Parroting the others after the fact, he hoped no one had noticed his gaffe.

Daniel wiped tears from his eyes with the back of a sleeve. Alana wept openly into a tissue. Mitch actually felt a sadness watching her in such pain and wanted to do something, but had no idea what. Something stirred within him, some unfamiliar emotion for Mitch. Empathy? He shifted uneasily. He was way, way out of his comfort zone.

Alana, trying to compose herself, took a deep breath and squared her shoulders. For some reason, this moved Mitch deeply. She still had bruises from her assault, she just lost her sister and brother-in-law in a bizarre storm, she came halfway across the country to escape the madness to a place she'd never been—and yet, not one complaint out of her. She wasn't just gorgeous, she had guts, and Mitch found himself feeling things he was unaccustomed to feeling. For a man who based attraction solely on physical attributes, he found himself drawn to this woman in a way that left him feeling strangely out of his depth and suddenly shy.

Alana walked past Mitch. Her nearness sent his pulse soaring. Looking down, he mumbled, "I'm—I'm really sorry about your loss," then glanced bashfully up.

She looked straight at him with her bright green heartbroken eyes. Tears shimmered at the edges, threatening to spill over. He found himself captivated by her gaze.

157

All of a sudden, he wished he were more of a man. Her eyes were the clearest and deepest emerald green he had ever seen. Her cheekbones were high and chiseled, her neck long and graceful. His gaze went to her sensual lips. They were perfection. Angelina Jolie had nothing on Alana. Women paid big bucks for plastic surgeons to try and duplicate what Alana had been born with. Her skin, like flawless porcelain, at the same time appeared luminous and soft. As she spoke, her voice sounded like musical notes to his ears. Even with the bruises and swollen lip, she was stunning and he knew he wanted to be someone she'd find irresistible. He tried to concentrate on what she was saying.

"How kind of you to come to the burial Mitch, especially after your accident yesterday. How are you feeling?"

Miraculously he found his voice again. "I'm doing OK, actually."

They walked the rest of the way back to the main house in silence accompanied only by birdsong. He tried to think of something to say, but couldn't. Her nearness caused his mind to go blank and his face to flush hotly. Maybe with just a little careful planning, he could be more than OK with some help from Alana.

CHAPTER 24

When the group approached the porch, John said, "I can get the cabins ready for everyone if you'd like to move your things there."

This comforted Alana. He was so take-charge and she needed that right now.

"John, would it be all right if I stayed in the main house? That won't be putting you out, would it?" She loved her room and felt secure there. She hoped John wouldn't mind.

"Yeah, I'd like to stay where I am, too," Daniel chimed in.

"Me too. I don't have to stay in the suite. If you want, I can move to another room, but I'd prefer staying with everyone else as well." Mitch said.

"Of course. I'm glad to hear all of you like the accommodations. That sound like a plan, Pop and Lizzy?"

"Yep!" Parson answered with a smile.

John smiled broadly. "Time to see what I can rustle up for us to eat. I'll meet everyone in the kitchen after I take a quick trip to the freezer."

Before he turned to go back toward the outbuilding, John put his hands on Alana and Daniel's shoulders. "Are you two going to be all right? If you'd like to be alone, we'd understand if you went to your rooms. I'd be happy to bring you whatever you want."

Alana and Daniel assured John that they would be fine. John said, "I'll keep praying for you both. If there's anything you need, please don't hesitate to let me know." John bent slightly to make his gaze even with theirs.

Alana found herself very taken by John's care and concern. She was virtually a stranger to him, and yet he treated her and Daniel like family.

Daniel expressed much of what Alana was thinking, "Thanks John. I can't tell you how much it means to have had your help. I had no idea how I was going to go about burying my father. I know I've already said this, but I really appreciate everything you and your dad have done."

"It's what the Bible tells us to do, Daniel. Do to others, as you would have them do to you. I'm sure you've heard that before."

"Sure, I've heard it before! But dude, you live it and I'm grateful."

John gave Daniel's shoulder a reassuring squeeze and headed off to the freezer.

Alana's gaze followed him as he walked away. She knew the Lord gave her a gift when she met this kind, gentle man who opened his home as a sanctuary to her.

They all went inside to wait for John to return and begin preparations for lunch. A few minutes later Alana thought she heard something. "Parson, I think someone's knocking."

Parson looked at her quizzically, then, unmistakably, the knock sounded again. Alana followed Parson to the entryway. Parson peeked through the small recessed trap door within the main door before opening it.

Standing on the porch was a handsome African American man, built like a linebacker. His cropped black hair was cut military style, providing an open canvas for light brown eyes and a smile that contained an overbite that gave him a boyish appearance. Next to him stood a young man, about 15 or 16 years old who resembled him. Both were solidly built and Alana liked them on sight.

"Hi, my name's Steve Hammersil, and this is my son Caleb. My wife Sarah is right behind us in another car with my daughter Meg. We've stayed at your resort a number of times in the past."

Parson asked, "Where are you from originally?"

"We're from the Detroit area. I was a GM vehicle assembly plant manager. I had hoped you were open again. I should have called, but we have family in Mackinaw City, so we thought we'd just keep going if you were closed. I remember this place was owned by a Christian family named—"

"Culver?"

"Yeah! I seem to remember one owner was a minister or something like that.

"That's me!" Parson stuck out his hand, "Parson Culver, nice to see you. My son John is in the pole barn. We don't have any of the cabins opened up yet, but if you don't mind waiting a bit, we can have you up and running in no time."

"Not at all, that would be great! How much will it be per night?

"Well – that's the thing. We're not actually open for guests. It's no longer 'business as usual' for us. If you're willing to help us lay in supplies for the winter and work around the resort, you can stay free of charge."

Steve shrugged and glanced at his son. "As long as my wife approves, I don't see why we can't do that."

Parson asked, "Do you hunt?"

"That would be a definite yes! I bagged the biggest buck of my life right here in Manistee National Forest the second time I ever stayed here! An eleven pointer, as a matter of fact. I bagged that baby just as the hunting season opened in November of 1999. The head is still mounted on my den wall."

"Outstanding! That's what we like to hear! John will like that story, and I'm sure he'll want more details as soon as he gets back. And here he is now."

John entered the kitchen with his arms full of food. "What do we have here Dad, guests?"

Once again, Alana was impressed by the sheer presence of the man.

Parson explained who their new guests were, and although John's arms were full and he couldn't shake hands, he welcomed them warmly. Just as he scattered the food on the counter, Daniel called from the living room, "Hey guys! Get in here! You'll want to hear this!"

They all moved quickly into the sprawling living room where Mitch and Daniel stared at a huge flat screen TV framed by split logs. Daniel was dividing his attention between something he was studying on the tablet and something on TV. The news was grim.

The asteroid would hit the earth soon. The force of its entry and impact could cause tidal waves and incalculable damage to any nearby coasts. If the asteroid broke into pieces prior to impact, the damage would extend beyond the current estimated radius. The science wasn't exact, and experts were unable to accurately assess the timing, location and level of damage. Accordingly, as a precautionary measure, coastlines deemed most likely at risk had begun to evacuate.

Daniel grabbed the remote off a coffee table that sat in front of matching denim sofas and pointed it at the TV. The screen segmented into two vertical portions: One was the cable signal; the other reflected exactly what Daniel had on his tablet.

He explained. "See, if we're talking about anything larger than a few hundred tons—which this sounds like it just may be—it's going to be traveling at about 10 to 70 kilometers a second."

He began using the remote as a laser pointer. "That's going to have a tremendous impact. The kinetic energy caused by an asteroid is determined by its mass and velocity, and this is what creates all the damage. We're talkin' a huge, huge impact."

The warm and welcoming atmosphere turned somber. Alana fought the fear rising within her. Lizzy spoke up, "What does that mean, Daddy?

John avoided Lizzy's question and shut off the TV. "Everyone, why don't we go into the kitchen without watching the TV for now while I make us a lunch." As they made their way to the kitchen, there was another knock—this time everyone heard it. Parson opened the door. "You must be Sarah and Megan!"

He ushered in a statuesque woman with cocoa latte skin and a short stylish bob, her pre-teen daughter beside her. Introductions were made all around, followed by a discussion concerning the latest news.

"Well, that's one of the reasons we decided to go north." Steve said, "First that storm, then the worldwide disasters followed by this bizarre aliens thing, now this doomsday rock that's ready to hit. I just felt the need to get my family out of the city and go somewhere away from it all and live off the land. So we took our savings and here we are. The resort being open is an answer to our prayers because, frankly, we don't have any relatives we'd actually *want* to stay with."

Daniel interrupted, "Well, I don't know if you'd call *this* an answer to prayer." He was peering intently at something on his tablet screen, which he then set up on a stand so everyone could see. "I hate to be the bearer of more bad news, but come here and take a look at this." Daniel touched something on the screen and a light emanated above it. Within the light, a 3-D hologram approximately two by three feet formed a tube that hovered just above the propped-up tablet. Within the light's sphere, they saw a full-color, digital enactment of an asteroid hitting the Earth, and the various cataclysmic consequences of such an event.

"Any type of asteroid—even the one they're saying will end up in the Atlantic—can be as powerful as several nuclear bombs. The U.S. Department of Energy and the U.S. Defense Department studied them way back in 2000. Of course, considering no one has ever witnessed an asteroid of this size colliding with Earth, it's only conjecture... still, it's a pretty educated guess. The prediction concerning this specific asteroid is also predicated on the assumption that it doesn't break up. If it does, there's no telling what kind of widespread damage it will cause."

Alana was impressed by the breadth of Daniel's knowledge on the subject and his ability to put it into laymen's terms.

John asked, "So what exactly are you saying, Daniel?"

Daniel pushed his glasses up his nose. He was so immersed in his thoughts, Alana wondered if he heard John's question. Then he said, "Well, obviously, this is not just some rock falling somewhere far away. It could dramatically affect the entire planet in any number of ways, and it will probably affect areas far beyond the initial site of impact. That it is predicted to land in the ocean will help prevent an enormous fireball of radiation, but in all probability, a fireball can't be avoided entirely. Add to that the fallout after impact will probably cause a massive counteraction sending who-knows-what into the air. One thing is pretty certain, though—whatever goes up into the air will be contaminated with radiation. Therein lies the problem, as they say. Tsunamis and earthquakes are just some of the expected after-effects, but we're also talking about severe atmospheric disturbances, to say nothing of the ocean becoming polluted. We've already got that red algae contamination. To what extent the damage will spread is anyone's guess.

John asked, "Daniel, will the debris that goes into the

air definitely be radioactive?"

Daniel jiggled his leg as he considered the question. "No... it depends on what the make-up of the asteroid is. If it's radioactive material, which some are—it will throw a pretty massive cloud of radioactive dust particles back up into the atmosphere.

There was a stunned silence for a few moments, and then John said, "Ahhh... well, Daniel, that certainly gives us something to think and pray about. For now though, first things first, let's eat then we need to get cabin twelve ready."

John put together a lunch of homemade chicken soup and two loaves of freshly baked bread. After everyone finished eating, he and Steve opened cabin twelve and all members of the Hammersil family pitched in to get it ready. In less than two hours, the Hammersils had it as cozy as home.

"I'll leave you so you can get settled in. You're welcome to join us for dinner at the main house around 6:30 if you'd like."

Steve and Sarah said they'd be happy to join them, thanking him again for his hospitality.

When John was coming back from preparing the Hammersil's cabin, he stepped over the threshold and saw Mitch go down one of the hallways. He resisted an urge to follow him and headed toward the kitchen instead. Alana was putting the finishing touches on cleaning up after lunch. John said, "Alana, I was going to do that, you don't need to clean up."

Daniel was the only other person left in the kitchen. "I tried to help but she insisted. She's pretty stubborn."

"You can do it next time, Daniel. Right now, the best thing for me is to keep busy. And anyway, we all have to pull our own weight around here—you wouldn't be cutting me some slack because I'm a woman now, would you John?" Alana cocked an eyebrow and, with one hand planted on her hip gave John a look of mock disapproval.

John got the biggest bang out of her. He laughed a hearty laugh. "No way! I wouldn't dream of it. You just have at those dishes."

"Besides, you're a much better cook than I am, and I'm feeling a tad inadequate. I figured I better do something I know I *can* do." She brushed a stray lock of hair out of her eyes. "I'm glad you're here though, John. What do you think about all of this, everything that's going on?"

Daniel interrupted, "Yeah, you said you might have a theory about what is happening."

John scratched the back of his neck before he spoke. "Well, Daniel, I believe I have some ideas, but they're based on the book of Revelation."

Daniel's gaze was skeptical. "Oh. So you're saying you think this is a God thing? No offense John, and you, too, Alana if you're religious, but that stuff just doesn't jive with science. It's essentially a collection of fantasy writing in my humble opinion. I mean, it's good for certain historical purposes, but this Jonah-in-the-belly-of-the-whale business—that's definitely the stuff of fiction. I'm not anti Judeo-Christian or anything, but to me, taking the Bible literally just isn't logical. I really don't mean any disrespect."

"None taken, Daniel." John answered.

"I understand your feelings. I'm not offended either." Alana added.

"So, Daniel, would you still be interested in hearing about my theory even though it's based on what the Bible says?"

Daniel nodded. "Sure, because frankly, I can't seem to make any sense of it, especially with these Martian men. I mean, what's up with that? Did you know these aliens are saying there are numerous other civilizations out there?"

"No, I hadn't heard that." John looked over at Alana.

"I didn't hear that either... wow..."

Daniel said, "So, I'm willing to at least listen."

A disheveled Mitch, hair askew, dark circles under his swollen, red eyes, came back into the kitchen at that moment. John wasn't surprised when he caught a faint whiff of alcohol.

"Want to join us Mitch?" John gestured to a stool at

the kitchen counter area.

Mitch mumbled something and almost missed the stool as he straddled it. John stood on the other side of the counter and pulled his Bible from one of the kitchen cabinet drawers. Alana finished the last dish and walked over to stand next to Mitch, prompting him to sit up a little straighter.

"I was just about to explain my take on what I think is going on these days, and I firmly believe the source of my information can be found in the Bible's Book of Revelation. I happened to be in an intensive Bible study group discussing the book of Revelation prior to all of this. It seems the strange phenomena we are experiencing lately could be traced back to the book of Revelation, particularly chapter eight."

Daniel held up his hand. "Whoa, wait a sec, hold on, let me bring that book of the Bible up on my screen here. You said Revelation, chapter eight, right?" John nodded.

Mitch's head hung slightly, his slouched body indicating a sleepy boredom. The only sounds were the snapping and crackling of the fire in the fireplace and Daniel's tapping of the virtual screen keys. Then Mitch surprised everyone by asking, "So are you saying you think this has to do with that rupture thing?"

Alana and John both tried to stifle a laugh. Then John clarified, "It's 'rapture' Mitch."

Mitch smiled sheepishly. "Oh..."

John continued, "I believe it's possible we are in what many Christians refer to as *the end times*. I'm also quite certain that—and this is according to the Bible—a lot of Christians will not recognize the so-called *signs of the times* because they believe the *rapture*—or, as it is also referred to, the *second coming of Christ*—hasn't preceded these signs."

John felt a sudden chill in the room, as if he'd let the fire die out. Alana's eyes were wide. "John, you mean the end is here without the rapture happening first? You think it's already begun?"

Mitch broke in. "Wait a minute, hold on here. What is the rapture? You don't mean you think that it's the end of the world do you? Translate into English please for those of us who aren't too familiar with this stuff…"

From the kitchen entrance, Parson spoke. "That's exactly what he means, Mitch. This life as we know it may be coming to an end, and the Bible tells us that what's coming next is going to be the worst kind of death and destruction that the world has ever seen."

CHAPTER 25

"I suspected something like this, but wasn't sure since the rapture didn't occur." Alana's legs suddenly didn't seem too reliable. She chewed on an already nonexistent thumbnail as she walked to the couch, and then sat down carefully. "I just thought—well I'm not sure what I thought. To tell you the truth, I've been a little consumed with just trying to keep it together. It was in the back of my mind though. The signs seemed familiar and yet, I definitely expected a different order of events."

Mitch's eyes turned hard. "Yeah well, that's good for people like you who believe this cra—uh—Christian stuff, but just because the Bible says something, doesn't make it true." Then, realizing the harshness of his words, he added, "With all due respect."

John replied reasonably, "Well, Daniel asked what I thought, and this is what I think is going on. Should I continue?"

Alana was impressed by John's patience with the three of them.

Mitch nodded, and Daniel opined, "Well, John, you're not the first person in history to predict the end of the world. Philosophers and religious leaders have been predicting it all along. But go ahead. You definitely have my attention."

"All right. First, I believe that the Bible is not only true, but it is the Word of God and, on top of that, a living document. What I mean by that is that it is applicable through all time—past, present, and future. While I don't know with certainty that what is happening in the world today *is* related to what it says in Revelation—in fact, I definitely have my doubts that it is—the signs still seem to point in that direction."

"Okeydokey. So the stories in the Bible are real for you," Mitch said. "Now, what does that have to do with what is happening today? Are you saying that the Bible tells us space invaders are going to visit earth from another galaxy? I'm not trying to be obnoxious here, but give me a break. I may not be a Bible scholar, but I'm pretty sure the Bible doesn't say anything about that."

Alana wanted to be annoyed with Mitch for his antagonistic stance, but found she empathized with him instead. She could see by his face that he asked in earnest, although the way he cynically expressed his questions set her teeth on edge. Again, she was impressed with John's calm demeanor and his neutral tone. She wasn't however, prepared when Mitch's next question was lobbed in her direction.

"Do you believe all of this too, Alana? Do you get where John is going with all this?"

Caught off guard, she didn't know what to say, but managed to stutter, "Uh—I—I'm not quite sure what John means or where he's leading, but I do know that all of this, no matter how strange to us, is part of God's plan. That is something I'm certain of." Mitch was staring at her and the intensity of his gaze made her cheeks flush crimson. She cast her eyes down to her hands.

John continued. "Without going into detail or reading to you from the Bible—I'm going to encourage you to do so yourself. If you don't have a Bible, we have extras here and you're more than welcome to use them. Or, of course, you can go online. But if you turn to Revelation, chapter eight, and start reading, you'll see a correlation between what is written and what is happening in the world today. It also appears that the correlation is in the same sequence as laid out in that chapter—at least as far as verses seven through nine show us."

Daniel quickly began typing something on his tablet as he said; "I can look that up right here."

John continued. "The most important thing to know though is that the Bible also clearly tells us no one will know the time or the day of the End Times. Both Matthew 24:36 and Mark 13:32 tell us: 'But of that day or hour no one knows, not even the angels in heaven, nor the Son, but the Father alone.' There are more references, Acts 1:7 'He said to them, "It is not for you to know times or epochs which the Father has fixed by His own authority."'

Daniel scratched his head. "So you're saying this could be the 'End Times' according to the Bible, but you're also saying the same Bible tells us it's impossible to know the time or the day?"

"That's not exactly what I was trying to say, Daniel, but I understand your confusion. It's complicated, not quite that simplistic, as you pointed out."

Daniel started to say something but stopped. John urged him to continue. "Well, I was just going to say, it sounds to me like you're saying the Bible contradicts itself, which, quite frankly, I've always believed."

Alana had to interject. "Daniel, the Bible doesn't contradict itself. I could try to help explain for you what John is talking about." She looked to John for approval and with a nod he gave it.

Mitch began squirming in his seat. "Before we go into that—I have something I want to talk about—ask you about. Is that OK?" As he spoke, Daniel looked up warily from his tablet.

"Sure Mitch, we're listening." Parson's kindness and attention gave Mitch the courage to continue.

"I know you're probably going to think I'm completely nuts, but I think—I hope Daniel will back me up on some of this."

Daniel tentatively nodded his head.

Then Mitch described for Parson, John and Alana the eerie phone call, the robed being who caused the accident, and lastly, the encounter Mitch had the night before.

"I thought I was just having a nightmare, naturally. But when I saw that thing hovering over my bed, even though I think I was dreaming, I don't know—I can't explain it. Remember how I couldn't remember the accident Daniel? The second I saw him—it—I knew he was the one in the road. I'm telling you, man, I know this dude's supposed to be an alien, but there's something more. He changed into something—something I don't think I could even begin to explain, but suffice to say it was hideous. I've never felt so—so scared of anything in my life." Telling his story left Mitch visibly shaken.

Alana rubbed her arms in an attempt to rid herself of the goose flesh that had arisen while Mitch spoke.

John's voice was grave. "What do you think, Pop?"

Parson said, "Daniel, you saw this alien in the road too?"

Daniel nodded.

"Well, son, I'm of the notion that these aliens aren't really aliens at all."

John's reply was quick, "I agree, Dad."

Mitch looked one to the other quizzically. "What are they if they aren't aliens?"

There was a silence in the room for a few seconds. "I think John and Parson believe they're demons." Alana said softly, then looked to them both as they nodded in unison.

"I'm afraid so," said Parson.

Alana continued. "The Bible isn't especially detailed about something like what's happening to us now. Correct me if I'm wrong, John."

John eyed Alana with admiration. "Alana's right. According to some passages in the Old Testament and a passage in the New Testament we can find some clues as to current events. Jude chapter one, for example, tells us there were giants. The actual word for these beings were Nephilim, which in Hebrew translates to 'giants.' There are other words in the Bible that have sometimes been used as a translation for 'giants.' There's Emim, which are the fearful ones' or Rephaim, which are 'the dead ones' or Anakim, which are 'the long necked ones.' There are some historical writings that also call them 'The Watchers'."

Mitch's mouth was slightly agape as he listened to John.

Parson added, "Many scholars believe these giants are a race that came about when fallen angels—or, as they are also known, demons—came to earth and coupled with human women."

Daniel's response was direct. "What the... are you kidding me? The Bible talks about bad angels who did the wild thing with humans? Mind explaining to me why demons would need space ships for crying out loud?"

"Hold on, Daniel," John broke in, "That's the entire point here. Deception. They don't *need* a spacecraft; they could use them, though, to help perpetuate a gigantic ruse. It's a good plan, wouldn't you say?"

Alana noticed Mitch sitting there looking stupefied and not a little unhinged. "I need to just think about all of this, I guess—I just need to... sorry you guys, you're gonna have to excuse me. No offense, John, but this is just too much to process for now..."

Mitch got up so quickly he almost tipped his chair over, and then strode out of the room.

CHAPTER 26

Alana immediately followed Mitch calling out to him, "Mitch, wait a second."

When Mitch heard her call his name he didn't take another step, but turned around.

"Mitch, this is a lot for anyone to take in. So much has happened—so much is still happening. I hope you didn't feel ganged up on in there."

His focus on getting himself a drink was momentarily supplanted by his attraction to Alana. As she walked toward him, he became immobile, her warm green eyes rooting him to the spot. He felt vulnerable and transparent. The realization caused a flush to spread from his neck and face down his arms, and he hoped she didn't notice.

"I—ah—I—"

Terrific, now I'm going to be so tongue-tied I'll sound like I'm imitating Porky Pig. Get a grip Mitch, get a grip.

He tried again. "No, it's not that. I didn't feel cornered at all. What you, John and Parson were talking about though, is just tough to swallow... for me, anyway. No offense, but I'm more of a 'proof' guy, so it's hard for me to accept religion. Sorry."

Alana's heart seemed to be right there in her enormous eyes. Mitch tried to hold her gaze, longing to figure out what she was really thinking. Suddenly, knowing what Alana thought was of paramount importance, more important than anything else in the world. A butterfly started flitting around in his stomach. He felt his entire body becoming warm and it had nothing to do with the temperature of the room or the whiskey; it had to do with the quickening of his pulse.

His hands felt clammy. Impulsively he rubbed his palms together. This definitely was uncharted territory. He actually felt something—something beyond physical attraction. Mitch was fully aware he objectified the opposite sex. He never cared what a woman was thinking—as long as they both were in it for a good time, why should he? This thing with Alana, though, was something different altogether.

"That's okay, I'm not offended at all." She smiled kindly and Mitch went weak in the knees. He found his eyes fixated on her perfectly white teeth, her sumptuous full lips. What was going on? Women didn't do this to him... even the beautiful ones. *He* was the seducer; always confident in his ability to draw any woman he wanted to him with lightening speed. He had the gift of gab, he was charming, and he knew women and how to play them.

Alana's beauty was undeniable and he understood that, but there was something more that he couldn't put his finger on. He wanted to be near her, not merely seduce her. He wanted to find out all about her. He wanted to talk to her. He wanted to listen to anything and everything she had to say. He wanted to get lost in her eyes and smell the intoxicating perfume of her. With a start, he realized— for the first time in far too long— that he wanted to stop drinking so he would be worthy of her.

She tossed her hair out of her eyes as she spoke, the shiny gold of it resettling on her shoulders. His gaze returned to her lips, watching them as she talked. She was the most stunning woman he had ever seen.

Focus! You're not going to hear one word she says and then you'll really look like an imbecile.

"When you're ready, I'd love to share a bit of the Bible with you, if you'd let me. I promise you can tell me to stop any time. I'd also like to share what having faith and relying on my faith has done for my life. You never know, it just might help you put all of what has been going on into perspective. There's a lot of wisdom in the Bible. It's a great resource, especially given the times."

She could read the phone book and I'd listen. Anything

coming from those lips would be heaven...

He swallowed drily before speaking. "Sure, I'd like that. I can't promise you'll convert me, but I'll at least listen." He hoped his attraction for her wasn't too glaringly obvious. Old habits die hard and Mitch gave her one of his signature grins.

"Great! See you later then, you know—for dinner. We can pick a time to start after we all get more settled."

Mitch tried to sound indifferent, "I... sounds like a p—plan!"

He looked down quickly, embarrassed by the unusual stutter he seemed to have developed in the past five minutes.

Well... so much for avoiding playing Porky's understudy...

As Mitch watched her turn around toward the kitchen, he thought being isolated in northern Nowhere Land might turn out more pleasant than he initially guessed. Study time, one-on-one with her? Hmm... even recalling the boogey man of last night's nightmares couldn't dim the excitement of *that* enticing engagement.

CHAPTER 27

The threat of the coming asteroid prompted the residents of Sleeping Bear to take stockpiling supplies seriously. For weeks, each resident pitched in to help prepare for a possible survival mode existence. Wood was chopped every day, stacked and covered with tarpaulins or put in sheds. Those who could cook took turns making meals for either immediate consumption or freezing. Long term plans for gardens and the possibility of keeping cows for milk, chicken and geese for eggs, and other livestock on the property were discussed.

Scheduled trips to the nearest warehouse food store for supplies were carefully planned. On this particular trip, John took Alana along. He found himself charged by the fact he had her company to himself while they waited in long lines to get into the store, then more lines to get two carts. Once they had their carts, only a few customers were allowed to go down the aisles at a time, only to find the shelves poorly stocked. At one point, a harried woman pushing a cart down the produce aisle ran over Alana's foot.

"Ouch!" Alana started hopping up and down on the foot that wasn't run over, and tucked the other one up under her bottom like she was playing hopscotch. The hit-and-run driver disappeared with her offending cart, not bothering to look back.

"Are you OK?" John began to bend down to examine her foot.

"No, don't bother, I'll live. Let's just go through our list and get this over with."

John hesitated. Alana waved him off. "John, really, my foot's fine. Let's get back to work." She stood on both feet and turned a smile on him that lit up her face. John was surprised that something as simple as her smiling at him could make this mundane and often irritating chore something he hoped would last.

Each cart was soon filled with the personal items requested by the Sleeping Bear residents as well as down comforters, thick socks, thermal underwear, lanterns, batteries, four small generators, camping equipment, and other survival gear. John made a mental note that they needed to prepare their lists in a more organized manner and consider doubling or tripling what they picked up on these trips. Restocking of store shelves seemed slow, with John and Alana often completely buying out existing stock.

John said, "You know, it's a good thing we're up here in the boondocks. I think that's the only reason there's merchandise on store shelves. I've heard stores in many of the major cities have simply closed because they can't get supplies."

Alana put something in her cart. "Well, that means we'll probably not only have to plant some gardens to make us more independent, but we should also think about adding a greenhouse. Don't you think?"

"That's a great idea considering we have some pretty tough winters up here. But we'll have to see what happens when that asteroid hits and if we'll be able to maintain a garden. Maybe we should think about something inside a pole barn… I'll put my head together with the others and start working on that right away." John grinned, "You know, you're pretty smart… for a *lawyer.*"

Alana dropped a can of stewed tomatoes into her cart. "Excuse me?" She spun around, placed a hand on her hip, and faked being hugely annoyed.

John backed up. "Whoa, OK, I'm sorry! You're very smart. I guess I just don't have a soft spot for lawyers."

She raised an eyebrow.

He put both his hands up backing farther away, "OK, OK, that is, until *now!*"

She frowned, her lips pressed together sternly.

John continued his faux *mea culpa*. "Seriously! I humbly apologize and admit you are a *genius* lawyer!" He looked up hopefully.

Channeling a queen pardoning a supplicant, Alana nodded serenely. "Well... I shall accept your apology and forgive your transgression." She turned back to her shopping and looked behind her only once with a delightful twinkle in her eyes.

Over an hour later, after loading the truck, John hopped into the driver's seat. Alana was fiddling with something in her lap when she said, "John, the seat belt seems to be stuck."

Instinctively, he moved to assist her and inadvertently pressed his chest against hers as he reached for the belt. The unexpected contact with her body caused a jolt of desire so sudden, he abruptly sat back, walloping his head on the rearview mirror. Alana seemed unaware of her effect on him. "What happened? Are you all right?"

John rubbed his head. "Uh... sure, I... just... um..." He sat back in his own seat and reached over backwards with his right arm trying to reach the belt buckle without touching any part of her body while doing so. Beads of sweat began dappling his forehead. Despite his efforts, his elbow brushed up against her causing new delicious sensations. His arousal shocked and humiliated him. He closed his eyes as he fumbled around and tried to think about hunting season. When he finally disengaged her buckle he sat back hard, drawing in deep breaths and trying not to be obvious about it.

"Thanks!" She wiggled herself into a comfortable position in the seat, completely oblivious to John's struggle. He said a silent prayer of thanks for that.

He couldn't speak. He knew if he tried, it would come out as a croak.

He was befuddled and silent on the ride home as Alana chattered away. John nodded as if listening, but he was far more focused on his disturbing physical reaction to her.

She finally stopped mid-sentence. "John, what's wrong?"

Snapping to attention he said, "Hmmm? I'm fine, fine..." She didn't believe him and smiled skeptically. After hesitating a moment, she decided to fill the uncomfortable silence with more chatter, and John continued to pretend he was listening intently. After a short while she said, "OK John, I'm talking too much, aren't I? I do that sometimes. I'm sorry..."

"Oh, no! No, Alana, I like... you're fine. It's fine... that you... ah... like to talk. I like listening—"

A little smile accompanied by a quizzical frown indicated she still remained unconvinced. To his increased discomfort, she became quiet.

He tried to make amends. "Alana, I'm sorry. I guess I did allow my mind to wander a little. I'm trying to figure out a way to get the supplies we need so we can stock up on more, but make fewer trips. I really am interested in what you're saying, though—" He took his eyes off the road and glanced over at her trying to convey the sincerity of his words.

She gave him one of her mega-watt smiles and went back to enthusiastically describing a college internship the law firm was sponsoring.

They had to take several detours due to roadblocks set up by the National Guard, who had been called in to restore order after some local rioting and looting in the hamlet of Manistee. This devastated the community residents as the town had already been in a depressed state even before the power outages.

When they arrived back at the resort and began unloading the car, Daniel was there to greet them. "The generators had to pop back on again. They've been on for almost three hours now."

John said, "I'll go check how they're all running once we get these things put away."

They had a specific routine—the fresh meat would go immediately to the large freezer in the pole barn, with the exception of any food planned for the day's meals. All of the other items—except for the personal ones—were taken to another pole barn that was used for dry and nonperishable goods. John was glad for this organized routine as it always made these large shopping trips much easier.

When Alana was transferring some of the things in

her arms to Daniel, a thermal blanket fell to the ground and she bent over to retrieve it. With a herculean act of willpower, John averted his eyes from her very shapely bottom. He could feel, however, that his cheeks were burning red hot with shame.

Later, when everything was put away in its place and Alana was off somewhere, John wrestled alone with his distressing thoughts.

She's a young, gorgeous woman I'm forced—given the situation—to live with. I'm just not used to it. There are only guys at the firehouse. My normal daily interactions don't include incredibly gorgeous women. That's all it is. I just have to stop my thoughts when they drift inappropriately. I'll be all right. I've just got to adjust to living with her, that's all.

As John walked into the kitchen to prepare for dinner, he was painfully aware his self-analysis and pep talk were probably useless.

CHAPTER 28

"So why is this a bad thing?" asked Daniel carefully. "Instead of news about widespread looting or the asteroid, I'd say this was pretty upbeat in comparison."

Mitch felt the same as Daniel. Steve was rubbing his forehead, and Sarah looked stricken, her eyes full of fear. Parson was sitting in a chair shaking his head, John looked miserable, and Alana was wringing her hands.

Mitch took a drink from the bottle of beer he was holding, making sure his face was inscrutable.

The reaction was caused by news that the alien Visitors would be conducting a nation-wide census.

"What's going on Daddy?" Lizzy asked, with what clearly sounded to Mitch like apprehension.

"Not to worry, baby. Listen, why don't you, Megan and Caleb go outside for awhile? Caleb, will you keep an eye on them?"

"Daddy, I don't need a babysitter!" Lizzy protested.

"I know, I wasn't saying you couldn't take care of yourself, Honey, but until things settle down a little, I think we all should keep an eye out for each other."

Caleb, proud of being assigned this important duty said, "Sure, Mr. Culver. If I see anyone on the property, I'll alert you immediately."

"Thanks, Caleb." John said, giving him a pat on the back.

Steve looked over at his son and nodded. "Go ahead, Caleb, and make sure the girls stay in your sight."

Mitch waited until the children were safely out of earshot before he spoke his mind. "Why are you worried about them being out there alone? I thought you said this was a safe area?"

Parson answered, "Well, it *is* under normal circumstances, but the world has turned topsy-turvy... proof of that is what we just saw on TV a few moments ago. While the looting seems to be limited to Lansing and south of Lansing in Detroit, we need to be vigilant. Security fence or no, a pair of wire cutters would take care of that obstacle in short order."

"Oh, I see..." Mitch said a little sheepishly.

"I still don't get why these so-called Visitors going house to house for a census is such a terrible thing." Daniel said.

Mitch agreed. "I admit I'm a little confused too."

Steve spoke up. "Daniel, there is no doubt you're a smart guy, probably smarter than any of us here in this room. Do you really think aliens have been watching the earth and have decided to visit us because they want to be here for the second coming of Christ? And just as important, do you really believe that aliens interfering in our constitutional process is something to be celebrated?" His questions carried an angry edge.

Daniel responded sarcastically, "Well, it's better than thinking they're 'fallen angels.' You know, I've seen a lot of them now and I still haven't caught a glimpse of their pretty feathered wings."

With balled fists, Steve glared at Daniel. "What the Bible talks about is real, whether you believe it or not. There is so much about the spiritual world we don't know. If the aliens are manifestations of demonic forces that have chosen to walk boldly amongst us, this is nothing to be scoffed at. You don't have children. You don't have a clue what such a danger feels like to a parent." Steve thrust his finger close to Daniel's chest.

Sarah stepped close to her husband's side, gently touching the crook of his arm, which immediately seemed to cool his temper.

"Whoa—hold on here. We're not the enemy. This is a lot for any of us to take in no matter what our beliefs are." Parson looked genially at both men.

"Sorry, man," Steve said apologetically.

"No problem," Daniel replied. "Guess we're all a little on edge. Sorry if I sounded like I was being disrespectful about your religion."

Despite a calm discussion that continued for the better part of an hour, Mitch felt no closer to any real answers than he had before they started—but there was one small difference. Mitch began to feel the stirrings of something. He wanted to believe like they did. He wanted to have the same kind of strength Alana, Parson, John, Steve, and Sarah had. Heck, even their kids had this unshakable faith. They seemed so strong and able to cope with all that came their way, and they were kids! He wanted whatever they had, and he felt an increasing need to find out how to get it. He was so tired of feeling frightened and miserable.

"Listen, man—I'm getting a headache with all of this. I gotta tell ya, I really want to be able to put this all together the way you guys seem able to, but I can't. I just can't get my mind to think that way. I don't know, maybe I'm hopeless…"

Alana moved to his side and put her hand on his arm, "No one is hopeless, Mitch. Don't think that way. You're doing fine. Why don't we take a walk and talk about this?"

When Alana touched his sleeve, Mitch felt her

fingers through the fabric like a mild electric shock. All of his senses were heightened. His grandmother used to call it "sparks flying." He stared down at her hand as if it held some magical power. When he turned and met Alana's eyes, he looked down again immediately, and stammered, "S—sure."

He wanted to smack himself on the forehead for sounding so stupid. His fears were baseless. Alana, as usual, seemed to have no idea of the affect she had on him, and this greatly reduced his anxiety. His intuition told him she saw him myopically, her vision of him strictly that of a conquest-for-Christ-conversion and nothing more.

John's voice was calm but to the point. "Listen everybody, I have to take an inventory of the food we have on the shelves. The date of the asteroid hit isn't too far away. While I don't believe we're in any imminent danger, the strike might diminish what little food supply we have. Why don't we all go about our chores and take some time to think things over?" John had resumed his "take-charge" mode and Mitch was glad.

"Good idea," Parson said. "I'm the cook tonight, so I better start the preparations."

"I'd like to help Parson, but since I'm a horrible cook, it's probably best if I just assist," Daniel said.

"Sounds great, Daniel my man! You can start chopping the vegetables for the salad. You don't have to be a great chef to do that." Parson gave Mitch an exaggerated wink.

The others dispersed except for Alana and Mitch who temporarily put their duties on hold to take a walk.

When they got to the foyer, Alana said, "I'm just going to run to my room and get my Bible in case you have any questions."

"No problem, I'll wait for you right out front." Mitch was surprised he was able to say a complete sentence without stammering. *Atta boy Mitch-er-roo—keep dazzling her with your monosyllabic replies. She's sure to fall hard-core for that kind of brilliance.*

He let out a huge sigh. *I am such an idiot! Why would she be interested in a guy who's acting like a tongue-tied fourteen year-old? I need to start acting like the old Mitch, the guy who'd lure any babe with ease.*

As he walked across the grass, he tugged at his white, green and blue striped Polo dress shirt to straighten it. *Man, I wish I had thought to iron this thing.*

He smoothed his designer jeans, wishing he had a chance to change into something she'd like. *What did she like?* All he knew was that he intended to find out. His heartbeat kicked up a notch when she returned.

She rushed out the door with her hair flying, scattered wisps floating behind her. She was a little winded when she reached his side. "I ran all the way! I still have to get the laundry done, so we can't take too much time."

Mitch was riveted by her. She had run those few steps to him like a gazelle and now stood before him in a red tank top and cute navy sweater that fit as if they were made just for her. He had never seen anyone look better in a pair of jeans. Was there even one thing less than perfect about her?

She was close enough for him to smell lilacs and, he thought, maybe baby powder. Whatever it was, it smelled warm and sensual and clean, and Mitch experienced a fresh shot of adrenaline and heat coursing his body like a current.

Alana asked, "Ah—where did we leave off? Oh wait—I remember—you asked me about forgiveness. Do you want to talk about that or something else?" Her voice held a lyrical sweetness, and listening to it, Mitch finally understood what the saying *music to my ears* meant.

He jammed his hands into his front pockets and wondered how he could make this walk with her last. He knew if he kept asking her questions about the Bible, she'd stay to answer them. His attempts to prolong their other meetings had resulted in his not only enjoying her company, but coming away with a strange feeling of contentment irrespective of his attraction to her. It all seemed intertwined, but he knew that there was something more to these exchanges than just the boy-girl chemistry. He just didn't know what that "something" was yet.

He decided on the spot he was going for broke. Why not? What did he have to lose? Their earlier talks led him to believe that while Alana didn't seem necessarily attracted to him, she liked him and felt at ease around him.

On several prior occasions he had drawn her out about dating and dating fiascos. Doing so, he had discovered she didn't like men who drank. She didn't come right out and say as much, but she had told him about a particularly horrific and frightening night when her date drank to excess and almost killed them both. Most revealing of all, Alana had never fallen in love... and this offered Mitch hope.

So he took the leap. "Alana, I was thinking I wanted to—ummm—I was thinking maybe I should give up drinking..."

Mitch paused. They were standing on the banks of Little Lake Manistee surrounded by pine trees so lush, their needles had the appearance of fur. The reflection of the sun off the lake made it sparkle like etched crystal. A breeze ruffled Alana's hair, causing single tendrils to dance around her face. She used a hand to shade her eyes from the sun and Mitch marveled at its slender beauty. Fluffy cumulus clouds floated in the clear azure skies above them. If Mitch could have frozen this moment—the lake, the sun, the trees, Alana standing next to him—he would have. Feeling uncharacteristically vulnerable, he knew he was about to venture into dangerous and unknown territory. If he did, there would be no turning back—but he also realized he'd do pretty much anything for Alana at this point. He had to know if there was a chance.

And so he resolutely continued, "I mean—if I stopped drinking, would I be the kind of guy you'd consider going... uh... maybe... like dating?"

CHAPTER 29

Alana held her breath for a few seconds of stunned silence. "Oh! Oh... I didn't know—I had no idea..."

He interrupted. "I'm not trying to push you into anything. But if I stopped drinking—would you want to— do you think you'd consider giving us a try?"

Alana looked down and was surprised to see her hands trembling. "Mitch it would be good for you to stop drinking, of course. I'm sure John could help you with that. I don't think you're supposed to go cold turkey without taking precautions of some kind, but as I said, John could probably advise you." She hesitated before going on.

Mitch seemed intent on convincing her of his sincerity. "You can tell me anything you want, I'm pretty hard to scare."

A mischievous smile played about his lips, and although it was cute, she felt torn. On the one hand, her greatest desire was to lead a lost soul to the Lord. On the other, she felt a sudden thrill that he thought of her this way. It hadn't crossed her mind. He had always been polite and attentive, but didn't seem to indicate anything beyond that. Here he was admitting as much, which made it all the more difficult for her to say what came next. "Mitch, I—I can't date you. You're not a Christian."

Mitch's smile faded instantly. "Why can't you date someone who isn't a Christian? People do it all the time."

Alana struggled to explain. "I know, but people do a lot of things they aren't supposed to do. Christians—*true* Christians—aren't supposed to date someone who isn't a Christian. The Bible says this plainly. Dating is what we do to find a marriage partner, and we are not supposed to marry someone who the Bible tells us is 'unequally yoked.'" Here Alana pantomimed quotation marks.

Mitch grabbed her gently but firmly by both arms, and stared intensely into her eyes "Alana, I don't really understand what you're saying. I mean, I haven't been to church in a really long time. I guess I believe there's a god of some kind. But tell me this: since it appears I'm not the Christian you want me to be, if I became a Christian, if I converted and believed—as you've told me before—in my *heart of hearts* that Jesus Christ is Lord, then would you go out with me?"

Alana stared back at Mitch wordlessly. The last time

she had had any real feelings for someone of the opposite sex was in law school, where she had met a fellow student at church. They had dated for over six months, and at first she believed she genuinely was falling in love with him. Over time, however, it became clear that she was working too hard to keep it afloat. Since then, she had dated few men because she found that, in general, they either didn't measure up or were intimidated by her beauty; the latter made no sense to her. She wanted to hand them the mirror with which she saw all her flaws magnified and in Technicolor.

This entreaty by Mitch caught Alana by surprise and she found herself vaguely excited by his touch, his earnestness, his eagerness and intensity. *Lord, what do I say? What do I do?* Then, before the words formed in her head, they tumbled out of her mouth.

"Well—yes. If you accepted Christ as your Savior and endeavored to stop drinking, I guess I would consider going on a... date with you." As she said this she realized the idea of seeing Mitch as more than a friend suddenly seemed quite appealing.

"Then I'll do it! I'll become a Christian and I'll stop drinking. Where do I sign?"

Alana found herself giggling, something she wasn't prone to do. "Mitch, I'm serious, you can't make this one big joke."

"I'm sorry, I really am. I'm an idiot sometimes—it's the way I handle things when I'm nervous. This is a huge step, I mean, for me to even say these things, you know. But I mean it. I want to do this, all of it. I just don't know how to go about this whole Christian thing. Is there some sort of instruction book? I'm good at following directions."

"Yes, as a matter of fact there is. It's called the Bible," Alana said cheekily.

"Good, I'll get one. Check. What else do I do? Just tell me boss, I'm at your command."

Despite her usual elegant demeanor, Alana found herself giggling like a tween. Embarrassed by this juvenile silliness, she abruptly turned away from him and studied the lake as if the Loch Ness monster was making an appearance. There was a strange fluttering around her insides. She liked this sensation, but wasn't sure she should. *Steady, Alana. Steady.*

"Well Mitch, it's not so easy. You can't just say you're a Christian and voilà! You are one. It takes study and repentance. You and I could keep having our talks, but I'd also bring in John and Parson and maybe Steve or Sarah to help. In other words, you'd need other seasoned Christians to help lead you to the Lord."

He grabbed her again by her shoulders. "I'll do it. Name the day and time. I'll do it for you, Alana—that is, if you'll have me." The passion and plea in his brown eyes gripped her heart. Her first thought was, *He really wants to do all of this just for me? But he can't do this just for me. He has to do this for himself! Without faith in God, no matter how eager he is, kicking his alcoholism will be almost impossible.*

Still, a relationship had to be premised on both.

She found his willingness to change his life just for her endearing and at the same time, a little frightening. The only person in her life who had ever exhibited such devotion and passion toward her was her sister, Bianca. And of course, a sister's affection was something altogether different.

Next to Mitch, the pursuers of her past were obscure, faceless, and lifeless and she felt wholly disconnected from them, like some casual observer looking at a film of someone else's life. Mitch was something new, something forbidden... something she wanted to run from as much as she wanted to run to.

Trying to rein in her thoughts and feelings and this heady conversation, Alana said, "Mitch, before we embark on any type of personal adventure—so to speak—these things you said you would do *have* to be done. Do you understand what I'm saying? Do you understand what you're agreeing to?"

He reached down and took both her hands in his. "I got it. No conversion, no deal." Alana raised an eyebrow.

"Seriously, though," Mitch lowered his gaze. "I really don't get the full extent of it all. I have to admit that because I want to be totally honest here. But I'll try to do what you ask harder than I've tried to do anything—and I mean anything—in my life. I want this to work—the whole thing, especially the part about you and me. We can start by going to John and asking him how I can stop drinking, because right now that idea is scaring my socks off. But I'll try. So what do we do to get started?"

His hands were warm, his eyes solemn. Despite her better instincts, Alana decided to believe him. "Let's see if John has a few minutes where we can talk this out with him."

He made two fists, brought them up in the air and threw his head back, "Yesssss!" Alana laughed at his happiness, happy herself that she was so much the cause of it.

They began walking slowly back to the lodge. "Mitch, you know that it isn't just going to be the drinking. I can't... I won't... I mean... you have to become a Christian. That is key. We can't be together if you don't know the Lord as Lord of your life."

"I understand. With your help, I'm going to take that big step too. I can do this, I want to do this, I *will* do this."

CHAPTER 30

They found John in one of the storage buildings and told him what their plans were, taking care to leave out the dating aspect. Intuitively he knew. Alana, glowing, kept her eyes averted. He could hardly blame Mitch; any man of flesh and blood would fall for her. They already made a great looking couple.

John felt heaviness in his chest. He knew if he allowed himself to consider its source, he'd discover jealousy, so he immediately put it out of his mind and said, "Mitch, you have to realize a couple of things. I've seen detox before. It's not a pretty sight. The determination you feel now is going to take a powder once your body begins withdrawal."

John assumed his professional tone, which enabled

him to talk to the young man in front of him with dispassionate authority. He ran a hand through his hair. "My suggestion is that you do not go cold turkey, but do an accelerated withdrawal, with alcohol being doled out incrementally in smaller and smaller amounts. But it's not going to be enough. You will crave and, I promise you, *demand* more. How are we going to handle that?"

Alana interrupted, "Maybe we should look into rehabilitation facilities. Do you know of any in the area, John?"

Mitch's response was immediate and adamant. "No. No way. I mean… I want to be here, I want to stay here. I don't want to go to any facility."

John replied evenly, "I hear what you're saying, but you need to understand you're going to want more than you'll get. And after being weaned, after you're cut off completely, your craving will intensify. My suggestion is for you to stay in one of the cabins away from the rest with someone there with you, 24/7. I realize, though, that there's a fine line between helping you and holding you hostage. So what is your suggestion for getting around that?"

Alana answered instead. "Mitch, call it my lawyer training, but we should draw up an agreement that spells out your commitment and our part in it so that there will be no questions in the future. If you weaken in your resolve and believe you are being held against your will, it can be read back to you. We'll have the others witness the signing if they are comfortable doing so."

Without hesitation, Mitch eagerly responded, "I'll sign on the dotted line! When can we write it up?"

CHAPTER 31

Mitch stayed up until the wee hours drinking the last of his stash. To conserve energy, there had been a voluntary blackout imposed in Manistee county starting at 10:00 pm every night. Mitch was therefore drinking alone by candlelight. He hated himself for doing it; sitting in that dim puddle of light made him feel pathetic as he compulsively poured shot after shot. He had to use up what he had before he tried to go dry. The thought of not being able to reach for a bottle of alcohol any time he wanted tormented him. The idea became more inconceivable as the hours ticked by. What would he do without that pint secreted away in his back pocket? How would he get to sleep at night without a drink? He had real doubts he'd be able to do this. What had possessed him to think he could?

The first three days weren't as difficult as Mitch had expected. The constant vigil and steady praying in his room gave him some comfort. He was surprised that he found any comfort at all in someone praying for him, but the fact was he did. When Steve and Sarah were with him, they prayed silently and read from their Bibles; Parson, Alana and John often did the same. On the occasions when they prayed aloud for him, however, he had to admit something happened. He became calmer—almost peaceful—and his fears weren't quite so overwhelming.

Physically, he felt like he had the flu. One minute he was freezing, shaking like a leaf, and the next he was burning up and throwing off the covers. He vomited relentlessly until there was nothing left to vomit, subjecting him to the dry heaves. Eventually this subsided. Although he was weak, he showered frequently because it made him feel more human and because he thought given his current state Alana might begin to find him repellant. Mitch was also painfully aware that in 48 hours he'd have consumed his very last drop of alcohol and the pain and discomfort he felt now might escalate into agony. Although he tried to put a good face on it, he was tormented by the very real possibility that he was about to enter a personal hell over which he had no control. While Alana sat by his side that first afternoon, she reminded him gently that he had to do this for himself, he couldn't do this for her. He assured her that he understood and was definitely doing this for himself. But he knew if he were being completely honest, he'd tell her his primary motivation for becoming sober was so they could be together. What was wrong with being motivated by a woman who turned him into a bowl of Jell-O whenever she was near? When Alana was in the cabin with him, her beautiful face etched with worry, he believed he could do anything, endure anything for her sake.

Mitch also realized he was becoming more open to knowing Jesus, a savior all his minders seemed to know on an intensely personal level. At first his interest was tied to the promise he had made to Alana, but as the hours passed, he found himself curious despite how awful he felt, indeed, often *because* of how awful he felt. He asked questions. Not the perfunctory ones of a child, but deep, life-probing questions—the ones that he really wanted to know the answers to—and one in particular that had haunted him for years.

This last question had become the biggest obstacle in his life. But to ask it, he had to tell a story, a terrible, secret story, one he had spent years hiding. Although his guts twisted at the prospect conversely, for the first time, he felt the stirrings of hope.

Alana was in an easy chair next to Mitch's bed sewing some warm weather garments. John was quietly reading his Bible across the room next to the fireplace.

Mitch began tentatively. "John, I have a question."

John set aside his Bible, "Sure, Mitch. Shoot. What's on your mind?"

Mitch didn't know where or how to begin. Worse,

he realized that once he finished what he had to say, Alana would probably never want anything to do with him. Maybe this wasn't such a good idea after all. Mitch began to lose his nerve. "Ahhh… I don't know…"

Alana said softly, "Go on, Mitch, and say whatever you need to say."

He took a deep breath and began. "If someone did something—something really horrible—how could God forgive them for it when it's impossible to fix?"

John sat back in his chair. "Well, the Bible tells us that there is no sin that His sacrifice doesn't cover. There is nothing you could have done that can't be forgiven. Christ died as the sacrifice—the *complete* sacrifice—for the sins of the world. It is finished. He didn't leave anyone out of that sacrifice. It's all-inclusive. Jesus didn't die for just *some* sins, He died for them all."

Fighting a wave of nausea, Mitch spoke haltingly. "Not this. It can't be fixed. There's nothing anyone can do to fix what I—what happened. There's no way to make it right. Ever."

"Mitch, there's always a way with Christ. It's not something I can easily explain to you, it's something you have to take on faith. I know that's a hard thing to do, but it's something you must come to terms with yourself… believing, in faith, that Jesus Christ died for your sins— even *your* sins—and that those sins are forgiven once you accept him as Lord." John was leaning forward now, elbows on his thighs, intensity narrowing his eyes.

Alana put down her sewing.

John asked Mitch quietly, "Do you want to tell us what it is that you feel is unforgivable?"

Drawing in a deep breath, Mitch began shakily, "I haven't spoken about it since my sentencing in court. Not even to my parole officer."

CHAPTER 32

Mitch sat silent for a few moments. He wondered what Alana was thinking now that he had let the cat out of the bag. He had a criminal record.

He sighed, running a hand through his hair. "I don't think I know how to talk about it. I haven't been able to even *think* about it for years. I guess that's why I drink. It's the only way I can get to sleep at night..."

"It's up to you. I'll listen and I won't judge you. I'd be more than happy to hear what you have on your conscience, and you don't have to fear my disapproval." John was now sitting so close to the edge of his chair, he was in danger of falling off.

Alana added, "I'm here for you if you want to unburden yourself. It might do you some good, Mitch."

Mitch turned to her quickly. "You're never going to accept this about me, Alana. It will probably scare you away."

Remarkably, he saw only compassion on her face. She reached out and took his hand in hers. "That's not true. All sin is the same to the Lord. All sin is equal. My sin is no worse than yours. Yours is no worse than mine in the eyes of the Lord. He died so that we would no longer be separated from Him because of sin. No matter what it is you have to say, I will not sit in judgment of you."

Mitch gripped her hand like a lifeline. With her words giving him courage, Mitch began telling the story he had tried so long to forget, the one that forever after had corrupted every chance of happiness.

"I was in Princeton, it was my third year. We all were out barhopping. I only had three drinks, the third one after dinner. I had the fourth drink hours after the third. At 3:00 in the morning, I felt perfectly capable of driving. My buddies were visibly incapacitated, so I got behind the wheel of the car to take us back to our fraternity house less than two miles away.

We were almost there, just a block away from our frat house when a woman ran a stop sign right in front of me. I had already stopped and hit the gas to go on through even before she reached the stop sign. I had the right of way. She never stopped. She just blew through the intersection, making a left turn right in front of me. I hit the back end of the passenger side. I almost missed her—if she had gotten there just a split second earlier she would have cleared the intersection."

Mitch paused. The scene wasn't unfamiliar, playing as it did over and over through the years. His jaw ached and he realized he was clenching it. He took another deep breath and continued.

"She spun out of control—it had rained earlier and the roads were slick. It was so fast. The next thing I knew, her front end was facing mine and her back end was wrapped around a telephone pole. We knew right away it was bad. The van was—just hammered—I'll never forget it..."

Saying the words, having an audience—the silent film of his mind became unbearably real and Mitch felt strangled by the lump forming in his throat. He beat back the urge to break down and continued doggedly on.

"I immediately got out of the car and ran over to the van. The woman driving—there was so much blood—she was slumped over the steering wheel. Her air bag had opened and partially deflated. The white bag was almost obliterated by blood. The whole side of her head looked caved in. I called out to her, but she didn't respond. Then... then my eyes—like it was slow motion—moved to the back seat on the passenger side. I saw blood dripping from a jagged piece of the window. Most of the window was gone. Just this one jagged piece—the point half way up the window. In the night, the blood looked like chocolate syrup. My mind didn't register what I was seeing, you know? Then one of the guys hollered—I don't remember who— 'There's a kid—a baby—over there! Look!'

We all ran to the car seat that had been thrown from the car. When we got there, not even thinking—I grabbed the car seat to lift the baby up and—and…

A sob escaped him and Alana placed a hand on his shoulder. They both waited in silence for Mitch to collect himself, then John said gently, "Go on Mitch—if you can."

Mitch took a deep shaky breath and let it out slowly. He let go of Alana's hand and lowered his eyes. "The baby's head—her little head just rolled off her shoulders. She—she was almost totally decapitated…" Mitch dropped his head and covered his face with both hands as an inhuman sound came from deep within his throat. His shoulders shook as he tried desperately to control the first crying jag he'd had while sober since the accident.

CHAPTER 33

Alana wept quietly. She swiped at the tears with one hand, gripping Mitch's hand with the other.

John lowered his head and said a quick prayer. "Lord, help this man find your peace with these memories. We ask you to give him your strength, Father, to overcome what he has done, and we also pray for the family. In Jesus' Name." He then asked Mitch, "Are you able to go on?"

Mitch nodded and swallowed several times trying to corral the emotions churning inside him. "I almost dropped the car seat. I guess I set it back down and tried—I tried—I thought I could put her head back on her neck. Her little face—I'll never forget it as long as I live—was untouched somehow. Her eyes were closed, she looked so peaceful, like a little doll, but she was—she was dead and her head was only attached by a strip of skin!" Mitch cried again, but worse, much worse this time, an unbearable keening sound. He heard the howling from far away before realizing, horrified, that it was he.

Alana squeezed his hand and protested, "But Mitch, the accident wasn't your fault. You said the woman ran the stop sign!" Mitch hiccupped, raised a wet face, his eyes suddenly hard.

"Yeah well, I'm getting to that." He wanted to finish this confession but on his terms. No pity, no cutting himself any slack. He sat up, roughly wiped his nose with an arm and kept going, "The guys were just screaming in panic. I guess I was too, but I really don't remember that part too clearly. It was pretty much chaos from that moment on. One of them called 911 on his phone and just about that time, we heard a pop and a sizzling sound. We looked back and saw flames had started coming from the back of the woman's van. I just stood there. The rest of the guys ran back to the van to try and get the woman out. They couldn't open the door, but Bill got inside it somehow. As carefully as they could, with flames shooting up all around them, they got her out and carried her away from the van. Then it went completely up in flames. All for nothing. She didn't make it. The police and rescue workers got there pretty quick, but she was pronounced DOA. Of course, so was the little girl..."

"But I don't understand why you're still blaming yourself for this Mitch. She was at fault..." Alana tried again. "I mean—I understand why this haunts you… I can't imagine going through what you did, but why do you feel such incredible guilt? You didn't cause the accident."

Nausea crawled up from his stomach and burned in his throat. He shivered cold and clammy as if ceiling sprinklers had burst open drenching him. Despite the nausea and chills, his need to tell the story completely had become compulsive. Everything had to be told.

"That's really sweet of you to try and take me off the hook, Alana." He gave her hand a squeeze and let go. "But I'm not finished. There's quite a bit more to the story." Mitch swallowed down the rising bile. "When the police arrived, they immediately could smell the alcohol on the guys, except I wasn't worried because I was positive I was perfectly sober, right? I had not only given it enough time before driving, but I had eaten dinner before the last drink. Well—I was wrong. Dead wrong as they say, pun intended." Mitch used a towel near the bed to wipe his face. "I willingly took a Breathalyzer test, and much to my complete shock, I didn't pass. I was one-tenth of a point past the limit. I was legally drunk. The strange thing was I never felt so sober in my life."

John still had his elbows on his knees, leaning forward, hanging on every word Mitch said. With this last revelation, John slowly shook his head back and forth.

Mitch noticed. "I know, man, you must think I'm scum."

John didn't hesitate. "No, Mitch, not at all. I'm just

so sorry that this happened to you, and to that woman and baby. I'm sorry for you, I'm sorry for your family and I'm sorry for that woman's family. It's a terrible, terrible tragedy. But you can't change any of that now. It's something that happened in the past. You're right; you can't fix that particular situation. But you can fix the way you live your life, by giving it over to Christ. It's the only way you'll learn to forgive yourself. I can tell you that with absolute certainty; it's the only way you'll ever know true peace of mind."

Mitch wanted to trust him more than he wanted to trust anyone in his entire life. Looking into John's eyes, somehow Mitch knew he was telling him the truth. Before he realized he was saying the words, he uttered, "You know something? I believe you…"

Alana grabbed Mitch's hand and squeezed. That small gesture brought renewed tears to his eyes.

"Let's concentrate on getting you sober, Mitch. Wait until after you've gone through this drying out. One ordeal at a time, one step at a time. You have to make this commitment clean and sober and with a clear mind."

Alana still had more questions. "Mitch, what happened after you took the Breathalyzer?"

"I was handcuffed right there on the spot. There was a witness, unable to sleep who saw everything from her bedroom window. She told the officers the woman caused the accident, and while the accident itself wasn't my fault, I was beyond the legal limit. It didn't matter what the other driver did, I was legally drunk. I had to go to jail. I used my savings and raised bail but had to spend that night in jail. An experience I'd never, ever want to repeat. There I was in a cell that reeked of vomit and urine so acrid it burned your eyes. And there I stayed with the rest of the drunks and thieves and criminals."

Mitch leaned back on the pillows suddenly tired. He kept his gaze fixed on the ceiling, too afraid to look at Alana. All three were quiet for a moment. Alana whispered, "Then what happened, Mitch?"

"Well—the trial was set pretty quickly. Of course, it made all the New Jersey papers. 'Princeton frat boy kills mother of four.' I made my family proud," he said acidly.

Alana stammered, "She was a—a mother of four children?"

"Yep, and in one fell swoop, I killed her and one of her kids." He was wondering which nail would be the one to permanently seal the coffin on their nascent relationship. Was it murdering the baby? Not dragging the mother out of the van? Murdering the mother of four? Oh well, there was no turning back now.

"Regardless of your responsibility in the matter, you never set out to take anyone's life, Mitch. You're being too hard on yourself," John said.

"Yeah, well, you didn't see that little baby's head roll off—you don't understand, man. Nothing, nothing they could have done to me could have been worse than what I was doing to myself. I haven't slept a solid night since. The only way I can even get to sleep is if I—"

He didn't have to finish his sentence; he knew Alana and John both knew where that was going.

"Because I had excellent grades and a perfectly clean record—not even a traffic ticket—the judge gave me five years probation and a ton of community service where I talked to classrooms full of students about the dangers of drinking and driving. The irony though, was after awhile, I went to these classes pretty smashed. I also had to pay restitution to the family and go to a drug and alcohol program for 90 days. I went to the program pretty smashed too." Mitch paused, staring into space for a few moments, then he continued. "The woman's husband was given the opportunity to speak at the hearing. It was the most unbelievable thing—" Mitch felt tears coming on and pinched the bridge of his nose. "He got up and spoke *on my behalf.* He begged the court for mercy, asking the judge not to go too hard on me. I just couldn't believe what I was hearing. Here he is in *tears* and he says this about the guy who killed his wife. They'd been married for eight years. Their seven, four, and two year old would grow up without their baby sister and their Mamma. He said his family forgave me and wanted the judge to give me a light sentence. I don't think I could have felt any worse."

Alana and John didn't speak in the long silence that followed but sat quietly, their understanding and empathy palpably filling the room.

John finally spoke. "Mitch, I'm not trying to tell you that I understand all of what you've been through and what it must be like. But what I *can* tell you is that even with what happened, all of it can and will be forgiven through Christ. If you take Jesus Christ into your heart, confess that you know you are a sinner and mean it, even that accident will be forgiven. All of your sins will be forgiven, Mitch."

Mitch hung his head. "I'll definitely try to get my head wrapped around that. I can promise you I'll try, because I'm sick and tired of living in hell."

Finally, exhausted and completely drained, he leaned against the headboard, a bank of pillows cradling his head. He wouldn't look at Alana, he couldn't. He was too afraid of what he'd see in her eyes. Sure, she told him he was forgiven, but by *God*. Could *she* forget everything he had just confessed? She probably despised him.

And yet, as he lay there feeling shaky and fragile, he was aware of feeling something else. Comfortable maybe? Safe? What was it they said in the program? *You're as sick as your secrets?* Maybe they were right. He did feel as if a weight had been lifted—that the horror of that night and all that followed was no longer so formidable. His past could be conquered. For the first time in years, Mitch allowed himself to feel something foreign—hope. As he drifted off to sleep, he found himself thinking that it actually might be possible for him to commit to a God who forgives the unforgivable.

CHAPTER 34

The Sleeping Bear residents concluded that Parson and John were right to refuse to participate in the census, but this was at odds with the rest of the world, where it was reported that the vast majority of the American people were cooperating with the mandate.

In related news, a hastily arranged press conference was organized. A human spokesperson announced that the Visitors had indicated they might be able to stop the asteroid's impact, but that they were waiting for it to be in a particular orbit before they could attempt to do so.

They already were international sensations, with world leaders fawning over them and entertaining them as heads of state. The small group at Sleeping Bear, however, remained wary, skeptical.

Mitch found global events the least of his concerns. Forty-eight hours into his dry-out, he'd taken his last swallow of alcohol. Now his flu-like symptoms had worsened and more misery was in store. John tried to prepare him, and Mitch tried to believe he was ready for it, but Mitch had underestimated the extent of his addiction. Part of the written agreement was that he could be taken to a hospital facility if his condition warranted it, but Mitch didn't want that—he was determined to remain at the lodge whatever it took.

He felt at home at the resort, more so than he had felt anywhere in a long time. The thought of some antiseptic room with white-coated strangers bearing clipboards wasn't a feasible choice for Mitch and he had made that clear right from the start.

For John, however, a hospital stay with medical experts and devices definitely was an option and he told Mitch so in no uncertain terms. Mitch agreed that John and Parson would be the final decision makers if it came down to it.

Steve was about to relinquish his shift to Alana and John when Mitch cried out from a fitful sleep.

Quickly putting down his Ereader, Steve left the small living room where he had been sitting and headed toward Mitch's bedroom. Just as he got to him, Alana and John arrived for their shift. John cracked the cabin door open and stuck his head in. "Ready for us Steve?"

"Yeah, John! I'm in here with Mitch!" Mitch was

waking up, still groggy and disoriented. "You were dreaming Mitch, you okay?"

"Oh, I'm just peachy Steve, just peachy." Mitch retorted sarcastically as he tried to prop himself up on one elbow. Sleep was an escape, doing little to improve his physical symptoms. He was in a very sour mood.

Alana entered the room and Mitch self-consciously fingered his wild hair into place and wiped his oily face with a towel. A stomach cramp stopped him mid-wipe and he crumpled into a fetal position stifling a moan.

John brushed past Alana and Steve to check Mitch's pulse. "A little weak, but steady," he murmured.

"All right Mitch. My shift is over, you're in good hands now with John and Alana."

Alana sat down on the side of the bed and put her hand gently on Mitch's arm, giving him a tender squeeze. Without taking her eyes off his face she said softly, "We're going to take great care of you."

Mitch wanted to say something to her, but kept himself wrapped up in a self-embrace as his body shook violently.

Alana carefully pulled the blanket around his neck and tucked it beneath his shoulders.

Finally, the trembling and pain abated enough for Mitch to whisper, "Hey you guys, I—I'm not sure I'm gonna make this. I'm—I'm not strong enough. What about a few more days of… of some beer or something?" A spasm of pain gripped his stomach. He burrowed his face in the sheets and kept his back turned toward Alana and John as he moaned softly.

"You can do this, you're strong enough Mitch. All of us have been praying for you." John motioned for Steve to go ahead and leave. Steve clasped his hands together and mouthed, *I'll be praying*, then left, padding out in his socks.

John took the Bible he was holding and opened it. "Mind if I read something to you right now?"

"Go ahead, you've got a captive audience here," came Mitch's muffled reply.

"'Yes, the Lord hears the good man when he calls to Him for help and saves him out of all his troubles. The Lord is close to those whose hearts are breaking; He rescues those who are humbly sorry for their sins.'"

"I'm not a good man though, John, ole boy—I'm a piece of..."

Alana interrupted sharply, "Mitch, don't say that! Stop it this second! We're all filled with sin. We're all objectionable to the Lord before we know Him as our Savior. None of us measure up. The choice is ours, *yours* to make."

Mitch was silent for a few moments, then replied, "Okay both of you, I get it, but right now, I don't want to talk about this or listen to anymore... anymore anything. No offense..." Mitch rocked back and forth as raw nerve endings flared like millions of electrical shocks throughout his body. He was covered in sweat, his shirt sticking to him as if he'd worn it during a swim, and he couldn't stop his teeth from chattering.

For the next three hours John and Alana slipped into what had become a regular routine during their watch. John was tinkering, fixing an old transistor radio in the cabin's small kitchenette while Alana sat in a Lazy Boy in the bedroom reading a novel on her Ereader. Suddenly Mitch awoke and propped himself up, looking around disoriented.

"Do you need anything?" Alana asked.

"Yeah, I need a drink."

Alana didn't reply, the only indication she heard him her pained expression.

"Alana," Mitch whispered, "Come here."

She looked at him, unsure. He patted the mattress next to his side, "Come here, next to me on the bed, I want to tell you something..." As she neared the bed, Mitch grasped her wrist in a surprisingly firm grip.

He felt her pulse quicken. In a lowered voice she asked, "Why are you whispering?" as she sat down gingerly on the edge of the bed as if it might explode.

Mitch gestured for her to lean close, and then said, conspiratorially, "Listen, I give up—I'm toast. I don't want to do this anymore. I can't—I can't do this. Just a drink to get me through. I'll cut down; I know I can do it. You'll help me do it." A new tremor coursed through his body and he released her wrist to contain the shaking.

Her anguish was evident.

"Mitch, you think having a drink will make this all go away, but it won't. It can't. You've come so far. Don't give up now."

With power and energy he didn't know he had, Mitch launched himself upright and grabbed her by both arms. Looking over her shoulder to see if John was coming, he pleaded feverishly, "I know what you're saying, but you don't get it—just a little drink, you don't even have to bring me a whole bottle, just a half of one—I'm not ready to go cold turkey. I thought I was, but I'm not. Please Alana, what could just a half bottle hurt?"

Grief swallowed her eyes and for a brief moment, Mitch was aware of the position he'd put her in and felt shame.

"Mitch, if I thought giving you a drink would help, I'd get it for you. But you don't want a drink. Trust me, it's the addiction talking. You don't want this."

Enraged, Mitch shook her roughly and said louder than he meant to, "Don't tell me what I want!" followed by a flurry of curses. "Just get me a drink, Alana! Just do it! Sneak it past John and..."

"Take your hands off her, Mitch." John had suddenly appeared in the doorway, pinning Mitch to the bed with a menacing glare.

CHAPTER 35

"It's all right John, I'm fine…" Alana began.

"Mitch, take your hands off of her or I'll do it for you." John's voice was icily calm, his eyes lethal.

Mitch instantly let go and crumpled into a heap, turning away from Alana.

"John, really, he wasn't hurting me…"

Mitch turned around to face her. "Just go. John's right, I shouldn't have laid a hand on you. I was out of line. I lost my head…"

"I understand. Really, you didn't do any harm. I—I just wish there was something more I could do for you…"

Alana's face was sad and confused. John gently took her by the hand and pulled her to her feet. Bending down slightly he said tenderly, "I'm sorry, I was just outside throwing away some trash. I should have been here." He put both hands on her shoulders and looked at her intently. "Are you all right?"

She was trembling. The look on John's face, the pulse in his temple, told Mitch that he'd like to beat him senseless but was keeping his fury in check. When John looked again at Alana, the hard lines of his countenance softened.

She glanced over her shoulder at Mitch. "I'm—I'm fine, John, thanks." But her green eyes were moist and troubled. Mitch wanted to find a very deep hole and crawl into it. He should have been the one comforting her, telling her how sorry he was, but he was too ashamed.

John moved his hands down her arms until they lightly held hers. "How about I sit in here with Mitch for awhile? You could go back to the main house if you want."

Tears welled and threatened to spill over. With a blink, a single drop escaped and slid down Alana's right cheek. Mitch didn't think he could possibly feel any lower than he already did until he witnessed this. Then he knew he could.

John kept trying to persuade her. "Alana, you've done a great job here, why not take a break?"

Alana nodded mutely, gathered up her Ereader and left the room. As she headed out the cabin door she turned back, her voice tremulous, "Don't give up Mitch, you're stronger than you think you are!"

When the door closed, John's cheery tone seemed forced. "Mind if I play some music for you? I'm hoping since we can't give you any degree of physical comfort, that maybe some music can—as they say—soothe the savage beast.'"

Mitch didn't respond with anything other than a soft moan. As he hugged a pillow to himself, he rocked back and forth trying to will the pain and discomfort away.

But nothing's going to get rid of my humiliation. Alana will never speak to me again, and I don't blame her at all.

"I'm taking no response as an affirmative. I think some classical music from the old masters might help."

For the next twenty minutes, music played in the cabin but Mitch remained unresponsive except for teeth chattering and occasional grunts and moans. John checked on him periodically, but spent most of his time in the kitchenette fiddling with the old transistor.

CHAPTER 36

Alone, Mitch tried to ignore the aches and raging tremors that racked his body.

Overwhelmed by pain and shame, he began to weep. His head felt like someone had used it for batting practice, he had alternating hot and cold sweats that left the sheets damp no matter how many times they were changed, insomnia that gave way to nightmares, and cramping that knotted his stomach with breathless intensity.

Why go through this? It might not even work. The only real desire he had right now was for a drink. Would his cravings—*could* his cravings—ever end?

He had had some terribly down times in his life, but this was so deep a pit of hopelessness and despair, he thought he'd never be able to claw his way out.

Then, Mitch heard calming words inside his head: a voice—not his own—was tenderly speaking to him, reaching for him through an abyss of darkness.

Trust Me, Mitch with all your heart. Put your trust and faith in Me and not in the things of this world. Do not lean on your own understanding, in all your ways, acknowledge Me, and I will make your paths straight.

He opened his eyes wide and peered around the room, but a leg cramp sent him spiraling into agony.

After it passed, he lay back, exhausted, trying to figure out what that voice was and if he had really heard it or, more accurately, sensed it.

He whispered, "God? Is that you?"

Silence.

"Trust you? How do I do that?"

Only the sibilant sounds of a breeze through the pines answered him.

John wasn't sitting more than thirty feet away in the kitchenette, but Mitch couldn't have felt more alone. The shadows lengthening, his body woven with steel-like threads of pain, Mitch quietly wept himself into a dreamless sleep.

CHAPTER 37

Two weeks later, a paler, weaker, but sober Mitch emerged from his cabin to sit outside and enjoy the changing leaves and fresh air. The all night vigils were no longer necessary, but Mitch was rarely alone for long.

A tapestry of multicolored leaves filtered a brilliant sun, but it was still bright enough to force Mitch to wear sunglasses. He inhaled the pine-scented air deeply. A crisp cool breeze ruffled his hair as he reveled in the picture-perfect fall day. The sun was so warm he considered removing the jacket he was wearing.

As Mitch stuffed a third huge chocolate chip cookie into his mouth, he saw Parson coming up the walk. Earlier, John had warned Mitch that addicts usually end up craving sweets, and he was right. These days, the only reason Mitch ate regular food was so he could have something sweet afterwards. *I'm thinking I found a new addiction, and it's sugar...* He had to be careful because until he felt strong enough, there was no way he'd be able to work out and all this sugar would put the weight on fast.

"So, how are you doing today, Mr. Abbot?" Parson extended his hand, ready for a shake. "It's a great blessing to see you up and about!" he added heartily.

After wiping his hand on a pant leg and standing, Mitch gave Parson's hand a robust pumping. "Pretty good, pretty good. Thanks Parson, it's really great to see you too."

"What a day. Isn't it something? The boys are out hunting so we can get a freezer full of venison and anything else they can bag. John is a little rusty, but Steve and Caleb are seasoned hunters. I'm sure they'll bring us back something. What a day for it!"

"Yeah, I guess I'm just grateful I can stand here and enjoy it. For a while there, I didn't think I'd be able to enjoy anything again..."

"It's a courageous thing you've done, Mitch. Everyone is proud to have been a part of it. There have been a lot of prayers going up for your situation... and it would appear our prayers were answered."

"I guess so. You know, this whole thing has been pretty awesome. I can't believe how generous you all have been with your time, and how you've cared for me. I—I can't possibly begin to thank you all." Mitch found himself blushing, something he didn't think he was capable of doing.

Parson put his hand on Mitch's shoulder, "You don't have to thank us. All of us wanted to help you get through this, and if we've played even a small part, we're happy."

"Not a small part, a huge part. I couldn't have done it alone, I can tell you that."

They stood there quietly, enjoying a comfortable lag in the conversation when they heard the sound of a large vehicle coming up the winding private road leading to the resort.

The others in the kitchen heard it as well, and Alana, Daniel, Sarah, Megan and Lizzy came to the front porch to see who was coming.

"Looks like we've got company." Parson started on his way to the main cabin, but stopped at the crest of the hill to get a glimpse of who was coming up.

The rumble of several engines grew louder the closer they came. Shading his eyes with a hand, Mitch could see a large SUV followed by two other Sport Utility vehicles. Mitch was unable to make out who the occupants were due to the tinted windows.

All the SUVs rolled to a stop in front of the lodge. The driver of the first SUV jumped out and immediately opened the door behind his own. A magnificently clad Visitor stepped out and put on a gem-encrusted headdress that rose at least three feet from his head. The headdress's flattened top was angled with the alien emblem prominently displayed on the front and framed in what appeared to be diamonds.

The intricate patterns of the Visitor's garment and headdress were fashioned of gold and silver brocade embedded with various gemstones, all of which glittered blindingly in the sun. He smiled broadly, extending both hands outward in welcome.

"Hello, hello, dear people! How wonderful it is to see you! What a lovely place you have here. I am continually amazed by your race. You have such an incredible work ethic, which is evident by what I see around me here."

Once again, Mitch observed that these Visitors spoke like BBC commentators.

"Please allow me to introduce myself. My name is Elam. I come to bring you pleasant tidings and also to ask for your assistance."

Parson's face was emotionless. "My name is Parson Culver. Just what is it you think I can do for you, Mr. Elam?"

"Please, please call me Elam. There is no need for such formality. May I be introduced to everyone else here before we tell you why we've come?"

Mitch was slowly coming up behind Parson "I'm Mitch Abbot... I think it would be best for you to answer Mr. Culver's question like he asked."

Elam's expression never wavered. His chocolate,

almond shaped eyes flickered briefly, but his smile remained. At that moment, two additional Visitors emerged from their vehicles along with men in dark suits wearing CIA-style sunglasses. These Visitors were dressed like Elam, but Elam's costume had a greater quantity and variety of precious stones. Mitch wondered if this indicated that he was their leader.

"I understand your concern—we are, after all, strangers. But I assure you, we're friendly strangers," Elam replied smoothly.

"I see." Parson still did not make a move to welcome the group.

"My contingent landed in the Leavenworth, Kansas area. Our assignment was to become better acquainted with the local citizens, and that is what we set out to do these past few months. However, in doing so, we found that some of the Leavenworth citizenry had left, and it would appear they left rather hastily. I think that would be you, Mr. Culver, am I correct? Ah... may I call you Parson?" Elam tilted his head politely, seeking confirmation.

Mitch tried again. "What I think Mr. Culver is trying to convey is that you are uninvited guests and it would be a good idea for you to explain why you've come. The best way to get on the good side of people is to state your business, especially in times like these."

Even though Mitch was speaking, Elam's gaze moved over to the front porch and found its mark: Alana. Looking at her steadily for some moments, he finally returned his attention to Mitch. "Of course, of course. Forgive my rudeness." The other Visitors came to either side of Elam and bowed deeply.

"Please allow me to introduce my colleagues, Hazael and Merari." As they heard their name they each bowed again.

"We noticed you and your son left Kansas the morning after our arrival, Mr. Culver. We came here in the hopes of finding out why. Then, of course, there was your refusal to take part in the census…" Mitch thought he caught the slightest hint of an implied threat there.

The alien continued. "We came here because we have seen the signs of the times; we have studied what the ancient text says, and everything on earth points to the return of the Messiah. We want to make certain that all those who await His return are protected." The Visitor paused. "We want to be sure we know the whereabouts of all U.S. citizens in order to be better able to offer assistance, especially in emergency situations or natural disasters." When the Visitor finished speaking, he smiled reassuringly and folded his hands in front of him.

Parson seemed to be considering the Visitor's words when he replied equably, "I'm not sure why our refusal to take the census is any of your business. Please forgive my frankness, but we did nothing wrong or illegal. This is our property and we chose to come here to use it. I don't quite understand why I have to tell you anything at all." The lodge guests stood transfixed, each wondering if Parson had just sealed their doom.

Instead, Elam's smile grew wider, if possible. "I can appreciate your perplexity. Let me attempt to explain. We have joined with the local Kansas government in a combined effort to ensure that services are expertly and efficiently provided for all citizens of Leavenworth and other surrounding counties. We have, of course, done this strictly as volunteers. To properly carry out our mission, we must conduct a type of census—if you will—and when the Leavenworth census was taken, we realized you and some others were missing. Further investigation revealed you came here to northern Michigan." Again, he smiled congenially. Mitch was beginning to find this incessant smiling intensely creepy.

CHAPTER 38

I'm really starting not to like this. Mitch shifted his weight from one foot to the other uncomfortably. Hazael spoke for the first time. "It may seem drastic, this attempt to locate residents of Leavenworth, but if you've had access to any media outlets, you would know there is a danger of the water supply becoming contaminated. In order to maintain order and to make certain everyone has his or her needs met regarding water use, a report of everyone in each city and county across this great nation of yours is underway even as we speak. Armed with this information, your government will be equipped to take care of everyone who might need supplies or assistance in the near or distant future."

"Well, as you can see, we're self-sufficient here, and

since we're in Michigan rather than Kansas, I would say we are now out of your jurisdiction. As far as contaminated water is concerned, we not only have our own water supply," Parson pointed to the water tower in the background, "but we also have access to a private lake. We don't anticipate any problems, at least not in the foreseeable future, as long as we are careful. It is doubtful we will be looking to the government for assistance. We believe the Lord will provide for our needs, not any local or federal government."

There was something going on here. Nothing Mitch could put his finger on, but once again, he sensed that the presence of the Visitors was ominous—maybe even dangerous.

Merari addressed them all, "Well then, we can see that you are well prepared and will not require Kansas government assistance. Accordingly, our job is done. We were hoping, however, to have accommodations just for the night. Then we will begin our journey back tomorrow so as not to inconvenience you any longer than necessary. We are prepared to pay you, of course." "Oh yes, indeed, quite handsomely!" interjected Elam. "Above what your normal rates would be, because we understand we have intruded without any prior notice or reservation."

Everyone had their eyes on Parson. Lizzy stood sandwiched tightly against Alana's legs, and Sarah held Megan in a similar fashion. Daniel was in front of all of them. Mitch moved up next to Parson. Even though he was still weak as a kitten, something rose up in him that wanted to protect the older man—or at least try—if he had to.

"My son will have to make the determination whether or not we'll be able to offer you accommodations for the night, but my guess is that it will be all right with him." Parson looked directly at Elam's face; he may have been a senior citizen, but now he spoke with unbreachable authority.

Elam and his colleagues smiled cordially. "We would be most grateful for the hospitality. One of our escorts is a chef and he'd be happy to prepare our meals so as not to disturb your customary practices." Elam bowed deferentially but when he came back up, his gaze once again locked on Alana like a laser.

She closed her eyes and put her fingertips to her temple as if trying to ward off a migraine. When he spoke, Elam's voice visibly jarred her.

"May we be introduced? You must be Miss Engels." He walked up to the porch and extended his hand.

She ignored his hand, a slight intake of breath betraying her alarm. "How do you know my name?"

"It is our job to know all of the residents to whom we have been assigned. You were not in your New York home, and your neighbors told our friends in that region that you had come to Kansas for your sister and brother-in-law's remains. We are aware, of course, of your loss and extend our deepest sympathy, Miss Engels. So many have lost loved ones, it's such a shame."

Mitch found the fact that they had tracked Alana from New York to Kansas and then from Kansas all the way to Michigan more than a little disturbing. *How could they possibly know?*

"Thank you," Alana replied curtly.

Sarah stepped forward. "I'm Sarah, and this is my daughter, Megan. Nice to meet you." Her demeanor was that of someone simply paying heed to social conventions and held little warmth. Daniel followed suit.

"I'm Daniel, he said coolly, but the Visitors seemed unaware or purposefully ignoring their chilly reception.

"Excellent." Elam turned his attention back to Parson. "We'll look forward to meeting your son, Mr. Culver. Now, might you have a place for us to freshen up?"

CHAPTER 39

"Since I'm quite certain my son will allow you to stay with us overnight, you can use some of our cabins. How many will you need?" Parson spoke with business-like brusqueness.

"Oh, that is wonderful! We would need four cabins, Mr. Culver. Thank you so much for your hospitality." Elam, Hazael and Merari once again bowed deeply.

Mitch watched as the suits, apparently bodyguards, opened vehicle doors and retrieved luggage, then followed behind as Parson escorted the Visitors down a pine-needled path to the cabins.

Alana, Sarah, Daniel and the two girls watched them go. "I don't like this one bit. I wonder why Parson is letting them stay," Sarah said.

"I don't know, but he must have his reasons. We're just going to have to trust that for now," Alana said, without conviction.

"When that Elam guy looked at you and started talking to you, what happened?" asked Mitch.

"You know, I have no idea. I can't explain it. It was like he was able to touch the inside of my head!" Alana rubbed her eye with the heel of her hand, her fingertips tangling in her hair.

"Huh?" Mitch bent slightly trying to see her downturned face. "What do you mean?"

"I don't know what I mean—he was sort of rummaging around inside my head!" Alana blurted, her voice sounding bewildered and laced with exhaustion, then added softly, "That sounds crazy, doesn't it?"

Mitch touched her arm gently. "You're not crazy, Alana. What's crazy is that we have aliens running the planet, poking around inside our skulls."

"They give me the creeps. I don't know why I ever thought it was okay that they do the census or have anything to do with our lives in the first place," Daniel whispered.

"Me too," Alana replied as they all went back into the main house. Mitch came up behind her. "Are you all right?"

Alana shook her head. "Well, sort of, but no. I don't like them being here at all. I'm not sure I'm going to sleep too well tonight."

"Want some company then?" Mitch grinned a bad boy grin. Her indignant cry of "Mitch!" accompanied by a swat prompted the quick retort, "Just kidding! I swear, I was just kidding!" Even though it was obvious she didn't believe him, it suddenly occurred to him that he really *was* kidding.

CHAPTER 40

A mist hung like a hazy blanket over the Manistee National forest floor, the air still, and heavy with cool late-morning moisture. As John hoisted two deer onto the back of his truck, the call of a young bald eagle high atop a birch tree broke the tranquility. John paused for a moment to look at the beautiful bird.

"You'd like some of this, wouldn't you?"

Steve followed John's gaze, "That's a bald eagle, isn't it?"

"We don't usually see them come this close—well, relatively close, but I think he's a bit envious of our morning's bounty." Caleb said, "His feathers look funny."

Steve replied, "He's a young one, probably close to a

year old. So he's still molting."

"Your dad's right. They don't get that white head you're used to seeing until they've matured."

Caleb looked up thoughtfully. "Man, they look really busted until they grow up."

Steve and John both chuckled as the three of them finished loading the rest of the game and fowl. John's black down vest and insulated red plaid shirt were starting to feel too warm with the exertion of the hunt and loading of the truck. He also noted his work boots were worse for the wear and would need a good cleaning. Removing one of his broken-in sheepskin gloves, he slid off his watchman's cap and tossed it onto the backpack on the ground near the truck.

Using the back of his hand, John wiped the sweat off his forehead. He felt fairly confident that with the take of the day plus what they already had stocked in the freezer, would make it through to the spring thaw, even if the grocery stores closed down and it turned out to be a long winter.

In less than an hour they had gotten the truck's load secure. John grabbed his cap, fit it back snugly on his head, and jumped into the driver's seat. Caleb took the middle of the front bench seat while Steve sat shotgun.

During the drive back to Sleeping Bear, Steve noted that they seemed to be isolated in the Manistee National Forest area. "Isn't this unusual this time of year? I'd have thought we'd see more people up here during hunting season, right?"

John agreed. "Sure, usually this place is actually pretty crowded. There are countless cabins and hunting shacks in the area, and hunting season usually sees quite a bit of activity. I'm surprised we haven't seen more people, now that you mention it. But then again—most of these places aren't going to be nearly as self-sufficient as Sleeping Bear is. It's one thing for a hunter or outdoorsman who wants to rough it. It's another to come up here with your family and try to stay for any length of time the way some of these places were made. They're just meant for short seasonal stays."

Two hours later they pulled up the driveway to the front of Sleeping Bear. John saw the three identical SUV's lined up, one behind the other, parked in front of the lodge. "I guess we've got company." John's voice held an edge of uneasiness.

"Were you expecting anyone?" Steve asked.

"No, no we weren't. I don't have any idea who this could be. Let's see who it is before unloading the truck."

John, Steve and Caleb went into the main house and headed straight to the kitchen. Not seeing anyone, John called out, "Hello!"

Parson responded from the living room area. When John walked in, despite a roaring fire in the fireplace, he felt a distinct chill.

Parson stood when he saw his son. "Oh good, you're back. We have a situation here."

275

John swiped his cap off with one quick motion ruffling his plastered down hair. "What's going on?" With Steve and Caleb flanking either side of him, it appeared as if the cavalry had arrived.

Speaking quietly, John asked, "Where are the girls, Dad?"

"They're in my room, coloring," Alana replied. "We thought it would be better to stay under the same roof until you got back.

Sarah walked up and stood in-between Steve and Caleb, putting her arms around both. "I think we're all going to remain in the main house at least while the Visitors are here, if that is all right with everyone."

"We have some aliens here? Why?" John looked concerned, then grim, his right cheek muscle twitching.

Parson told them everything that happened. "Son, to be fair, I didn't feel threatened, but by the same token, I didn't feel we could refuse them. However, I made it clear you were the last word on whether they could stay or not."

John hesitated a moment then said, "I think we should allow them to stay here." His announcement was met with a chorus of protest.

Alana's stomach twisted.

John held up his hands, palms outward, "Hold on, now hold on..."

Mitch said, "John, these—these Visitors are unnerving

to say the least. And I thought you said they might be demons anyway, why take a chance?

"I know, I get that Mitch, but this is the way I see it. While Dad and I think that this whole visiting from another solar system thing is a ruse, we don't know that for sure. What if they are God's creatures after all?"

Parson sided with his son, "He has a point. While I don't get a great feeling about them either, we have no real evidence that these aliens are anything but who they say they are."

"Let me just handle this for now. I'll try to... let's just say, I'll do my best to encourage them to stay for just one night. I guess that's one way to play it safe. The main thing is, we've already stood our ground about the census, and I think it's wise to avoid stirring up anything more."

This approach seemed reasonable to the rest, but left Alana feeling deeply uneasy.

At that moment, they all heard a voice from the front of the house. "It sounds like it's coming from the foyer," John said as he headed to the lodge entrance.

"Hello! Anyone here?" Elam was standing at the front entrance with Hazael and Merari. Parson did the introductions. "It is nice to finally meet you, Mr. Culver."

"I understand you wish to stay here at the resort. Why don't we go to the front desk and I can get you checked in? How many nights do you think you'll need accommodations?" Although John's voice carried its usual polite professionalism, Alana could hear an undercurrent of unease.

While Elam accompanied John to the check-in area, Hazael made an attempt at small talk with Sarah. She abruptly excused herself saying she had to see about the girls and took Caleb with her, leaving Steve, Daniel, Mitch, and Alana. Unfazed, Hazael turned his attention to Alana. He spoke softly, almost tenderly. "Miss Engels, I understand you were assaulted on your trip to the state you call Kansas. What a terrifying experience that must have been for you."

Alana was too stunned to speak, her mouth forming a small, silent "o." "I imagine you're wondering how I might know these details. It's a bit difficult to explain, but our people have an advanced ability to understand the spirit world."

Mitch blurted, "What spirit world? What are you talking about? What is he talking about Alana?"

Parson responded, "Perhaps Hazael is referring to what the Bible says in Ephesians chapter six verse twelve: 'For we wrestle not against flesh and blood, but against principalities, against powers, against the rulers of the darkness of this world, against spiritual wickedness in high places.'

This verse explains that there is another world, so to speak. A world we can't see, but the Bible tells us it definitely exists."

Alana found her voice. "And it would seem the Visitors

have a way of seeing this world, as well as interpreting it."

"Yes, yes, quite so Miss Engels! Bravo, Mr. Culver, that is precisely what I am trying to convey. I wanted to talk to Miss Engels about what I was able to discern from her assault. You see, we are able to see glimpses into those 'spiritual high places' and I believe you'll find it intriguing— Might we go someplace where we can be more comfortable?" Hazael gestured expansively toward the formal living room area.

Mitch and Daniel immediately stepped in front of Alana to form a protective shield—an almost comical show of bravado given their Hobbit-like size compared to the aliens.

Merari bowed slightly toward Alana. "I'm sure my colleague intends that we *all* go to an area where we can be more comfortable, isn't that right Hazael?"

"Of course! Yes, indeed. I have so much to talk to you about, Miss Engels, if you would permit me some of your time. It is a sensitive topic, however, so I defer to you whether or not we should keep our conversation private."

Alana eyed him warily. "I'd prefer that my friends stay with us."

"Delightful! Then let us go in here where we can be much more comfortable." Acting as if he were the lodge's proprietor, Hazael swept ahead of them into the living room area.

CHAPTER 41

As they filed into the living room, Alana's pulse began to accelerate. Each took a seat around the fire. Hazael sat next to Alana on the large brown leather couch and turned to face her. His extremely long legs ate up the space in the center of the room between the couch and loveseat. His size dwarfed Alana and everyone else for that matter, making Alana that much more uncomfortable.

She attempted to disguise the fact that all she wanted to do was recoil from him. "Now, what is it you have to tell me about my assault? I'm sorry if I sound a bit rude, but dredging up these memories is difficult for me, so if you could get to the point, I'd appreciate it."

"Oh, most certainly, Miss Engels. We understand," said Merari with what seemed to be counterfeit sympathy.

"I'm wondering if you remember the exact moment when this man brought you into his truck?"

Despite Alana's new awareness that these beings seemed to have a supernatural grip on a whole other realm, she was still taken aback by what he said. She tried to see some type of expression in his huge black/brown eyes. Oddly, the almond shape of his eyes was pleasing. She wasn't certain it was because his lashes were so thick they almost looked feminine, or if it was something else. His high cheekbones, and chiseled prominent features gave his face sharp, angular lines. She had to admit, the Visitors were beautiful and graceful beings in a way. Still...

"How... how do you know these details?" She couldn't help asking although she wasn't at all sure she wanted to know the answer.

Hazel leaned even closer to her. "It is as if we can see it on a type of screen, like in one of your movie theaters. The image or scene comes before our inner vision when we probe the mind of another. It's completely under our control. We can bring the screen up in our mind and at will, make it transparent, make it opaque, fill our field of vision in real time, or just in the background." He was moving his hands animatedly as he spoke.

"What else did you see that you wish to tell me?" Alana asked, trying to focus the conversation back onto the matter at hand. Her gut did a few somersaults as dread crawled its way up her throat.

Hazael seemed eager to continue. "Well at the

precise moment when you were in the most danger, and this man was about to attack you in an unspeakable way, I am pleased to inform you that angels came to your rescue, Miss Engels. That is what stopped this man from doing any further harm to you. When you called out to the Lord as you did, you summoned angels and this man saw them standing on either side of you, as well as behind you. That is what ultimately stopped his evil intent."

Alana suddenly had a crystal clear recall of the assault. It flashed before her eyes like a digital video. She could see her attacker's hate-filled, crazed face as if he were standing before her. She saw his eyes ablaze with maddening rage and other inexplicable dark things. Then she remembered all at once his entire expression changed. His eyes became larger, he almost tripped as he stepped back a half step. His arms went to his sides, flailing outwards, palms facing backwards, his neck craned as if he wanted to turn away, but couldn't.

Alana uttered in a far away voice. "I remember—"

Hazael continued on. "This man who was going to do you harm saw a miraculous apparition of angels behind you and by your side. He became so terrified; he lost all sense of what his intended evil plan was. Thus he let you go. The poor soul, he's never been quite the same since. And it might please you to know he has not harmed anyone else after his encounter with you."

Alana tried to absorb everything he said.

Mitch said, "So you're telling us you can read Alana's

thoughts, as if you were watching a digital playback or hologram?"

"Well, not quite. It must be an imprint upon your mind for us to really see the memory. We do not read thoughts as they are formed, but we can read memory stamps—so to speak, similar to digital images in your mind's storage capabilities. We merely have an advanced usage of extra sensory ability. We have this and so much more we wish to share with your civilization."

Hazael said, "We do indeed! And it is our hope, nay, our plan—to convince every person of the human race that our goal is to enhance the earthly living experience as we await the return of the Son of God."

Elam and John came into the room at that moment. Elam had an expression of triumph on his face. He held his staff as if he were royalty, holding court. His free arm moved with a sweeping gesture. "Mr. Culver has been kind enough to check us all in and give us access to his spacious kitchen and supplies. If you wish to hear more about the great things we can offer your people, please join us for dinner tonight. It will be our pleasure to cook for everyone."

Parson didn't hesitate in giving his answer. "I think I might be taking dinner in my room, but thanks for the invitation all the same."

The chorus of "me toos" from those gathered followed.

The jovial expression in Elam's eyes altered ever so slightly, but his voice conveyed nothing different in his mood. "That is most unfortunate, we would have loved your company while we dined. If you should change your minds, please feel free to join us at 6:30."

With that, he gave a low bow and with a staged turn, left the room. Hazael and Merari immediately followed, briefly bowing before their exit.

CHAPTER 42

Alana remained seated. John came to her side. "Alana, you're trembling, what's wrong? What happened?"

Without hesitation, he sat down next to her and put his arm around her shoulder hugging her close to him. Her answer was rapid shallow breathing as she gnawed on a thumbnail.

He said soothingly, "Alana, take some deep breaths for me—will you do that? When you can, tell me what happened. They didn't hurt you did they?"

Parson filled John in as they all gathered around Alana trying to ease her obvious distress. John listened, never taking his eyes off her. His voice was gentle, like a caress.

"Alana, I'm sorry you had to go through that. How frightening it must have been listening to their account of that night."

Daniel was ready to sprint to the kitchen. "Alana, let me get you some water or something."

She finally spoke. "I—I'm fine… it's just the things he said—dredging up those memories, that night—it's all a little overwhelming." Alana was fidgeting with her hands while she kept her head down trying to take longer deeper breaths.

Mitch got down on his haunches directly in front of her. "Want me to go beat those big bad aliens up for ya?"

Alana burst into a fit of laughter mixed with coughing and sputtering. Everyone else joined the comic relief except for John. A smile barely creased his lips as he concentrated on Alana.

Daniel pointed at Mitch. "Dude! I can just see your pasty, weak be-hind strutting up to those guys and giving them a huge swift kick in the knee, or you could just stick your tongue out at them I'm sure then they'd know you the man!"

This brought even more laughter from everyone and broke the strange atmosphere that still lingered. Steve broke into the reverie. "I think I should get Sarah and the kids and bring our things to the main house here, as long as that's still fine for you, John."

John addressed the rest, "Why not make it a

permanent move? We have plenty of rooms that should be suitable enough for your whole family."

"That would be great. Thanks so much." Steve gave John a slap on the back as he headed out the door.

John yelled after him, "You've earned your keep, Pal. Your aim is flawless. What did you end up getting, a dozen deer?"

"Ahhh, I think that's a bit of an exaggeration there, try three."

"Well regardless, we're going to be pretty good for venison this winter thanks to you!"

"The Lord gets all the glory John. He surely provided for us today with a bountiful hunt. And I mean that. I've never seen so many deer on a hunting trip in my life. It was like shooting fish in a barrel."

John addressed the rest when Steve left. "Tomorrow we can try more fishing. But right now, I have to prepare what we brought back in the truck for freezing, that is, if you think you'll be all right, Alana."

When Alana tilted her face upwards, the unexpected charge of emotion he felt astounded him. Her vulnerability, mixed with the apparent pain of the memory of that night, made him want to sweep her into his arms and protect her from everything. He tore himself from her scrutiny. The room suddenly seemed hot and close. He absently rubbed the side of his leg where their thighs had touched.

"I'll be all right, don't worry. Thanks though, that's

really sweet of you." She put her hand on John's arm.

He had to get away from her. He bolted to his feet, rubbing his palms together, unsure of where to put his hands. "Good, ah—glad you'll be—that you're... well, if you're sure you're all right."

"Yo! What are we, chopped liver here?" Mitch protested. "Is John the only good-guy here? Daniel and I can take those alien dudes on for you, Alana. Can't we Danny boy?"

"You got that right! Tell Stretch and his pals to *bring it*! I am *so* ready!" Daniel was sticking out his chest, flexing his nonexistent biceps in a mock display of machismo.

"Okay, okay, I think there's enough testosterone spilling out into the room for now." Alana was taking her hands and wiping her palms across her face, traveling up her forehead, then pulling her fingers through her hair. She momentarily arched her back and it was this graceful movement, a seemingly insignificant action, which John found absolutely absorbing. The room became much warmer.

Mitch directed his question to John. "Hey, I was thinking of bringing my stuff in here, too. I take it there'll be enough room for me?"

John was still unable to regain his composure but managed a reply. "Ah—sure, we have over sixty rooms and a third of those are suites designed for long-term stay. You're welcome to any one of them. Bring your things into the lobby and I'll get your key and have it ready for you."

As John raced from the room he gave one last glance back toward Alana. Mitch and Daniel were hovering over her, both talking to her at once. Alana looked up from between them and lasered in on John flashing a huge sad smile. He turned and rushed from the room as if it were on fire.

CHAPTER 43

John's mind wasn't on unloading the truck or carting the deer into the pole barn. He went through the motions to prepare it all for the freezer, bringing in the deer, hanging a carcass on a hook so that he could clean and cut up the meat. He began to portion the animal into package-sized pieces for freezing. As he stripped and cut away the hide, he barely realized what he was doing. His mind was a million miles away.

Racing from jumbled memories of his wife to how he reacted when he sat next to Alana, he tried to brush it off again as just being in close proximity to such a stunning young woman. But this argument was becoming very weak. He was loath to admit, this wasn't the first time he found himself pulled in by her.

He tried sorting through all of these things while he arduously prepared the meat for the freezer, putting much more gusto into the task at hand than was necessary, but unable to resolve any of them adequately. This frustrated and confused him. His attempt to convince himself he was reacting in a very human way, a natural physical reaction— wasn't working. He thought that part of him had died with Katie. Her memory still lived and breathed, as it had for so many years. How could this be happening to him? It's not as if he had never been around beautiful women since Katie died. He stopped what he was doing and said a silent prayer.

Father God, what do I do? What can I do to clear my mind of these feelings? Help me Lord, please help me, my flesh is weak. I need your strength and your wisdom. Please Father, make me strong in you. Keep my mind stayed on the things of you and keep me from the trappings of sin. Amen

Steve and Caleb joined John after moving their things into the main house. Together they finished all the packaging of the meat, cleaned up the mess and then headed into the lodge. Passing through the lobby on their way to take showers, Steve and Caleb continued on to the kitchen when Elam stopped John in the lobby.

"Oh, Mr. Culver, I'm glad I found you. Would it be all right if our chef began his meal preparation?"

"Sure, you're welcome to use the kitchen." John tried to sound as cordial as he possibly could.

"Are you sure you won't be joining us?" Elam's

expression was all warmth and friendliness.

"I'm sorry, but we have chores we should finish up before our meals. Enjoy yourselves." And with that John, Steve, and Caleb headed toward their rooms.

John needed a shower and planned to spend time alone reading his Bible before doing anything else.

While he was heading to his apartment, he saw Mitch and Alana deep in conversation in the hallway. For the first time he felt deeply uncomfortable around them and tried to duck into his apartment, but Alana called to him. "John, could we talk to you for a moment?"

John hoped his discomfort wasn't as obvious as he felt it was. "Sure, what do you need?"

As they both approached him, his eyes fell on the way Alana filled out her tightly fitted pale yellow sweater. He realized with shame that he was tracing every soft curve of her. He tried to bring his gaze over her head, as if examining the framed prints he had on the log walls of the long hallway.

"We'd like to talk privately. Can we go into your apartment?" Mitch asked.

He focused on Mitch. "Ah... sure thing, come on in."

John opened the door to his apartment. "Listen, make yourself at home, but do you both mind if I jump into the shower? I'll just be a second. I'm a mess from getting the deer packaged and into the freezer. Just have a seat, I won't be but a minute."

He didn't wait for their answer. He couldn't. He ducked into his bedroom and closed the door behind him. He couldn't believe it, his heart was racing. Maybe that shower would have to be a cold one. He prayed again.

After his shower, he was feeling refreshed and much stronger. He emerged from his room drying his hair with a large white towel. "Thanks for waiting. As soon as we're finished here I need to get to my Bible reading, I haven't had a chance today."

"Perfect! That's exactly what I have questions about, things in the Bible!" Mitch exclaimed as he plopped down on the tan leather couch. John noticed Alana slid closer, leaning into him. Her body language spoke volumes. He felt his fresher outlook dissipate like a puff of cigar smoke.

"Alana's been answering some questions for me, but I wanted to hear what you both have to say. So I'm on the tail end of being clean and sober. I really think I'm going to make it."

Alana's adoring smile as she gazed proudly at Mitch made John want to squirm. This was going to be a big test of his self-control. "Well thanks be to God, Mitch, that's wonderful." His voice sounded flat, even to himself.

Mitch didn't seem to notice. "I've been thinking long and hard about this commitment Alana has talked to me about—this commitment to Christ. I admit, first off, I wanted to do this because I ah—wanted to ah—well—impress Alana." Mitch paused and gave Alana a knowing glance. She grinned and flushed over her neck and face.

Oh this definitely feels like jealousy all right...

John quickly got up to stir the embers in the fireplace. He busied himself with adding a log that when jostled, reignited the fire. *Great, a cozy fire for the lovebirds to sit in front of.*

Mitch continued. "Well, now I think I really want to make that commitment because this may be the next right move for my life. While I was lying there day after day feeling like I'd rather die instead of go dry, I had a lot of time to think. I guess I was the lowest I had ever been, you know... facing, really for the first time my past..." Mitch heaved a sigh. "Then it just... it hit me, I guess..." He looked down at his hands. "For the first time in I can't remember when, I felt a sort of quiet inside me, like a calm."

"We know just exactly what you're talking about. That's the inner peace of knowing Christ." John could see Alana's eyes sparkle with anticipation, catching the firelight, glowing like two flawless Columbian emeralds.

"And I didn't really consider it before, but those aliens, I don't know, I think it's way more than what we're seeing on T.V. I got that creepy phone call. Then I know what I saw on the road, because Daniel saw it too. Next I had that dream that I don't think was a dream at all, because the thing was in the room earlier—I felt it. I'm beginning to realize there's much more to this whole thing you talked about in Ephesians. If there's aliens or evil spirits as you told me about, then there must be a God. I even actually picked up one of the Bibles you have in each room and read a little about it after you told me some chapters and verses. Maybe this stuff is real. It sure seems real to me now."

Normally, John would have an overwhelming desire to take this opportunity to lead someone to Christ. In this case, he didn't want to do anything. He closed his eyes for a moment to collect himself. "Oh, it's real alright. I can tell you from personal experience." John reached for his well-worn leather Bible on an end table near the fireplace and opened it. "I have a portion of the Bible I want to read to you right now, if that'll be all right. Romans chapter ten, verses nine through ten:

> *If you declare with your mouth, Jesus is Lord, and believe in your heart that God raised him from the dead, you will be saved. [10] For it is with your heart that you believe and are justified, and it is with your mouth that you profess your faith and are saved.[11] As Scripture says, anyone who believes in him will never be put to shame. [12] For there is no difference between Jew and Gentile—the same Lord is Lord of all and richly blesses all who call on him, [13] for, everyone who calls on the name of the Lord will be saved."*

"Are you telling me that if I say that in some kind of prayer, I'm all set? Alana's already told me a lot about this, but I really don't quite get it. Not exactly..." Mitch trailed off. Again, John felt conflicted. He was on the verge of leading someone to Christ. This should have been a pulse-pounding moment. Yet he felt oddly reticent. He tried to concentrate and focus on parsing his words carefully, listening to the voice of the Holy Spirit as he answered Mitch, but he found he was unable to center his thoughts. Why wouldn't he want to lead Mitch to Christ? What was the matter with him?

"Uh… well… almost." John fumbled around for more words trying to focus when Alana interrupted. "Mitch, if you proclaim what those verses in Romans say and truly mean what you are saying in your heart of hearts, then yes, you will be saved."

John said, "We could pray with you, Mitch. If you think you're ready, you could repeat the prayer, and as long as you really mean it, you can become a Christian right now."

With a dream-like quality to his voice as he looked into Alana's eyes Mitch said, "Sure, sure, right now, I'm ready. Just tell me what to do."

John, Alana and Mitch knelt in a semi-circle. They all bowed their heads and with eyes closed, John told Mitch to repeat the sinner's prayer after him.

"Lord, I am a sinner and I ask your forgiveness. I know you have sent your son Jesus Christ to atone for my sins. Thank you for the sacrifice your son made for my sins. I ask that you become my Lord and Savior, come into my life and take control of it. I ask you to make me the kind of person you want me to become so that I may serve you according to your will for my life. I thank you Lord for your forgiveness and for your Son Jesus Christ our Lord and our Savior. Amen."

John said a portion of the prayer then paused, allowing Mitch to repeat the prayer after him, line by line. When they finished, John recommended, "Mitch, you should read this passage in the Bible, right now to yourself. You should make certain that you have taken this into your heart of hearts—this can't be faked. Ultimately, only you and the Lord know for sure if this is an honest conversion."

"Sure John." Mitch took John's Bible, already opened to Romans chapter ten, sat down on a nearby lounge chair and silently began reading the passage.

Alana and John stood across the room. Alana looked at Mitch with eyes gleaming and filled with exhilaration. John was calmly observant.

"Isn't this wonderful?" Alana whispered.

"There is rejoicing in heaven today." John snuck a peek at Alana who was still staring at Mitch. He felt hurt and a little sad. Something so incongruent to the feelings he knew he should be having at such a moment. The love in Alana's eyes was so obvious. He silently prayed he would have a right heart instead of this painful feeling of envy.

At that moment Parson came into the room. John mustered up some cheer, "Hey Dad, say hi to your new brother in Christ!" John pointed at Mitch.

Parson's eyes widened, "No!"

"Yes! I'm afraid I'm a new member of the flock Parson, if you'll have me."

"Have you? Well son, I think that the Lord is the one

who has you now. What welcome news! Praise God!"

Parson walked over to Mitch with an extended hand. Mitch took it with an enthusiastic shake.

"Welcome to the family of God, Mitch!"

"Yeah well, after what I went through, I want to make sure I don't ever go through it again. I'd say it's a good idea to have God on my side right? I like to hedge my bets." Mitch winked at Parson.

The three of them laughed, even John was able to chuckle. Then Alana threw her arms around Mitch's neck and gave him a huge hug. Her enthusiasm was so strong she almost knocked Mitch off his feet.

John turned away trying to occupy himself with his Bible case but not before noticing Parson's knowing gaze.

Keeping his eyes on John, Parson bellowed, "Why don't we tell Sarah and Steve, I know they'll want to hear about this." Heading for the door, Parson put his hand on Mitch's shoulder. Alana gave Mitch's arm an affectionate squeeze, saying how proud she was of him. With great effort, John tried to put a smile on his face as he trailed behind.

CHAPTER 44

After all the congratulations and a check to ensure the kitchen was empty of Visitors, the Sleeping Bear family filed into the kitchen for a celebration. Sarah and Steve prepared the fresh venison with potatoes, green beans, freshly baked bread, and an enormous salad. The mood was festive, the conversation cheery. All over-ate shamelessly.

During the after dinner cleanup Alana asked Mitch to accompany her on a walk to the lake.

"Hey, do you think I might need a chaperone?" Mitch whispered.

Alana stifled a giggle and punched him in the arm, "You dope!"

Mitch wasn't just feeling good about himself; he was

feeling great about life. While still a little on the thin side, the emotional strength deep inside him was something he had never experienced before. Now he knew what it meant when people said they were walking on air. Everything seemed new, and for the first time in his adult life, he felt at peace. He couldn't explain how, but he knew that saying the prayer of salvation, confessing his sins, and believing in his heart that Jesus was Lord had changed his life forever.

"I still have some questions for you —a lot of them, in fact," Mitch said as they started out the door.

The weather had been unusually dry for days. The night sky was sparkling like a canopy of countless diamonds against black velvet. The crisp, chilly night air was so clean it felt like breathing purified oxygen. Mitch tried to absorb the tremendous beauty around him. A full moon mirrored off the lake, creating a luminous path of light that cut across its entire length. He wanted to run wildly across it. He felt so deliciously alive.

They were strolling slowly along. "Alana, what exactly do I do now? What is the next step in this?"

"Well, it's important to read the Bible. You should try to every day. The Bible is the Word of God. John chapter one tells us that in the beginning was the Word, the Word was with God and God is the word. So it's not just a book of books, it's a living document the Lord uses to communicate his will for our lives and to teach us everything we need to know about life. It's like an instruction book for Christian living."

"Okay. I'll start doing that. I don't have a Bible though, not one of my own. Is there one you would recommend?"

"The next time we're out running errands, we'll get you a good study one, but for now, use the Bible in your room."

There was a rustling behind them. They turned. Elam stood looming in the darkness, this time without his headdress. His head was as smooth as a billiard ball; from the back, a single thick braid of black hair fell all the way to his waist. This evening, he wore a less ornate robe and the light reflecting off the lake made its fabric shimmer as it fluttered gently in the breeze. The top of his polished head also shone in an unsettling sort of way.

"I hope I didn't startle you," he said, bowing.

Once again, Mitch felt the need to shield Alana. He took a step in front of her. Somewhere nearby, an owl hooted eerily, the sound chilling him. Elam walked closer, enabling them to see his face. He looked at Mitch intently, as if he wanted to bore a hole right through him, then blinked twice—deliberately, theatrically. When he spoke it made the hair on the back of Mitch's neck stand up. "I see you have gone over to the side of Christ. You are a Christian now, aren't you Mitch?" The question seemed more like an accusation.

CHAPTER 45

He could not articulate why, exactly, this seemingly innocent comment sounded so sinister, but it caused the blood in his veins to turn to ice water.

Feeling protective of Alana, Mitch felt a surge of daring. "You 'see' I'm a Christian now?" Mitch made quotation marks midair. "What the—look, I know you're a paying guest of the Culvers here, but frankly, I don't see how that's any of your *business*." He said the last word with particular emphasis, grabbed Alana's arm and began moving past Elam back up the path. "I'm afraid we have something we have to get to, if you'll excuse us."

"Why certainly, I wouldn't wish to intrude," Elam said gravely. He gave another deep bow.

"Well, you did, so like I said, excuse us." Mitch and

Alana went quickly up the path.

"Please accept my humblest apology for any inconvenience I may have caused you!" Elam said to their retreating forms as they quickly made their way back to the main lodge.

"Just ignore him," Mitch told Alana. "Man, that guy—Visitor—thing—whatever he is—gives me the creeps!" Mitch shuddered.

"I feel the same way. I hope they leave tomorrow like they promised. I can't believe they're considered heads of state and some countries are actually inviting them to become members of their government. Why would they do such a thing?"

"Well, I guess because the Visitors are contributing lots of stuff to local communities, and they're super smart with technology.

"No wonder everyone thinks they're the hottest thing since Elvis." Alana chewed a nail thoughtfully.

"There's a whole group-think that government—and this includes the Visitors—should now take complete care of us, from cradle to grave."

Alana thought about this. "I guess once Michelle Crowley—you know, Oprah's heir apparent—had some of them on her talk show, it was like bestowing a seal of approval. Millions became convinced that they're fabulous and it just snowballed from there. When Visitors talk, everybody seems to listen."

Once they arrived back at the Lodge, Mitch was relieved. He stood just outside the door before going in, shaking his head. "I don't know, I just get the feeling there's some sort of unspoken threat coming off them."

"I do too. Let's get inside." When they both entered the dimly lit lobby, it was empty and quiet. Everyone seemed to have gone to his room.

"So, getting back to what we were talking about, other than reading the Bible, what else can I do? I feel like I want to do something. I don't really believe I'm worthy yet."

"Do you think you're not worthy because of the accident?"

"Well—yeah—I guess. I get that God forgives me. I get that the creator of the universe somehow can forgive what I've done. But I'm not God. What I don't understand is how to forgive myself. Don't get me wrong. Somehow... I feel peaceful. But I still feel a lot of guilt, and I want to be able to hold onto this idea that my sins really are forgiven. I don't know, I'm babbling. I guess I'm not making any sense, am I?"

"Sure you are, just don't be so hard on yourself. It's a process. Every Christian is at some stage of this process, some are just a little farther along than others, but always, it's a process until we take our last breath. You're just at the beginning stages and I'm sure with time, you're going to be able to reconcile these inner doubts." He was just slightly taller than she was, allowing them eye-to-eye contact.

Mitch could see genuine compassion flowing from her earnest green eyes and it touched him deeply.

How remarkable she was. He owed her his life. Well—he owed her for leading him to the God who gave him life—and he had no idea how he could ever thank her. He wanted to say something, but the words eluded him. "It's late, we better get some sleep. I've got to start pulling my weight more around here, so I vowed to get up early and help out." He hung his head, trying again to reach for the words. "How do I thank you, Alana? I just have no idea how to express my gratitude."

"Shhh—" In one smooth movement she placed her index finger against his lips and stepped closer. "Mitch, it was my honor to help lead you to the Kingdom of God. I'm just thrilled the Lord chose to use me—use all of us here, really—to guide you to Him. I'm so proud of all that you've done." She moved closer, "You're an extremely courageous man." Her eyelids were half-closed and provocative, her intent unmistakable.

She was so close. Mitch could feel the heat of her. Her breath smelled sweet, like lilacs, or was that the scent of her hair? Mystified, he wondered why her nearness didn't stir him. No carnal thoughts entered his mind despite there being less than an inch between them. At no time in recent memory had a woman gotten even half as close without eliciting a response from him, much less someone as beautiful as Alana. He realized what he felt was tremendous affection for her, untouched by any sexual desire. This was unchartered territory for him.

Well, she is my sister. Parson and John and the rest always said things like 'sister in Christ' or 'my sister in the Lord.' So that must be what I'm feeling. Then a troubling thought came to him: *Does a conversion mean you become like a monk or something? Or was it the alcohol? Did my withdrawal do something chemically to my brain... or worse?*

"You're amazing Alana, you really are." In the pale light of the lobby, the pupils of her eyes had become large, soft, and warm. There was such love in them, Mitch knew no one had ever looked at him that way before. The sisterly affection in his voice surprised him. "I'd say God gave me a miracle by bringing you into my life. You really are my angel."

With a deep intake of breath as if she were struggling with something, she said, "You're right, it's late and we should be getting to our rooms. We all have an early day tomorrow." She stepped away from him.

"Good night, Alana, and thanks again—so much—I couldn't have done this without you." He gently took both her hands in his.

"Sure you could have, Mitch. If it hadn't been me, the Lord would have put someone else in your path. I can't take any of the credit. It's the Holy Spirit that changes hearts, not me."

"Yeah, but there is no way I would have even considered that there *was* a God without you coming into my life. The others helped toward that goal of course, but you fascinated me and made me want to at least explore this God of yours." Mitch hesitated and his face brightened when he exclaimed. "Hey, I guess he's my God now too!"

This brought tears to Alana's eyes. Her voice choked with emotion. "I'm so blessed you know the Lord. It's amazing to me that God used me in such a way."

Mitch was still bumbling around trying to find the words to thank Alana sufficiently. "Thank you for your patience in helping me get clean and sober, and being my guide as it were." He paused waiting for more inspiration, but the enormity of what he felt was too daunting. Finally, he gave up. "Well, like I said, we both better get some sleep. Good night, Alana."

Mitch leaned over and kissed her sweetly on her forehead.

She blushed and stammered, "G—good night, Mitch." before turning around and walking quickly down the hallway to her room.

Mitch stood there baffled as to why the contact with her skin hadn't set him ablaze.

CHAPTER 46

Diminutive, dark, leathery-skinned man-creatures with fangs, tails, and clawed hands began tearing at his flesh. He tried to swat them away, but there were hundreds of them, multiplying into thousands. They swarmed everywhere, crawled over his bed, onto his chest, legs and arms, heading upwards, biting and pulling off small pieces of skin as they climbed. He kept trying to slap them away, but the creatures were relentless. The sound they made was an unintelligible high-pitched laughter, like a soundtrack on fast forward. Ones that weren't clawing at him were writhing and undulating as if engaged in grotesque sexual acts. As they ripped off each piece of skin with their razor teeth, he felt like they dropped acid on the resulting wound. They made their way to his eyes, crawling, biting, and snarling. Just before he succumbed to the terror, his own screaming woke him.

"Mitch, what is it man? Lemmie in!" Daniel pounded on his door.

A shaken Mitch unlocked and opened the door as Daniel burst in. "What is it? Was it another nightmare?"

Mitch fumbled ineffectually with some matches. He was trying to light candles to add warmth to the room, which felt numbingly cold to him.

He sat down hard on the edge of his bed. "I had a dream—a—a nightmare, but I'm telling you, Danny—it was so real." Mitch examined his arms and legs to be sure.

Daniel sat down next to him on the bed, his glasses more askew than usual. "You gave me a heart attack. We're the only ones down here on this end and it sounded like you were almost next to me. Man, you were screaming so loud. What the heck was it?"

"I don't know, I really don't know, but it came from hell whatever it was. And I mean directly from hell and they didn't pass go…"

Daniel sat in worried silence, then tried to right his glasses by removing them and putting them back on.

"Why don't I just bunk in here for tonight? There is no way I'm going back to my room alone and I don't think leaving you alone is a good idea either. You're creeping me out, man…" Daniel shuddered.

"I'm creeping myself out, trust me! And you sleeping

in here with me sounds like a plan. I'll take the lounge chair, you can have the bed."

"What, and sleep on that nastiness? Man, you must have a bucket of sweat on those sheets. No thanks. The Lazy-boy will do just fine." Daniel got up and went to the closet to pull down another pillow and blanket.

Mitch snorted softly. "You're just what the doctor ordered— a little comic relief."

Daniel prepared a makeshift bed for himself and settled in. The silence between them was comfortable, each wrapped in their own thoughts. Then Daniel spoke.

"Mitch, I don't know how to ask you this because actually I don't really know what I'm asking—but did you really become a Christian, or is this whole thing just so you can score with Miss Hottie?"

Mitch was astonished by his question but answered gamely. "I guess I can see why you'd say that. I am—or was, I should say—quite the player, always have been. No, it's real all right. More real than anything I've ever done in my life. Now, I admit—initially my motives weren't pure. Anything but. Then a number of things happened. I started to see what this Christian stuff might be all about. I liked it too. Not just because Alana was into it, but because everyone else was, and they were all so genuinely nice. Not fake nice, but really decent, kind people. I could see that even in the midst of all this insanity in the world, they had this tranquility thing going on. I wanted some of that. I haven't known any kind of inner, outer, or any other kind of peace in a long, long time. I at least wanted to find out more, that much I knew. Although to tell you the truth, I doubted anything would ever lift the black cloud that seemed to be following me."

Daniel listened, propped up on one elbow. "So you're saying these really cool people convinced you that there's a God?"

"No, it's not that simple. Now, I *can* tell you that my main motivation in the beginning was to be whatever Alana needed me to be so we could hook up. That was my first and primary motivation. But then I realized—I couldn't fake this. It had to be real. More importantly, I *wanted* it to be real. So I stopped trying to rush things and I just watched and listened. I asked questions, lots of them, and not just of Alana." Mitch sat forward, his body leaning toward Daniel, eagerly trying to express himself.

"The big 'moment' came when I was in the middle of the DT's. Something happened to me in there. Yeah, I went through physical torture, but I also know my resolve changed. Not just my resolve, *I* changed. When I'd talk to John or Parson or Steve and Sarah about it, they'd say 'We're praying for you'. And the weird thing is—it worked! Like one night—one of the worst nights—Sarah was in the kitchen and Steve was sitting across from me reading his Bible. I told him I felt like someone had beaten me with a baseball bat then set the bed on fire. He prayed out loud. At first I was so wrapped around feeling miserable, I didn't notice that the feeling like all my nerve endings were in flames had subsided. Steve kept praying and asking the Lord to intervene and give me a release from the withdrawal symptoms, and dang if I didn't get relief! Am I saying I felt fantastic? Not at all, but it somehow became bearable."

"Is it possible we're talking about a coincidence here? Don't the DTs come and go?" Daniel raised an eyebrow. "I mean, I don't know much about this sort of thing, but couldn't it just have been a temporary cessation of your withdrawal symptoms that just happened to coincide with Steve praying for you?"

"Yeah, that's possible, but when I think about everything that happened day after day during my detox, and everything leading up to and after detox, it all can't be chalked up to coincidence. Listen my scientific friend, I don't expect you to believe me. Trust me, I understand. If you were me and I were you, I'd be a total skeptic."

"Okay, let's just say I buy all of this for argument's sake. Why are you still having these hideous nightmares? Isn't life supposed to be perfection when you became a Christian?"

"Well, I'm pretty new to all of this, but I don't think that's the deal. I now know there's a dark spiritual world you and I can't normally see. It's really like all the stories say— it's good against evil. I think evil wants me to change my mind or something. Not too sure, but that's my take from what I've been reading in the Bible. There's no guarantee life will be smooth sailing. But the promise is that you'll have peace inside you, so deep it can't be shaken. The promise is God will never forsake you no matter what you're going through. And what's really cool is that when you die, you're going to go to heaven. And you know something? Not too long ago that going to heaven stuff meant absolutely zero to me. Now it means everything. It means so much that my original motives not only seems lame, but I'm ashamed of them. That kind of thing is *so* not my goal anymore."

"Are you trying to say that you don't think Alana's hot now?" Daniel pushed off his elbow and sat up.

"I'm saying that I now have a much better perspective on things, and trying to get into Alana's pants definitely doesn't top my to-do list anymore."

"Oh man, that's scary dude. So this Jesus-freaky stuff—it just sucks out all of your testosterone or something?"

Mitch laughed out loud. "No! That's not it at all you jerk! Believe me, it's hard for me to get a full grip on this too. I'm so new at this, but I know it's about getting your priorities straight. And now that I've done the Jesus thing—my greatest desire has nothing to do with chasing women. I just want to become a better Christian. It's sort of like my goal in life now instead of getting Alana to—shall we say, fall for my charms."

"Cool, can I have her then?" Daniel smiled craftily through glasses again lopsided.

"Cute, very cute. Hey, it's up to her, Danny boy. She's not mine to give."

"Yeah, well, I saw the look in her eyes at dinner,

and for all intents and purposes, she's yours. So it's pretty unlikely I'd ever have a chance to score. I'm resigned to the fact that this fuzzy-headed geek isn't going to make Alana's heart go all aflutter."

Mitch was sitting back against the headboard with several overstuffed pillows propping him up. "You know, there's more to this than what I used to think—this whole 'life' trip. I haven't told anyone, but you know when John came up to me in that diner? I actually was thinking of offing myself. I was just going to take a bunch of pills and a bottle of Jim Beam and say *hasta la vista,* baby. I was sort of planning it the night before, but I got too drunk to think it all through."

Mitch laughed softly once and went on. "So when John came up to me, I was nursing the mother of all hangovers. I felt so bad that I just might have gone home and ended it all that day. I don't know, maybe not. But I do know this: the minute John walked up to me, I somehow felt better about my life. I could feel a tiny bit of optimism. And I'll tell ya, the sunny side of life hadn't been in my part of town for a really long time. All because he was so nice to me. What was so cool was I knew he didn't pity me. He was just being a really good guy. In retrospect, I firmly believe God sent him to me, to bring me here to get sober and to become a servant of Christ."

Daniel had resumed a reclining position and stared pensively at the ceiling. He looked about ready to fall back to sleep when he mumbled, "That's really good for you,

Mitch. But why were you feeling so miserable in the first place? You seemed to be fairly successful, judging by that loaded SUV you drove. What was your problem?"

With a long sigh, Mitch told him about the car accident and the downward spiral his life had subsequently taken.

"So you went from crashing—to burning—to Jesus? Is that what you're trying to tell me? You're saying a prayer really made this difference in you?"

"Well... yes—no—not exactly. Nothing over night or anything. More like a process. I don't know, Danny... it's too hard to explain."

Daniel pushed his unruly fro away from his face, removed his glasses, and yawned noisily. "How about we chew this over tomorrow or something?"

Mitch leaned forward to blow the candles on the nightstand out. "Yeah, you're right. I'm definitely tired, and I planned on getting up and doing my part around the resort. But at this rate, I'm going to do the usual Mitch-sleep-in routine."

Daniel chuckled, "Yeah, it's about time you put your useless self to work around here, you slacker."

Mitch cried out a weak, "Heyyyy," but soon both were snoring.

From the vent just above the bed where Mitch slept, two crimson eyes glowed.

CHAPTER 47

The Visitors loaded up their vehicles early the next morning. John offered to help them, but his offer was politely declined—he had hoped to get a good look inside the vehicles, but after their refusal he knew that wasn't going to happen. Elam was standing off to the side as the last of the luggage was placed in the SUV. He asked John, "Has Miss Alana been around yet this morning?"

"Yes, she's taking inventory and making up our shopping list. I just came from there." John moved slowly to block Elam's path to the pole barn where Alana was.

Undeterred, Elam looked directly at him. "Mr. Culver, I was hoping to speak with her before leaving."

Not intimidated in the least, he replied evenly, "The ladies don't like to be disturbed when they do their work.

I'm sure you understand."

In a flash, a millisecond, the face of a hideous monster burst into being and glared at him. Glowing reptilian eyes met his, their irises cesspool green. A burgundy tongue writhed out of a raw hole of tobacco-colored fangs. The sight should have sent John reeling, but somehow he half expected the sudden appearance of Elam as he truly was. John's voice was low, almost a growl when he gave the order: "In the name of Christ Jesus, our Lord and our God, I command you to leave this place."

The vision was gone. Elam stood before him once again in his former incarnation. "Why, Mr. Culver! I'm not sure I understand the need for such inhospitality. We are all brothers in the Lord here, are we not?" Hazael and Merari now joined Elam on either side, Hazael on the right, and Merari on the left. Each wore a frozen visage of innocent congeniality.

"Thank you for your patronage, Gentlemen, but I'm afraid from now on everyone will need to call ahead for a reservation." John's jaw was hard. He stood with his feet planted wide, hands on hips, his posture unyielding.

"Yes, I suppose we do need to carry on with our journey back to Kansas, don't we? Once again, we thank you for allowing us to stay at your charming retreat." Elam bowed quickly and backed away toward the SUV. Hazael and Merari did the same. The Visitors' escorts and chauffeurs materialized silently to hold doors and slide into driver's seats; the vehicles departed noisily, tires spitting pebbles and kicking up dust.

As the last SUV drove away, John was certain he saw the reptilian eyes of Elam glowering at him through the rear window of blackened glass. A hand on his shoulder made him jump a half-foot.

"Holy cow! Where did you come from?" John exclaimed, stepping back and trying to regain his footing.

"Sorry, Son, I didn't mean to scare you. Are you all right?"

"I am, now that they're gone!" John started walking down the long driveway with Parson following. "I think it's time to close the front security gate. No more uninvited visitors."

"I remember thinking the gate was an unnecessary expense at first, given the lack of crime in this area, and I hated the barbed wire along the top, but once we started hosting the kids' summer camps, we needed to be careful. Now I'm really glad we installed it, an eyesore though it is."

They reached the road and each took one side of the sliding gate, then pushed it together until the chain-link sides met with a very loud clang. John secured the electronic lock.

"Do you think they'll be back?"

"I don't know, Dad, but let's pray the answer to that is a great big negative."

CHAPTER 48

Alana and Sarah were working hard to inventory their stockpiled items. Alana was trying to focus, but like a schoolgirl with a crush, her mind strayed. With the holidays fast approaching, it was important she concentrate, but her thoughts kept drifting back to Mitch. The droning of the small generator that powered the lights was just another distraction.

Sarah teased. "Looks like somebody has a happy little secret they're not tellin'."

Alana stopped in the middle of writing *canned tomatoes*. "Huh?"

"That smile on your face. But of course I don't mean to pry!" Sarah kept moving cans, calling out their contents and how many they had. She had a sly smile of her own.

"Oh, wow—I'm not concentrating." Alana blushed as a smile lit up her face.

"You're doing a good job with the inventory, but your face is saying you've got a secret you're dying to tell. I am a good listener, and I admit I'm curious, but I think I already know what this is about." Sarah announced her latest count: "Thirty, thirty-two ounce cans of peaches."

Alana made a note and then looked up from her tablet. "I guess I have some strong feelings for Mitch I'm trying to understand. I'm on shaky ground here, I honestly don't know what I'm doing."

"Do you want to talk about it?"

Alana was looking at the screen without really seeing it. She replied absently, "Yes, I think I do, actually."

"Well, what are you confused about?"

Alana shook her head. "I don't know. It seems like everything is turned upside down. I do know this though, I can't get him off of my mind, and frankly, I'm not sure I want to."

Sarah chuckled softly. "Been there done that! Sounds just like how I felt about Steve—once I knew I was in love with him anyway."

Alana looked up startled. "In love? Do you think I'm in love? I know I've never felt like this way before about anyone but..."

"It sure seems to me like you are Alana. You show all

the signs."

Alana said, "On the one hand, I like this feeling. On another, I really dislike the lack of control I'm displaying. I'm acting so... so... well, juvenile. But it's like I'm powerless to stop it."

Sarah gave another count again before replying. "Forty-two sixteen ounce cans of green beans and the same for potatoes. I think we're good to go with the beans and potatoes, but maybe we ought to stock up more on corn because we only have seventeen of those. Anyway, everything you say just keeps telling me that it's love."

Sarah turned around and pulled up a small chair next to one of the metal-shelving units and sat down. "How about a little break and we can talk about this?"

Alana grabbed another chair and sat down. "I don't know... he pulled me in... he was so sincere. He told me that he was attracted to me and that he'd stop drinking and even become a Christian for me. It sounds really wild, but if you could have seen him, he was so intense and incredibly—vulnerable. But I was cautious. I never thought he'd do either, much less both. Now I have to admit that somehow during it all, he stole my heart away."

"So, what's the problem?"

"I can't put my finger on it. He's different. He's, of course, *good* different. He's sober, which is definitely a good thing. But I also sense that he's, well—sort of holding me at arm's length. He's gone from fawning over me to holding back. So I just feel funny about it. I don't know how to put the brakes on the way I feel, if he's changed his mind."

"Oh, I doubt he's changed his mind. He's probably just being respectful, now that he's beginning to live as a Christian instead of giving in to matters of the flesh. Hey, I have an idea. Why don't you just ask him?"

Alana looked at Sarah as if she had just sprouted two heads. "Ask him? What do I say? 'Gee Mitch, don't you like me anymore?'"

Sarah's laughter bounced off the pole barn walls. "Not exactly like that. Come on, are you telling me you're in love—or you *think* you're in love—and you can't *talk* to the guy?"

"I guess I see what you mean. You're right, I'll talk to him. Somehow I'll figure out a way to broach the subject. It's better than just mulling over it and driving myself crazy, that's for sure. Gosh, I feel like a teenager with her first crush."

Just then, Lizzy and Megan flew into the pole barn, giggling and running at top speed. "Well, speaking of pubescence, look who just arrived." Sarah pointed at the girls who were gasping dizzily for breath.

"Whoa, you two! If you have that much energy, you can help Alana and me count our supplies here."

Deflated, Megan replied, "I guess we can help, Mommy."

"Good, now Lizzy, you go over there with Miss

Alana and do those shelves, and Megan and I can finish these shelves over here."

John stood in the doorway of the pole barn and watched his daughter working alongside Alana. Lizzy was so pleased to be helping, and Alana had a way of including her without being patronizing. The simple scene before John's eyes endeared Alana to him even more than he thought possible. He recognized a pain—a longing—welling up in his heart.

Just as he was about to say something, he heard yelling from the main lodge. Alana and Sarah heard it as well and both looked up. Alana said, "I didn't see you there John, what's all the yelling about?"

"I have no idea, but I better go find out."

Alana and Sarah moved to the doorway as John trotted toward the lodge.

"What's going on, Dad?" John yelled, as he came through the door.

Parson's alarmed and agitated voice shouted back, "John! Iran just launched a nuclear attack on Israel!"

CHAPTER 49

The Sleeping Bear family stood in the kitchen, eyes glued to the TV, awaiting additional information. The news was so alarming; no one thought to sit down except for Daniel, who was furiously typing away on his virtual tablet keyboard.

First reports indicated the casualties were likely to number in the hundreds of thousands. No official count was available at this time, and none was anticipated any time soon due to the horrific devastation. Multiple air strikes had been launched against various Israeli military installations in the predawn hours; the most destruction, however, came from several suicide bombers who set off a thermal nuclear bomb in downtown Tel Aviv at noon.

Lizzy and Megan were playing a board game on the

floor of the Great Room, seemingly oblivious to what was going on. John had placed them in an area of the room where they weren't able to see the television.

Steve and Caleb were deep in hushed conversation. The fire crackling in the grate did little to dispel the sudden chill.

"Daniel, what do you have there?" Parson walked over to Daniel and began reading over his shoulder.

Daniel hesitated before replying, as he gathered his thoughts. "I think I've come up with some fairly accurate calculations as to the possible damage done based on my research."

Everyone else joined Parson behind Daniel. "Now. Apparently the bomb was a 200-kiloton HEU, or Highly Enriched Uranium, thermal nuclear bomb. From what anyone can tell, the terrorists drove an eighteen-wheeler right into the middle of downtown and then detonated it. Of course, no one on the scene is alive to verify that. Anyway, due to the buildings in downtown Tel Aviv, we're going to assume that the shock waves were blocked to some—albeit small—extent. Within the first second, the pressure of the first shock wave, we're talking at least 20 psi, or pounds per square inch, would extend about four tenths of a mile from detonation or ground zero. Everything, and I mean every single thing within that radius is destroyed. Buildings, structures, gone. People are instantly destroyed—before they even know what's happened to them. They're the lucky ones. We're already talking some 75,000 to 100,000 killed here. Those outside that radius but in direct line with the blast will be vaporized from the heat. Those in buildings outside the radius will survive the blast but will be killed when the buildings collapse."

Daniel glanced over at Lizzy and Megan to make sure they hadn't overheard his commentary. They were still absorbed in their game.

"All communication—radio, TV, cell phones, and land lines stop immediately as the mushroom cloud expands upwards. It's not like 9/11, where the rest of the world can turn on their TV's and there are cameras on the ground recording what's happening. There is nothing—that's why there's no live coverage TV right now—nothing's coming out of Tel Aviv, and I'm guessing that's going to be the case for quite awhile."

Alana said, "I just don't believe this is happening… I can't believe it…"

"Neither can I. I think we're all in shock." Sarah put an arm around Alana and gave her a hug. They stayed that way as Daniel continued.

"Now we're at only four seconds since detonation. The shock wave extends for at least a mile, with an overpressure of 10 psi."

"Danny, What does 'overpressure' mean?" Mitch interrupted.

"Oh yeah, sorry. Overpressure means pressure that's over normal air pressure—so this is the blast—the tremendous pressure of air pressing on people and objects. That's what the 'psi' is."

"Got it."

"Now, like I said, we're only in the first four or five seconds since the bomb was detonated. At this stage, those on the outer ring of the shock wave in buildings have survived, but because of windows blasted out and other interior destruction, flying debris kills them. We're looking at probably 300,000 more killed at this point.

Listen, I could go minute by minute, but by my estimation by the end of the day, at least a million and a half people are going to be dead."

There was stunned silence. Finally Parson spoke softly, "I think we all should pray, if you don't mind, Daniel. Can we gather in a circle and hold hands?"

John called to the children, "Lizzy, come on over with us for a prayer, all right, Honey?" Parson held out his hand. "You too, Megan."

Both girls obediently jumped to their feet and came over to the adults. Parson said a short prayer after which they all disbanded with the promise to meet back for lunch in a few hours.

Daniel closed the cover of his tablet, drew in a deep breath, and let it out slowly. While there was no immediate danger to them at Sleeping Bear, he didn't feel safe. Fear gnawed at his stomach, mocked his intellect, and he had no idea what to do about it.

CHAPTER 50

The group went about their regular chores quietly. John had just finished an inventory of the survival packets, hunting clothing, ammunition, oil, and other stockpiled necessities. The last three trips to the local warehouses had been in vain; they had to travel farther and farther now to replenish their provisions. There could be no rest when it came to preparing—not only for the winter, but for a self-sufficient future.

A nip in the air reminded John to retrieve some extra blankets and down comforters from one of the climate-controlled storage barns. Gathering several vacuum-sealed covers in his arms, he carried them into the back entrance of the lodge. The plastic-y tower of covers slipped this way and that, proving difficult to keep upright. On his way to the walk-in linen closet, John was peering around the stack when he passed the gym and glanced in. His heart stopped. Evidently finished with her laundry chores, Alana was working out alone. Not entirely conscious of what he was doing, John stood and stared.

Alana wasn't aware of John's watchful gaze as she concentrated on her exercise regimen. A narrow horizontal hall window ran the entire length of the gym opposite the floor-to-ceiling mirrors she faced, but she still didn't see John studying her every move.

He wanted desperately to turn away, but his feet felt rooted to the spot. Guilt overwhelmed him. He had never before experienced anything like this in his life. His mouth parted with a soft intake of breath as his pulse quickened.

How could this be happening?

He had avoided the whole adolescent hormonal-overdrive experience. Katie and he had met in a church youth group when they were both eighteen. They were good friends months before they realized their friendship had grown into a romantic attraction. Even so, they hadn't experienced the molten-hot passion of first love, and John always treated Katie with the utmost respect. Both had been virgins when they married and after he had lost her, John had never known another woman intimately or otherwise—he simply never wanted to.

This reaction to Alana was a raw, grating, insistent, and powerful thing that had taken on a life of its own, and he didn't like the out-of-control feeling one bit.

He watched her bring the hand weights in front and do alternating lifts with her elbows hugging her sides just above the hips. She concentrated on her arms instead of her reflection.

Her workout clothing wasn't particularly revealing, but her yoga style pants and tank top fit like a second skin, hugging every curve of her beautiful form. Distant memories of what it was like to be intimate with a woman and yearnings long dormant—at least until he met Alana—resurfaced. His mind conjured up carnal images, and his face flushed with acute embarrassment.

For her next exercise she took the weights and used them to do the butterfly, an exercise he was familiar with from his own routine. She bent her arms at the elbows, brought the weights to her eye level, swung her elbows together and then out again, arching her back as she did so. John's desire roared though him like a wild animal.

Finally guilt trumped desire and he quickly walked down the hall to the linen closet. It was a large windowless room filled with stainless steel shelving that covered all four of its walls. After he put the blankets away, he gripped one of the shelves, arms outstretched with his head lowered, trying to catch his breath. He hadn't bothered to turn on the overhead lights, the iridescent emergency light was sufficient. Besides, the dark seemed to help hide his disgrace. He was panting like he'd taken a long run. His arms quivered as he clutched the shelf like a lifeline and tried to steady his uneven breathing and clamoring heartbeat.

What am I going to do? I can't act like I don't care. How can I keep how I feel a secret when I have to see her every day? If I try to avoid her, it would be obvious... John whispered an urgent prayer. "Lord, please take this longing from me. Help me to be stronger than this—this—urge—my life is in chaos and you are not the Father of chaos. Please remove these thoughts from my mind. Help me keep my thoughts stayed on you Lord, instead of desires I should not have. In Christ Jesus' name I pray, Amen."

John began to feel calmer, more in control as he turned the knob of the linen closet door, opening it inward. Just as he was about to step into the hallway, he bumped smack into Alana. The force of the collision caused Alana to stumble and John caught her before she fell.

"Oh, John! I'm so sorry! I guess I was lost in thought about all that's happened."

"That's—it's—ah—no problem... totally my fault. Guess my mind was elsewhere too." He almost laughed at the irony of that statement.

The instant she steadied herself he drew back as if he had grabbed a live wire.

He jammed his hands in his pockets to quell the sensation of touching her bare arms.

Alana looked up at him, and again John was drawn into those brilliant green eyes. She began patting her face with a towel that was draped around her neck, and he found himself oddly captivated by the motion.

"John, do you think we're safe here?"

Lost in his reverie, he pulled himself back to her question and wracked his mind for an answer. He was about to reply when Alana placed her hand on his upper arm, sending his head spinning. He looked at her blankly.

"John, are you all right? Is it that you're worried about the asteroid and everything? We all are."

Just her touch, something so simple, sent a shock wave through his body.

"Ah... Alana, I think for now, we're definitely safe." *Not sure I am though, not with you so close to me. Not with you touching me...*

She gazed at him earnestly. "Do you really think so? You're not just saying that to make me feel better, are you?"

John barely heard her voice—he saw her mouth *saying* the words but they didn't register. He saw her lips: their fullness, their softness... he wanted to bend down and kiss them... *Holy cow, what on earth was happening to him?*

He cleared his throat and averted his eyes to somewhere above her head. "No, Alana, I'm telling you the truth," he said reassuringly. "I really believe for now we're safe here at Sleeping Bear. I don't know about the future—that's in the Lord's hands—but for now, the fall-out won't affect us. We're half way around the world. By the time anything reaches us it will be in miniscule amounts."

Alana's grip on his arm tightened. "Oh, what a relief. I didn't want to say anything in front of the girls, and yet I needed to know what you thought. Do they understand what's going on?"

"Not really. They know something serious has happened. But they know it isn't threatening to us. Steve, Sarah and I talked to them."

"How's Caleb doing?"

"Steve said he's pretty upset, but Steve and Sarah are keeping a close eye on him. I'm sure he'll be fine once he realizes he's safe here."

"Oh good." Alana kept her hand firmly on his bicep. John was afraid she might feel the heat he was sure was emanating from every part of him. He looked away and prayed she wouldn't detect his discomfort.

She seemed to want to linger. As much as John wanted to prolong this moment too, he knew he needed to distance himself from her—and fast. Images of her flooded his fevered imagination, making it almost impossible to concentrate.

"You know, John, I don't know what would have happened to us without you. You've done so much. There is no way we could ever repay you and your father. Just being around you gives me a—a peace. The world is in such chaos, but being here I feel safe. Just talking to you like this, I feel so much calmer."

Alana went up on her tiptoes. He stood paralyzed.

He should have offered her his cheek, but instead, her chaste kiss landed dangerously close to his own lips. Her scent was slightly musky with overtones of lilacs, and when she kissed him, he closed his eyes involuntarily and took a sharp breath.

"John Culver, don't be so modest. Take my gratitude and accept it, for all that you and Parson have done for us. I probably would have fallen apart, and Lord knows what else, if I had stayed alone in Leavenworth. I probably would have gone back to New York, alone, and wallowed in my grief. Now I feel part of a family again. Being here has helped heal my heart after losing Bianca and Dom—"

Her voice trailed off and her eyes softened with tears. Seeing her so defenseless, so fragile, was about to send John over the edge.

Tears trembled at the rim of her lower eyelids. "You have such a heavy burden to bear running the resort and taking care of Lizzy, yet you care about everyone here selflessly, working so hard every day, and well into the night. What a sweet, thoughtful man you are. Beneath that gruff and macho exterior, you're just a great big teddy bear. I don't know how I'll ever be able to show you how grateful I am, ever." Now the tears fell freely. She loosened her hold on his arm to wipe them away with the towel.

John nearly choked. "I—I know how you feel, and I'm glad you believe I—we helped in some small way."

"No small way, John Culver! Big way!"

John avoided her gaze. "Well it's been wonderful having you here, Alana. I'm glad we were able to help." He was amazed he was able to form a cogent thought between the kiss and the weeping that tore at his heart.

Regaining her composure, she said lightly, "Well, I better snag a shower so I can get cleaned up in time for dinner. I didn't feel much like eating before, but now I'm starving! Boy, I shouldn't have gotten so close to you, I probably stink to high heaven."

His imagination helpfully conjured up images of Alana in the shower. "No, ah—not at all, you actually smell a little like lilacs or something."

She brightened, her eyes sparkling with recent tears, and smiled at him. She looked luminous. "Really?" She tilted her head coyly, obviously taken by his remark. John could feel perspiration tickling down his ribcage. *Oh this will never, never do. I have to overcome this.*

"Aw, you're just being kind! I *do* wear perfume called, 'White Lilac Dreams.' But regardless, I'll smell like an old gym bag if I don't get a shower soon. Hey, thanks again for being such a sweetheart." Reaching up, she brushed his cheek with her fingertips, her fingers remaining a beat too long, as if she were reluctant to remove them. Then she withdrew her hand quickly.

"See you for dinner?"

John opened his mouth to say something and his voice cracked, "Su—sure."

He wasn't sure his legs could still hold him up, but blessedly she turned on her heel and walked away. He watched her as she went down the hallway until he could see her no more.

Then he prayed again silently. *Oh Lord, I have to be delivered from this. Father, please, please help me regain control of my thoughts. Help me focus all my thoughts on You.*

He touched the place on his cheek where her lips had been and thought he could still feel them there.

As Alana disappeared around the corner on her way to her room she found herself oddly stirred by the innocent contact with John. Generally she wasn't "physical." She wasn't a "touchy feely" type of person. Yet with John it seemed perfectly natural, and this was puzzling to her.

CHAPTER 51

The early morning sun threw golden geometric shards across the log-hewn kitchen island. John was preparing breakfast while Parson sat across from him, elbows on the granite countertop. A large fire in the fireplace snapped and crackled in the grate, warming the room.

Parson's words seemed to lower the temperature in the room a degree or two. "I'm afraid the news is still pretty disheartening." He was using his digital reader to access a number of newspapers and publications wirelessly. "You know, I realize this is the way to read newspapers now, but I sure miss the smell of newsprint in the morning while reading the paper over a cup of coffee."

John deftly cracked two eggs at once into a speckled bowl. "I know Dad, I understand. I also understand why you still use a non-digital Bible. You're lucky it's one of the few books they still actually print these days. I guess we're both getting old."

Parson chuckled, looking at John over his reading glasses. "I'm afraid I've got a good jump on you there..." He pushed his glasses back up and stared at the reader. "What I especially don't like is that ever since the census was changed and digitalized, the government knows my every move as it is—what, with the IRS expansion and the NSA's unconstitutional intrusion into our private communications, the government knows everything we do. It's like being under constant surveillance. How did we ever let it come to this? So much for 'centralization.' I was never one of those conspiracy theory types, but no matter what administration is in power now, they'll know what we do, where we live, and where we buy our groceries; they'll know when I fill up or charge my car or even what I just bought at my local store. They'll know it all, including what credit card we use and precisely when we use it. I guess I was complacent because I didn't know the extent of it all— that is, until the Visitors showed up. Now the government must be using them to read the minds of its citizens. The founding fathers are probably rolling over in their graves. It sure keeps me on my knees in prayer, I can tell you that much."

John stopped whisking the eggs and wiped up some yolk that had splattered on the counter. "I know, Pop, I know. I think a lot of people feel as you do. I'm guessing more people will want to stay with us as the days go by.

I think we should remain open to all, at least for now. Especially given what the future may hold with the coming asteroid."

Parson stared off, as if trying to count the stones of the fireplace. "I believe you're right. We will keep our doors open to the public, unless for some reason that becomes impossible."

John ground some fresh pepper into the bowl. "Anyway, Dad—what is the grim news? I can take it, I've already had my first cup of coffee."

Parson adjusted his reading glasses. "Well, it's not all grim. Electricity has been restored throughout most of the country except for some outlying areas. They're predicting more and more townships will regain power daily. And if it hadn't been for satellite internet connection, we wouldn't have had the information we did get, spotty though it was due to overloading the system. Looting is continuing to be a widespread problem. Martial law is still being imposed on many cities across the nation. All the more reason to stay safely tucked away at Sleeping Bear."

"Do we have any recent news about what the Visitors are up to? Is any one of them going to be our new President come the next election?" John smiled sardonically.

"Well, one columnist wrote 'While American life limps back to some semblance of normality, the Visitors have gradually and persistently injected themselves into many aspects of our communities. The United States is not alone in this: the Visitors have also ingratiated themselves in almost every civilized country of the world.' Talk about disturbing."

"I'm pretty sure that we are in the end times, Pop. I just never dreamed it would come down like this—aliens, asteroids, catastrophic natural disasters everywhere…"

Parson again looked at John over the top of his glasses. "Want me to continue?"

John nodded, and with a sigh Parson continued, giving him a synopsis of what he read. "Close to two million people in Israel lost their lives as a result of Iran's nuclear attack on Tel Aviv. The final count won't be known for months as people continue to succumb either to related injuries or radiation sickness. Hospitals are severely overcrowded…" Parson's eyes filled with tears. "I can't even imagine this type of devastation. I intend to pray about it every day."

"Any news about the asteroid?" John asked. Parson scrolled through the news.

"Nothing we don't already know: it's huge, it's going to hit, and it will cause mass devastation."

Alana wandered into the kitchen with her hair askew and yawning. She wore a bright red fitted hoody and black yoga pants. The tiny sweatshirt allowed John a glimpse of her flat stomach, and the stretchy pants accentuated her toned and shapely legs. Even her messy hair was cute. John busied himself with flipping the last of the pancakes and turning the sausage, but Alana's presence in the room made it twice as hard to concentrate.

"I can't believe you can cook up all this food for so many. You make it seem easy. Everyone else has to have two or three others helping them when it's their turn to cook, including me." Alana stood opposite John admiring the sumptuous meal of pancakes, scrambled eggs, fresh fruit salad, sausage, and buttermilk biscuits.

"When firemen aren't out chasing fires, we cook up meals for everyone on duty. It's just practice. Not really that much to it."

"Don't let him kid you, Alana. John's a great chef." Parson's eyes glowed with pride.

"Oh, I know. I've had the gustatory pleasure of John's meals many times." She looked straight at John and flashed him a teasing smile. "I always thought it would be fantastic to find a guy who would cook for me. You're quite the catch, John Culver. Don't you think so, Parson?"

Parson took off his reading glasses. "Oh, he's a real sweetie all right."

John was dumbstruck. He could feel his face growing redder by the second while Alana and Parson traded gleeful smiles.

CHAPTER 52

Everyone at Sleeping Bear was determined that Christmas Eve and Christmas Day would be days of joy and celebrated by shutting out the world. In remembrance of the birth of Christ, global disasters, asteroids, and the threat of world war would have to wait. For almost two glorious days, TVs, tablets and radios were shut off.

A nine-foot blue spruce from the Manistee National Forest stood majestically near the fireplace, resplendent with homemade decorations. The kitchen was busy from morning to night with everyone making his or her own specialty. Even Daniel, who professed to be "cooking challenged," made rolls from scratch with only moderate coaching from Sarah. Megan and Lizzy baked shortbread cookies in the shape of stars.

Gift-giving Christmas morning was a special and touching event. All had agreed that presents were to be from the heart, not from a store, and for weeks the lodge had become a bastion of industry with sewing and knitting, carving and baking.

Parson said the blessing over Christmas dinner and then all dug into the feast: turkey with crisp brown skin, buttery mashed potatoes, homemade dressing by John, fresh cranberry sauce from a generation's-old family recipe by Parson, Sarah's famous green bean casserole, and Steve's velvety gravy. The aroma of pecan, pumpkin and apple pies waiting in warm ovens wafted through the room enticing those not over-full from dinner.

Wiping his lips on a napkin, Parson said, "We all should thank Steve's hunting prowess for providing such a huge and delicious turkey for our table. From the looks of it, we just may have some leftovers!"

With a mouth so full of food he looked like a chipmunk storing nuts for the winter Daniel said, "Not if I have anything to say about it!"

After a few hours of good food, good company, and lively discussion, the problems of the world seemed to drift away. The atmosphere was warm with the kindliness of the season and the genuine affection they held for each other.

John leaned back in his chair taking in the scene before him. Stuffed to the gills, he watched everyone almost as if from a distance.

He thought about the past few months. He was particularly thankful that the unwelcome and inappropriate thoughts he had for Alana had become fewer and less intense. But the disturbing reality was, he knew this was only a reprieve.

Face it. What would she want with a guy almost fifteen years her senior? It's only a matter of time before she and Mitch make it official.

The constant struggle of keeping his attraction under control and under wraps was beginning to take its toll. The nights were the worst. No matter how exhausted he was from the day's work, Alana rarely failed to come to mind. Even when he finally slept, she figured in his dreams. He knew it because every morning when he opened his eyes— while he was still in that fugue state between sleep and waking—his first clear thought was of her.

John unintentionally let out a long sigh. "What's the matter, Son, too much great food?" Parson asked with a twinkle in his eye. But Parson's expression swiftly changed when he observed John's overplayed reaction.

"Yep, I'm just about as stuffed as I can be." Parson recognized a familiar family trick as John rose from the table and lifted his shirt to reveal a protruding belly. In reality, John had such control over his stomach muscles, he was able to make it only *seem* as if he had a paunch.

"Daddy! You are *so* gross!" yelled Lizzy.

Everyone burst into laughter. Once the table quieted

down, Parson said, "I think it's time to clear the table. If someone wants to get a fire going in the living room, we could play some old fashioned board games like checkers or Pictionary or Life—or whatever everyone wants to do."

Chairs scraped back as everyone picked up plates and utensils and brought them into the kitchen. Steve and Caleb offered to get the fire going and Parson and John volunteered to wash the dishes. Soon they were alone in the kitchen, John up to his elbows in suds and Parson holding a towel.

In a low voice Parson asked, "So, Son, are you ever going to tell me what's eating you? I've held my tongue for months now, but enough is enough. Something is heavy on your mind, and I'd really like it if you'd talk to me about it."

John stopped scrubbing dishes for a moment, considering what to say. "Everything's fine, it's just... you know... everything. And Lizzy—making sure she's shielded from as much as possible. Wondering what will happen to us... trying to trust in the Lord and maintain that trust."

Parson didn't let John finish. "Son, you and I are fortunate to have a very close relationship. I know you have these things on your mind, we all do. But this is something different. It's all right if you don't want to talk about it, but you might feel better if you do. Up to you."

John stared down into the soapy water. "Pop, I trust you with my life. It's not something I'm hiding from you, it's—something I'm trying to hide from myself. I can't talk about it. I can't—I don't even want to say the words. It would make it somehow real. I just want the whole thing to stop. I've been praying the Lord would deliver me, and lately I've gotten sort of a grip on things."

Parson said nothing, he just continued drying dishes, waiting patiently as John handed him plate after plate. Suddenly John stopped scrubbing. "All right, I give. I'll tell you." He spoke just above a whisper. "I'm not big on talking about my feelings, you know that. But maybe I'm supposed to air this out. Sometimes it's difficult to remember that you're not just my father, but a wise and seasoned man of the cloth as well."

"A retired man of the cloth, but I'm still a good listener. I should tell you first, though, I think I know."

John turned to face Parson so quickly; he sloshed water onto the floor with the dishrag. "What?"

"Well, Son, you're attracted to Alana."

John knew his expression of shock probably made him look uncannily like a wide mouthed bass. "Oh, no! Tell me I'm not that obvious!"

"I'm sure no one else has noticed. I just happen to know you like the back of my hand. Sometimes, on rare occasions, you wear your heart on your sleeve. This is one of those times. The last time I saw what I'm seeing now, Katie was alive."

John dropped the dishrag in the sink and walked over to the Great Room's oversized couch where he began pacing, using the length of it as his boundary.

"Dad, are you sure no one else knows?"

"Why, John? Would it be so horrible if Alana knew?"

John stopped and twisted around, "Yes! Of course it would be horrible! I'd be humiliated."

"Why?"

His hands balled into fists at his sides as he said emphatically through clenched teeth, "Because I'm old enough to be her... her... she'd laugh herself sick at the thought of someone as old as me—caring—attracted to—arrrggg—you know what I mean!" He resumed pacing again. "And you know what else? I wouldn't blame her. I'd feel like such a chump!" He sat down hard on the couch, his splayed fingers digging into his thighs angrily. Parson put the dishtowel down, came and sat next to him.

John leaned forward, his elbows on his knees. His head down, he folded his hands and rested his mouth on his knuckles. Parson put his arm around his son's shoulders. Finally John said in a strangled whisper, "I have to get over this, I have to conquer it, Dad. I can and I will. I can't keep acting like this, it's got to stop."

"Son, why are you so sure Alana would be repulsed by how you feel?"

When John looked up, his frustration boiled over. "I just know Dad. *I just know.* I'm like a big brother to her or—or worse." Then the rest came tumbling out of his mouth in an anguished rush. "She—she's everything I could ever want. I never gave women a thought after Katie, you know that, Dad. I realize you tried to find another mother for Lizzy—a suitable companion for me, and I appreciated your efforts, but what you hoped wasn't for me. I didn't even feel friendly affection for the women you tried to steer my way from church, even though I really tried. What I ended up feeling was resentment. I'm sorry to confess that to you, Dad. I know you only meant well, but that's the truth of the matter. Sometimes I'd sense their attraction to me and it would make me feel awful, like I was letting them down. Kate just filled me up, she was all I ever needed, all I ever wanted and then—and then she was gone."

Parson gripped John's shoulder. "I know, Son, I know. And I'm sorry if I was insensitive to your feelings after losing Katie. I finally did pick up on your lack of interest, I just wish I had realized sooner. I'm sorry."

"I know, Dad. I know you only meant well. There's really nothing to be sorry for." Then, determined to tell it all, he continued. "I have always been able to shut down that part of me and keep it shut. Even thinking about another woman... well, it felt like I was somehow cheating on Kate. I know that sounds strange, but it's honestly how I felt."

"I do know what you're talking about. It's the reason I didn't remarry after your Mom died. I just never had the desire. But I was much older than you when we lost your Mom. I guess I thought you still had so much to live for and that you should share it with someone," Parson smiled sadly.

John met Parson's sad smile with one of his own. "I

understand, Dad. Once I made the decision to concentrate on Lizzy and her upbringing—and, of course, my career as a firefighter, it was actually easy. I went about my life and remained in love with Kate, she just wasn't there anymore."

He looked down sheepishly. "But you know, even as an adolescent, I was never tempted when the other guys were looking at those magazines like *Penthouse*. If a friend pulled one out, I'd tell him to put it away in no uncertain terms. I was always in control with that kind of thing."

Parson replied, "It's good to know your Mom instilled a real respect for women in you."

"That she did, Dad, that she did." John stared across the room at nothing in particular, then resumed his confession.

"But everything changed when I saw Alana. She was—is—so incredibly beautiful. At first, I didn't know I felt this—this powerful attraction, at least not for a while. I didn't recognize it for what it was. And as corny as it sounds, like the sappy love stories Kate used to read, it was like this ember that suddenly ignited. The first time it really hit me was the day the Visitors arrived. When Elam upset her, I wanted to protect her. I wanted to kill that... that... *thing*. It was overwhelming—it just blew me away. It hit me so hard. God knows how I've tried to get her out of my mind since then. God knows because I've prayed about it non-stop. But I feel like I'm losing control. You know, I've always prided myself in my ability to control my emotions... that is, up until now."

The only sounds were the crackling fire as Parson quietly digested this information. He nodded his head thoughtfully before speaking. "Son, maybe the Lord brought you this trial so that you would come to realize that He is in control, not us. We're never really in charge of anything in this life."

John hung his head, clasping his hands before him. "Well, maybe you're right, Dad. I hadn't thought of that." Then he shook his head. "But Dad, I keep asking the Lord to take these thoughts from my mind. They torment me. It's exhausting because I'm forced to push away these feelings and thoughts every single day. I don't understand why God won't deliver me, Dad. It's driving me crazy." John wasn't sure it was possible to convey how he felt in words without sounding overly dramatic.

"Did you ever consider that maybe your prayers haven't been answered because you're asking for something that is different from God's plan for your life? You have made the decision already that these feelings you have for Alana are wrong. Have you asked the Lord what *He* wants for your life?"

"With all due respect, I'm pretty darn sure she loves Mitch, and I'm just as sure he loves her," John said dismissively. "God didn't mean for me to get brainless over someone who doesn't care for me in return. No. It's wrong, and I know it's wrong. And trust me, some of the ways I think of her are definitely wrong. The whole thing is stupid!"

Parson looked pensive for a moment. "I'm not advocating inappropriate thoughts and desires, so you're right, those kinds of thoughts are wrong. But perhaps your feelings for Alana aren't altogether wrong. Maybe she's worth fighting for? *That's* what I'm asking you to consider, John."

"Consider what? That the most gorgeous, fantastic woman I have ever laid eyes on would find someone like me attractive or desirable? I really don't think so."

"I'm not going to argue with you. Let me ask you this, though. Did your feelings start out as inappropriate?"

John didn't hesitate when he answered. "No!"

"Just think about that." Parson gave John a pat on the back. "You know I love you. You and Lizzy mean the entire world to me. It breaks my heart to see you so unhappy and torn up. I'm grateful you were able to talk to me about this—now I know more specifically how to pray. And I *will* pray about this whole situation, John. That much you can count on."

John turned and gave his father a big bear hug. "Thanks, Dad. You were right. I feel better having talked about it." He gave a relieved sigh that came from his toes. "Thanks for listening to my nonsense. Now, let's finish up the dishes and get into the living room with the rest."

As John and Parson returned to the kitchen, they were unaware that someone had been in the shadows listening, just beyond the doorway. The unseen figure slowly turned and walked into the living room.

"Well, are they coming?" Alana asked.

"Ummm—they're a—they're still finishing up. They were talking about something and I, ah—didn't want to interrupt. But it looked like they're almost done. Why don't we just play a practice game while we wait? I just want to know if Lizzy has the guts to take me on. I'm the master when it comes to Uno, ya know." Mitch gave Lizzy a playful wink.

From the floor Lizzy grinned up at him. "Oh yeah? Just bring it, Mr. Mitch, that's all I've got to say!"

Everyone laughed, and Alana and Sarah yelled in unison, "You go girl!"

As Alana dealt the cards, Mitch's thoughts were elsewhere. He was sorting out why the conversation he'd just overheard didn't make him feel jealous or threatened. To the contrary, it gave him an idea.

CHAPTER 53

Supplies lasted through the winter, and the first blush of spring began to periodically warm their days as the Sleeping Bear residents made preparations for extended farming and the replenishment of their supplies.

Breaking news: Hezbollah invaded northern Israel from Lebanon in the early morning hours. The recent nuclear strikes on Israeli military compounds from Iran have rendered Israel powerless to stop the invasion. Israel's Prime Minister Moshe Itzik has called upon the United States to send troops to assist in the conflict. There is no official word yet from the White House concerning American involvement in the conflict, but a press conference is scheduled for 5:00 p.m. eastern standard time today.

The unexpected and disturbing news cast a pall over

the kitchen's inhabitants.

Mitch, still holding the morning's breakfast dishes, hastily put them on the counter and apologized as he fled the room. Elbow deep in dishwater, Alana was startled by Mitch's sudden reaction and called after him. "Mitch! Where are you going?" but he was already gone.

"What do you think that's all about?" she asked Sarah, who was putting leftovers away.

"Honey, I don't have a clue. Why don't you go ask him?"

A premonition of dread turned the breakfast she had just enjoyed into a leaden lump in her stomach. "I think I will, but I'll finish up here first."

Everyone else continued the breakfast clean up while discussing the news. When they had finished, each went about his normal daily tasks.

John went straight away to cut more wood. The weather was unusually warm and dry for early April in northern Michigan, and John wanted to take full advantage of it.

He was shirtless, his torso glistening in the gold and pink watercolor wash of the sunrise. He found chopping wood useful in expending some of the energy he needed to redirect, particularly on days when he was forced to be around Alana more than usual.

Normally when he worked outside, he would take in the scene around him, admiring God's beautiful creation.

Today he was only distantly aware.

He stopped and leaned on his axe handle, distracted by thoughts of Alana.

Massive White and Northern Pines surrounded a circular, cleared-out section of about a quarter acre, providing shade as well as shelter from harsh winter winds. Although some deciduous trees dotted the interior, the White Pines dominated the perimeter, like Sentinels guarding the soft grass below. These trees were so uniformly immense, John felt insignificant among their towering majesty. This place, this chopping wood, was a familiar comfort for him, but today he found he longed to share it with Alana. He was proud of this private sanctuary in the woods. He took care in keeping the area pristine. The large stump he used to chop wood was de-barked all around from years of missing the mark. A smaller stump next to it served as a worktable. Near the north edge of the clearing stood a structure that resembled a miniature Lincoln Log cabin with a blue gabled roof; this cabin not only held an array of tools and equipment, but it also provided Lizzy with the perfect playhouse while her daddy chopped wood.

John realized he didn't simply want to share this private spot with Alana, he wanted to share everything with her... he wanted a future with her. The improbability of this made him pull in long a breath, shake his head and sigh hopelessly. He heaved his axe and began chopping with renewed vigor.

John had found breakfast with Alana more stressful

than usual that morning. When Mitch had rushed off, John stepped in to take his place drying the dishes. Try as he might, he could not help stealing sidelong glances at her. Her nonchalant style was disarmingly attractive, and even the sound of her voice was utterly beguiling, although he'd be hard pressed to remember anything she'd actually said. At one point he'd reached for a fresh towel and his arm brushed hers. His heart began pounding so thunderously he wondered if it might just burst altogether. There he was, going stupid again. Knowing that, as much as he wanted to forestall wood chopping, he also knew he had to get away as quickly as possible if he were to maintain any semblance of sanity.

John had already blazed through almost a fourth of a cord of wood and had started another when Mitch came down the path.

John spoke as he continued to chop. "I guess I really need to think about buying a chain saw. This is great for a workout and I like chopping, but it's not practical for the amounts we go through, in the winter. I should think of the others who might not like it as much as I do."

"Yeah—you're probably right... Ah... hey, can I talk to you?"

John looked stopped swinging the ax and looked up quizzically. "Sure, Mitch. What's on your mind?"

"Guess I'm going to have to cut to the chase here." Mitch had one hand tucked in his back pocket, and fingered the collar of his black and red tartan shirt nervously with the other. Sighing heavily, he continued. "I have a strong sense that our President is going to commit U.S. troops to the conflict in Israel. I also have a strong—*extremely* strong feeling, in fact—that *I'm* supposed to go." John squinted at Mitch, confused. He clarified: "I think I'm supposed to join the Army to help defend Israel."

CHAPTER 54

John didn't try to hide his surprise, "Mitch, wow…" He scratched his head. "I'm not sure why you would think that."

"I guess I've known for a while now—not exactly that I'd join the Army, but that I'd play some part in the Middle East conflict. It started almost as soon as I became sober. Then, after I gave my life over to Christ, the feeling became stronger with every passing day. I finally realized my life had some kind of meaning. I don't mean the every-Christian-has-a-purpose kind of meaning. I'm talking about what I heard Sarah say once—it's a calling. The thing of it is, I had no idea what that calling was—that is, until this morning when I heard Prime Minister Itzik was seeking U.S. military aid. In that instant, I was sure I was supposed to go back to

Leavenworth and join up. I recognize now why I was put on this planet. I never stood for anything. I never took a stand about anything—politically or otherwise—in my entire life. I'm taking a stand now. For Israel."

John was still stunned. "I don't know what to say, Mitch…"

"Well, I've pretty much made up my mind. But what I'm also here to tell you is that I want you to pursue your feelings for Alana. I have no claim to her."

John froze, one hand on the upturned axe, the other on his hip and his eyes as wide as saucers as Mitch broke out into song:

"I'm just a love machine, and I can't work for nobody but you—" Then he added some sliding disco dance steps before holding up his hands as if to put a hasty end to his own performance. "Not to worry. You weren't obvious. In fact, I had no idea, really. I overheard you and your dad talking Christmas day. I didn't mean to eavesdrop, I swear, it was totally accidental. I apologize for that, but I think I heard your whole conversation. Then afterwards, what began as a thought in the back of my mind became something I mulled over these past few months." He took a wider stance and folded his arms simultaneously. "You know, I didn't feel even the tiniest bit of jealousy when I was listening to you. I felt nothing except a kind of relief—but I didn't understand why at the time. Then I began really studying the Old Testament. I started with Genesis and kept reading and reading, like I was cramming for finals. And in a way, I was I guess. I

discovered some things I'm sure you already know. The Jews are God's people. They are our heritage, the foundation of Christianity. They are the bloodline to Jesus Christ. And, of course, it's because of the death and resurrection of Christ that we were grafted into this promise of a Holy and blessed people."

Mitch paused and nudged the soft green grass with the toe of his boot. John waited.

"During all of this reflection and studying of the Bible, I kept feeling like God was preparing me for something. Today I believe I found out what that something was." Mitch looked off at the White Pines thoughtfully, and then continued. "There is something else. I realized that while I love Alana, I don't love her like you do. She was just an angel the Lord sent to guide me straight to Him. She was my 'Do not pass Go, do not collect $200.00, go directly to Jesus ticket.' She was designed to get my attention, and man, did she ever. She was supposed to lead me out of the pits of hell and onto the path of righteousness. However, we weren't meant for each other—at least, not romantically. So she's yours, John. I mean, not that she's mine to give in the first place. You know what I mean."

John stuttered, "I... Mitch... I wouldn't... I mean— there's—there's no way I... I never tried anything..."

"Whoa man! Take it easy. First of all, I know you weren't trying anything at all. You thought Alana and I were hooked up, and you're such a man of integrity, you'd never try anything to undermine that. The thing of it is, we're not hooked up. I don't think you're hearing me here. The whole family unit scene isn't in the cards for me, not with Alana or anyone else. Although, my choice? Believe me, she'd be the one I'd want to have the whole two-point-five-kids-white-picket-fence-thing with, no question." Mitch paused and John wondered if he saw sadness cloud his eyes. An instant later, Mitch looked straight at him with quiet intensity.

"The really bad news is I haven't told Alana. Not because I wanted to string her along, but because I didn't understand it myself. That is, not until now. I won't lie to you—for a while there, I definitely was attracted to her. Talk about one desirable hottie... and I don't mean that disrespectfully. Well—ah—maybe I did initially..." Mitch scratched his head and flashed a sheepish grin. "Anyway—she's of course drop dead gorgeous. But she's also on fire for God. Hey, she's on fire for life in general. She's sweet, and kind, and so innocent. I've come to realize that she has the kindest heart of anyone I have ever known. And she's strong as an ox. She's a perfect combination that essentially plays out to her being the perfect woman."

John, still mystified by this seemingly out-of-nowhere conversation, managed to utter a noncommittal sounding "Yes..."

"Yes, indeed. But—and that's a big but—she's not for me. This morning I knew it, just like that." He snapped his fingers. "All of it fit together and everything became clear to me."

John protested. "Mitch, I get it, you have a calling.

You really believe God has given you this calling. So, go after that calling in your life, it's the right thing to do. When you get back..."

Mitch interrupted him abruptly. "That's the thing, John. I somehow know I'm not coming back."

"What are you saying?"

"Well, John, my-man—just what you think I'm saying. And trust me, I was a little shocked by this disclosure myself. There have been other things. I'm not *of* this world... I'm not really meant for this world. This isn't my 'home,' as it isn't for all Christians. The difference for me is that I know this, and not merely in the abstract sense. I'm aware of this in the here and now and it's become almost an integral part of who I am. Number two—some of us, not all of us in the Body of Christ, but some—are called out to do 'extraordinary' things. Then today in my Bible reading I saw these passages." Mitch reached into his back pocket for his digital reader, then recited, "'But man dies and is laid low; man breathes his last, and where is he? As waters fail from a lake, and a river wastes away and dries up, so man lies down and rises not again: till the heavens are no more he will not awake or be aroused out of his sleep.'" Mitch turned the pages on the touch-screen. "There's more. 'Now we know that if the earthly tent we live in is destroyed, we have a building from God, an eternal house in heaven, not built by human hands.' And then my last reading for the morning was, 'Precious in the sight of the LORD is the death of his saints.' I don't know, given this, the news, and how I've been feeling lately,

I'd say it's all pretty darn clear."

John said, "Mitch, these passages are what you've read recently? I'm guessing they come from that digital download credit we gave you for Christmas, *How To Read Your Bible Daily*. So I can see why you'd think random readings that have the same central theme might be some type of sign. But Mitch, are you sure the Lord is telling you to join the Army now and that it will lead to your death? Are you absolutely sure?"

"No, I'm not sure of any of it. I just get this strong sense of it. I kind of know I'm not going to come back if I actually end up being deployed to Israel. But what's even more bizarre is, I'm good with it. I'm ready I guess. Don't get me wrong—for so many years I was just this side of suicidal. Nothing dramatic, the slow way. The one-drink-at-a-time way. No. Make that one bottle at a time." Mitch smiled ruefully. "But this is not at all like that. This is something totally different. It blows my mind really, but it gives me an even deeper peace than I've come to know in these last several months. Some people go their whole lives wondering what the heck they've been put on the planet to do. I think I know my purpose now. Unfortunately, it isn't going to include Alana. So John, one of the most important things I'm trying to say here is take good care of her, will you?"

John put down the axe and approached him. "Mitch, you're assuming a whole number of things here. I'm still not as convinced as you are that even if you do join the Army you won't come back. And then there's another problem with your plan. You're forgetting one thing: whether I want her or not is not the point. She doesn't want me. You're her guy. She's in love with you—or haven't you noticed?"

Mitch's face broke into a boyish grin, "What was it you said? 'God wouldn't have you getting all stupid over someone you shouldn't care for?' Or something like that? Anyway—she only *thinks* she's ga-ga over me. I thought I was ga-ga over her too. Now I'm able to recognize the true shallowness of my original feelings. Could we have had something more if I wanted it? You bet. What's not to love? But by the time I understood how you felt, I was already on this fast track with God. When I heard you and your dad talking, the pieces started to fall into place. Maybe this means your feelings aren't so stupid after all."

John took his T-shirt off the small stump and wiped his neck. "Mitch, I'm not going to argue about what you feel called to do. All I can say is it's amazing the miracle the Lord has worked in you. I'm in awe of God's power in your life and your commitment to Him. It came about so quickly. Your life has been completely transformed."

"Yeah, it amazes me too, but you're a huge part of that, you know. God sure did use you to get me to where I am today. If you hadn't invited me so generously and graciously, we wouldn't be standing here having this conversation."

"Mitch if I do anything right, it's because of God. When I don't follow him every single day, I screw things up. It's just that simple. And I always fall short. So I can't take any of the credit. I was just listening to that still small voice when I approached you at that diner. I sure am glad I listened and obeyed." John reached out to shake Mitch's hand. Mitch accepted it, then warmly clasped both their hands with his other.

"Mitch, I hate to beat a dead horse, but there is no way she's going to go for me. She only sees you. You have a personal engraving on her heart."

"Don't sell yourself short, John." Mitch freed a hand and gave John's stomach a hard smack. "I'd kill for these abs!" John doubled over in case another smack was headed his way. "She's going to take notice, trust me. I've got nothing on you. She just doesn't know it yet. Give her a little time and she'll see what's been right in front of her all these months."

John studied the young man before him, and his respect for him knew no bounds. "I'll pray for you every day, Mitch. If this is the path you believe the Lord has put you on, you have my deepest admiration," he said gruffly, his eyes watering.

"Let's not get all sloppy and sappy here, John boy." Mitch flushed. "Look, I have to do a few things, then I better find Alana and tell her. I'll make the announcement to everyone else tonight at dinner. It's important to me that I have your support. Can I count on that?"

"You bet you can."

"Great." Mitch turned to go, turned back. "I'll see you around. Everybody's on their own for lunch today, right? That works for me because I've got chores to do and I need to tackle some other things like finding a way to Leavenworth. That ought to take me the rest of the day. Public transportation isn't as easy as it used to be."

"Take my truck. Dad and I have another vehicle between us."

"Wow, John, that's amazingly generous, but I think they're still running some buses on their regular routes. I'd rather do that anyway so I don't have to drive all that distance by myself. I never was good behind the wheel for long distances, sober or otherwise…" A bemused snort accompanied a self-deprecating smile.

"If you're sure, but know that you're welcome to the truck. I know Dad would feel the same."

"I'm sure. But thanks so much anyway." Mitch clapped his hands, then rubbed them together briskly. "Good—this was a productive talk. I'm glad we had it. I have that and so much more to thank you for, John!"

"Not at all, not at all. It has been my heartfelt pleasure—our heartfelt pleasure—to see the man you've become. If I had any part in that, I'm humbled."

Mitch stepped over to John and hugged him with surprising ferocity. The bond that had developed between the two of them was unmistakable. They parted then, each to his own thoughts as Mitch turned and started down the tree-lined path toward the lake.

CHAPTER 55

Before resuming chopping, John had turned on some music that started through the Bluetooth speakers. Now Alana came down the path to the clearing following the blaring noise of his remarkably tiny speakers. Still shirtless, John was swinging the axe, his muscles looking oiled and well defined. He hadn't noticed her. But Alana noticed him.

"Oh my..." Alana said under her breath. *He's completely ripped. I never realized...* Her pulse quickened and a warmness crept up her neck and spread to her face.

She hid behind the trunk of one of the massive Northern Pines and commenced staring at John's bronzed torso, broad chiseled shoulders and six-pack abs. Her stomach did a jig.

She was admiring—for the first time—the sheer physicality of the man. As he swung the axe, the highlights in his dark blond hair shimmered in the early morning sun. At six foot three, he had a commanding presence with the requisite square jaw and cleft chin... and the intelligence to go with it. And yet, he could be silly, too, like when he teased her about being a lawyer. She had to admit, this was one extremely attractive package. And, he *cooked*, too.

"John?"

John's cerulean eyes locked onto hers. *How had she never noticed how striking they were?*

She forced herself to focus. "Have you seen Mitch by any chance?"

"Ah... yeah, he was just here a few minutes ago. He went down toward the lake."

"He asked me to meet him. Do you know what he wants?" She noticed John's eyes went quickly to the axe he was holding.

"Maybe that's something you'd better ask him..." his voice trailed off.

"John, what's going on?" Alana's smile began to fade. When John looked up again, his eyes were troubled. He quickly resumed examining something on the axe handle.

"Uh... you really better ask him."

Puzzled, she decided to do just that.

"Well, all right, I guess..."

With a quick wave, she hurried down the path.

John energetically attacked a log as Alana strode away, trying to shake the image of his muscled arms and perfect abs from her mind.

CHAPTER 56

Busy readying the fishing nets for later in the day, Mitch was singing along with a contemporary Christian tune that floated over the pines from the cabin in the clearing. He stopped for a moment to inhale the pungent smell of the evergreens and listen to the soft lapping of the lake.

He would miss this place.

He saw Alana coming down the path.

Well, now is as good a time as any. Oh Lord, give me your words to say to her. Help me make her understand what it is I have to do.

"There you are. I saw your note. What's up?"

"Mitch fixed his gaze on the lake. "You know, this

music seems to make a difference in the atmosphere."

"I know. I listened to the Christian satellite station driving from New York to Kansas. It was after my sister died, and after I was attacked. I thought I couldn't feel any lower. But somehow the music lifted me up." Alana's look of heartbreaking sadness as she stared out over the water almost made Mitch lose his nerve.

She broke the moment. "So, what was it you wanted to talk to me about?" She wore a multi-colored scarf with a swath of emerald green that accentuated her eyes, and when she smiled at him, Mitch felt his stomach sink to his ankles. He took a moment to study her: under a heavy Irish cardigan she wore a form-fitting navy turtleneck that made her waist look like he could encircle it with one hand. Boot cut jeans of faded denim tapered down endless legs, flaring over light brown high-heeled boots. Mitch soaked in every detail, committing her to memory.

She tossed her head to remove the tendrils of hair on her face carried there by a lazy breeze. Putting her hands on her hips, she said saucily, "Well? What's on your mind?"

Again, she dazzled him with a fetching smile. Like the sun ducking behind a cloud, his resolve began to fade.

Mitch gestured toward a bench near the end of the dock. "C'mon over here. Let's talk."

As he watched a Great Blue Heron take flight from the top of a low hanging tree, its massive wingspan making it appear as if the bird was flying in slow motion, he wished with all his heart he could forestall this moment. Those trusting eyes...

He faced her squarely. "I don't know how to tell you this any other way but the fastest way. Alana, I'm going to join the Army." Alana blanched, looked stricken. Bowing his head, he added, "I'll probably leave before the end of the week. This is something I've thought about and prayed about for a long time. I'm sorry. I'm really sorry."

"You... you're going to join the Army? Are you serious?"

"Yeah. I'm serious Alana. I'm so sorry for springing this on you— I'm sorry there wasn't any way to let you down softly."

"Wha... what about..." Alana's bottom lip started to quiver.

Mitch wanted to stop then, to say it was a bad joke, but it was too late now. "Listen, Alana—you came into my life and saved me from drowning at the bottom of a whisky bottle. You also led me to the most important thing in life—God." Mitch paused a moment and lovingly brushed a strand of hair from her eyes.

"For such a long dark time, I was aimless. I wasn't only aimless, but as you know, a barely functioning alcoholic in the fast lane to total self-destruction. I held a pretty good job, and I saw a little success with it. But my life was completely empty. Now, all that has changed. My life has purpose. I know why I was created, and that's to worship and serve a totally awesome God. There aren't enough words to thank you for that. I guess you could say that I have a mission now. That's what makes what I'm about to say even harder."

A single tear slid down Alana's cheek. Mitch tried not to notice.

"Alana, I don't think you and me are a 'you and me' any more. We danced around the whole thing and believe me, I enjoyed the dance. Being with you... becoming... well... let's just say, it was one of the best things that ever happened to me. But once I make this commitment with the Army, I'm going to stay in the military. I'm not going to come back to Sleeping Bear to live... I won't be coming back to you."

Alana started hyperventilating. Mitch felt like a knife sliced into his gut. "Alana, Alana, whoa... please— holy cow. Oh, wow, Alana I'm so sorry."

Her shoulders sagged and she spoke to him through hands that covered her face. "You mean, you don't... this was all a ruse—you never really..." Wracking sobs rocked her as she rose from the bench. "I gave you my heart—I allowed myself to—to—fall in lo..." She abruptly turned and started up the path.

Mitch grabbed for her arm. "Alana, please! I'm begging you! Please listen to me! It's not what you think. Don't go. Please Alana, just hear me out."

"I... I need a tissue." Alana began patting herself

down in search of a nonexistent tissue.

"Hold on a sec, we have paper towels over by the fishing gear." He scrambled down near the water's edge and came running back with a paper towel. Alana took it and dabbed at her eyes, blowing her nose noisily.

"Please, let me try to explain. I'm going to lay it all out for you in sequence, so hopefully you can understand." Mitch gently led Alana back to the bench. She sat down carefully, gingerly, as if the slightest movement might break her.

Mitch continued. "Alana, when I first laid eyes on you, I didn't exactly have—ah, well—let's just say—wholesome thoughts about you. I'm admitting that. My motivation to get to know you was far from pure. Then, as I *did* get to know you, I fell in love with you. Now, the way it started was definitely all wrong, I'll confess that. I actually considered faking a conversion just to be near you. Then I realized you didn't like guys who drank. At that point what I felt for you was real enough to give up drinking. I meant everything I said to you that day when I told you everything. Every word was true. What I didn't know was that my conversion would end up starting a chain of events that would change the inner most part of who I am."

Alana interrupted, "I think I sort of suspected your motives weren't honest." She smiled weakly.

"Well, yeah, but only in the very beginning. What it eventually became was something quite different. Everything changed while I was drying out. I wanted to know about this God that you, John, Parson, Steve, and Sarah knew about. I wanted to know what this redemption and forgiveness felt like. I really became curious about a God who could forgive someone like me. You guys convinced me that even I could be forgiven for the unspeakable nightmare I had caused. The nightmare I never seemed able to wake up from."

Mitch found himself becoming emotional; tears bit his eyes and he blinked hard to keep them in check. "And that day when I was with you and John and I gave my life to a God who was not only capable of forgiving me, but who could lead me to actually forgiving myself—well— talk about life changing! Things slowly came together. And during that transformation, I started having this odd sense that my life had a specific purpose. I didn't know what that purpose was at all, but the more I read the Bible and those eBooks you and everyone gave me to read, the more I slowly came to the realization that I have a place in this world and a mission. I just didn't know what that mission was—until now." He grabbed the paper towel from Alana with a "May I borrow this?" and wiped his nose.

In a choked voice, Mitch went on. "Alana, when I heard that announcement about Hezbollah invading Israel, I knew. Everyone else was horrified, but I could see God at work in this and I saw my place in these events. For the first time in my formerly wretched, worthless life, I knew that I was made for something—something good and right." Mitch snorted into the paper towel.

"Ah… you can keep that now…" Alana said pointing to the paper towel.

Mitch looked up at her, perplexed.

"You asked to 'borrow' the paper towel—it's all yours now—"

"Oh! Let me get you a new one!" Mitch jumped up ran down to the fishing gear again and came back with a fresh paper towel for her. When he handed it to her, he noticed with relief a faint smile on her angelic face as she stared straight ahead over the lake. A woodpecker hammered away near-by. Another gentle breeze tossed wisps of hair into her eyes. He wanted to take her face and kiss the hair away, but erased the thought with a determined shake of his head.

Focus, focus. This is the first time you can do something with your life. Don't chicken out now, bedazzled by the wonder of Alana.

"So do you see what I'm saying here, Alana?"

Alana sniffed, cleared her throat and blew her nose. "Well, I have to admit, what you're telling me is a good thing. But are you sure it isn't because you've practically lived with me now for all these months and you've seen me at my worst—I mean—there aren't too many times I can actually wear make-up and fix my hair."

Mitch impulsively grabbed her by the shoulders and made her face him.

"Alana, are you kidding me? How can you possibly

be that clueless about how beautiful you are? Don't you understand how breathtaking you are with make-up, without make-up, no matter what you wear or what you do? And by 'breath-taking' I mean literally—you take a man's breath away!"

Alana looked down at her hands.

"How can you *not* know this?" he asked incredulously. "You're just like Keira Knightly's character, Lizzy, in *Pride and Prejudice*. I'm sure you've seen it, every chick has. Do you remember when Darcy rushes toward her through the mist at sunrise with his coat tails floating behind him in the breeze? When he reaches her he confesses, 'You have bewitched me body and soul...'" Mitch imitated Darcy with a perfect British accent. "That's exactly what you do to any man who lays eyes on you!"

Alana looked at him curiously. "You actually know about Jane Austen's *Pride and Prejudice*? I would have never taken you for an Austen fan."

Mitch smiled guiltily.

"Well, I'm not exactly a fan. Ah... I told some girl I was because I knew she was a Jane Austen freak and I wanted to hook up with her. It—eh—worked I guess. When I asked her to go see that movie, she said yes."

To Mitch's relief, Alana tossed her head back and laughed a hearty, loud laugh.

"See! I told you I was a scum-sucking bottom crawler." Mitch hurriedly clarified, "That is—until I met you. Alana, this isn't a rejection, I'm just choosing to take the path God has put me on. There is no competition here—who can compete with the creator of the universe anyway?" Mitch searched her face for anything to quell the sorrow welling up inside. "I have to do this, Alana—I feel it in the marrow of my bones."

He needed to know that she believed him.

"I don't understand why I just can't wait for you to come back." She looked straight at him again, fresh tears pooling at the lower lids of her heartbroken eyes.

Mitch tipped his chin toward the sky, his gesture a request to the Almighty. The pain and vulnerability in her eyes was ripping him up. He made a silent plea. *You're killing me here! Please help me out, give me your strength to get through this.*

Facing her again, he whispered hoarsely, "Alana... dear, sweet Alana. I won't be coming back even if I don't end up staying in the military. I'm going to remain in that part of the world where I now believe it is my place to be, side by side with the Jews, in both physical and spiritual battle."

Thank you Father, the truth, but not the whole truth...

Alana said in a small voice. "Is there anything I can do to make you stay?

She was shredding his heart to pieces and he didn't think he could stand it a second longer. Mitch suddenly stood and began pacing. "It's not that I don't want to stay,

Alana. It's that I'm in His grip now, the grip of the great I Am, and I have to follow His lead. I absolutely have to." He wanted to hug her close and squeeze away the hurt he knew he was inflicting on her.

"Alana, you're the very first person to ever tell me about God 'calling' a person, and that God has a purpose for every single soul. It's all a matter of whether or not we find that purpose and allow Him to use us to His greater glory. Don't you remember that?"

Alana's eyes were glistening, magnified. "Ah, foiled by my own words... yes. I guess I understand... I just don't like the part about you leaving me."

"I know, that's really tough for me too. I had a long talk with God about that as a matter of fact. But this is how it has to be..." Mitch trailed off, suddenly tired. He sat back down next to her. The only sounds for a few moments were the staccato call of a loon and Alana's sniffling.

With forced cheeriness, Mitch tried a different tact. "Well, the good news is, you won't be alone. There's someone here who hasn't been immune to your considerable charms."

Alana sniffed into the paper towel. "What?"

"I'm talking about John. He's lost his mind. He's coo-coo for Cocoa Puffs, totally mad cow."

"Mad cow?"

"Alana, John is in love with you."

Alana frowned at the absurdity of this. "Oh Mitch, don't be silly. John just cares for me like a sister!"

"Alana, *no man* feels like that about his sister, I can promise you that." He gave a low chuckle.

"Stop being ridiculous. How could you know such a thing anyway?"

"I heard him spilling his guts to Parson on Christmas Eve, that's how. Remember when you told me to see what was keeping them? I got to the doorway and overheard John telling his father how he felt about you. I heard it all—I couldn't help myself. He has been torturing himself over his feelings for you for a very long time. But he thinks you could never be interested in him. And, of course, he thought you and I were together, so he wouldn't consider coming between us. He's a good guy.

"But... but... I don't have feelings for him like I do for..."

"For me?" Mitch finished her sentence for her.

Alana didn't reply, but fixed her gaze on the crumpled paper towel in her hand.

"Alana, you don't have feelings for me. You just *think* you do, and I have to hold myself accountable for that because I led you on even after I started to realize that you might not be part of what God planned for my life. I couldn't tell you until now because I wasn't sure of the specifics until today. I'm sorry. " Mitch rubbed the back of his neck, wishing there were an easier way.

"And as far as your feelings for me go—Alana, we weren't meant to be, don't you see that? Otherwise God played a really dirty trick on us, and I just don't believe He'd do that. Mitch turned and grabbed both her hands in his. "You were sent by God to me because the Lord knew—in his infinite wisdom—that I would find you so captivating, so enthralling that I'd immediately be drawn to you and all that you are. But what really happened was—God was drawing me to *Him*."

New tears trickled down Alana's cheeks, but she made no attempt to wipe them away. Mitch gently took the paper towel from her and tenderly wiped them away for her.

She looked at him defiantly. "I didn't really love you after all? Interesting. Well. Then you better explain that to my heart." Her huge wounded eyes, wet and full of pain, hit him again like a body blow.

She took back the paper towel and wiped her nose. "That's a line from a song by the band Chicago. My sister used to listen to it. It sure fits."

Mitch didn't know how much more he could take— he had nothing more to say. He never meant to hurt her and he had. He sat there feeling sad and defeated.

Quite abruptly, Alana dried her tears, sat taller, squared her shoulders, and faced him "I *do* see what you're saying and I understand," she said bravely. "From the onset, my greatest desire was for you to come to know and love God with a powerful conviction. That obviously happened. How can I possibly be upset?"

At that moment Mitch couldn't have loved her more. Her desire to not inflict pain on him, even though he was the cause of it, was heart wrenching. For the tiniest slice of time, he allowed himself to envision a future that included Alana... and his heart hurt more than he'd ever thought possible.

CHAPTER 57

Everyone was seated at the rustic Great Room table just off the kitchen. They were almost finished with dinner when Mitch announced his intention to enlist in the Army immediately and hopefully assist in the Israeli conflict. Everyone reacted with surprise except John, who moved his food around on his plate, and Alana, who disconsolately stared into her lap.

"Dude, you *really* don't want to do that," Daniel said, elongating the word *really*. "We're talking about the most violent part of the world right now. You're walking right into a melee of chaos and death."

"Well, there's no guarantee I'll be sent to Israel, but at today's press conference the President indicated he would send troops there, and I'm willing to go."

John glanced obliquely at Alana to see how she was taking the news, but a sheaf of blonde hair hid her face. Afterwards, as everyone went up to embrace Mitch, offer him words of encouragement, or tell him he would be in their prayers, John watched Alana quietly leave the room.

After some had retired to their rooms and others had gone to the living room to relax, John, Mitch, and Parson were alone in the kitchen. John put his hand on Mitch's shoulder and gave it a good squeeze. "You sure are going to be missed around here. I don't know what to say, other than it's an amazing thing you're going to do."

Mitch leaned in close to John, confiding in a low voice, "Hey listen, Alana isn't taking all of this too well—you know, she's had so many losses. I think she's seeing this as the Sleeping Bear family breaking up, but she might still believe it's something else—if you follow me. She'll need someone to lean on, John. I know you'll be there for her."

John's grip on Mitch's shoulder tightened, but he said nothing. Seeing the emotion in John's eyes, Mitch drew himself up tall and said sternly, "Hey now, John, don't start going all gooey on me 'cause then we'll both end up crying like *girls*. Let's not go there."

They laughed then and Parson added, "So how is it you've come to know so much about my son's inner workings? Sorry, couldn't help overhearing."

Mitch winked at John, "Well, a little birdie told me, I guess."

"It is a miracle what the Lord has worked in you, Mitch Abbott. A wondrous miracle," Parson said proudly.

"I guess God knew it would take a miracle to fix me!"

"He worked a miracle on that cross, shedding his blood to fix us all, Mitch. No one is less worthy than the next. Every one of us needs His miracle. He died for us all."

"I've come to learn that, Parson, and it's still absolutely mind boggling to me. I actually really get the words to the hymn *Amazing Grace* now."

"When do you leave, Mitch?" John asked.

"Day after tomorrow the bus comes at 7:30 a.m. If I can get a lift to the bus stop, I'd appreciate it."

"I'd be honored to take you." Once again, John gave Mitch's shoulder a warm squeeze.

"That sounds great. All right, I have a few chores and things I need to do before turning in tonight."

John immediately protested, "Mitch, you're exempt from any chores. We'll have to pick up the slack anyway, why not start now? You just take it easy until you have to leave."

"John's right, go about your business, Mitch. Leave it to us. Please, let that be our parting gift to you, so to speak."

After some back and forth, Mitch finally gave in. "Thanks guys. Well then, I think I'll head down to the lake. Oh, before I do, may I borrow one of the vehicles? I need to pick up a few things."

John handed him the keys, then he was gone. "It's going to be a little empty around here without him," Parson said.

John's eyes remained fixed on the doorway where Mitch had departed. He already felt a certain emptiness, and Mitch hadn't even gotten on the bus yet.

CHAPTER 58

"Well, Dad, there are other things besides Mitch leaving us that we need to consider. I did some calculations last night before turning in. We can handle running the place maybe another year, year-and-a-half tops, then we run out of money. I think we're going to have to figure out if we can build our own hydro generator or find some other way of making our own electricity permanently. I'm getting the feeling we are definitely going to have to become survivalists. We need to plant more gardens, maybe consider growing our own crops. I'm going to triple up on our supplies this spring and summer. We need to build up our canned and dried goods, stock more survival kits, batteries, you know..."

"I think you're absolutely right, Son."

"Anyway—I'm thinking with Mitch gone, there's going to be one less body to help us prepare to live up here long-term... *and* we have to consider school for Lizzy, Megan and Caleb. There's a lot we need to talk to the others about."

"We'll call a meeting tomorrow after Mitch leaves. In the meantime, try to remember that God will provide for our needs. We're going to have to trust that."

"I know he will, Dad. It's just this starts to weigh heavy sometimes."

"I know, and you're doing a terrific job, son."

"Something else—I think we're not going to stay this tight knit group, Dad. Eventually we're going to become a sanctuary, in a sense, for Christians who won't comply with the new rules and are persecuted—forced to go underground or seek out places like ours. The news about that summit coming up—I forget what they're calling it, *Religion and the World*?"

"Right, I read that on-line yesterday."

"Well, it's not looking good for our constitutional rights with regard to freedom of religion. As I understand it, world leaders and the UN want to prohibit church gatherings and sanction use of the Bible."

"You know, I was thinking about that myself. But it's out of our hands for now. We have no control over when it will happen, if it happens at all. What we *can* do is like you said, prepare and be prepared."

John and Parson exchanged a few ideas about the meeting before both went off to finish up their chores and turn in.

The next morning, John spent hours chopping wood. Despite wearing gloves, he developed new blisters alongside tough old calluses. Returning the axe to a nearby shed, he turned up the path to the lodge. As was his habit, he mopped his face using his shirt as a towel. He was dripping wet with sweat and decided to go directly into the laundry room to throw his dirty clothes in a washer and grab a pair of painter's pants and t-shirt from a small locker there.

He pushed open the industrial laundry room door and saw Alana folding her laundry. At that moment she happened to have a navy blue bra with an abundance of lace suspended above her head that she was folding in half. Imagining her in it seared a visual impression onto his brain.

"Oh! I'm sorry!" Embarrassed, he quickly turned to retreat and managed to smash headfirst into the edge of the partially open door. The impact sent him staggering back into a laundry cart that wheeled away and left him in free-fall. He landed on the cement floor hard.

"John! Are you all right?" Alana knelt beside him.

John took stock of all his limbs and everything seemed in order, then he reached up and gingerly touched his forehead.

"I'm sorry, I didn't know you were in here... I was just

coming in to… to…"

"What are you so upset about? That I'm in here? And why do you keep apologizing?"

John's eyes moved over to see where the source of his trouble had landed. Alana followed his gaze to the floor and saw the lacy, demi-cup bra. "Oh, I see." She laughed to herself as she deftly picked it up and buried it discretely under some socks in the laundry basket. "The offending items have been safely tucked away, I assure you. I knew you were a modest gentleman, but I didn't know just *how* modest you were! There now, all safely hidden."

John sat up feeling keenly humiliated. He covered his eyes and shook his head slowly, feeling beyond witless.

"Oh, John, you're going to have a huge goose egg on your head. Let me get some ice." He started to object that he certainly didn't need any, but Alana cut him short with, "Don't be silly, I'll be right back with an ice pack. Don't move."

John started to pull his hand away from his face. With mock annoyance Alana demanded, "And for heaven's sake, take your hand away. It's safe, really it is." Laughing, she left to find some ice. John got up and sat down at the folding table in a metal chair. In a few minutes Alana was back with ice wrapped in a terry towel.

"Here, put this on your bump. Wow—it's gotten huge!"

"I'm okay, Alana, don't fuss over me really—I'm just

a clumsy dolt." Annoyed with himself, he started to stand. Alana pushed him back down.

"John, will you *please* sit still for one second? Honestly! Just use this, will you?" She handed the towel-wrapped ice to John, and then reached over his shoulder to set down a bottle of painkillers. "I have an anti-inflammatory for you. Let me get you a glass of water, I think we have a few plastic cups in the cupboard here." Alana began rummaging around in the cabinet above John's head.

As Alana leaned over him, her hair brushed his forehead like silken fingers and her chest was merely an inch away from his face. Again his senses ran riot, and he closed his eyes to capture the wonder of her nearness: her scent, the feathery touch of her hair on his face.

He jumped up suddenly almost knocking Alana over.

"I'm sorry. I have chores to fin—"

"Honestly, John, what is the matter with you? Will you sit down and put this on your head? Let someone take care of *you* for a change! Now sit down!"

"I'm sorry, I'm really sorry," John repeated.

"And for crying out loud, will you stop being sorry? I'm not going to tell you again." Alana tried to look imperious, but it was no use. She looked so cute that it brought a crooked smile to John's face. He sheepishly sat down and sent up a silent prayer that he go numb, deaf and blind so he wouldn't react to her like a cretin. *Some former fire chief. I couldn't be chief of a hill of baked beans right now.*

Holding the ice to his head, John allowed Alana to minister to him. She brought him a cup of water. "Take the anti-inflammatory and just hold that ice on your head for a while."

With his free hand John took the pills.

She bent to get a better look at his face, "If I carried a flashlight, I'd be checking *your* pupils," she smiled. "Are you feeling all right?"

No, actually I'm not. I am absolutely certain I'm crazy, madly, head over heels in love with you. And I act like a blithering idiot when I'm near you, much to my chagrin.

Instead John replied, "I'm all right. I'll live. Thanks, Alana." He remembered, then, that Alana had her own, recent sorrows. "So how are you doing—you know—since Mitch's announcement?" As soon as he said it, he noticed her eyes were red-rimmed and a little swollen. How did he not see this? He could have kicked himself.

"I'll be fine. I guess I—I saw it coming in a way. He had been pulling back for a while. I was just in denial about it for a long time. I definitely didn't understand at first, you know, when he first told me. It hurt. It hurt a lot. Almost like a betrayal." She walked across the room and dragged a chair over to sit across from him.

As she sat down and smiled wistfully at him, John wished with all his being he could stop the hurt in her eyes. "Alana, I'm so sorry. I can't imagine what that must have felt like for you."

"You're being sweet John, thanks." She paused thoughtfully. "I don't understand how the rest of the world does it—you know—the ones without faith."

"I know what you mean. Without my faith, I would have lost my mind when Kate died. I'm sure I would have gone stark raving mad with grief. But somehow, I got through each day. Sometimes it was hour by hour, sometimes minute by minute, but I got through it with God's strength." John couldn't understand why the words were coming so easily to him now, while a moment ago, he was completely stupefied.

A comfortable silence had passed between them when Alana said, "He was my first love."

Her confession was startling, something John hadn't considered. The enormity of it felt like a presence in the room. He waited a moment before saying softly, "It's difficult to lose your first love. Kate was mine."

Alana's gaze met his—she reached over and took his hand. Sighing, she said, "Now it's my turn to say I can't imagine what that must have felt like—losing your wife and having to raise a new baby all by yourself. That your faith was enough to carry you through such a shattering loss is remarkable. I'm glad." She gave his hand a squeeze, and let it go.

"But you braved an enormous loss too, Alana—losing Bianca and Dominic was losing your entire family. I at least had Lizzy and Dad."

"Well, I'm not going to sit here and argue with you about who had the harder time of it." She gave him a sad smile. "But I will tell you that while losing my sister has definitely left a void in my life, losing a sister just doesn't compare with losing a wife. You become one. And while I've never experienced this myself, of course, Bianca told me that at a certain point she didn't know where she left off and Dom began. The two become one she said, in every sense of the word. She told me she was unable to understand how people actually go through with a divorce. She used to say, 'How do you separate what no man can separate? How do you divorce a part of yourself?' So in a way, I'm glad they went together. She loved him with all her heart."

John's eyes blurred with tears and he looked away hastily, afraid she'd notice. When he looked at her again, her brilliant green eyes were wet with unshed tears as well. Neither of them spoke. They had no need for words, and for one golden moment, John Culver felt what it might be like to become one with Alana Engels.

CHAPTER 59

"Mitch, there is still time. Allow us to protect you and care for you. Don't go on this fool's errand." He smiled cloyingly.

Ranulf, the apparition Mitch had seen in several nightmares, stood at the foot of his bed levitating five inches from the floor. This time, however, instead of being scared senseless, Mitch was just plain mad.

"I serve someone else. I serve the One True Living God, not you or anyone you're affiliated with. Sorry, Bub."

Instantaneously, Ranulf's face became a repugnant leathery visage covered in seeping boils—just as quickly it returned to its former incarnation. Still, Mitch was unperturbed.

Seemingly aggrieved, Ranulf inquired, "Mitch, why are you risking your life like this? For what? For a people deserving of annihilation? Who never should have existed in the first place? They are nothing but human waste. They are a worthless, vile and destructive race." Ranulf unnecessarily adjusted the cuff of his robe. "We understand your historians have vilified Hitler over the years, but his belief in a master race and eradicating the unfit was not without merit." He waved his hand peremptorily. "But let's not go into that now. *You* could have a global impact—*would* have a global impact—if you chose to serve with us. I'm asking you to reconsider for yourself and for all of humanity. If you serve us—that is, come and work for us—I can assure you, you will be completely protected."

Mitch threw off the covers and stood. "Listen, I really hate to disappoint you," he said sarcastically, "but the best thing I can do for mankind is to tell them about Jesus Christ." Ranulf blanched at the sound of the name and moved his hovering self back a foot. Emboldened, Mitch went on, "There is nothing you can offer that can top eternal life, so you're wasting your time. Now get out of my dreams and out of my life. Go back to that rock you crawled out from under. You don't scare me anymore."

Enraged, Ranulf became hideous again, with skin covered in oozing pustules, eyes yellow except for the black pinpoints that served as pupils, and a lipless mouth filled with stunted brown teeth and slimy gray stalactites. A sulfurous odor filled the room. Mitch frowned slightly at the rank smell—a frown that Ranulf mistook for fear.

420

"Mitch! Don't be a fool! You cannot stand against us, we are powerful beyond anything you can imagine."

"And your point, you heap of stinking decay? Guess I'm not following you."

Ranulf thundered, "Mitch! You are not listening to what I'm telling you!" The lampshades swayed and every object lying on a lateral surface rattled. Then, closing the gap between himself and Mitch, Ranulf snarled, "You should listen very, very carefully to what I am telling you." Ranulf emphasized the word "very" by jutting his head even closer to Mitch. Slime and spit dripped between Ranulf's upper and lower teeth and Mitch tried not to gag. Waving a hand in front of his face, Mitch sputtered, "Phew! Dude, you *really* need to brush your teeth or suck on a case of Tic-Tacs or something..."

Then Mitch became deadly serious. "Listen you stinking pile of fish guts—You. Don't. Scare. Me. Any. More. Savvy?" Mitch paused and looked Ranulf squarely in his yellow eyes. "I know *exactly* what you are, and you have zero, zip-o, nada power over me. I'm a soldier of Christ the King. You are nothing but a foul smelling vapor, so vanish, will ya? I'm not buyin' what you're sellin." Mitch turned back to his bed and sat on it. He picked up the Bible from the nightstand, ignoring Ranulf.

With his arms spread wide and his head tilted toward the ceiling, Ranulf let out a keening wail that shook the plaster from the walls and jostled the bed Mitch was sitting on. And then he was gone.

Mitch awoke with his heart slamming against his rib cage. He bolted to a sitting position and surveyed the room. All appeared in order, except his bed was at a crazy angle and several feet from where it had been. Shaken, but resolute, Mitch now believed this latest encounter with Ranulf merely confirmed what he already knew: he was following God's ordained plan for his life.

CHAPTER 60

Alana watched John load Mitch's bags into the back of the truck while the Sleeping Bear residents all stood outside the front of the lodge saying their goodbyes. As was typical for spring in northern Michigan, warm days could suddenly be swept away as a fierce snowstorm barreled in. Today was no exception; almost two feet of new snow had fallen in a record amount of time creating waist-high drifts. The sun hid behind dull gray clouds, their color befitting Alana's mood. John had warned her not to be seduced by the recent gorgeously warm days, they were probably in for one last gasp of winter. Well, here it was.

A strong gust of wind whipped snow off the top of a drift, creating a swirling icy mist through the air. Alana distantly noted the pristine beauty of her surroundings, but could find no joy or wonder in it. Mitch moved from Sarah to Parson to Caleb while John sat in the idling truck.

When Mitch came to Alana, he said quietly, "Guess I saved the best for last," with a brave smile that didn't quite reach his eyes.

They embraced. With his thumb, he gently brushed a hair from her cheek that had escaped the hood of her down jacket. Grasping both her gloved hands in his, he whispered "Check your room, I left something on your pillow. No big deal, but I thought it might explain things a little better."

He paused, looked away, looked back at her. "I'll be back after basic training, unless they send me straight to my unit. So this really isn't goodbye, just *see ya later.*"

He pulled her into his arms then, and as he held her, Alana tried valiantly to swallow past the painful lump in her throat. She couldn't say a word, but she understood she didn't need to.

They parted and Mitch walked over to the truck. As he hoisted himself into the passenger seat, his Sleeping Bear family waved and kept on waving until the truck was no longer in sight. Daniel wiped his eyes on his sleeve. Alana, who had waved only once when Mitch smiled at her out the back window of the truck, turned and walked quickly back to the lodge and her room. There, lying on her pillow, was a small package and folded note.

She sat down and opened the note with shaking hands.

ALANA,

I can't find the words to explain how I feel about you. I only know I have to follow my heart, and thanks to you and your obedience to God, my heart now belongs to Jesus Christ. I hope these lyrics explain it better— it expresses what I can't really put into words. Remember, you'll always be my first love, Alana. Never forget that.

Love, M

With head bowed, she held the note to her breast for a moment before opening the package. Inside she found a small media card with another note, this one explaining that the recording was *Angels Brought Me Here*, by Jörgen Elofsson and sung by Carrie Underwood. Mitch had also painstakingly written out the lyrics.

◊ ◊ ◊

Alana stood up and walked over to her bureau. She had to rummage around in several drawers before she found her multi-media digital player. Carefully placing the foam ear buds in her ears and inserting the media card in the player, she pushed "play".

It's been a long and winding journey,
But I'm finally here tonight picking up the
pieces walking back into the light
Into the sunset of your glory where my heart
and future lies
There's nothing like that feeling when I looked
into your eyes

My dreams came true when I found you; I
found you, my miracle

If you could see what I see
That you're the answer to my prayers
And if you could feel the tenderness I feel
You would know it would be clear, that angels
brought me here

Nothing here before you
Feels like I've been born again
Every breath is your LOVE
Every heartbeat speaks your name

My dreams came true right here in front of you
my miracle

If you could see what I see
You're the answer to my prayers
And if you could feel the tenderness I feel
You would know it would be clear, that angels

brought me here

It brought me here, to be with you
I'll be forever grateful, forever thankful
My dreams came true when I found you my
miracle

If you could see what I see
You're the answer to my prayers, oh…
And if you could feel the tenderness I feel
You would know it would be clear that angels
brought me here

You know I love you baby
And if you could feel the tenderness I feel
You would know it would be clear, that angels
brought me here

Crumpled in half, tears flowed down Alana's face, dripping onto her jeans. When the song ended she hit *Play* again… and then again. An overwhelming ache swelled the walls of her chest, escaping as a sob. Woodenly, she sat down on the edge of her bed. She laid her head on her pillow, curled up tightly and felt the waves of grief wash over her, unable to stop the sounds of her shattered heart.

CHAPTER 61

The bus stop was just under a mile from the resort. After they arrived, John sat with Mitch until the green and white bus came rolling up to the wait shelter. He watched Mitch board, the hinged doors closing behind him. In less than 30 minutes he was back at the lodge. When he entered the main room, he saw everyone milling around, except Alana. "Where's Alana?"

A little flustered, Sarah said, "What was I thinking? I never even thought to check on her." Both she and John walked down the hallway toward Alana's room.

"John, is that Alana?" Faintly, they heard the sound of weeping and hurried to her door.

Sarah knocked. "Alana, Honey? Are you all right?" There was silence followed by a muffled, "I'm... I'll be all right..."

John was ready to break the door down to get to Alana, but instead clenched his fists and took a deep breath. He knew Sarah noticed his agitation, but she said nothing. She said to the still closed door, "Alana, may we come in? It's just John and me."

Her reply was so soft; they barely heard it, "Sure."

When Sarah opened the door, John rushed passed her, almost colliding with Alana, who had come to let them in. In one hand she held her digital music player, in the other, a tissue she held up to her reddened nose. John stood there awkwardly.

"Oh, Honey, I'm so sorry." Sarah put her arms around Alana.

Alana tried to explain, "It's... Mitch left me a note—and a recording—it." To put words to her pain was apparently suddenly more than she could bear. She turned and leaned heavily against Sarah's shoulder as more tears fell. Sarah led her to a suede loveseat. "Sit down, Honey. How about I make you a mug of hot tea?" She headed toward the tiny kitchenette, and John immediately sat next to Alana, grabbing an afghan to tuck around her as he did so.

"Do you want to tell us about it?" Sarah asked tenderly as she prepared the tea.

"Mitch left—a—sweet note." She handed it to John. "I was actually fine until I listened to the song he mentions in his letter. It's so..." She shook her head and looked at John bleakly. "Could you just hold me, please?" John carefully turned to fully take her into his arms, and there they sat—he rubbing her back, she trying to quiet her heart. Every few moments, Alana would try to say she was sorry, she was acting like a baby, and John would say softly, "Shhh—shhh, it's going to be all right."

Sarah brought over the mug of tea and set it down, then dragged an armchair closer to the settee. John could feel her gaze and knew she was conjecturing about the two of them. He studiously ignored her.

Engulfed in John's solid arms, Alana found great solace, when it occurred to her that she hadn't been held like this since she was a child. How wonderfully soothing it felt just to let go and be comforted. Gradually her weeping subsided and she pulled back from John's embrace. "Sorry you guys—the words, the music, it just struck a chord inside me that I didn't expect."

"It's understandable Alana, you've suffered a loss." Sarah leaned forward and gave Alana's thigh a little squeeze.

"Well, I guess maybe you're right. It *is* another loss in its way."

Alana looked at John seeking affirmation and found only profound kindness in his lapis blue eyes. Mitch was absolutely right: Mitch and she had been drawn together for a much higher purpose, perhaps merely as a prelude to something better for her life. Could she possibly be looking into the eyes of the man God planned for her future?

433

"Alana, we're here for you. We'll be praying for you too, Honey. Now, how about taking a sip of this hot tea, hmm? Then how about taking that skinny self of yours to the kitchen where you'll find some of my gooey brownies waiting for you." Sarah smiled maternally and tilted her head, causing her silver hoop earrings to dance. Her mahogany eyes twinkled. "You know what they say— chocolate is cheaper than therapy, and you don't need an appointment."

The corners of Alana's mouth lifted, and in portentous tones she added, "And on the eighth day God created chocolate."

John stood and Alana felt a little gust of air as he did. With exaggerated cheeriness, he said, "All right you two, now you've got me salivating. Put your money where your mouth is and let's see which one of us can eat the most brownies. Onward! To the kitchen!" He turned and strode purposefully toward the door. Alana was a little crestfallen. She had hoped when Sarah left for the kitchen, John might stay behind. Clearly he was uncomfortable with her proximity. *What feels so right to me doesn't seem to feel so right to him.* Alana had to wonder if his hasty retreat had more to do with running away from her or the siren call of brownies.

CHAPTER 62

Mary Bristol pulled her car into her own designated spot in front of the church, a spot that had been hers for as long as anyone could remember. For almost 62 years, she had been a member of the church and was on the church board, consistently elected to the position when the congregation voted annually.

Walking past the front church doors, Mary headed toward the side office door, the entrance used by church staff. Her 89-year-old body was slightly hunched from spinal arthritis, and of late, she had to use a cane. This annoyed her, but only mildly. She still had enough pep to do her gardening, take a daily walk once around her neighborhood, and stop at Meredith's for a game of Scrabble. On the whole, life was good and she thanked the

Lord she had the means to own a modest home in Florida, especially when she heard how dreary and cold it was up north. No thank you! She had been a snowbird for years when her husband James had been alive. But now she was a full time Florida resident living comfortably on her college professor pension, and she wouldn't have it any other way.

A gecko skittered across and dodged into the bushes lining the side of the cement walkway. A smile creased her deeply lined face. She even loved the lizards and the bugs here. Not quite noon, the sun was already sending the mercury to over 80 degrees. This was pleasing to Mary— she relished the heat even when the humidity was sky high. She quite simply loved every little thing about Florida.

The church, solidly built in the late 1960's, was not in disrepair but in need of a few major renovations. Recently the board had voted to replace the roof and proceed with bringing the electrical wiring up to code. However, for reasons Mary couldn't fathom, an alien "Visitor" had been allowed to become not only part of the congregation, but to assume responsibility for making some Pastoral budgetary decisions. This Visitor thought it "best for everyone involved" that the money allocated for the renovations be used for other things. Why the Pastor had kowtowed to the Visitor's suggestion was beyond Mary. What did it matter that this *Visitor*—a term that Mary found suspiciously benign—had been performing miracles? That could be a bunch of hocus-pocus. She didn't trust this pulpit magic act one bit. But she *could* understand the fascination, the wish to believe. After all, the lame walked, the blind saw, and the deaf could hear. The fact was, this *was* amazing. She couldn't explain it except to say that Satan could also do mighty signs and wonders. Just because they happened didn't necessarily mean they were signs from God.

Now, instead of a new roof, they wanted to build a TV Studio to broadcast their message and any miraculous healings the Visitor might perform. And *perform* was the key word as far as Mary was concerned.

Just what kind of nonsense was that? Mary had held her tongue long enough. She was going to give Pastor a piece of her mind, and she was going to do it today. People were placing far too much stock in the alleged abilities of the aliens. Their church had taken its focus from Christ and placed it in the things the Visitor had suggested. To Mary's mind, this had to come to an end. Of his own volition, Pastor Mike Hughes had given up his duties almost entirely, handing them over to the Visitor who called himself Jericho. She had prayed about the Visitors, too, asking the Lord if she was supposed to love them as her brothers in Christ—as she was finding the 'loving' part supremely difficult. She just couldn't believe these beings—or aliens, or whatever one wanted to call them—could be members of the body of Christ. Something about them definitely wasn't right. So while she was never one to remain silent too long about most matters, on this one she had taken a wait-and-see attitude due to her deep respect for Pastor Hughes. Now however, it had gone too far.

Mary hadn't made an appointment, but Pastor

Hughes usually had lunch somewhere on the church grounds between noon and one. She was confident she'd find him.

Mary was within feet of the double wooden office door when she felt, more than saw, something out of her peripheral vision. Something flashed by one of the church hall windows adjacent to the doors. She shivered. It was probably Jericho. She often felt a chill whenever he was around.

Jockeying her purse, cane, and the small canvas tote she had embroidered with *You Have a Friend in Jesus,* Mary struggled to pull the heavy right-hand door open. When she finally did, she made a beeline to Judy McDonald's office. Judy was the church secretary, a flawless typist despite three-inch nails. As Mary approached, she looked toward the paned window of the Pastor's office door and noticed the lights were turned off.

"Hi Judy, is the Pastor in?"

"Hi Mary! How's your back today?" Judy stopped her typing and looked pleased for the interruption, her florid plump face crinkling with delight. Not for the first time, Mary noticed Judy's age-inappropriate and thinning golden blonde hair; she reached up absently and touched her own white coif, which was twisted into an elegant knot at the nape of her neck.

"Having a good day today, praise the Lord. Thanks, Dear. Now, is the Pastor gone for the day?"

Judy lumbered to her feet and stood on impossibly tiny shoes. She reached for a manila folder in the filing cabinet. "Nope, he just ran out to give Mrs. Coldwell a ride to her doctor—she missed the shuttle today. He said she's going to catch the shuttle back so he won't have to stay with her. We're expecting him back any minute now. Did you want to wait in his office until he gets back?"

"Yes, I'd like that very much, young lady." Mary decided she would sit and read her Bible while she waited. It didn't matter how long—she was determined to speak her mind today.

Judy smiled broadly. She was well past her youth, but Mary knew Judy loved being called *young lady*, and so she persisted in doing so.

"Then come with me. I'll get the keys and unlock the door for you. Want any coffee or tea?"

Mary decided the bottled tap water she carried in her tote bag would be enough. "No, I'm fine for now. Thanks."

Judy slipped a bundle of keys off a peg, unlocked the door, and turned on the lights for Mary.

"Now you go ahead and make yourself comfortable. I'm sure the Pastor will be back in just a few minutes." Turning, she pulled the door partially closed and went back to her desk.

Mary settled into one of two green paisley upholstered chairs that sat facing Pastor Hugh's desk and took out her Bible. She was reading Matthew Chapter fifteen verse one, when she felt the presence of Jericho behind her. Startled, but not frightened, she turned and stared at him up and down. *Look at him in all of his fancy finery. He's just a tall homely thing. Everyone else seems smitten by these creatures, but I think they're simply funny looking. Look at this one, with his enormous egg-shaped head and silly little chin. And those black eyes. I do not see how they can remotely be called attractive.* What she said out loud was, "Oh, it's you. It's a good day in the Lord today. Praise Him. I am waiting for Pastor Hughes." She returned to her reading in Matthew.

Standing in the doorway, Jericho placed the tips of his fingers together to form a pyramid, and tapped them thoughtfully.

"How nice to see you, Mrs. Bristol." Mary kept her back to him and continued reading.

Jericho glided to the Pastor's chair and sat down. Mary looked up, and with that unmistakable resolve shining in her faded gray eyes, said evenly, "I'm waiting for the Pastor—so, if you'll excuse me, I'm in no need of a babysitter. I'll be quite fine on my own."

Jericho rose from the chair and swooped in front of her, the attenuated fingers of one hand pressing into the desk. "Why not tell me the reason behind your visit? I think you'll find I am exceptionally open to all of the parishioners' ideas and concerns, especially one as powerful as you."

"Why not tell you?" Mary was in no mood for games. "Quite frankly, because it's none of your business, Mister, that's why." She held his gaze.

Jericho's eyes narrowed almost imperceptibly. "I get the feeling that you don't like me, Mrs. Bristol. That would be a shame. I could be your greatest ally."

The hackles rose on Mary's neck. "My ally?" She sat forward in her chair. "Listen to me carefully. You may have charmed almost everyone around here, but you don't fool me. Not for one single second. In fact, that's exactly why I'm here today. I'm going to tell Pastor Hughes that he had better start listening to the board instead of taking directions from the powers of darkness. And yes, I'm referring to the likes of you."

Jericho became visibly displeased, drawing in his cheeks, elongating his already long face. "Oh, I see. Well that is most unfortunate... most unfortunate indeed Mrs. Bristol. My suggestion to you is that you do nothing of the kind."

"It doesn't matter to me one whit what *you* suggest. *Your* suggestions are meaningless to me. Now *I* suggest you leave." She waved her hand dismissively and settled back in the chair, holding his gaze defiantly for a few seconds before returning to Matthew.

The alien stood still for several moments without blinking. Mary continued to ignore him. She glanced up once in time to see Jericho with his palms turned heavenward as if accepting a present. And then she felt an explosive pain in her head. She never formed a last thought; she was dead before her chin hit her chest.

Playing the part of a concerned parishioner he yelled, "Mrs. McDonald! Call 911! Something is wrong with Mrs. Bristol!" Making a conscious effort to wipe the smile from his face, he hurried out of the Pastor's office. The only sound he made as he left Mary's body slumped in the chair was the rustling of his robes.

CHAPTER 63

Siena Montanari dabbed a tissue at the corners of her eyes as she listened to the minister deliver the eulogy. It didn't matter that her Grandmother was 89 when she died so suddenly; the fact she was alone in a church office with one of the aliens seemed deeply suspicious to Siena. It was true, she didn't have one shred of evidence that Jericho had done anything to her Grandmother, but in her gut she knew, she just knew something wasn't right.

The mourners were clustered around Mary Bristol's closed, white mother-of-pearl casket, which would soon be lowered into the freshly dug grave. Siena smiled to herself through her tears knowing her grandmother would have fussed at them for picking out such a pretty, elaborate casket for her final resting place. They were very fortunate to have been able to arrange a normal burial as there were so many who had been forced to bury their loved ones on their own these days. The funeral homes were still overwhelmed, yet they were able to follow all the traditional steps to lay Grammy to rest in the plot she had purchased long before her death and that was a relief.

As Siena wiped the moisture from her brow, she knew her Grammy would have loved the blazing hot Florida sun beating down on the graveside service. Despite the fact that the mourners were sheltered beneath a tent, it was nonetheless stifling, a hot and humid 86 degrees. Grammy would have loved it.

The grounds of the cemetery were well kept, with mature palm trees and other local vegetation that afforded shade and variety to the expanse of green that looked disconcertingly like a golf course. It was a peaceful setting— no wonder Grammy had chosen it.

Siena saw her brother fighting back tears as he tried to comfort their father. Grammy had been the matriarch of the family and now she was gone. She had had an impact on the lives of every member of their family and she would be greatly missed, of this there was no doubt. Her only son, Siena's father, was taking her passing especially hard. She had been in perfect health; there hadn't been any warning. Regardless of her advanced years, or perhaps because of them, Siena knew her father had expected Grammy to simply live forever. As her only child, they had been exceptionally close.

Jericho stood across from Siena, in the midst of family and friends paying their respects, dwarfing all those around him. He was wearing a golden silk garment much like a sari, with one panel elegantly swept over his shoulder.

Siena studied him. What was it about him that made her uneasy? She was unable to put her finger on it, not that she had any desire to pursue her intuition.

Under her scrutiny, Jericho's lowered head slowly began to lift until his eyes were level with Siena's. A chill swift and sudden gripped her despite the oppressive heat, and she shuddered.

She met his stare. Jericho's long slender arms and fingers were clasped in front of him, motionless. His expression revealed nothing, which was troubling to Siena.

Then she saw it.

He blinked once, twice, a third time. Deep within the recesses of his oversized obsidian eyes, Siena thought she saw not sympathy, but a malevolent satisfaction.

CHAPTER 64

Alana went over Mitch's schedule by reading the email he had sent her. He would be at basic training for thirteen weeks and then immediately go to Airborne School for three more weeks. His letters, emails and text messages to everyone were sent from Fort Benning, Georgia. Even Lizzy, Megan and Caleb heard from him. He wasn't able to write often, but he wrote whenever possible, and when the kids got his letters they couldn't be more thrilled. He also included photographs of himself and his new friends in the basic training section. He wrote that he if he wasn't deployed immediately to his permanent unit, he planned to return to Sleeping Bear right after his graduation.

At the lodge, the after-breakfast clean up was underway. Daniel sat at the granite island with a plethora of electronics displayed neatly before him on the counter: his Sat-phone, Digi-reader, large-screened periodical e-reader, wireless tablet, and wireless Silbuds—small silicone disks that stuck to his ear lobe and delivered wireless sound from any device.

Sarah and Steve stood side by side washing dishes in adjoining sinks, while Alana was drying and putting them away. Daniel had helped clear the table, and then got right down to what had become a familiar ritual of his morning—perusing the headlines. Lizzie and Megan had gone off to play and John was somewhere on the grounds fixing a faulty generator.

Looking up from a screen, Daniel said, "NASA is reportedly going to make an attempt to send an unmanned space shuttle armed with nuclear explosives into the path of the asteroid, in the hopes of blowing it into tiny pieces outside of the earth's atmosphere."

He continued his synthesis of world news; "Officials from the administration have reported that Iran is supplying Hezbollah with weapons and supplies through Syria. This information was obtained by secret intelligence and made public. Reaction was swift. Israel demanded that Syria immediately and unconditionally cease its support of Hezbollah. Despite heavy casualties due to repeated strikes on their military bases, Israel is threatening to launch a nuclear attack on unspecified Syrian targets if their demands are not met."

Alana's stomach tensed. She wished John were there

to offer a word of hope. Instead, Parson piped up from the couch where he had been reading from his leather bound Bible, "Well, that was to be expected."

Daniel went on, "The Visitors have been given a place at the table for the upcoming U.N. summit and are expected to address world hunger, AIDS and religious liberties."

"Now *that* troubles me even more than the Middle East news..." Parson glanced at the others over his reading glasses with a look of concern. For the second time, Alana wished John were there. She always felt calmer listening to the morning news if he was present.

Daniel cleared his throat, "Should I go on? The rest doesn't seem to be as upsetting."

"Go ahead, Daniel." Alana waved her drying towel at him indicating she wanted him to go on.

Pushing his glasses up and peering at the screen once again, Daniel continued. "Well, so far the Visitors seem to be doing pretty benign things, but this one editorial did note they are getting fairly involved in American and European culture. We know they've avoided political causes for the most part, but they're saying many Visitors have gotten intimately involved on the local, state and even Federal government level."

Parson sighed, took of his glasses and rubbed his eyes. Daniel cast a glance his way and added, "If you think that was interesting, Dude, get this—*more* Visitors have made their way into religious movements. There's an entire page devoted to the pros and cons of this infiltration on the opinion page of *The Wall Street Journal*. You guys know about that really popular Visitor?" No one in the kitchen seemed to. "The media superstar, remember? From that huge church in Sacramento, California? Well, he calls himself Rotem and now he's co-pastor of the church. The congregation has grown from just a few hundred to over 15,000, and now they're talking about needing something like a mega-church to accommodate the deluge of people cramming into the services. They're also planning a program on the Christian channel, Religious Broadcast Network, that Rotem would host."

Parson nodded and said, "I've heard of that church. They used to abide by Biblical principles, but not anymore. They've become very New Age."

Daniel read a moment more, then said, "Apparently a bunch of the aliens have become members of school boards across the country. Harvard, Yale, Michigan State University, Notre Dame, Texas A&M, Berkeley, and other well known colleges have allowed the Visitors to be guest professors. Some institutions have found imaginative ways to make them full or part-time faculty members."

Scanning more items of interest, Daniel continued, "Remember that commercial by Ford? That one where three Visitors go on and on about the virtues of the new solar powered SUV, the Aurora? Apparently the alien scientists helped develop the technology that allows the Aurora to run completely on solar energy—and now the rest of the world is clamoring for it. Ford can't make cars fast enough to meet the demand and so they're expected to make trillions in profit. *Trillions!*"

Alana turned to Daniel as she placed a juice glass in the cabinet. "I forgot, how is the car actually powered?"

Steve replied, "It's in the paint. The solar chips are so small, they just mix it into the paint of the car."

Sarah stopped washing dishes and interjected, "What is also irritating is Hollywood embracing the Visitors like A-list movie stars. They literally get the red carpet treatment. That Visitor, the one who co-hosted the last Academy Awards, I mean what is up with that?"

Steve sighed, "And our great 'lame stream media' is completely complicit with the public image the Visitors portray. I mean, I *know* the media have been a lost cause for years now—Hey, remember that Visitor making the talk-show circuit? I can't think of the name—he's going to have a starring role in George Clooney's upcoming Ocean's 19!"

Sarah put a third mug of coffee at Daniel's elbow and read over his shoulder, "Locally, even though electricity has been restored to most towns and cities, daily life is hardly back to normal, looting and violent unrest remain widespread."

Daniel said grumpily, "Well, that's what you get when unemployment is 22% and rising." He read from the screen again, "Due to the catastrophic loss of trees that burnt to the ground after the hailstorms, timber production has ground to a halt and industries that rely on it have suffered substantial losses. Furniture stores have been particularly hard hit, forced to either close or raise prices so high that only the well heeled can afford furnishings. Paper goods have achieved luxury status, if you are lucky enough to find it. The limited availability and skyrocketing costs has had a tremendous impact on everyday life from toilet paper to paper towels. Countless food manufacturers are scrambling to find alternative packaging materials."

Daniel took a swig of coffee. "The blood colored algae that developed after the volcanic eruptions has spilled into the oceans and seas, causing immense loss of sea life. The really bad news is, the algae is spreading and killing off more and more sea life. Marine biologists are unable to find a way to stop the spread." He paused thoughtfully, and then shrugged. "Without a sample, I can't even begin to speculate on the origins of this new species."

Sarah quickly added, "And I hope you never do see a specimen! That would mean it's spread here, and that's the last thing we need."

Parson put down his Bible and ambled over to the others gathered around the island. "I'm surprised we haven't had more people show up here. People are leaving their homes and towns in search of work, and when that doesn't pan out, they end up moving in with family members. And then, of course, you've got more and more people becoming survivalists, even stockpiling weapons. Those who own land are, in many cases, being forced to parcel it off, or sell it off in trade for other goods or services."

Parson was about to go on when there was a loud knock on the main lodge doors.

CHAPTER 65

The influx of new Sleeping Bear residents that Parson predicted had materialized.

Alana was pleased on the one hand, but on the other, her pleasure quickly soured when she met Siena Montanari. Siena arrived with her brother Matthew, his wife Christina, their three-year-old daughter Marta, and their three-month old baby, Abby. As the residents helped the newcomers take their belongings from their cars, Alana overheard Siena tell Sarah that she was a military brat who had moved with her parents to Ft. Leavenworth—it was there she and her family had met Parson and become members of his church.

Siena was striking. Long strawberry blonde hair framed a peaches and cream complexion, and a smattering of freckles fell lightly across the bridge of a perfect nose. Large light blue eyes were set just wide enough apart to be alluring. Perfectly fitted jeans revealed the most voluptuous body Alana had ever seen this side of Hollywood. A lavender V-neck angora sweater showcased every ample curve and emphasized her nonexistent waist. She was the kind of woman who elicited whistles from men when she passed by. For this reason—and the fact that she seemed to be genuinely sweet—Alana, to her dismay, instantly disliked her.

Parson played host and gave them a warm welcome, as did Daniel, Sarah and Steve, but Alana found herself having to make a concerted effort to be cordial.

Everyone but Siena looked tired from their journey, so Parson immediately assigned cabins. Though John wasn't available for their welcome, Alana noted that Siena had an inordinate interest in pumping Sarah and Steve for information about him, and it irked her.

After some brief introductions, everyone pitched in to help divest the cars of suitcases and assorted baby paraphernalia. Alana was assisting Matthew and his wife, Cristina, when Siena walked up to her, hips swaying in a way Alana wanted to describe as unnecessarily sensual. Deep down, however, she knew she wanted to pick at everything, find some flaw in this seemingly flawless creature. Siena probably moved that way naturally.

"Hi, I'm Siena—I know Parson introduced us all, but I wanted to introduce myself to you personally. You're Alana, right? I remembered your name because it's such a pretty and unique one." Siena's grin revealed two rows of perfectly even white teeth.

Couldn't her teeth at least have been imperfect? An overlapping tooth or something?

"Hi, Siena, it's nice to meet you... again. Welcome to Sleeping Bear." Alana held out her hand, and managed a tepid smile.

"Are you and John related?" For a second, Siena's question confused Alana until she realized how it must look to an outsider: why would she be here unless, perhaps, she was family?

"No—we met right around the time the Visitors came. He was kind enough to help me with the burial of my sister and brother-in-law. He invited me up to Sleeping Bear and buried them on his property for me. He's been so kind to me." Alana felt awkward explaining her situation to a complete stranger. "Anyway, I've been here since early last spring. I guess I sort of consider it home now. I'm... sure you'll find it a lovely place."

"Oh, I *know* it is. We've stayed here before. It is absolutely beautiful, isn't it? Such peaceful, amazing surroundings, tucked away right next to the Manistee National Forest. I've always loved it here. I'm so sorry to hear about your loss, though. How did they die?"

So she'd been here before. Maybe she was something more than just a guest. Hmm.

Alana told her about Bianca and Dominic's deaths

461

during the storm.

"Oh, no. I'm really so sorry. I almost went nuts trying to find out how my brother and family were. We were awfully blessed nothing major happened to anyone. We just lost our Grandmother, though." Siena's face unexpectedly turned dark and angry. "The doctor said it was old age, but I don't think so. Unfortunately, I have no way of proving anything; there wasn't a mark on her. She lived in Florida and was 89, bless her heart. She lived a good long life, but the last person—I mean, *creature*—to see her alive was a Visitor. I don't know..." Siena gave her head a quick shake as if to dislodge the disturbing thought from her head. "Regardless, that's a whole other matter, and obviously nothing like what you've been through. I'm so sorry about the loss of your sister."

"Thank you. I'm thankful I was able to find refuge here from everything that's been going on. And I'm sorry about your grandmother, too. Were you close to her?"

"Well, she was not only the matriarch of the family, but she practically helped raise my brother and me. I really miss her wise, Godly counsel." Siena looked away.

Alana's jealous heart began to thaw. "I still miss Bianca, too. I think of her every day. Time really does ease the pain, though. One day at a time, I guess."

There was a short silence between them when Siena asked, "So, are you and John—ah, seeing each other?"

Alana was so startled by the unexpected question she

visibly jerked her head back and frowned.

"Uh—no, not at all. Just friends." Alana turned her head away, wincing at how lame that sounded.

"Oh, good!" Siena's chuckled, soft, rich, throaty, "I mean—well, I guess I've been what you could call 'sweet' on John ever since I was church secretary. He never really noticed me, but I sure noticed him." Her cheeks flushed with this admission. "I think he's never quite gotten over his wife. I waited and waited, but he was never interested. I guess his not noticing me didn't really hurt, because he didn't seem to notice anyone. Bless his heart. Do you think—I mean—you being here with him for so long—do you think he's gotten over his wife's passing yet?"

"Ah… is John over Kate yet? Gee, I don't know Siena. Do you ever really get over it when your spouse dies?" Alana punched the words *over it* harder than she meant to.

The distress in Siena's eyes was immediate. "Oh! I guess that sounded really insensitive, please forgive me."

Alana instantly regretted her snarky remark. She wanted to dislike Siena in the worst way, but reluctantly she had to admit that Siena seemed to be a lovely woman. She felt guilty for allowing her jealousy to come out sideways.

"No… ah… I'm the one who should apologize. That wasn't fair of me. I'm sorry. I really am. I honestly don't know if John's completely over Kate. He's spoken to me about her a few times. Maybe his pain has eased a little. But you know what? I think it's probably best that you ask him about all that yourself."

Alana turned and lifted two small green and blue paisley suitcases from the trunk of a car and began carrying them down the path toward the cabins. Siena reached in and grabbed a larger matching suitcase and followed Alana, the valise bumping against her legs as she walked. "Well, I sure hope he has. He's definitely a keeper."

Alana struggled not to sound peevish. "I take it you're not married."

"No, not anymore." Siena paused as if to summon up the courage to say what she wanted to say. "I'm divorced. Gosh, I hate the sound of that. My husband left me for another woman... a much *younger* woman."

Alana was taken aback. She stopped trudging along and put the suitcases down. She looked again at Siena appraisingly. *How could any red-blooded man leave a woman with her faith and her brains all packaged into such a banging body?*

"Wow. That must have been awful." Alana felt genuinely empathetic. She had never experienced such a thing, of course, but the mere thought of being betrayed by someone with whom you took marriage vows made her feel compassionate. "How long ago did that happen?"

"Well, it seems like yesterday, but actually it happened over seven years ago." Siena stared down at her shoes, then returned Alana's gaze. "Seven years ago last month in fact... I don't believe in divorce, you know? But he really didn't leave me any choice. I meant, 'till death do us part.' He apparently didn't. To add insult to injury, he ran off with a teenager. She was a sickening 19 years old."

Embarrassed, Siena looked up at Alana and added, "Uh—no offense..."

Alana chuckled and smiled warmly, "I'm 28—a shade past teenager. No offense taken." She waited a beat before asking, "Do you have any children?"

Siena tossed her beautiful silky hair in what looked like a small act of defiance. "No. We never were able to, and now I thank God for that. I longed for children, but I could never get pregnant. Now I guess I know why. The Lord knew my husband would leave me. I'm pushing the clock though—I'm just shy of my 38th birthday. Not much time left for me to become a mother. I try to trust that God has His plan and it's, of course, the best plan. It's difficult sometimes though..." Siena trailed off.

Alana realized again this woman was very amiable.

"Then, the pièce de résistance was that immediately after they were married, his mistress-turned-wife got pregnant. Who says the Lord doesn't have a sense of humor?" Siena gave a small harsh laugh.

Alana couldn't believe she didn't sound any more bitter than she did. She was not only beginning to like this woman, but found herself admiring her as well.

"Well, this is your cabin, Siena, and I certainly hope that your time here is going to be a heck of a lot less stressful than that story you just told me."

Siena blushed, "I hope I didn't talk your head off."

"Hardly, I was the one asking the questions. Listen, I'll give you some time to get yourself settled. Dinnertime varies and you can make your own if you choose, but we usually end up eating together whenever possible. It's just the way we do it here, and I have to tell you, I think that's one of the reasons everyone seems like family to me now." Alana extended her hand. "I hope we can become the same for each other here, or least become good friends."

Siena took Alana's hand and pressed it between her own. "Thank you, Alana. I feel welcomed already. You've been most kind."

As Alana walked back to the main lodge she couldn't help wondering if the green-eyed monster she'd vanquished for now was going to take up residence at Sleeping Bear Lodge and ruin any chance of a friendship with Siena.

CHAPTER 66

It was already late August. With the asteroid impact mere months away, work for the Sleeping Bear residents increased in intensity. The new residents had quickly become acclimated and dispatched their assigned tasks with dedication and enthusiasm. The large basement of the lodge was prepared as an emergency fall-out shelter, and supplies that formerly would have been stocked in pole barns were stored on subterranean shelving built for that purpose. Four bathrooms had been plumbed and work was being completed on separate sleeping quarters for all of the residents.

For all the doomsday preparations, the first thing on Alana's mind that morning was Mitch would be coming home. She wondered about her own inner compass. Which direction was she going in? When Mitch told her he was going into the Army and she found the song on her pillow the day he left, she was positive her heart was broken. Since then, she had come to accept the things he told her and, in retrospect, knew the way things had turned out were for the best. She had misconstrued their strong attraction for each other. When she was able to accept that, it seemed she almost immediately felt attracted to John. How could her feelings have changed like that if she had really cared about Mitch?

About John, there was no denying she was jealous of Siena's obvious intentions. On the day of Siena's arrival, Alana had been outside the lodge and within sight of Siena's cabin when John returned. Their reunion was nothing out of the ordinary. But she still didn't like the way Siena practically threw herself into John's arms. Then, each time John and Siena were in the same room, or anywhere together for that matter, Siena's attraction to John was obvious. Alana found she was able to be cordial to Siena, but the seed of friendship she had hoped would take root quickly died when she witnessed Siena's incessant fawning. John would have to be dead not to respond to it. She was so self-assured, so completely comfortable in her own skin. She was such a—well—a *woman*. Alana felt young, inadequate and naive around her, as if she was someone's little sister hanging around the adults. Every time she saw Siena and John together, her self esteem took a major nose-dive.

Still, if she was over Mitch, why the butterflies

fluttering around her stomach at the thought of him coming home?

Finally, the wait was over. It was late morning when a mid-sized electric SUV wound its way up to the front of the lodge, crunching gravel as it pulled to a stop. Lizzy cried out, "It's Mr. Mitch!" Everyone who was working outside stopped, eager to either welcome the returning soldier home or meet him for the first time. Even those who didn't know Mitch wanted to say hello to the young man about whom they had heard so much. Everyone was proud of him for his commitment to the armed forces and the country.

Alana, Sarah, and Siena came up the path from the lake, having pulled in all the fishing gear and stowed it away. Alana's heart beat so strongly, she could barely hear beyond the pounding that reverberated in her ears.

Mitch emerged from the driver's side and looked every inch the conquering hero. When Alana first laid eyes on him, she was astonished: he'd never looked better. He was almost unrecognizable.

He wore desert fatigues tucked into black boots, and a black beret creased over the right side of his head. He stood absolutely ramrod straight, with broad shoulders and tanned skin. The patch on his beret and arm displayed the crossed rifles of the infantry. Although he was only a private, he stood as tall and commanding as a general. He looked amazing.

But she noticed that seeing him didn't tug at her heart, the tumultuous beating before was merely anticipating what her reaction might be. Now she found she was joyous, nothing more.

She broke into a run. When Mitch saw her, she noticed his eyes held an uncertainty, but this didn't impede her. When she reached him, she threw her arms around his neck, almost knocking him over as she squeezed for all she was worth.

"Welcome home, you crazy fool!" Alana said with jubilation in her voice and heart.

As Mitch regained his balance, he said choking and laughing at the same time, "I can tell you're still keeping long hours in the gym, eh, Blondie? Hey, you're cutting off my air supply here!" Then, despite his protest, he wrapped his arms around her waist, hugging her right back.

Parson and John emerged from the lodge in time to see Mitch and Alana entwined in each other's embrace.

With a lowered voice she said, "You know, you made me cry like a baby when I read your note and listened to that beautiful song."

Mitch looked into her eyes earnestly. "Alana, do you believe I never meant to..."

"You don't have to say anything. It's all good. I'm fine now. I admit—you broke my heart. Just a little—well, maybe more than a just a little—but I understand. I really do. You were right." She kissed him on the cheek.

Mitch's eyes shined with gratitude, "Alana, I prayed for this every single day. I would never want to hurt you."

"*Duuude!*" Daniel held up his hand to give Mitch a high five. "You look just as ugly as you ever did, only now you're wearing some sort of ninja pj's!"

Mitch returned the high five with a loud slap and then both of them embraced as Alana stood aside. "I'm just trying to compete with you, man, the Mack-Daddy of dating! I'm told the babes go for a guy in uniform. Hey man, you really are a sight for sore eyes." Then Mitch unexpectedly broke into song, "*Oh Danny boy, the pipes, the pipes are callin' from glen to glen, and down the mountain side...*"

Daniel plugged his ears in mock horror. "No, no, no! Stop the torture, I'll tell you anything you want to know!"

Everyone else approached Mitch now with congratulations and pats on the back. Alana stepped farther away, allowing the others time with him. As she did, she blew him a kiss and Mitch gave her a wink before returning his attention to the others.

John stood aside from the welcoming crowd waiting his turn. The new residents introduced themselves, and the original Sleeping Bear family fussed over Mitch like a long lost brother or son. John couldn't help but notice that Alana gazed at Mitch with what looked like adoration. An aching gripped his chest like a boa constrictor.

To his relief, by the time he strode over to Mitch,

the warmth and affection he felt for this young man came flooding back. John engulfed him in a manly bear hug. "Mitch, we're so proud of you. And believe me, even though the place is filling up, you've been missed."

Parson broke in, "You can say that again! I don't think I've laughed at all since you left, Mitch my boy!" More backslapping and hand shaking followed. Even the kids jumped around treating Mitch like a movie star.

"Wow, this is so nice! Hey, all I did was complete Army basic training and Airborne School." Then he let out a rousing, "Hooah!" much to the delight of all those around. While his words were modest, the tone in his voice carried great pride. John knew Mitch's status as returning hero was well deserved.

CHAPTER 67

"Dad, I know we told our guests we wouldn't take their money if they worked while staying here. And they've all kept their part of the bargain faithfully. They're family to us now. But we're going to run out of funds eventually." John was standing behind the Sleeping Bear front desk going through the mail.

"The bills keep coming in and our money keeps going out faster than I originally anticipated. John tapped an envelope on the desk and sighed. " I don't know how we can go back on what we promised."

Parson rested his elbows on top of the high gloss of the wood. "Son, if it comes down to us having to ask for a small fee to simply cover the costs of running this place, we'd give them a full accounting of the expenditures—

just like we did when we had the church. I think everyone would understand and be more than willing to pay a small offering."

John's brow furrowed. "I don't know, Dad... I guess if it comes down to that. Maybe we should sell our charter business in Mackinaw City? We might be able to sell to some residents on the islands near the Upper Peninsula, or even on Mac Island. If we could sell, then we could get along for a year or two after that and, in the meantime, set up an electrical system that would sustain us—at least keep us independent from the county. There are fireplaces in every room and throughout the lodge—we could wean off gas and use firewood for the fall and winter. I'm just not sure how we'd heat the water for showers and baths. We'll have to come up with something."

Mitch came out of the kitchen. "Hey, I was looking for you guys. May I interrupt, or is this personal?"

"Of course not, Private Abbott. No secrets between family members," Parson smiled.

Mitch came between them and put his hands on both their shoulders; in his right hand he also held a folder.

"Hey listen, I was going to do this later, but I guess I sort of can't wait. Just follow me into the main living room for a minute, would you mind?"

When they entered the living room, Mitch's voice became thick with emotion. "I knew I was going to do this before leaving for Ft. Benning, but I needed to get everything in order before I told you both. John, I know you know this already, but I believe I'm probably not going to come back once I get to my unit, especially if I'm deployed to Israel."

Parson looked at John, then back at Mitch. "Why won't you be coming back?"

Mitch smiled, "I just believe that God has prepared me for His mission over there and I won't be coming back." It took a moment before Mitch's meaning dawned on Parson. He asked carefully, "You mean... do you mean you think you'll be killed?"

"Ummm—I can't tell you that for certain. But I think that's the implication, yes." Sadness flickered across Mitch's eyes momentarily before he smiled kindly and added, "Parson—I spoke to John before I left. He can fill you in on the details later on."

Mitch handed the folder to John. "I want you both to know why I'm doing this. Read it."

John opened the folder and pulled out one of the documents. He looked up at Mitch quizzically.

"Go ahead, read that top paper, John," Mitch encouraged.

John read out loud. "I, Mitchell William Abbott, do hereby make, publish and declare this to be my Last Will and Testament, hereby revoking any previous Wills and Codicils made at any time heretofore by me. I hereby nominate, constitute and appoint John Culver, Jr. as the

Executor of this, my Last Will and Testament."

John stopped reading, "Mitch, what is this?"

"Read on, John. Just read it, please." Mitch winked reassuringly at Parson, whose face was a mask of apprehension.

Reluctantly John continued. "Should John Culver, Jr. predecease me or be unable or unwilling to serve as Executor of this, my Last Will and Testament, I hereby nominate, constitute and appoint John Culver, Sr. to act as Executor." John looked at Parson.

"Go on," Mitch prodded.

"I hereby direct the Executor to handle all funeral costs, any unpaid debts or taxes, and to pay these directly out of a savings account under my name at Western Savings and Loan." Then John read the essential bank account information.

"Keep going." Mitch was getting more excited.

"After all of my debts and expenses associated with my funeral and the administration of my estate have been paid, I give, devise and bequeath all the rest, residue and remainder of my estate, both real and personal, of any name, nature and kind whatsoever and where it may be situated to John Culver, Jr., same to be his, absolutely and forever."

Unable to contain himself, Mitch blurted, "This is the really cool thing—I have one piece of real estate I invested in when I sold my first home. It's a long story, but I got it for a song. It's a beachfront bungalow in Hawaii with a perfect view of Diamond Head, right on the bay. It's a 3,500 square foot, 3 bed, 3 ½ bath home overlooking the ocean with a pool. It's worth a small fortune, even in today's economy. If you sold it at cost, it's worth well over $3 million. If you find a good buyer, it could probably sell for triple that. And that's not all! I had savings of over thirty-five thousand dollars and when I sold another property, I made almost two hundred fifty thousand in profit. Plus, I have an IRA with about fifty-six thousand in it." He paused, doing some mental calculations. John ran his tongue over his lower lip and Parson shifted his weight from one foot to the other, neither man seemed particularly happy.

"I'm not through," Mitch plowed eagerly ahead. "The economy is in a total slump, but medical is doing fantastic. I had stocks in a pharmaceutical company that I had almost forgotten about. When I cashed them in, they were worth just slightly over seven million! They just invented some serum that cures all strains of the flu or something. It's phenomenal, isn't it? Hey, I was a total waste in my life about so many things, but the one thing I could do was sell real estate, and the other thing I could do was invest wisely. I just spent my money on Jim Beam and a decent car. Otherwise, I socked most of my money away. It's all yours John and Parson, and of course, Lizzy too." Mitch grinned at them like the Cheshire cat.

"Oh, and I don't have any debts. The car's paid for with cash, and I have no other debts whatsoever," he added enthusiastically.

"Mitch…" John began.

"Listen man, I know what you're going to say. But you have to take it. There is no arguing about this. It's in my will. It's a legal document, signed, sealed and delivered by JAG—the Judge Advocate General. You can sit here and argue all you want about it, but it won't change a thing. Or, you can just say *thanks!*"

Parson said, "Son—I don't understand how you can do this. Don't you have family of your own you should leave this—all this wealth to?"

"Frankly, no. I don't have any family I would feel right about leaving all this money and property to. No one in my family knows the Lord, and they can't stand me—they tossed me out when I was thrown in jail. And don't mistake this for my being unforgiving. At the time, I admit, I was miserable about it and just wrote them off and out of my life. Over the years, they didn't even feel like family to me. I've re-examined my true motives in this and I know I'm not doing this out of any sort of revenge. In fact, I was considering leaving at least a portion of my estate to some cousins, but then I had another one of those dreams. This time, though, the dream was from the good guys."

John said, "You think you had a dream that told you to leave your money to us?"

Mitch laughed a hearty laugh. "Not exactly, but I did have a dream right after I started Basic Training. We had just gotten off of a bear of a road march—eighteen miles—I think I was asleep before my butt hit the bunk. The next thing I know, I'm talking to, well... what I guess must have been an angel. He was bathed in this indescribable bright light. The brightest thing I'd ever seen... brighter than the sun, brighter than anything in this world, but it didn't hurt my eyes. It's too hard to describe. Anyway, I knew I was looking at a messenger from heaven. He said, 'Do not be afraid, Mitch. You are loved by God. You have pleased your Father. Continue to live your life serving The Lord your God. Remember the Great Commission the Lord gave the apostles. You have been called to a great and particular commission as well. Before your time is done, Mitch, remember those who led you to this path of righteousness and be generous to them.' He said all this without a sound. All of it inside my head, just as if he were talking to me. I didn't fully understand the message when he gave it, but as soon as I woke up, I knew."

"Mitch, I'm... I guess I'm pretty much speechless." John shook his head.

"We are unbelievably humbled by your generosity," Parson said. "This is such a powerful example of God's provision. John and I were literally just discussing how we were going to maintain the operating costs of the resort. Our resources were running dry so to speak." Parson smiled shyly at his inadvertent slip of the tongue.

"What Dad's trying to say is we were facing a future of being completely tapped out. We have depleted our savings between us, and didn't have much left other than the house in Leavenworth and a charter service we have in

Mackinaw City. We were going to have to sell our assets and property to make ends meet to pay the operating costs of Sleeping Bear."

Mitch looked at them. "You're kidding me. Really?"

"Really," Parson said.

"I always wondered how you guys were pulling it off. I mean, we paid some of our own groceries and personal items and other things, but I remember thinking about the costs of this place and wondering how you guys could do it. But you both never let on this was a problem. Wow—how cool is that? This all was really meant to be, wasn't it?"

John was still uncertain. "Mitch, are you absolutely sure you shouldn't attempt to reconcile with your family members and leave this to them instead?"

"I can honestly say, they are forgiven. In fact, while I was in basic, I started writing letters to family, even a few distant cousins I haven't seen since I was a kid. Just to—you know—sew things up neat and tidy. Forgiving them and reconnecting is one thing. Forgiveness doesn't mean I have to include them in my will. You all have become family to me in every sense of the word. What you and Parson just told me is confirmation that I was supposed to do this."

Parson interrupted, "And there is no guarantee that you won't be back once your tour is over, so this whole thing is probably going to be moot anyway."

Mitch and John looked at each other. "Well, if I, ah— come back, great, but I'm giving you the money anyway. I'm deploying as soon as I leave here, and it's a pretty dangerous part of the world, so I'm just covering my bases." Mitch handed a check to John; "Here's the money I just got for the house in Leavenworth, the IRA account I liquidated and from cleaning out my savings. I've also included a complete power of attorney should you need to sell the Hawaiian property before—you know—the will goes into effect."

Parson once again looked baffled, "Mitch what are you trying to say? Why don't you think you'll be coming back? You act as if it's a sure thing that you're going to…"

Again, Mitch and John exchanged glances, "You're right, Parson—just covering my bases, I guess. God's God, and I'm not, and He's in charge of whether I live or die." He looked at John. "So, will you be able to cash that check?"

John held the check in his hand tentatively. "Mitch, I just—I don't know what to say."

Mitch chuckled, "You said that already, old boy! It's yours. And now things are all fitting into place. There was no way I was going to be able to rest until I knew I had taken care of this. Once the idea came to my mind after the dream, I couldn't wait to tell you. This is my home, you are my earthly family, God is my father in heaven, and I absolutely want you to use that money for His purpose as I know you will." Mitch teased, "Hey, why don't you take some of that money and build a real church instead of holding services in a pole barn for instance? No offense, but Sunday services in that pole barn without any air conditioning during the summer was murder…"

Alana came into the living room just as Parson, John and Mitch were having a good laugh. "Hey! Everyone's wondering where our soldier boy is and I find him in here yucking it up with you two! Get yourself into the kitchen. Everyone wants to ask you about a million questions, especially the kids." She looped her arm through Mitch's and he immediately faked being dragged away against his will.

"Yes, Ma'am, Drill Sergeant!" Mitch gave a lopsided salute, and they disappeared into the kitchen.

John was still too much in shock over Mitch's gift to let their antics have an effect on him. He looked at his father in disbelief. "Dad, we didn't even get a chance to specifically pray about it and the Lord just dropped this into our laps. It's unbelievable how God's perfect timing works. I'm absolutely astounded."

Parson just shook his head and said, "As cliché as it sounds, our God truly is an awesome God! And even at this stage of my life, I can still be awed by His mighty provision.

CHAPTER 68

It was the eve before Mitch had to leave. The group, although larger, had simply become a bigger family and by the end of his stay Mitch realized he'd have a whole new set of added pen pals. He warmed to these new people as if he'd known them for years. It was difficult for him to pack his rucksack because as he packed each item, he knew it brought him closer to leaving. The atmosphere was surprisingly light and jovial as they cleaned up after the evening meal.

Mitch took John by the elbow. "John, let me have a word with you for a minute."

John joked, "Mitch if you have any more generous offerings, I don't think Dad's heart can take it!"

Mitch chuckled. "Nope, I'm tapped out actually!" He

gave John a wink. "It's something else."

John and Mitch walked out of the kitchen into the main lobby. "John, have you let Alana know how you feel?"

The look of surprise was evident on his face. "Well Mitch, why don't you stop beating around the bush?"

"I repeat, have you told Alana how you feel about her?"

"Mitch, she only cares about you. She's too far gone to even notice I'm alive. You've stolen her heart. And frankly, I can't blame her. You aren't only acting the hero, you *are* a hero."

Mitch didn't hide his frustration. "John, you've got this all wrong. She doesn't care for me like that any longer. She really doesn't!"

Siena entered the lobby looking for John. When she saw him she cried out, "Oh, there you are! John, you didn't finish your meal, and I worked so hard on the pasta Primavera for you and Mitch."

Mitch raised an eyebrow. *Man, this woman definitely has her flirt on.*

John blushed. "The meal was terrific Siena, I guess I ate too much at breakfast today. If there's any left, I'd be happy to have some. You're a great cook, you really are."

Sheesh, he's acting like she's he's wife. She's a hottie, all right. There's no doubt about that. But she's got nothing on Alana. Hmmmm... John is in love with Alana but Siena's

490

definitely moving in.

Mitch followed them back into the kitchen, and while Siena fussed over John, he quietly grabbed Alana and took her off to a corner of the great room. "Alana, listen to me. Do you care for John?"

Placing both his hands on either side of her shoulders, he gently pushed her against the log wall, his nose mere inches from hers.

His close proximity didn't seem to affect her in any way. She held his gaze. "What? What do you mean? Of course I do."

"No, I mean, do you have feelings for him, as in romance-novel type of feelings?"

Alana stole a glance in John and Siena's direction. "Mitch, what is this?"

"Look, I have a real good gut feeling about this. If you don't act on the fact that you care about that great big lug, you're going to lose him. It's as simple as that."

Alana kept her voice almost a whisper, "Lose him? Why? Tell me what you're talking about!"

"Well, for one thing, Miss Daisy May over there is all over him like ugly on an ape. He's only going to be able to hold out for so long with her full court press, if you catch my drift. She's a woman, he's a man, she wants him bad, he's human. Do the math! He thinks he doesn't have a chance with you. She's going to start looking real good to him after awhile, Alana. I mean she *is* pretty easy on the eyes."

Alana looked over at Siena again.

Mitch acted like he was doing a sit-up on the wall, "Never mind that! I meant it rhetorically. Listen—what does matter is, she's going to nab the guy if you don't make your move!"

Alana stared at him blankly.

"Don't you get it Alana? You're going to lose him if you don't do something!"

"Mitch, how can you be so sure he even wants me? Did he tell you he does? Did he say something to you?"

Mitch glanced at John, who still seemed unaware of their private talk, then looked back fiercely at Alana. "Alana! What are you, deaf, dumb and blind? He is crazy insane over you!"

"Well, he's not looking too terribly insane over me right now. He looks pretty smitten with Siena. And you didn't answer my question. Did he tell you he—he's interested in me?"

Mitch stammered. "Well—yes—ah—well—no, not recently—but..."

"Exactly. I think 'Miss Daisy May' as you call her, is his love interest now, Mitch. Have you looked at the woman? Well, obviously you have. I think it's too late for me—even if there ever was a chance." she drifted off, suddenly finding something on the floor fascinating.

Mitch moved his finger to her chin and made her

face him again. "How do you know? Have you told him how you feel? Have you actually *told* him that you love him, Alana?"

Alana's stunned expression almost cracked Mitch up. "Love him?" she repeated softly.

"Yeah, you nut and a half, as in those silly love songs love. But actually, I'm talking about a life-long commitment. You love him, Alana, I've seen it just in the few days since I've been home. I've watched you." Mitch got a sly grin on his face, "You've always been pretty easy on *my* eyes." She hit him in the shoulder.

Mitch recoiled as if seriously wounded. "No kidding around, Alana—we have a—you know—connection and I see the way you check him out." His voice turned tender, "Your eyes used to have that look for me. I recognize those twinkly stars in your emerald gems all too well. Now the only thing you need to do is tell John how you feel."

Mitch watched her creamy skin flush from her neck to her forehead. "Umm... sure Mitch, I'll tell him."

"Promise?"

Now he was holding her to her word and he could see that it made her uncomfortable. "I'll tell you what, I'll keep you in the loop. I promise to text you the moment I profess my undying love for John and I'll provide every juicy detail."

"Good. Don't wait, Alana. Ole Daisy May is moving

in for the kill." Mitch made a chomping sound as if he was a wild animal biting into its prey.

◊   ◊   ◊

Alana laughed a huge laugh, throwing her head back, causing John to freeze mid-forkful to watch her. He was sitting at the table, allowing Siena to make a fuss over him and forcing himself to eat the food she prepared. *What was it that Warren Beatty said about Annette Bening when they first met?* he wondered. *'I dare anyone to leave the room when she's laughing' or something like that. Well, I dare anyone to leave the room when Alana's in it. How can a single male with a beating heart resist her?*

Siena was talking sweetly in his ear, "Earth to John!" It sent a shiver up his back.

John quickly focused on the plate she had prepared for him and continued to shove food in his mouth, but he wasn't tasting anything. His mind was on how Alana was going to react to Mitch leaving again.

CHAPTER 69

The skies swirled and churned with gunmetal gray and black clouds. The wind bent the top of the pines and swept through Sleeping Bear with a sudden chilling drop in temperature even though it was August. John could feel the heaviness in the air as the sky prepared its release. The rule was work could continue outdoors unless thunder was heard. John tried to speed up his repair job on one of the two docks on the lake but a faint rumble in the distance forced him to reconsider. Mitch's visit had caused a welcome delay in chores, but upon his departure work had begun again in earnest, as there was much to be done around the resort. This new delay only added to his stress. Another long rumble, much closer now, caused John to collect his tools and put them away. With toolbox in hand, he set off for one of the pole barns. He figured he'd busy himself with something there in the hopes that the storm would blow over quickly. He reached the pole barn just as the bottom of a heavenly lakebed burst open.

As he rushed through the front entrance, he couldn't believe how soaked he had gotten just in the few seconds he had been caught in the downpour. Slamming the door behind him, the sound reverberated off the twelve-foot high steel ceiling. Out of habit, John did a quick mental inventory in case there was something that needed tending to. The arched perma-columns that ran the length of the entire 30 x 64 x 12 foot structure made up the frame of the building. It was sound in almost any weather, so no matter how nasty this one got, he knew he'd be safe. On the farthest end all the heavy equipment that was used for maintaining the resort grounds was stored. There were various snow blowers, a huge commercial lawn mower covered with a tan canvas tarp and several large bags of salt. Snow shovels lined the walls, along with various gardening equipment hanging on hooks that protruded from one of the long seams that ran horizontally along the walls, the entire length of the barn. John made a mental note to secure some of those hooks and to tie down tarps over the equipment, but first he wanted to get out of his wet clothes.

He put his toolbox on a small metal shelf unit he had right next to the door and was shaking off the water when the door opened behind him. Siena hurried in, bent over so that the rain ran off her yellow hooded slicker. "Wowee, it sure is raining cats and dogs out there!" She pulled her hood off and John couldn't help but observe what a natural beauty she was even without make-up. She was all woman in every way, yet freckles dotting her nose and cheeks gave the appearance of a woman much younger than her age.

She's pretty, she's nice, she's a Christian, and I'm sure she'd make a nice mother for Lizzy— He stopped himself mid-thought. *What am I thinking?*

He knew he shouldn't even go there. A marriage of convenience was out of the question. He had managed without a woman in his life this long. If he couldn't have Alana, then he'd just let things go on the way they were. And that was that. Still, she *was* a deliciously beautiful, sensuous woman.

"My goodness, John, you're soaked through. Why didn't you wear a rain coat?"

"Well, I guess I didn't think it would rain, at least, not as hard as it is now."

She walked seductively toward him, hips rocking side to side. Her eyes locked onto his. John wanted to look away but couldn't.

"Let me get you into some dry clothes, you'll freeze. I'm sure we can find something around here. Take off your shirt. "

He snapped back to reality. "Siena, I'll be fine. If I get cold I'll get something to put on. I'll take care of it myself."

Giving up on that angle she tried to make small talk. The pelting of the rain on the steel roof forced her to raise her voice. "Did the forecast say this would blow over, or are we in for a good long northern Michigan drenching?" Just then an enormous crack of thunder simultaneously sounded with a flash of lightening. Siena screamed and somehow managed to throw herself into John's arms.

John found himself holding her and awkward wasn't even in the ballpark to describe how he felt. He made an effort to gently push her away. "Wow, that one was close... nothing to be frightened about, though. I'm sure it'll..." There was another deafening crack, and a flash that seemed to scorch its way through the only window in the barn. Siena squealed and clung closer to John.

He decided to give in and just pat her on the back while allowing her to clutch him. He compensated for his discomfort by standing perfectly straight, and made a fruitless, yet valiant effort, not to touch her with any other part of his body.

"I just hate these kinds of storms, they're so frightening. They make me feel so small and helpless. You know, it's really nice to be in such strong arms like yours."

Sweat traced thin rivulets down his neck and sides. How could he possibly extract himself from this?

The metallic tap-tap-tapping seemed to dissipate, evidence the storm might be passing but Siena still clung to him for dear life. *Now what the heck can I do to get myself out of this mess?* John's frustration seemed to jump from every pore.

Then suddenly, Siena stepped back and put her hands

on her hips, her feet splayed wide. "John Culver, I may be just a hairdresser—a hairdresser with her own shop for your information, but I'm no idiot. I get the distinct impression my close proximity isn't exactly a thrill for you. What gives here, Bucko?"

John couldn't have been more surprised or more flustered.

"Cat got your tongue?" She asked with an unpleasant edge to her voice.

John just stood still, unable to say anything. The pelting rain on the metal roof was the only sound in the pole barn.

"John, I think I've made it pretty obvious, I like you. You're a single man. I'm a single woman. Life is short and my clock is *definitely* ticking. What is it? Am I too old for you?"

John finally found his tongue. "No, Siena, that's not it at all. Of course not... please... I'm sorry..."

"Perhaps I'm not pretty enough?"

"No—you're—you're gorgeous... I... you..." John trailed off, deflated, unable to finish the sentence.

"Not exactly the words I was hoping to hear." Siena heaved a heavy sigh. "I guess I was looking for something more along the lines of, 'Oh, you like me? I like you too. Let's get together—'" Siena looked completely crushed. "What is it about me? Some people tell me I'm... well... attractive. I'm a good cook, I'm hard working, I'm honest

501

and I love the Lord. So what the heck is it, bad breath?"

John wanted to dig a hole in the concrete floor and jump right in. *Where's that ax when I need it?* Out loud he said, "Siena it's not you, it's me."

She didn't try to hide the impatience in her voice. "It's not Kate anymore either, is it? It's something—or should I say *someone* else, right?"

John looked down at his feet, his hands hung limply at his sides. He felt like a little kid who had just come back from the worst T-ball defeat of his career, and he was the strikeout king.

"John, is it Alana? Do you care for her? Is that it? And listen to me, you better tell me if it *is* her because I'm getting a monster complex here! My husband leaves me for practically a child—and now someone of the opposite sex I find—well—really nice—runs from me whenever I come into a room. At least give me a reason, will ya? So I'm going to ask you once again, *is it Alana?*"

John still couldn't speak he just held her gaze.

"Bingo. It is Alana, isn't it? I can tell by your eyes, they do say they are a window to the soul..."

John still didn't say a word; he just looked down at the floor in silence.

"Sheeze, John, why didn't you say so? You let me chase after you making a fool of myself, and all along you have it bad for Alana. Why the heck didn't you just say something?"

He finally spoke. "I thought maybe I'd get over it."

"What? And I'd be sloppy seconds? No thanks, John Culver. Brother! You could have at least given me a hint for crying out loud! You seemed to like it when I—well fussed all over you."

"I did—I do like it," John said sheepishly.

"Just not enough..." She let out another huge sigh. "Oh well, that's that I guess. I knew I could never compete with Kate—she was a memory you worshipped. It's pretty tough on the ego to be rejected by a man who worships the dead, on the heels of another rejection by my own husband." She stopped, "Oh crud, I'm sorry, John. I never should have said that about Kate. I didn't mean it."

"No need to be sorry, Siena, I'm the one who should be sorry."

She stared off past him, tears wetting her eyes. "You are the only two men I've ever really wanted." Siena started to snap up her slicker.

John felt like the biggest heel.

"Tell me something, and don't spare my feelings—if you didn't have your heart set on Alana, would you—do you think we would have had a shot at it?"

John regained some of his composure and assurance. "Sure, Siena. I wasn't just saying it, you are beautiful. Your ex was a fool. Any man would be proud to have someone like you to call his wife. You're a very sweet, Godly woman. It's just that, I—I..." he trailed off.

"You what? Finish it John! For crying out loud, you what?"

John struggled with what he was trying to say but finally came out with it as if telling himself more than Siena. "Since Kate, there's never been another woman. Not until I met Alana..."

Siena let loose a groan of frustration. "Arrrrgggggg. Okay—well, time to put a stop to my abject humiliation. Sorry John, forgive me, I definitely didn't want to make things awkward between us. Let's just pretend this didn't happen. Can we keep it our little secret?"

John felt compassion for her. "Siena, there's really nothing at all to be humiliated about. I'm very flattered. This will of course stay between us." He opened his arms to invite an embrace. Siena took the offer and they gave each other a brief, chaste hug.

Siena said longingly rubbing her eyes, "I know God has a plan, and I know His plan is perfect, but I sure wish He'd give me just a little preview—you know—like a coming attraction—into what He's got in store for my life."

With a wink and a wave she was out the door into the diminished storm. John raked his hand through his hair, picked up his toolbox and followed her into the drizzling rain.

From the wooded area across from the pole barn Alana was

adjusting the hood of her rain slicker when she caught sight first of Siena, then John who emerged soon after her. He was glancing around in a guilt-ridden fashion. Holding her breath, she watched John go right up the path toward the Lodge. Siena cut left on the path that went to the lake. As disappointment swelled in her heart, she was absolutely convinced she had just witnessed a secret romantic tryst.

CHAPTER 70

Late September turned the leaves vivid golden yellows, tomato reds and burnt orange, almost at their peak for the fall season. The resort was buzzing with activity as everyone prepared for the pending winter. The urgency was unspoken as each day seemed to bring with it news of world events filled with catastrophes, danger and the looming asteroid impact. Most Americans felt an impending threat to U.S. soil due to the war in Israel. Even though the war was being fought across the world, the war seemed somehow much closer. Sleeping Bear's family used their anxiety in a positive way to reinforce their determination to become self-sufficient.

As part of their plan, a small school had been set up in one of the pole barns. Siena's sister-in-law, Christina, was a middle school teacher by trade and conducted classes each weekday.

The breaking news of that rainy dreary and chilly fall day was that Israel had launched a nuclear strike on Damascus in the region's early morning hours. As every nation watched and waited, the expected negative reaction from the Arab world had already begun to trickle in. The first American troops had been committed to the area one-month prior as a nervous nation watched events unfold. Rumors of wars filled cable and network newscasts and digital newspaper headlines. The home front reflected the world's unrest. The price of oil hit a record $175.63 a barrel and the stock market was tanking. Each day, the tension of world events seemed almost palatable.

John was unloading the truck of supplies from the local hardware do-it-yourself store chain. He had almost finished organizing the lumber, tools, and other equipment in one of the pole barns when a blood-curdling scream pierced the sound of the steady rain. John froze for a millisecond then dropped the new yard tools, and took off running toward the lodge. Several of the others who had been working outside came running too. As they all burst into the foyer, John called out, "What happened?"

Then they heard Alana's agonized cry, "John, in here!"

They all ran into the kitchen to see everyone staring up at the T.V. in the Great Room, and the scene was more horrific than John could have ever imagined possible. Blindfolded, hands bound behind him, was Mitch in his

Army fatigues, forced to kneel in front of a hooded terrorist. An AK-47 was held to his head.

"Take any of the children old enough to understand out of the kitchen please," John said. Next, John called to his father, "Dad?"

"Here, Son."

"Where's Lizzy? Do you know?" John looked around anxiously.

Parson said, "She's with Theresa at the school."

John's attention turned toward the sound of a muffled sob. Alana stood directly in front of the screen, so close her head was tilted up as far as it could possibly go. Both her hands were clutched across her mouth, her eyes wide. John came up behind her and gently placed his hands on her shoulders. "Alana, come and sit down, you'll still be able to see the screen from the couch." He led her trembling body away from the screen and helped her to the large couch. Alana sat on the edge, her eyes glued to the screen.

The female news anchor reported that four soldiers were being held hostage by a group calling itself The New Palestinian Liberators, or TNPL, who also claimed ties to Hezbollah. Their demands were simple; a complete pullout of all American troops from the region within 72 hours or they would begin killing the hostages.

The soldiers had been captured when their convoy ran over a roadside bomb in Ramat Gan, a city near Tel Aviv. After a skirmish, one soldier was killed and four soldiers, including Mitch, had been taken hostage.

The news anchor said a response from the White House would be released soon, but there were no details as to exactly when that would happen.

Alana was ghostly white. John sat with her, agonized that he had no consoling words. By this time, Sarah had come into the kitchen and thrown her arms around Alana.

"Oh Sweetie, this is horrible."

Alana tried to choke out the words, "Sarah, where are Lizzy and Megan and Caleb? Oh my gosh, he'll be so upset!"

"In the classroom with Christiana and Steve—that's where they're going to bring all the kids who are old enough. That was sweet of you to ask Honey but don't you worry about them right now. We'll talk to them once we know more."

Alana's voice trembled, "I—I just can't believe it. This can't possibly be real."

John knew she was in good hands with Sarah and stood up to go find Lizzy.

Alana immediately put her hand on his, her eyes huge, tormented. In a panicked voice she asked, "Where are you going?" He didn't know what hurt his heart more, the fact that she was so distressed, and he was incapable of comforting her, or that Mitch had been taken hostage by the terrorists.

"Alana, I have to go check on Lizzy."

Alana seemed reluctant to let him go leaving John deeply conflicted.

Alana said, "Oh, of course. Are you going to—to tell her?"

"I really don't know what I'm going to do right now." He smiled warmly at her. He felt powerless, wanting to shield her just as badly as he wanted to shield Lizzy, but unable to do this for either of them. "Will you be all right?"

Alana nodded then asked, "Will you come back? Please?"

"Sure, I'll come right back."

John knew he had to go to his daughter, but he lingered for a moment. He felt much better about leaving when Sarah caught his eye over Alana's head with a wink and a nod, as if to say she'd take care of Alana.

Siena found John just as he came out of the kitchen.

"John, you're going to the kids, right? Let me go with you and help. My nieces and nephews are there and this way I can be there for them when you break the news, or were you just going to take Lizzy aside and tell her privately?"

"I don't know, Siena, I really don't know what to do. I'll talk to Christina when I get there and ask what she thinks is best for the kids. My impulse is to tell them, but we need to have all the parents present if we do."

"I'm sure Christina will know what to do. I have an

idea, I know all the kids at the school, how about I round up the parents, then meet you there as soon as I talk to everyone."

"Sounds like a plan, Siena. I'll see you there."

John gave one last look into the kitchen and caught a glimpse of Alana with her face buried in her hands weeping, then hurried to Lizzy.

CHAPTER 71

Every T.V. at the resort was connected to one of five satellite dishes the entire resort used. Day and night, all screens were tuned to one of many 24-hour news channels as they waited for any updates. The adults tried to shield the children from what was happening as best they could. The children were informed about Mitch to a certain extent; the information about the threat to kill him was not shared.

John hadn't been getting much sleep and he knew that was the case with most of the adults. Sleep deprived and in a state somewhere between grief and anger, he knew the wait would have been impossible without his faith.

The day for the first deadline came. The White House officially announced they would not negotiate. The tension in the air was a tangible presence with the Sleeping Bear residents. The hour of the threat came and went then the news went into an excruciating black out. Other news of the day was reported, but suddenly there wasn't anything at all regarding the soldiers who were held by the terrorists.

Little resort work was getting done. Everything revolved around waiting for word about the hostages. The atmosphere was like that of a wake.

Daniel wouldn't stop pacing. His habit of pushing his glasses up his nose went into max overdrive. He complained that he had been unable to eat or sleep since he heard the news of Mitch's abduction and looked as if he had dropped ten pounds. Face gaunt, the dark under-eye circles were magnified through his thick lenses.

John dreaded what he now had come to accept as inevitable. He believed Mitch's premonition was in motion and would be fulfilled. In one way, he knew where Mitch would go when he died, yet in another way, Mitch's imminent death filled John with a dread that was matched only by his wife's death. He didn't know how to pray any longer. He found himself repeating under his breath, "Thy will be done, thy will be done."

Breaking news finally interrupted the regular broadcast. It felt as if all the air had been sucked out of the room, while every eye was glued to the screen.

The demands of the terrorists had not been met by the deadline, but the news in from several sources said the soldiers were still alive.

An audible sigh of relief sounded throughout the room. Many prayed.

There was another development; a video of the hostages was going viral on WIGAPS. A popular news blog reported one clip contained an alleged "confession" by one of the soldiers.

"I can't imagine what they must be going through at the hands of these monsters..." Daniel blurted, his voice laden with fury and frustration.

Sarah came to him and stood by his side. She gingerly took his hand. "I know, I know Danny. All I've been doing, all many of us have been doing, is praying about it..."

Daniel's face contorted in anger as he threw her hand away and spat out a string of expletives. "Pray? What good is praying going to do? Want to tell me that? What possible good can you guys muttering some deals with God do for Mitch? No offense, but it's your God that is either causing what's going on, or more than likely, is out of the office with no forwarding address because what kind of so-called loving God would let this happen if he was actually on the job?"

Sarah tried to say something when Parson broke in, "Daniel, I understand your frustration. Christians don't always have a handle on everything simply because they believe in a God who does."

Alana was chopping some vegetables on the counter. She stopped. "Danny, no one can understand all the things that happen in this world. The Lord never promised us that we wouldn't have trials. Sometimes we have terrible trials—this thing with Mitch I think can definitely qualify as one of the worst ones ever..." Her voice became choked with emotion but she continued. "God's promises aren't that we will have an easy life. His promise is that when we do face life's trials, he'll be there with us all the way."

John didn't attempt to hide his admiration as a smile creased his face. What a wise thing to say. He added. "If you don't have God to turn to during life's most difficult trials, who can you turn to Daniel?"

Daniel gave John a blank stare. After a few seconds he spoke. "Are you asking me as in, you expect an answer?"

"Not exactly Daniel, it's just something to ask yourself, that's all I'm saying. We can't understand everything that happens in this world because we didn't create it. If you really try to think about it Daniel, a much higher intelligence than us made the universe. Even Einstein believed in God. What logic is there in thinking that something as complex as the human eye, for instance, was made all by happenstance? Believing in God doesn't guarantee we will have perfect knowledge of everything that happens in our lifetime. We do not have the mind of God—we can't possibly fathom the mind of a God who can create the stars and star systems filled with planets. I do know this though, through the times that were rough—and I have had my share of rough times—the Lord was there for me. I could feel it even through my own circumstance no matter how heavy the burden. Without it, without my faith—I would have been toast. It would have destroyed me. God truly can be our strong tower."

Parson jumped in. "Proverbs 18:10 tells us, 'The name of the LORD is a strong tower: the righteous runneth into it, and are safe.'"

This sparked Daniel to say, "How safe then is Mitch? Isn't he now one of those righteous? Why isn't he safe?"

For a reason he didn't understand, John glanced at Alana. Her expression conveyed an unspoken *tell him*.

This encouraged him. "He is safe Danny. He's safe in the arms of the Lord whether he's captured by men doing evil things, or whether he's in a capsizing boat, or on top of a mountain in a blizzard. It doesn't matter where he is. In this world or the next one—God is with him. As a member of the Body of Christ, the next world is eternal. So even if... he..." John struggled to say the rest.

Alana finished it for him, "Even if Mitch should be killed, Danny, he'll be with the Lord. I know he will be. I don't want that to happen—to lose him so soon. It would be—it's terribly painful to even think about for those of us who care for him. We don't want to lose him, naturally. But if that should happen, if the Lord decides to call him home, I know Mitch will be with Jesus and I will be able to gain comfort from that knowledge."

Daniel's shoulders sagged and he let out a shaky sigh before he said, "I don't get it. I really don't. He looked up sheepishly at Sarah, "And I'm sorry I did that. You know, tossing your hand like that. I'm sorry, too, for my outburst."

"I think we're all a little overwrought, Daniel. Don't give it another thought."

Daniel continued, "But I have to admit, in a way I sorta wish I had the faith you guys have, because this whole thing is just killing me."

John said, 'It's hard on us all Daniel. But we're together and we're going to pray together that Mitch comes home safely."

But even as John said it, he knew that his words were merely to comfort the others because he really didn't believe he'd ever see Mitch this side of heaven again.

CHAPTER 72

Three additional deadlines came and went and the Sleeping Bear family continued to live in a state of emotional siege, mindlessly carrying out tasks with eyes and ears attuned to the TV or radio. Tensions eased fractionally when a fourth deadline was proffered, and the residents almost began to believe the extensions would go on ad infinitum when suddenly the regular broadcasting was interrupted by a voice flatly announcing the news.

We have just received word that all of the hostages held by the New Palestinian Liberators have been killed and that their bodies have been left in several sites in Lebanon. Again, initial reports are that all hostages—Private Mitch Abbott, Sergeant Bill Bennett, Sergeant Thomas Thompson, and Corporal Sanchez Gonzalas—have been executed. We will bring you further information on this breaking story as it develops. We now return to regular programming already in progress.

Daniel and Alana sank to their knees in the middle of the Great Room floor and embraced, each weeping into the other's shoulder.

John's hands turned to fists by his side, his throat tight. He knelt next to the grieving pair and helped them both to their feet. Daniel removed his glasses and wiped the tears streaming from his eyes with a sleeve.

John was angry and sick. He knew there was evil—the kind of evil no mortal could begin to imagine. But this was proving beyond his reckoning. The barbaric, despicable act of viciously killing these vital young men with so much to live for was unconscionable—nothing but the deepest, darkest evil.

Still, Mitch had known it would happen. And that would mean this—even this—was all a part of God's plan.

John stood before Alana, gently bringing her to her feet. As he held her in his arms, he felt lost and bewildered. A tremendous feeling of emptiness washed over him, leaving him chilled and numb. Mitch was gone. Alana was gone now, too, in a way. Mitch would live in her mind and heart for a lifetime, and he would never be able to compete with the memory of such a remarkable, now larger-than-life hero. He wouldn't even try. Mitch's memory should remain untouchable, virtuous. Now any chance he might have had with Alana was dead, too. He closed his eyes against the thought, ashamed of his selfishness.

"I don't get it, I don't get this whole crazy world!" Daniel exploded, interrupting his thoughts. "Why did he do this? Why did he even go there? He didn't have to. None of this had to happen!"

Parson spoke, his voice thick and breaking with emotion.

"Everyone, everyone please—I know this is terribly tragic news, but we must remember that God is the God of—even this." He paused, swallowing hard. "Let us be reminded that the Lord has his perfect plan, and while we may not be able to see how any of this could possibly play a part in glorifying God, all things lead to that ultimate outcome. And so, if we could, let's come together in a circle. Please hold the hand of the person next to you and let us pray for the families of the soldiers who were lost to us."

The TV volume was muted as they gathered around and grasped the hand next to them. Parson began, his voice just above a whisper.

"Father, help us with the shocking news of Mitch's death. He embraced us as his family, and now we are bereft of his presence. We reach out to you Lord, to seek comfort and healing. Some of us feel lost and frightened, Lord. When the power goes out we search for something to give us light—a lamp, a flashlight, even a small candle will do. Now we reach out to You, Jesus, the light of our world, to help us during this dark, dark time. You tell us in your Word, 'The Lord is close to the broken-hearted'. 'Blessed are those who mourn, they shall be comforted.' We beseech you, Father, to show us your way and to help each of us deal with this tragedy in the days to come. We ask for your comfort, healing and peace for the families of the fallen soldiers as well. We pray these things giving Praise to the Lord who knows our great pain in this time of sorrow. In the Holy Name of Christ Jesus, our Lord, Amen."

Parson lifted his head. "Don't be afraid to share your grief with others. A trouble shared is halved. As a family here at Sleeping Bear, we should be helping each other with our burdens. Tragedy brings people together, but sometimes only for a little while. I trust and pray that we will help each other carry the cross of grief for as long it is needed."

When Parson finished, the room was quiet.

Daniel's narrow shoulders slumped, tears flowing freely under his glasses. Sarah and Steve came and stood by his side, Sarah silently offering him a box of tissues that he accepted gratefully. Steve asked, "Daniel, are you going to be O.K.?"

Swabbing at his nose, Daniel answered angrily, "No Dude, I'm not O.K. Why didn't he... why didn't God stop this? He could have, if he's God! What kind of sick twisted *father* would let this happen?" Without waiting for a response, he suddenly turned on his heel and stormed out of the room.

Alana huddled into the sofa, weeping quietly into her hands. Her profound grief was gut wrenching to John and he longed to put his arms around her. He was heartsick for her and the whole situation. Even though Mitch had prepared them for this day, believing unshakably as he did in the premonition of his own God-breathed fate, John had held out hope that Mitch was somehow mistaken. Now John felt like he was dangling from a cliff, barely able to hang onto the thin thread of hope that somehow, someday, they'd come out better servants of God as a result of this awful trial.

Overpowering sadness, despair and resignation threatened to overwhelm him. He needed air. Tearing himself away from Alana, he left the room to search for his own relief—but had no expectation of finding it.

CHAPTER 73

Within days, a digital video made available by the New Palestinian Liberators was released on Arab television. It detailed the prisoner executions. Daniel's anguished cry followed by the sounds of chairs being thrown around brought a number of the residents running into the kitchen. John was one of the first to arrive with Parson close on his heels. The moment John realized what was being televised, he turned and ran to Alana, preventing her from entering the room with a body block.

"Alana, it's a video..."

Alana's hand flew to her lips and misery filled her eyes. "When will this end? When will this nightmare end?"

Without thinking, John put his arms around her and

drew her to him—she leaned heavily against him. She felt thin, frail. He didn't think his heart could hurt any more than it already did, but between holding her close and the video of Mitch's death, a fresh wave of pain came over him and tears stabbed at his eyes.

"John? I just came from the kids—Lizzy wants you." John heard Siena's voice at his back. He stiffened, dropped his arms and turned to face Siena. "Tell her I'll be right there, will you?" Facing Alana, he said, "Will you be okay, Alana?" Staring dismally at the floor she replied, "Of course, John. Go to Lizzy. I'll be fine."

John walked hastily out of the kitchen followed by Siena. Alana felt crushed. When John was holding her, she had found a respite from the pain and grief. But when Siena arrived, he abruptly became rigid and pulled away. *I'll bet he didn't like it when Siena saw us. He acted exactly like a guilty boyfriend getting caught doing something he shouldn't be doing.*

Despite the devastation of Mitch's death, she felt a sharp pierce of jealousy as she watched Siena beckon and John willingly go.

John returned from the classroom to seek out Alana as soon as he was able to, but she was gone. Lizzy had only needed a little reassurance that everything was okay. Ever since Mitch's death, she'd been a little needy that way, worrying when John was out of sight. She was unaware of the video's existence as were all the children; the adults were keeping the children well cloistered.

When he didn't find Alana in the kitchen, John assumed she went to her room and set out in that direction. He found her talking to Danny in the hallway just outside her door.

"I'm gonna miss Mitch calling me Danny boy. He used to..." Daniel stopped, unable to go on, his face haggard with pain.

Alana put her arms around him and Danny hugged her back, "I know, I know, Danny, he really loved you. I think he pretty much adopted you as the brother he never had."

John interrupted softly, "How are you both doing?"

"I don't know how I'm doing." Daniel re-adjusted the glasses that had gotten skewed against Alana's shoulder. "These terrorist kidnappings have seriously been a way of life for us since 9/11. But I guess it's a whole new surreal horror when it happens to someone you know—and... and love..." Daniel looked away. When his gaze returned, it held a sad desperation. "I never told him I loved him. I never said those words. I should have told him he was just like a brother to me. How could I have been so stupid?" He looked at them as if seeking absolution from some terrible crime.

"Danny, he knew. He sang to you, Danny! He never

sang to me!" Alana smiled lopsidedly at him as if trying to un-break his heart.

She opened her door, "Why don't you come in? We don't need to stand in the hallway." As they filed into Alana's room, a familiar stirring of peace and comfort came over John. He liked going into her suite. On one hand, he felt slightly uncomfortable; on the other, he enjoyed being around her things. Even though he had been in her living quarters a number of times before, he was still impressed by how she had personalized the room.

Just beyond the living room area they were sitting in, he noticed two of Lizzy's drawings on the small refrigerator in the efficiency kitchen. They were positioned front and center and held in place by two colorful fruit magnets. That touched him. He could also see a framed photo of Alana and Mitch sitting on the end table next to the loveseat Daniel sat on. Alana had chosen the matching loveseat next to Daniel and John sat across from them in an easy chair. The loveseat could easily accommodate two and he found himself wanting to share it with her, wanting to hold her, wanting to tell her everything was going to be all right. But he couldn't. He didn't truly believe that himself.

Alana asked John how Lizzy was.

"She's fine. The kids are all doing just fine. Sarah and Christina have kept them occupied with their school studies, and of course, no TV." After a pause, John said, "I saw the video."

Alana and Daniel both went wide-eyed.

"Did you... did they—"

"No, Alana. They moved the camera away. I'm sure we could find the entire clip online if we chose to, but I'm choosing not to." John sat forward, his elbows on his knees, examining his hands.

With a dogged determination sounding in his voice, Daniel said quietly, "Tell me what you saw."

John looked up and searched Alana's face before he began. She gave a curt nod. "I want to know too."

John's answer was hesitant. "I can't explain this to you because how can anything like what happened turn into something positive? But I saw something—or at least something in the portion I was able to see..."

Alana sat on the edge of the love seat. She exchanged a glance with Daniel, then turned to John. "G—go ahead." She reached for Daniel's hand as she said it. John began. "There were three other soldiers with Mitch. The video showed them all. I was in the Army for six years, so I recognized their ranks. They all—ah—seemed pretty banged up, but otherwise fine considering. The four of them were kneeling, but straight, defiant, and under their own strength. Because of that, I'm praying maybe what Mitch went through up to that point wasn't—ah—too terrible." John cleared his throat. "They didn't allow any of them to speak, at least not on camera. One hooded terrorist stood behind each of them holding an AK-47 rifle across his chest. You could hear the terrorists giving orders in Arabic off camera before... before the video cut away."

John watched Alana and Daniel carefully while he spoke. Alana's face had paled and her only movement was to squeeze Daniel's hand hard. They both looked determined to hear it all.

John continued. "This is what I think might be of some comfort to you. All of it went pretty much the same: there was the soldier kneeling in front of the camera, then orders barked in Arabic off camera, then one of the terrorists would walk up to the prisoner's side and put a hood on him before the camera cut away. Each soldier kneeled stoically, arms bound behind him, head held up. They were defiant until the end, God bless them." John stopped for a moment to collect himself, and then continued. "Mitch was last. Just before the terrorist came to place the hood over his head, something utterly remarkable happened. He—he actually smiled."

John stopped. Alana's eyes had welled with tears, but Daniel just stared at John, his expression inscrutable.

"It wasn't a nervous, brave smile. It was a genuine, warm, well—joyous smile. It was the most incredible thing. You could only see this very briefly—but as clearly as I can see you two right now, I saw for one dreamlike moment his whole countenance radiating pure joy. I know that sounds crazy, but there really was no mistaking it. Then the hood was placed over his head and there wasn't any more to see. Thanks be to God."

Just then, they heard Steve calling outside of Alana's room, "Has anyone seen John?" John replied loudly, "I'm in here Steve! I'm in Alana's room!"

Alana added, "Come on in, Steve!"

Steve opened the door and poked his head in. "John, the outboard motor on the small fishing boat gave out right in the middle of the lake and stranded Marta and Matt. Do you have the keys to the other boat?"

John fished around in his pockets and came up with a keychain. "Shoot, I forgot to put these on the key hook." He jumped up. "Let me help you tow them in."

As he headed for the door, John took a quick glance back and saw Alana and Daniel getting ready to follow him. Alana was blotting under her nose with a tissue but met his glance straight on. "If it's all right, I'll go with you, John. Helping out will do me good." She was trying to be so strong. How many different ways could his heart break for her?

Behind her, Daniel said, "Yeah, I'd like to go too."

"Sure, sure. That—that sounds like a good idea."

As Alana brushed passed him through the doorway, their bodies touched briefly. John was surprised and embarrassed that quite autonomous of his brain, he had an immediate physical response to her. *Yeah, this joint rescue might be a good idea for Alana, but for me? Not so much.*

CHAPTER 74

Weeks after Mitch's death, Sleeping Bear was limping back to normal when a Fox news anchor announced that a spokesperson for the "Visitors"—as they had become known—had asked to address all the nations regarding an issue of "immediate, vital, global importance." The picture on screen then changed to a Fox studio affiliate in Washington D.C. A Visitor stood at the podium, resplendent in a dramatic robe of shimmering deep purple paisley. An undergarment, also floor-length, was like liquid sliver, fluorescing with his every move. John noticed the Visitor exuded complete confidence in his mastery of the medium.

The alien's jeweled headdress stood a foot high. John remembered Elam's headdress was much higher, and idly wondered if this alien was a lesser rank. The alien's skin was a warm cocoa color and his eyes large and almond shaped with thick, brush-like lashes. His face was ageless, without a wrinkle or flaw. As he spoke, his long slender hands gestured gracefully; he was the epitome of regal bearing.

"Fair people of the planet earth, we bid you good tidings. First, allow me to introduce myself. My name is Malachi—like the Judeo-Christian prophet." He paused comfortably, blinking into the light a few times, a good-humored expression warming his luminous black eyes.

"My people have come from a galaxy system—as many of you may know by now—called M104, or The Sombrero galaxy. We have chosen to make a pilgrimage to your world to await the arrival of the Messiah, an arrival we believe is imminent, as we have been observing the signs and monitoring your planet. Based on what we have seen, there is every indication the time is near for Yeshua's return. Again, Malachi paused, tapped the podium once, and looked directly into the camera.

"That explains why we've come. Today, however, we wish to impress upon you that not only have we come in peace, but our greatest desire is to earn the trust of all inhabitants of the earth. We wish to offer mankind protection, and we can prove to you today— unequivocally—that we come in peace and friendship. We are here as grateful guests, and, as proof of our benevolent intentions, we wish to show you our gratitude."

His eyes fixed on the TV, Steve murmured, "I don't

know about you, but I'm getting a bad feeling about this..."
His comment met with several heads nodding in agreement.

The Visitor continued. "It is common knowledge that an asteroid is hurtling toward earth, and when it makes impact, it will cause indescribable damage. My people know the potential destruction something like this can cause. We know this because in our solar system, collisions like this have happened to inhabited planets for millions of years and we have closely studied their aftermath. The alien paused for emphasis, then leaned forward and grasped the edges of the podium. "We know it will be far worse than all of the estimates. Far, far worse." The alien leaned back and rocked on his heels for a moment, as if in thought. Then, he threw his arms wide and beamed.

And yet, we bring good news! Our advanced race has the scientific capacity to prevent the asteroid from colliding with earth!"

CHAPTER 75

The alien's statement met with gasps followed by a cacophony of shouted questions from the media that filled the newsroom.

Malachi lifted his hands to quiet them. "I will be more than pleased to answer your questions, but ask that you wait until I am finished speaking." Malachi waited patiently for everyone to be seated then continued. "The anticipated time of impact has been reported as twenty-four hours from now, but our instruments indicate that this is incorrect—the asteroid is actually much closer. According to our calculations, we expect the impact within six hours."

The press corps immediately jumped as one to its feet at that and Malachi had to again quiet them by raising his purple sleeves as if bestowing a benediction. "Quiet, please. Quiet. Quiet, please. I am here to tell you the projected impact will not take place. We can prevent it. When I give the signal, a sophisticated laser device on our mother ship will send a charge to the asteroid that will pulverize its mass into such tiny pieces that most, if not all, will burn up upon entering your atmosphere. Thus, the laser will remove the threat completely."

The press corps were again on their feet, clamoring questions. "How will we know that what you claim has actually happened?"

"Where is the mother ship?"

"What signal will you give?"

Malachi calmly held up his hand to quiet the crowd. When the din subsided he continued. "We have a live satellite feed with NASA right now." He motioned toward two flat screens behind him. "Dr. Goldstein, can you hear me?"

"Yes, yes, I can hear you clearly," was the reply.

"Ladies and gentlemen and citizens of the world, we have with us via satellite Doctor Harvey Goldstein, who is currently the top Administrator for NASA, and Dr. Robert Coldwater, from Cape Canaveral. I'm certain many of you will recognize these men as being the best in their respective fields of Aeronautics Research and Space Operations. We also have Aidan McCafferty from Armagh Observatory, in Ireland. They were the first to discover the asteroid."

"But how do we know it's really them?" came a shouted question from the press corps.

"I'm certain you will be able to confirm the legitimacy of these men and their credentials later. But there is little time left to do what must be done while the asteroid is within range. We have only a small window of opportunity, so I'm sure you'd like me to use it to our greatest advantage."

Before anyone could grasp what was happening, Malachi raised his sleeved arms into the air, crossed them back and forth once and commanded, "It is done!"

The room went silent. After a long moment, Malachi spoke placidly, "Let us allow some time for Messrs, Goldstein, Coldwater and McCafferty to gather their data to support our claims that the asteroid is no longer a threat. Dr. Goldstein, are you able to determine anything yet?" Malachi turned his attention to Dr. Goldstein who was busily examining his portable PC.

"Yes, preliminary data shows that the asteroid has— ah—disappeared. " Dr. Goldstein's face filled the screen; he seemed stunned by this news. While the press became agitated again, Malachi serenely turned to the second screen.

"Let us verify this information with Dr. Coldwater. Dr. Coldwater, can you hear me?"

A video image of Dr. Coldwater showed him standing

in front of his desk. Puzzlement and awe colored his voice. "This is absolutely amazing! Yes! Yes! I can definitely hear you! It would appear from our data as well that the asteroid has broken up into such small fragments that it will no longer pose a danger once it hits our atmosphere!"

"I can verify the same information the others have stated," came Aidan's thick Irish brogue.

Back in the Great Room at Sleeping Bear, Parson sat down hard in a chair. "Just when I thought I'd seen everything..."

John remained standing, his head bowed in prayer.

Malachi had departed the newsroom at Fox's Washington D.C. station affiliate and the regular Fox News channel anchor returned. Plugging in his earpiece, he began.

This is Robert O'Hara with Fox news, and in case you've just joined us, a news conference held by a Visitor calling himself Malachi has just ended. The Visitor announced that a mother ship just outside the earth's atmosphere was capable of stopping the asteroid that was hurtling toward us, and this has apparently happened. Experts from NASA, Cape Canaveral, and an observatory in Ireland confirm that the asteroid is gone. We are now awaiting confirmation of the asteroid's demise from our own sources.

He covered his earpiece and appeared to be listening. Then continued.

And now our own sources confirm that the impossible is

true! It would appear that a laser the Visitors have on their main ship has vaporized the asteroid—the asteroid no longer exists! The Visitors have literally saved our planet from destruction!

CHAPTER 76

Marta, one of the preschoolers at the resort, had fallen off the dock and had scraped both knees in the process. John tended to her, his paramedic bag at hand as he fished for alcohol wipes followed by two large Disney cartoon Band-Aids. "Nothing a little ice and TLC can't cure," he said.

As he sent her on her way to play with the other children, John wondered what it would take to cure his ills. Thoughts of Alana troubled him every day despite his most arduous efforts. In addition, although he thought he and Siena had reached an understanding that rainy day, her attentions toward him nevertheless seemed only slightly diminished. It appeared she was still holding out hope that they would ultimately end up together.

John felt like a trapped animal. He tried to hide his discomfort so as not to hurt her feelings, but was often wearied and drained by her daily ministrations.

And then, of course, there was the nearness of Alana. No matter what he was doing—repairing a faucet, chopping wood or preparing a meal—whenever she entered the room, he became a fumbling, bumbling idiot. If he wasn't already acting the fool, he knew he'd probably turn into one with just a glance his way. And lately, much to his distress, she seemed to seek him out. He assumed this was merely her need to have an authority figure—or worse, a "father figure" at this difficult time in her life. Given her need, he was accommodating. What else could he do? He wanted to be there for her, but doing so was killing him. He hadn't had a good night's sleep in a week.

Although he remained in continuous prayer—the only upside to his dilemma—it seemed his prayers were falling into a vast dark void. He knew the Lord was there, but he couldn't feel His presence. Desperation began to set in.

Why wouldn't the Lord answer his prayers? He didn't understand and had long ago given up trying to understand, but it still left him feeling frustrated. He told himself this trial was to test his self-control. But if this refiner's fire was supposed to perfect his self-control, John was convinced he was failing miserably.

Feeling bone-weary and defeated one sunny fall morning, John found himself walking by the weight room.

He spotted one of Alana's jackets. Drawn to it like the idiomatic moth to the flame, he slowly walked into the workout area and headed to the bench where it lay. Feeling exposed by the wall of mirrors and windows, he glanced around guiltily before bringing the jacket reverently to his face.

He closed his eyes and inhaled. Alana's lilac cologne and a bouquet of other scents he associated with her infused his senses. For one small slice of time, he felt completely connected to her. Vivid images of Alana crowded out all rational thought: Alana gazing up at him in his bed. John touching her soft skin, making love to her, holding her, pushing a stray hair from her emerald eyes. The ache of wanting her nearly drove him to his knees.

With a shake of his head, he came back to the present. Wracked with guilt, he prayed his embarrassing display had gone unnoticed. Surreptitiously glancing around him again, he carefully laid the jacket back on the bench and hurried out into the hallway. Once there, he leaned with his back against the wall breathing heavily as drops of sweat trickled down his forehead. He felt as if he had just finished running full bore on the treadmill for five miles.

Enough! This had gone on way too long! He had to end this and he had to end it *now*!

Then a thought occurred to him.

John and Parson's charter boat business was in Mackinaw City, about four hours north of Sleeping Bear. He meant to check on the business the previous year, but hadn't gotten around to it. Now was as good a time as any to go up north, examine the two boats in storage, and then take one out to Mackinac Island. There, family friends he'd known for years, Theresa and Bill Wallace, owned a fantastic resort called Mission Point. He'd find out if he could stay with them for a while. He wasn't sure their resort was even open—given the way things were going, the tourist industry in Michigan wasn't exactly thriving. But, whether Mission Point was open or not, he had to get away, at least for a week or two. Maybe he'd have to rough it, but it would be worth it to regain some peace of mind. John felt better just thinking about it.

Once he made his decision, he was ready within an hour. Before noon he had loaded up the truck. After hugging his dad and Lizzy goodbye, he jumped into the cab, zipped the window down, and promised to call once he arrived on Mac Island.

CHAPTER 77

Alana was mulching the vegetable garden, mud up to her knees. It was a chilly October morning, and even though she wore her Wellies with thick socks, they were doing little to keep her feet warm. She was lost in thought. Her grief for Mitch came unbidden and in uncontrollable waves it seemed. But whenever she found herself grieving for him, she immediately reminded herself that he was with God now. It was the only way she could deal with it. John's description of what he had seen on the video gave her hope that Mitch's last moments weren't nightmarish. She wondered if angels had come to minister to him right before he died. Or perhaps he had a vision of the Lord. She could only pray that one of these was the case, and forced herself to rely on God and trust in Him no matter what. She had to admit, this was no easy task.

John was also on her mind. It occurred to her that beyond the sheer physical presence of the man she found so comforting, he was kind. During the emotional upheaval surrounding Mitch's death, he had been solicitous and concerned about all members of the Sleeping Bear family, but he had been particularly worried about her. Not that he said so, she just *felt* it. She finally came to the realization she had become extremely attracted to John. This both excited and confused her. He had been so wonderful and considerate toward her during the whole ordeal with her family, and now with Mitch. He practically doted on her. He was her rock and she found she had grown dependent upon him. He had actually become like a best friend.

But this was the confusing part—there were times he seemed to avoid her. Did he have feelings for Siena? Was that the reason? He must have. What else could explain them leaving the pole barn together?

She was so engrossed in her thoughts; she didn't hear Sarah come up behind her. "Honey, we're all getting ready for lunch, do you want to join us?"

A little startled, Alana recovered and produced muddied hands and boots in answer. "Do I look ready?" They both laughed.

Sarah said, "Ready? No. Cute in those overalls and Wellingtons? Yes. I'm so sorry. I got busy with Megan and Lizzy and forgot to come and let you know lunch was almost ready. We can hold a plate for you if you want."

"That would be great. You go ahead and eat. I am

almost finished here anyway. I'll come in later to get it."

Sarah looked concerned, "You okay, Honey? You don't seem too perky."

"I don't want to hold you up from your lunch Sarah, I'm all right."

Sarah persisted. "Something's up. Tell you what. How about we both have lunch together later? Steve can take care of the kids. Now, why don't you tell me what's eating you? Is it Mitch?"

Alana hesitated, "Well, yes and no. It's more like—well—John, if you want to know the truth."

Sarah broke into a wide smile, and with one hand on a hip, she used the other to smack her forehead. "Duh-uh! I was wondering when you were going to open those baby blue… er… green eyes! He is *so* crazy about you!"

Alana protested. "No, you mean he's crazy about Siena."

"Really? You *are* joking, right? Oh my gosh, you're not joking! Hello! Whenever Siena comes into the room John looks like he can't make up his mind whether to run or crawl under something."

Alana was truly perplexed. "Sarah…" She stopped. She wanted to tell her about seeing them coming out of the pole barn, but knew that would be gossiping. She ended up saying, "Nope, I don't think so."

"*You* may not think so, but I *know* so! He acts like a

mouse in a python tank whenever she's around. How can you not see that? Now, don't get me wrong, Siena is a sweet woman. But she obviously cares for John in a way that John doesn't care back. Poor John. Steve and I just talked about this the other day. Alana, I don't know how you don't see this. Everyone else does."

Alana used the back of her hand to wipe away some hair that had fallen into her eyes and managed to smudge mud on her nose and chin. Sarah laughed, "Oh man, you're a sight!" They both laughed. "Seriously, it's so obvious Alana. Are you blind girl? John acts like a kid with a playground crush. The only thing he's not doing is chasing you around the swing set!"

Alana was completely stumped. "Sarah, I think you're exaggerating just a little bit here. There is no way John feels like that about me—trust me. I know—he—well—he already has a thing with Siena. I think it's been going on—in fact—I'm quite certain it's been going on for awhile now."

Exasperated, Sarah threw her hands into the air. "I don't know what to do with you! Are you serious?" She shook her head. "Okay. Let me suggest this. Tell John how you feel. If I'm wrong, you can smack me later. I know I'm right, though. And Alana? Hear me well—if you don't, *I will*! How's that?"

Alana stared at her, wanting to believe every word she said, but she still couldn't get the picture of John leaving the pole barn out of her mind. He looked positively guilty. She set her jaw, "Nope, I'm sure he and Siena are going to make some sort of an announcement any time now."

"Announcement?" Sarah asked incredulously. "Alana what are you talking about?"

"I can't really say."

"Have it your way. But I'm telling you this; you are the only one in the world that can't see John is head over heels in love with you. He's just waiting for you to make your move. He's probably a little insecure. I think he believes..." Sarah paused and her voice became softer, "I think he believes you're still in love with Mitch—or Mitch's memory, to be more exact. Or maybe he just figures your age difference is a barrier for you two. I don't know why he hasn't actually told you how he feels. I do know this—he is totally in love and I for one am sick and tired of watching him make those wounded puppy dog eyes at you. It's terrible watching the man suffer like that. Not when you could just fix it by telling him how you feel!"

Deep, very deep inside Alana believed what Sarah was saying but she fought the urge to accept it. Could it be? Could John really care for her that much? Did she just misunderstand everything she thought she had been witnessing between him and Siena? *No, that was ridiculous. I know what I saw. I know what I've seen almost daily. Well— maybe not lately—but there's no mistaking what I saw that day outside the pole barn.*

Abruptly Sarah turned and said over her shoulder, "Uh... well... gotta go. I guess there's just no convincing you."

Surprised, Alana called out, "Hey, what about lunch?" but Sarah was already quite a ways along the path.

Alana resumed her mulching with a shrug, but inside a tiny glimmer of hope began to shine.

CHAPTER 78

A few hours later, Alana went to her room to change into her workout gear. She was walking into the weight room and noticed Siena on the treadmill, with a mini satellite radio and ear buds. Siena looked up when Alana walked in.

"Oh." Siena quickly hit the stop button on the treadmill and pulled the ear buds from her ears. "Good, I was going to look for you after my workout. Now you saved me the time."

"Me?" Alana replied, concern creasing her brow. *Oh no, Sarah didn't talk to Siena about all this stuff with John did she?*

Siena stepped off the treadmill. Standing akimbo she said, "Look, John and I don't have a 'thing' going on. I sure wish we did, but fact is, we don't. John's got a 'thing' for you Alana, and that's the long and short of it."

The shock of what she said took Alana's breath away. She couldn't speak.

"Yeah, I know, I get right to the point, but a lot of people tell me that's a good thing. Good or not, it's pretty much the way I am. I hope this settles things for you." Siena examined her perfect French manicure, and in that gesture Alana realized this admission had been very difficult for her.

Suddenly, all the pent up emotions came rushing at her, making Alana's pulse race so hard she almost began to hyperventilate. It took several moments to rein them in. Blinking back tears and biting her lip she finally managed, "Siena—wow. I don't know what to say. That was such a selfless and gracious thing to do." She paused for a moment, and then said softly, "You really care for him, don't you?"

"Well, sure, I mean—he's practically perfect. But listen, a while ago he let me know in no uncertain terms that it's not me he's interested in. He's definitely all about you Alana. I guess I've had enough time to adjust to that. It's okay, Alana, really. No hard feelings. It just wasn't meant to be. I guess the Lord has other plans for my life." Siena shook her head and sighed. "I just wish the Great I Am would consider sending me some kind of outline with just a few of His future plans to make things a tad easier on the heart." She patted her chest twice and smiled ruefully.

Alana rushed toward Siena and crushed her in an

embrace. "You are so wonderful!"

"Yeah, yeah, I'm a peach. Now go find him and let him know how you feel. Someone told me that you two have been carrying the torch for each other but you've both been tiptoeing around the whole darned thing. It's about time you set things straight."

"That 'someone' wouldn't be Sarah, would it?"

"Well, I better not say, but she was tall, attractive and African American. Take it from there."

Alana threw back her head and laughed heartily. She'd have to give Sarah a great big hug too.

"I think I'll take your advice Siena." She turned to leave the weight room and with a glance back she stopped, then turned all the way back around. "Thank you is so in-adequate—but I still need to say it—thank you so much."

Siena waved her hand in a dismissive gesture, "Yeah, yeah, now get out of here. Go find lover boy." She returned the ear buds to her ears, and got back on the treadmill. After punching a few buttons, she went from a walk to a jog. She figured she'd run five miles instead of three. Maybe that would be long enough to burn off the hurt weighing on her heart.

CHAPTER 79

"Now, Master? Should we strike now?"

"How many times must I tell you she is a Protected One? Can you not see the host of Erelim Angelus surrounding her? Your efforts would be fruitless."

"Allow me to try again, my Lord. She is going to the other creature. What you so wisely anticipate might happen, *could* happen if we do not stop her! It would be disastrous! Allow me to thwart the progression of this threat, this blasphemy, my Lord!"

"FOOL!" The voice bellowed, casting fear through the subservient, who cowered groveling on the floor. "I will give the order when it is time! Do not test me! I warn you, WORM!"

"I am sorry, my Lord. Please don't punish me, my Lord. I am not worthy of your attention. Please, my Lord, I only wish to serve you. I am not worthy, I am not worthy." In his terror, the beastly fiend tried to flatten himself against the paving stones even further.

The Master appeared to settle. "I watch the female creature carefully. My eyes never rest. We will strike when the time is right and her spirit weakens. We almost had her when she traveled alone. I curse the host that saved her from the clutches of our human vessel. Her violent death would have given me such delight. When those who guard her revealed themselves, they frightened that useless creature from carrying out our mission. What a pity. Why does The Enemy love this race so? They are worthless. Did you dispose of the human after he failed us?"

"Yes, Master. He died in a fiery crash in the thing mankind calls 'truck.' There was nothing left of him, just cinders. He suffered greatly, my Lord."

"Good. We must be much more careful with our next attack. We must execute the plan perfectly to ensure we eliminate this female The Enemy wishes to protect. The human spirit always weakens. Keep whispering in her ear that she is not the male creature's choice. Cast doubts in her mind. Be persistent. She herself could be our ultimate tool IF YOU CAN DO YOUR JOB CORRECTLY!"

"Oh yes, Master! You are so wise! I will whisper. Yes! But she turns to that wretched book. I cannot go near her when she reads! But I will stand guard and watch her, my

Lord. I will watch her and whisper. I will wait for a moment of distraction and I will cast doubt in her mind."

"If whispered guidance does not work, use fear, even if it means revealing yourself to her. Keep suggesting she not read the filth The Enemy has provided these beastly creatures. The wretched BOOK He gives to the... the... paltry... these... arrrgggg! How I hate them all! We must succeed! We *must!* But all in good time."

"Yes, Master, the time must be right. Must be right. Yessssss..."

CHAPTER 80

I-75 north toward Mackinaw City was resplendent with the rich hunter green of the pines and shimmering gold and red leaves of the deciduous trees. John relaxed into his thoughts and tried to sort through how he felt and make some sense of it.

He was powerfully drawn to a woman he knew he could never have. And, despite his decision to put a physical distance between himself and Alana, he hadn't been on the road an hour when he realized he missed her. Seeing her at breakfast, working side-by-side doing some chore, or simply running into her by chance was something he seemed to live for each day. Although these encounters made him edgy, they also seemed to fuel his day. So far his plan of using a physical separation to distance her from his thoughts was backfiring badly. The opposite was true—he missed her more and more with each passing mile.

Lord, I know I don't always understand your ways. I don't understand why you'd bring Alana into my life just to allow me to suffer. But I ask you, with a broken and weary heart, to give me the strength to endure what I can't understand. If I'm to learn something from this trial, Father, please open my eyes so that I'll see it. I need your strength and your wisdom to know how to deal with this from here on in because I am tired and my spirit is empty. I ask you, Father, to please give me your perfect peace so I can be filled up with you, and live again focused on a life given in service to you. Giving you thanks and praise in the name of Christ Jesus, my Lord.

His faith was tested, but even in his unsettled and fatigued state, he trusted that somehow this was all part of God's plan. The Lord had to work a miracle in him, and the sooner the better.

John sighed and was mildly surprised that he felt a little better. He just had to keep praying that his faith and ability to cling to the Rock of his soul would remain unshaken and strong.

He used voice recognition to choose a song on his audio system. "Play *Rejoice* by Chris Tomlin." Within moments the selection was blaring through the truck. John had never been much of a singer—nonetheless he crooned along and became lighter of heart as he reflected on the words.

Lord God, there isn't anyone like you. I do rejoice because it is only you who can satisfy. Your hold on me is the only thing that matters in my life. I give you thanks and praise for every blessing you have given me and most of all I thank you for your Son, Jesus Christ, my Lord and my Redeemer. Amen

CHAPTER 81

When John pulled into the Mackinaw City Marina, he didn't expect much activity. It was late in the fall season, and even prior to current world events, this wouldn't be a busy time of year. Until the straits began to freeze, some boats would be ferrying back and forth to the island and today it seemed a little of that was still going on.

John parked and walked over to the adjoining dock with its familiar, weather-beaten slats, then straight up to the office. A few seagulls circled and squawked overhead. Bells attached to the old Dutch door alerted Jim Bostwick that someone had come into the small, nautically decorated building. A Formica counter decorated with fish netting, shells, and a replica of an old ship's wheel stood just inside the door. From waist-high to ceiling, the office's east wall held framed photos of numerous happy clients hoisting fish aloft, a haunting picture of the Mackinaw Bridge in the mist, and a distant shot of Mac Island, with an expanse of water glittering in the foreground. Behind the counter the only source of natural light was a small window badly in need of a cleaning.

John was just about to pull the chord on an ancient ship's dinner bell when Jim came through the back end of the office, a broad grin creasing his sun-grizzled face. "John Culver! Why, you sure are a sight for sore eyes!" He stuck his hand out and pumped John's heartily. "How have you been, old man? How's your Dad? And Lizzy, what's she up to?"

"Great to see you, Jim! We're all doing pretty well, actually. We're staying at Sleeping Bear now, and really trying to get ourselves self-sufficient, what with the way things are going in the world these days. Kind of in a survivalist mode. How are things with you? How's Ellen?"

"Our oldest just got married, right here on the dock a few months back. I think maybe they wouldn't have married so soon if things hadn't been the way they are." Jim absently rubbed the back of his neck under a burgundy plaid flannel shirt "I guess we're all seeing things differently now. Life is precious. So our daughter up and got married, and now Ellen's recuperating from that whole ordeal."

They spent a few more minutes catching up with each other's lives when John finally said, "Well Jim, by any chance do we have a crew that can go with me to take one of my charter boats out to Mac Island? Or am I too late in the season with such short notice? I'd need to get the boat out of storage, too, if that's possible."

"Oh, there are still plenty of guys around. Why don't you sit and have a cup of coffee while I make a few phone calls? I think we can round up a crew, get your boat in the water and have you headed out to the island in about an hour." Jim situated John at a small desk behind the counter, moving a mass of jumbled papers aside for him.

"That is, if you don't mind a little mess! Here—I've got a copy of *The Northern Express* for you right here, hot off the press as they used to say." Jim rearranged the newspaper so the front page was in its rightful place and handed it to John.

"Sounds great Jim thanks. I think I'll take you up on that cup of coffee too."

Less than two hours later, John was at the helm of his 84 foot twin engine vessel, Katie's Dream and the six-man crew was readying the boat to go out into the straits of Mackinaw. The sun reflected off the white-capped water in brilliant diamond patterns, and the chilly breeze felt invigorating. As the deck hands removed the mooring line from the dock, they threw it onto the bow where another crewmember swiftly secured it by wrapping it around a large bit in a figure eight. John slowly turned the wheel until the huge ferry was facing the open waters.

As he carefully and expertly moved the craft away from the pier and began heading toward Mackinac Island, he surveyed the incredible view of the straits. To his left was the Mackinaw Bridge. When the bridge was built in the 1950's, it was the largest suspension bridge in the world and remained so until 1998. Designed to connect the upper peninsula of Michigan to the lower part of the state, the bridge was suspended over the straits where the waters of Lake Huron and Lake Michigan meet. Enormous cargo ships and even ocean liners used the waterway through the straits to bring goods or passengers to and from their destinations. Once winter froze the straights, boat traffic would cease until the spring thaw. Mackinac Island had a small landing strip where supplies and mail would be delivered to the island inhabitants during the winter months, but tourism season ended by mid-October.

Bouncing over the rough waters with such a powerful and fast vessel was always a thrill for John. The bracing freshness of the air that carried a trace of pine was like a heady scent to him, and John physically and emotionally buoyant as Katie's Dream pounded up and down beneath his feet. While he sped past Round Island lighthouse, he thought he spotted a bald eagle just off the sandy bar that protruded from its base. He pulled the throttle back and brought the boat closer for a better view. Sure enough, the great bird was standing on the exposed tip of a submerged rock, one of many boulders scattered around the lighthouse. At first the eagle was concentrating on something in the water, but when John maneuvered the boat too close, the majestic bird spread its enormous wings and took off—its escape so graceful, it appeared to be in slow motion.

Amazing Lord. Your creation is amazing. Thank you for this glimpse of your spectacular creation. I do have so much to be thankful for. Please forgive my self-absorption and failings. I know in you I can be strong. Help me to overcome something I cannot do on my own. Please strengthen me, Lord. Help me resist my flesh and defeat my weaknesses.

John hoped that by the time he left this place, God would work a miracle in him. With every passing moment, he believed he was feeling stronger, more confident. He dared to believe this trip could restore his equilibrium and make him whole.

CHAPTER 82

The ferry pulled alongside the Mackinac Island dock. Some of the crew jumped onto the land while the rest remained topside to help John safely dock the boat. Plans had been made for John to be left on the island; the crew and ferry would return to Mackinaw City and wait for his call to be picked up.

After John thanked the ferry crew, he grabbed his duffle bag and backpack, jumped onto the dock, and headed toward the main thoroughfare. Immediately, the pungent odor of horse manure, bridle leather, hay, and other barnyard smells filled his nostrils. To some they would have been offensive, but to John, they meant he was back in one of his favorite places on earth.

The only place John loved as much as Sleeping

Bear was Mission Point resort. When he had spoken to the Wallace's earlier, John learned that the property was officially closed for the season, but they were still there finishing up winterizing the place. He was welcome to stay as long as he wished. He and Parson had always returned the courtesy, giving the Wallace's a cabin to stay in as their guests for hunting, snowmobiling and other activities that were limited on Mackinac Island during the winter months. Mackinac Island—known locally as Mac Island—is a Victorian City that decided to become a monument to a bygone era. In 1898, a city ordinance forbade the use of motorcars, and in 1923 that prohibition was made law. Other than emergency vehicles—hidden well away from the public eye—no cars exist. This was one of John's favorite things about the island. Instead of motor vehicles, horse drawn carriages and bicycles occupied the streets. As John walked along, he heard *'coming up on your left'* from several cyclists.

Built into a rocky hilltop overlooking Lake Huron, the views at Mission Point were breathtaking. Row upon row of white Adirondack chairs were strategically placed on the lawns to afford the best views, and John couldn't wait to relax in one and absorb the soul-soothing beauty.

Going through town, he passed fudge shops, cafés and other tourist establishments now closed for the season.

John finally came up the steep blacktopped driveway to the front doors of the main lodge. He gazed fondly at them. Imitation being the sincerest form of flattery,

John had incorporated some of the beautiful architectural elements of this very building in his designs at Sleeping Bear. But really, nothing could match the grandeur of the main lodge lobby, which had been built with nine-ton imperial trusses that converged at a height of thirty-six feet to resemble a sixteen-sided teepee.

John walked up to a capacious log front desk and rang the bell on its glossy veneer.

"Well, John, how wonderful it is to see you!" exclaimed Theresa as she came through swinging louvered doors to offer him a hug. "I trust your drive was a good one?" John could see Bill right behind her.

"Yes, it definitely was. But you know, good or bad, coming back here is always well worth it."

"Well, we think the same John. Great to see you!" Bill clapped him soundly on the back. "Can we get you anything, or do you just want to get yourself settled into your room?"

"If you're hungry, the café and kitchen are self-serve, you know, since the staff is gone for the season. The cupboards are still pretty well stocked, too. On the other hand, if you'd rather not cook for yourself, the Pink Pony is still open for a few weeks along with a few other favorites in town," Theresa offered helpfully.

John thanked them for their generous hospitality and said, "I think I'd like to go it alone, at least for now. I'm a little tired and probably a walk around the grounds and some rest before I get anything to eat would be good. I hope that's all right."

"The place is yours—you know that, John. You're our only guest so no one will bother you. Just let us know if you need anything. You remember where our living quarters are if we're not in the office? We still have a skeleton crew here to help us close the place up. We've just got a few things here we need to finish up and then we're through for the day. You've got our private number too, right?"

John checked to see if their number was in his phone contact list and found it. Within minutes he was pocketing a key and off to one of the rooms that had a magnificent view of the straits.

Theresa and Bill always gave him one of their best rooms. All of their suites were decorated differently, but each had a warmth and elegant simplicity. This was something John had also copied at Sleeping Bear. A plaid wool area rug in navy and hunter green hues lay at the foot of a king-sized, four-poster bed. Numerous pillows of varying sizes and shapes lay against the headboard, and a plush down comforter with matching duvet covered the bed itself. The sitting area contained an impossibly thin flat screen TV, and French doors led to a terrace with a dazzling view of the water and Mackinac Bridge.

John put down his bag and walked out onto the terrace. The view alone could soothe a battered soul. And soul soothing was something John desperately needed.

He stood there several minutes, letting the scene

quiet his mind. The day was unseasonably warm and the sun felt good. Finally, he turned to go back inside, leaving the doors open for the fresh air. He quickly unpacked, putting shirts and jeans on hangers and a few sundries in the bureau. Then, grabbing his Bible, he sat in a leather easy chair to read. After a half hour, he was surprised to find he was hungry, a sensation he hadn't felt for weeks. Just the thought of a meaty double-decker sandwich with a pile of chips and a big slice of pie for dessert had his mouth watering. He was starting to feel so good, he wondered if extending his stay at least another week would be possible. He'd have to ask the Wallace's about that later. John locked his door and headed out to the café.

After his meal, John went for a run around the grounds and read some more in his Bible. He felt energized, renewed. Yes indeed, coming to Mac Island was just what the doctor ordered, and minute-by-minute his aching and tattered heart was feeling stronger for it.

CHAPTER 83

Alana took special care in blow-drying her hair and applying her makeup. She got into her favorite low-rise jeans and a white, fitted, long-sleeved Henley paired with a navy hoody. Adjusting the neckline, she fastened the mother-of-pearl buttons leaving the top two open. She examined the look in the mirror, then with trembling fingers applied a shiny, sheer shade of pink lipstick. She had no idea what she was going to say, so she fixed her gaze on her reflection and practiced a few things out loud.

"Ah—John—I—ummm—"

She cleared her throat and tried again, sounding stronger this time. "John, I have something to tell you..." she began confidently, but quickly realized she hadn't formulated a sentence to follow. "I—ummm—you see—"

she faltered, then stared at herself in dismay.

She couldn't believe she was so jittery. Even when she interviewed for her college internship with a huge legal firm, she didn't feel as nervous as she did right now.

What if I make a fool of myself? I wonder if he really does care about me, or if Sarah and Steve just think he does. Maybe he acts that way... the way Sarah says he does, because—because why? Why would he act so unhinged around me if he wasn't attracted to me? Oh Lord, Oh Lord, God, if this is the man who is supposed to be the man you have set aside for me, help me to say and do the right things so that I may best follow Your will.

She decided a second coat of mascara was necessary and, opening her mouth to a small "o," applied it.

This was love, wasn't it? It felt strange and wonderful and new and exciting. On the one hand, what she felt for John was like what she felt for Mitch, but on the other, it was entirely different. The thrill was the same, but this felt *right*, like *coming home*. Still, she wasn't certain John felt the same about her, and that was what set her stomach all aflutter.

She looked at herself for the umpteenth time in the full-length mirror on the wall, adopting different poses before finally giving up and heading for the door. She stopped so suddenly she had to hold out both arms to balance herself. *I forgot to brush my teeth!* She ran back to the bathroom, grabbed her toothbrush and brushed, finishing off the process with a swirl of mouthwash and a fresh application of lipstick. She gave her face a final once-over, making a toothy grin and checking for pink smears on the enamel. She was ready, sort of. With a flip of her hair, she was out of the bathroom and out of her suite.

What were John's usual chores on a Monday? She racked her brain, but she was too excited to concentrate. *Think, Alana. Think!*

She decided to try the grounds first.

I'm going to tell this man I love him, and I'm not even one hundred percent sure he loves me back. But I still can't wait to do it! Am I totally insane?

He must be somewhere outside. On nice days he always tries to get the outdoor chores done first.

Almost an hour later, she'd seen just about everyone else who lived there, but not John. She went back into the lodge. *All right, plan B. Find Parson—he'll know where John is.*

She found Parson in the kitchen, stacking wood next to the fireplace. Out of breath, but trying to hide the fact, she sauntered up to him and said nonchalantly, "Hi Parson, have you seen John by any chance?"

Parson got up from his crouch and turned toward her. "Hi there!" He seemed glad to see her. "I'm afraid John's not here, Alana. He went up north."

All the air was suddenly sucked out of the room. "Wha—what? He's where?"

Brushing wood chips and dirt from his hands with

an old bandana, Parson explained, "We have a charter service up in Mackinaw City. We have boats that shuttle the tourists from Mackinaw City to Mackinac Island. John needed to check on the boats in storage since we didn't get to it last year. Why?"

"Oh—I—I—" Alana sat down hard on the couch. She tried to disguise how crestfallen she was by saying breezily, "So, when will he be back?"

"Well, he didn't say. I'm looking after Lizzy for him. I'm sure it won't be long—two, maybe three weeks?"

"Two or three weeks?" She was incapable of hiding the dismay from her voice.

Parson ambled over to the couch and sat down next to her. "Why don't you tell me what's going on, Alana?"

Alana sat quiet, completely deflated. Her exhilarating moment was over. *Maybe I'm being stupid. If he really had feelings for me, wouldn't he at least have said good-bye?*

There was no hiding her disappointment now.

"Alana?" Parson prompted again.

"Oh, nothing really. I just wanted to… talk. I had some things to say to, ah…" She started to get up to leave, but Parson laid a staying hand on her knee.

"Alana, could this have something to do with your feelings for my son?"

"My feelings?"

"Yes, your feelings for him and his feelings for you."

He paused for a beat. "Look, I may be stepping in the middle of something I shouldn't be stepping into, but I think it's about time I spoke my mind. He loves you, Alana. He left the resort because he's been agonizing over how he feels about you. He's completely convinced those feelings aren't reciprocal."

Alana's heart thrilled to what Parson was saying and her eyes beamed. Still, she proceeded cautiously, in case she had somehow misinterpreted Parson's words. "You mean—he..."

Parson interrupted thoughtfully, "I think I've known it for a much longer time than he has. Heck, we all know it. All of us, of course, with the exception of you two. Pretty silly when you think about it."

A small sob escaped Alana's mouth.

"There, there Alana. What is it? Isn't this good news?"

"But he left!" Alana was unable to make sense of what Parson was saying, and after so many recent losses, she clung to the belief that this was yet another. She set her jaw stubbornly, near tears.

"I know how much he cares for you, Alana. He took me into his confidence last Christmas. This isn't just a guess. He *told* me."

She so wanted to believe this.

"Alana, do you think you—well—do you think you care for him too, as we all suspect?"

Alana nodded, but before she could say a word, Parson continued gently,

"Might you even love him?"

She looked at Parson and no words were necessary. "Then Alana, don't you think you should tell him?"

Alana's answer was a long time in coming, but finally she managed brokenly, "I—came—here—to—to—tell him, but now he's—gone…" the word "gone" becoming a whisper of despair.

Parson smiled, "Alana, he's not gone forever. And I have a sneaking suspicion if you went up to Mackinac Island, you'd find him very receptive to this kind of news."

Alana brightened. "I could—I—I can go up there? It's not far away?"

"Nope. I won't let you go alone, though. How about we all go find John? We'll take the new solar bus we just got. What do you say?"

"Who—who would take care of Sleeping Bear? All the chores?"

Parson stood up. "Leave that to me. You just get going and pack your bags. I'll round everyone up and let them know. We'll leave first thing in the morning after breakfast if everyone agrees. Now scoot!"

At that moment, it seemed to Alana that she was in love with the whole world. She gave Parson a hug. John's would have to wait.

CHAPTER 84

Alana was beginning to think there wasn't a single part of Michigan that wasn't extraordinarily beautiful, with so many lakes, rivers and streams. Although she had already begun to feel Sleeping Bear was her home, now she was starting to feel the same way about the entire state. The farther north they drove, the more a sensational tapestry of turning leaves took her breath away. Then again, she was looking at everything through a love-induced haze, flying high and nervous as a cat. The only thing keeping her from catapulting off her seat was the seat belt.

None of the adults in the car had provided a reason for why they were all headed to Mackinac Island, so the children were pumped—excited that this trip would include boat rides and horse drawn carriages. For Alana, sometimes the three-and-a-half hour drive seemed lovely and she wanted to extend her happy anticipation, but at others, it seemed endless. Sometimes she gazed out the window in awe of the scenery, and sometimes she saw nothing at all, lost in a fretful blankness of *what ifs*. She had changed into warmer clothes and now wore jeans ironed with a crisp crease, a ribbed white turtleneck sweater, and a navy leather jacket. She knew leather wasn't the warmest option, but she wanted everything to look perfect, a decision she knew she might regret later. John had never commented on her attire. Or had he? Maybe he didn't really like jeans? Wasn't it the khakis and red polo shirt outfit he had complimented her on? Oh she was a mess! Her mind was a swirling jumble of mostly pointless chatter, but of one thing she was certain: love had filled her heart to overflowing.

When they finally arrived, Steve was at the wheel and Parson directed him to the parking lot of the marina boat launch. Parson then spoke to Jim Bostwick and arranged for the same crew that took John to the island to ferry the rest of the Sleeping Bear family over. After eagerly waiting on the dock and enjoying the beauty of the straits, they boarded the boat and headed toward Mackinac Island. Alana stood topside at the bow, both hands on the railing, the wind blowing through her hair. It actually was too cold to stand there, but she was happily oblivious. In her mind's eye she was standing with her arms outstretched, hollering, "I'm the queen of the world!" Next, she was Fanny Brice belting out "Don't Rain On My Parade." It was all very silly and wonderful and she giggled as Sarah came up to her. She leaned next to Alana's ear to be heard. Still she had to shout above the sounds of the wind and boat crashing through the rough waters. "So, Miss Alana, this is it, hmm? Going to get your man?"

Alana blushed. Sarah affectionately hugged her, "You look beautiful Alana, you're positively glowing. John's a lucky man."

"Sarah, you've been so wonderful to me. You know, if it weren't for you, I wouldn't be standing here. Do you think he'll be happy to see me? I just can't help thinking this is going to be too much..."

"Happy? Honey he'll do back flips when he sees you, especially after he hears what you have to tell him!"

Alana's smile couldn't have been broader. "I sure hope so, Sarah!"

When they arrived at the pier, Lizzy led the way as soon as they got off the ferry. She couldn't wait to show Megan and Caleb the horses. The rest grabbed their suitcases and followed after them. Lizzy, Megan and Caleb ran up to one of the carriages. Alana couldn't believe it. Right in front of her was a "Horse Taxi" that had three rows of bright red vinyl benches for passengers, like booths found in a restaurant. The driver sat up front grasping reins attached to two gorgeous Clydesdales. They all clambered aboard and soon were off toward Mission Point. Alana tried to take in every aspect of Main Street and all the magnificent homes. It was everything the brochures she grabbed on the dock promised. *Step back in time to a bygone era…*

One after the other, each home or building was a unique Victorian reproduction. She felt like she was on a movie set. In fact, while on the ferry, Parson had told them the movie "Somewhere in Time" had been filmed here, at the Island's historic Grand Hotel. She knew exactly why a wonderful love story would be shot in this place. She had never seen anything like it.

When the carriage drew near the Mission Point entrance, the driver clicked his tongue and the horses broke into a trot up the hill to the grand front doors. Even though Alana still had no idea where John was, she knew he was near and this was enough to set her heart hammering.

After everyone had disembarked with his or her luggage, Parson paid the driver, giving him a generous tip. He was an older gentleman, dressed unassumingly in denim overalls, with several layers of shirts covering a very ample belly. Alana thought he would make a great St. Nick during the holidays, with his white whiskers and shoulder-length, snow-white hair. He winked, his eyes twinkling as he pocketed his tip in a dark brown corduroy jacket.

"Well folks, I thank you very much and hope you have a pleasant stay. If you need a Taxi any time, just ask for Fred—and I'll come to get you!" He touched the brim of his brown leather cowboy hat and turned to Alana, "And may you receive everything you've prayed for, young lady!"

Alana was astonished that he seemed to know why

they were all there! He jumped up into his carriage and drove off before she could respond.

"Parson—?" She didn't get a chance to frame her question before he answered.

"Well, we wanted our driver to know we were here on a mission. I didn't reveal anything too personal, not to worry."

The Wallace's personally opened the huge double doors with a hearty greeting. Prior to making this trip, Parson had briefed them via a quick phone call why the Sleeping Bear family should be descending on them off-season. After the introductions, Theresa took Alana's arm and said in a conspiratorial whisper, "Alana, we tried to stall John, but he decided to go for a bike ride around the Island. There are a few permanent residents, but for the most part, his bike will probably be the only one out there. Take your Smartphone—and call if you get lost, but if you follow the road all the way around, you'll eventually come back to Main Street, and then if you keep going from there, you'll eventually find yourself back here. The road around the island is a complete circle, so you can't really get lost. I can show you where the bikes are if you want to try and find him. He left only about fifteen minutes ago."

Alana squeezed her hand, as she looked into kind light brown eyes, "Yes, please, if it's not too much trouble, I would like to try and find him."

Theresa said to her husband, "Bill? Take care of Alana's bags, I'm going to take her to the bike rack."

"Can do!" Bill was sporting a green down jacket and a driving cap sat nattily over salt and pepper hair. Steel gray eyes peeked out from under the brim as he gave them a knowing wink.

Theresa led Alana on a short walk and up some steps to a spacious open terrace where two rows of bike racks were available to guests of Mission Point. From this elevation, there were stunning views in all directions. "Wow, this place is amazing." Alana said in wonder.

Theresa couldn't hide the pride she felt for Mac Island or Mission Point. "Well, that's one of the things that makes it such a romantic getaway! We've actually had many weddings held here on the grounds." She brushed at the brown bangs of her short-cropped hair. "These bikes are easy. You brake with the pedals, not the handles, nothing to it! Just grab the one you want and head down the hill. Stay to the left around the first building you'll come to. Then in front of you the path splits back toward our grounds or onward to the road. Stay left again, and follow the road around the rock cliff. All you have to do is follow from there."

Alana thought Theresa reminded her a bit of her own mother, or at least, photos she'd seen of her mother. She had a kindly maternal quality about her.

Theresa suddenly became animated. "You know, I just thought of something. John always goes to the overlook when he comes here. He's been doing it for years. I'll bet you anything his bike is parked at the bottom of

Arch Rock. There's a sign that says Arch Rock. He'll be up there somewhere, I'm sure of it. He'll probably be on that bench he always sits on."

Alana hugged her, jumped on the bike and, after a little wobbly start, made her way slowly down the hill, testing her brakes and trying to yell "Thank you!" over her shoulder as she went.

CHAPTER 85

"It is time."

"It is time, Master? Now is the time?"

"That is what I said, you imbecilic slug! Remember to wait for a weakness. Watch the others and wait for a break in their ranks. Keep whispering doubts. This will fortify your position. Frighten her, as it may be all you'll need. Remember this: reveal yourself only as a last resort—and do not forget, you will not be alone."

"Oh yes, Master, I will do everything just as you command! The she-beast will be easy to frighten. I know just what I will do. Even with the host there to protect her, no matter their numbers, we will fight and we will be victorious, my Lord."

"You must be victorious," he hissed. "She is protected for a reason that has yet to be revealed. It must be vastly important for it to be held in such protected secrecy. That means she must be destroyed. *Do not fail!*"

"No, Master, I will not fail! I will return with news of a great victory!"

Then the fiendish incubus spread his massive ebony wings and flew off into the blackness.

CHAPTER 86

Alana followed Theresa's instructions, and less than half a mile down the road she saw only one bike, in the rack just as Theresa predicted. Her heart leapt in her already winded chest.

She parked her bike next to the one she assumed was John's and started ascending the stairs going up the cliff. They were quite steep, but a burst of adrenaline pushed her to the top swiftly. A wisp of hair blew in front of her eyes, and she worried if the wind was undoing her careful preparations. Glancing around, it was immediately evident why John liked to come here. What a view! She could see the water shimmering through the blue spruce that dotted the cliff's edge. The outline of Bois Blanc Island was to her left and the Mackinaw Bridge to her right, with its beautiful green latticework supporting the entire span. This was where Lake Michigan and Lake Huron met via the straits of Mackinaw, and she now fully understood why this area's beauty was legendary.

Theresa told her about a stone bench John always sat on. Alana looked but didn't see anything like it. There was, however, another path leading up to a steep incline that appeared to lead to another overlook. She decided to try it.

She powered straight up, and as she came over the crest with great anticipation, she saw the bench—but no John. A little deflated, she turned her back to the water and leaned against a low iron fence that kept pedestrians from getting too close to the edge of the overhang. From here she could see two paths: a short one that led away from the bench and another led to Arch Rock.

Just as she decided she'd try the Arch Rock path, she inexplicably felt she was not alone, and the presence was not a benign one. She pivoted her head slowly from left to right, but no one was there. Frightened, she gripped the safety railing behind her. The feeling was overwhelming. Danger. The hairs on the back of her neck prickled and goose bumps stood on her arms. Where was the danger coming from? How could she—

Suddenly before it was possible for her mind to register what was happening, she was in the air, her arms flailing, free falling backwards off the cliff.

CHAPTER 87

"Alana! Alana, can you hear me? Alana!"

Through a fog, Alana heard John's voice calling her name over and over. Coming to, she realized she was looking into John's fear-filled indigo eyes. She also realized John was holding her in his arms and she was lying on sand. How did she get here?

"Alana, what happened?" The alarm in John's voice helped in clearing her mind.

Her recall of events came back. She pushed herself up onto her elbows as John gently released her.

"I—I fell off the cliff."

"You what?"

"I... I was standing on the overlook." She pointed

upwards. "Right there, against the railing, and the next thing I know, I'm falling through the air. But that's all I remember until I heard your voice.

"But there isn't a scratch on you! You don't have any broken bones, that's—that's impossible! You must have fallen at least a hundred and twenty feet!"

"I know it's impossible, but that's what happened."

She started to get up.

"Careful Alana, I haven't checked you out."

"I think I'm okay, as strange as that sounds." She slowly stood up with John's agitated assistance and began dusting herself off. "I just had this sense of something evil present— that much I remember, and the next thing I knew, I was airborne."

John stood in front of her scratching his head. "I have no idea what on earth just happened, but I thank the Lord you're all right."

Shaken, Alana tried to adjust her clothing and do something about her hair. *I'm never going to get the sand off of me. I must look horrible...*

"Alana, what are you doing here in the first place? Are Lizzy and Pop okay? There's nothing wrong at Sleeping Bear, is there?"

Completely rattled and unable to collect her thoughts, she knew this wasn't the time to tell John why she really came.

"Everyone's fine, John. Danny, Sarah, Steve, Parson

and the kids are back at Mission Point."

Silence. The only thing she could hear were seagulls squawking, the wind through the pines, and the lake splashing against the rocks on the shore.

"Well... ah... not that it isn't nice to see you—but then why *did* you come?"

Alana couldn't look at him. Eyes cast downward she mumbled, "Well—you didn't say goodbye."

She wanted to slap her forehead with the stupidity of what just came out of her mouth. *That must have sounded infantile.* Wincing, she snuck a peak at him. For the first time since she had known him, she felt awkwardness between them.

He stood there still scratching his head, a perplexed but easy half smile on his face. He wore a white polo shirt, khakis, and a chocolate windbreaker. He looked like he had gotten a little sun. It struck her she had never seen any man look so jaw-dropping gorgeous.

"I didn't tell everyone goodbye. That's why you're here? Alana—I—I'm confused." He was holding both palms aloft, staring at her, waiting for a reasonable explanation.

Stall, stall somehow—

She looked up at the railing. "Hey—uh—the view up there is fantastic. I didn't really get to see Arch Rock. Will you show me? At least this time you'll be with me and I'm less likely to go over the edge. I still have no idea how any of that happened..." She trailed off completely befuddled.

His eyes lit with something, but she wasn't sure what it was.

"Alana, are you sure? I mean, after what just happened to you, maybe we should just go back to Mission Point."

Her heart sank. He didn't want to be around her. He felt uncomfortable.

"But—but if you feel all right, sure, I'll take you to the Arch. As long as you think you're okay."

She brightened. "I have no idea why, but I feel just fine John. While I have no clue how it happened, I do know that I'm in one piece and nothing's broken. So I'd love to go to the overlook."

His smile made her weak-kneed. How had she missed what was right in front of her all this time?

Reaching the top, Alana was surprised she had no fear of approaching where she had just fallen.

John stood, hands widely spaced on the railing, staring out over the waters. It looked as if he were trying to figure out the logistics of how she fell. He turned to her, concern etching his face.

"Really John, I'm fine!" Alana said, slightly exasperated. Chastened, he returned his gaze to the water.

She stood next to him in companionable silence and it felt natural, just as it always had.

After a few minutes, he turned toward her. "You're still feeling all right?"

She chuckled, "*Yes,* John, I'm just fine."

He took a strand of hair that was over her eyes and moved it out of the way. "I still don't know how it's possible, but you don't appear to have hit your head either." He was examining her, professionally—doing his paramedic thing—gently touching her head in various spots. It tickled in a good way. Goose bumps ran up and down her neck and arms. He was whisper close and she wanted to tell him why she had come.

He suddenly stepped back from her. "Hey, wait a minute. You're not leaving Sleeping Bear, are you? Are you going back to Kansas because of Mitch... and everything that happened? Is that why you're here?"

Alana frowned, then the corners of her lips lifted. "Uh, no—I'm not going back to Kansas—not unless you want me to. It's something I've—I've been meaning to tell you, but then I thought... I thought you and Siena were—"

"Siena? What are you talking about? What does Siena have to do with anything?"

"I don't know how to say this." Uncertainty lay like lead in her stomach as she searched his face for a sign she should go on.

"Alana. Tell me. What is it? Is something wrong? For you to come all the way out here..."

Summoning every ounce of courage she possessed, she squared her shoulders and declared, "I love you, John."

CHAPTER 88

It appeared as if John's mind went blank. Like he blew a circuit and it simply did not compute. He blinked but didn't make a sound.

Had she just made a colossal mistake?

Panic rose in her throat. He brought his face very near hers. "What did you say?" he asked quietly, while gazing at her intently.

She gulped. "I... I said *I love you.*"

"You love me?" He seemed uncertain, unwilling to believe what he'd heard. With growing confidence she clarified, "What I mean is, *I love you,* as in *you are the man of my dreams* and I'm... umm. Well, I guess I should say, I love you, John." She blushed at how inane she sounded.

"Alana, are you sure? Are you absolutely certain? This isn't a rebound after Mitch thing, is it?"

She felt a smile wash over her face. "No, John, because I didn't love Mitch the way I love you."

He didn't say a word. His deep blue eyes were striking in the late afternoon sun. For a few seconds, the only sounds were the light breeze and the ceaseless calling of the seagulls that seemed indigenous to the island. Then Alana said so softly he almost didn't hear, "John?" her face searching his.

John gripped her arms, the muscle in his cheek twitching. "I love you, Alana. I've loved you for so long, I've ached with the way I've loved you. It seems like I've loved you since the day we met. I just can't believe you feel the same way!"

He stood there, his mouth slightly agape. Then each of them tried to speak at once. "You go." Alana giggled.

"No, you go," John insisted, both of them laughing, but Alana prevailed.

His hands tightened slightly on her. "It's why I came here. My feelings were so overwhelming, I couldn't—I couldn't stand it any longer, I needed to get away."

She moved closer, stepped on her tiptoes and said, "Well, stop running away, John Culver. Those feelings are definitely mutual. I love you."

John swept her into his arms then, pulling her tightly to him. She placed her head on his chest and relaxed into his embrace. It had been so very long since she had been held—an eternity since she felt real happiness—now it almost seemed a guilty pleasure.

John pulled away from her gently. "Alana, we have to talk about this. There's our age difference. We have to be realistic."

"John, our age difference doesn't matter one bit to me. Why? Do you prefer younger women?" A teasing smile slid halfway up her cheek.

"Alana, I mean it. This is important. I'm nearly sixteen years older than you."

"Fifteen, but so what? Is it that you prefer your women to be older?"

John stifled a grin and held her at arm's length. "Alana, I'm not kidding about this."

"Neither am I! It's not an issue for me. That reminds me, speaking of older women—I thought you and Siena were... you know... together!"

He jerked his face back with an astonished frown. "What in the world made you think such a thing?"

"What made me think such a thing? Only her mooneyes and her *Oh John, you're so strong* or *John, I can't open this pickle jar, can you please come over here and help me?* Alana mimicked Siena's southern drawl and mannerisms.

John tried protesting through his laughter, "All right, all right, that's enough. Well... maybe she, well—sort of

617

liked me, I guess, but I was never comfortable with her attention."

John reached out, cupping her head with his hands, and brought his face even with hers. "I've never had eyes for anyone else since I saw you, Lana."

Alana felt a stab of remorse. "I guess I'm not being nice—I shouldn't have said that the way I did. She's actually one of the reasons I came here. She really cares for you, but was selfless enough to tell me it was a one-way street and that you were only interested in me."

"Well—I feel badly about that, I really do. She's such a sweet woman. But tell me, why in the world would you think I returned her feelings? I understand why you would have thought Siena was attracted to me. She's been... ah... well, let's just say attentive—but what made you think it was reciprocal?"

Alana flushed from her cheeks to the roots of her hair and knew it was apparent. She was doing a lot of that lately, blushing. "I saw you two come out of the pole barn right after that terrible storm. Remember that thunderstorm that knocked down one of the trees along the lake? I got caught outside that day and decided to wait it out in the boat supply shack. As soon as it let up, I was going up the path when I heard a door slam. Siena came out of the pole barn and then you followed right after her. I really thought something was going on."

"What do you mean you thought something was going on?"

"Something. Like when two people... you know—*something*. You two looked like something—well, like something happened in there."

With mock seriousness John said, "Counselor, care to define *something* for the court?"

Alana cracked up, "You know! *Something*!"

"Well that *something* was absolutely *nothing*. In fact, I made it clear that very day to Siena that you were the only woman on my mind. I felt terrible, but she had to know. I wasn't interested in anyone but you."

Alana tilted her head, reflecting on what she'd seen that day in light of what John had just told her. She finally was able to put it all together and felt a little foolish. "Oh."

"Oh." John was making fun of her.

"Well, how was I supposed to know?"

"How could you *not* know? I thought I was being so painfully obvious. I fought it for so long. I nearly went insane trying to get you off my mind. I just couldn't do it, though." Worry creased his brow. "But that still doesn't erase the fact that there are barriers between us."

Oh no, he must mean Lizzy. Maybe he thinks Lizzy won't want us to be together.

"Alana, I'm just a working stiff. I have a four-year degree, but I'm not like Daniel. I'm no scholar. You have a law degree. This could be a huge obstacle if we're to have a future together."

Alana was startled, "Law degree? Are you joking? John Joshua Culver Jr., what good does a law degree do for anyone in the world today? As far as I'm concerned, you have a PhD in survival. You taught me how to continue to exist John, and that's more important than anything I might have achieved on paper. You not only showed me a way to survive in this crazy world, but you helped strengthen my faith. You led by example. There's no end to the things you've taught me." She paused for effect, "Needless to say, I am confident you can teach me *much* more..."

John raised an eyebrow, *"Alana..."*

"What?" She asked innocently.

John slid his hands to either side of her face, his fingers grazing her temples and moving to the back of her neck as he pulled her to him. He brought his lips to hers gently, slowly exploring her lips with his. He pressed her body to his. The kiss became deeper and longer. The sheer force of his desire for her was startling, and the intensity of her response just as shocking. She began to forget they were in a public place.

She abandoned herself to his muscled arms, feeling overwhelmed and somehow fragile. His body molded itself to her as she freely succumbed to the sensations.

Without warning he pulled away, his lips still hovering close to hers when he said through labored breathing, "We have to go see Dad."

The only thought that penetrated Alana's swoon was

He's thinking about his father at a time like this?

She remained in his arms, but woozily removed her arms from around his neck. She did not want reality to intrude on this dream just yet.

"Lana—Lana..." John gently kissed her tenderly on her neck. In between his feather-light kisses, he spoke, his voice husky, "Lana, we need to first tell Lizzy, then we have to ask my father to perform the ceremony—that is, if you'll agree to marry me."

That woke her up.

"You want to marry me?"

"More than anything." A boyish grin lit his face, his blue eyes joyful, glittering in the sun.

Finding her feet quickly, she stood back a step and planted both hands on her hips, saying sternly, "Not unless you ask me properly."

John dropped to one knee with a flourish. He cupped both her hands in his and without hesitation said, "Lana, my beautiful, lovely, wonderful Lana—will you marry me?"

She squeezed his hands. "Yes, John Culver, I'll definitely marry you!"

He stood up and swept her back into his arms.

She could feel the drumbeat of his heart pounding beneath her cheek. She had been drawing on that strength all these months. He had become her earthly rock. Everything that had happened to her had led to this God-breathed moment. It was incredible. She knew if her heart broke free from her chest, it would fly over the Mackinac Bridge.

"Lana, I want you to be certain. I don't want to rush you—but if I'm going to trust myself even in the same room with you now—I—well—let's just say—I want to be married to you as soon as possible. I'm rushing you, but I'm not. If you tell me you have the slightest doubt, then we'll wait. I'll send you back with Dad until you're ready..."

She stood on tiptoe to be as close as she could to his lips. "Shhhh—Shhhh. John, I'm positive. I've never been so sure about anything in my life. You're the man God has chosen for me."

"But Mitch... it seems so soon..."

Alana paused for a few moments to think about how she would answer. Then she said with conviction, "John—Mitch was my first love, I'll admit that. But I promise, you'll be my last." She paused, tilting her head to the side quizzically.

"You called me Lana, why?"

He chuckled. "It just slipped out. I guess I've always had that pet name for you in my mind. I never felt free to use it—until now."

"I like it. Especially the way you say it." To her amazement, she blushed again, her cheeks hot despite the cool breeze.

John was staring at her so intently, it seemed he

wanted to touch her soul through her eyes. Then the boyish grin returned and he said, "I just can't believe you really love me."

"Unreservedly."

John shook his head, "I don't know how, I really don't… but I'm not going to question you anymore. And that means we need to get married. *Now!*"

Without another word, he took her hand and practically ran down the incline, taking the stairs so fast they both almost fell, laughing like giddy adolescents all the way.

When they reached the last step, they ran to their bikes. Before she could mount hers, John took her into his arms again and kissed her. Just as her lips yielded to his and her body began to melt into him, he stopped. "We have to stop this right now if we're ever going to get anywhere. First one back gets to tell Lizzy!"

As they pedaled off Alana called to John, "Oh no you don't! You're going to tell Lizzy, not me!" Then she added, "John! Do you think she'll be all right with this?"

Ahead of her, John swerved dangerously close to a ditch as he tried to look back at her. "She loves you as much as I do! She told me months ago you'd make a nice Mommy."

Alana's heart swelled. God's provision was almost too wonderful to believe! She was in love and he loved her back!

Thank you, Father, for saving me from the fall from the

cliff. I felt an evil presence and then… you must have intervened with a miracle. Now I'm riding down the road to my future wedding! You truly are the giver of life, and I thank You so much for giving me more time on earth so I can be joined with the man You reserved for me. Amen!

CHAPTER 89

Back at Mission Point Alana and John found Lizzy and immediately told her the news. She squealed with delight and whooped; "Now I get to have a Momma!" Alana took her into her arms, not even trying to hide the happy tears spilling from her eyes.

The three of them then sought out the rest of the Sleeping Bear family where their news elicited more tears of joy, hearty congratulations and warm wishes. Parson pulled out a handkerchief and blew his nose with a loud honk. John walked over to him, as they both watched Sarah and Theresa make a fuss over Alana. "Pop, you knew. How did you know? I couldn't even hope…"

"It's God, Son. Don't try to figure it out. It's just a *God-thing*, as the kids say."

"I think I've learned a valuable lesson from this Pop. I assessed the situation and made up my own mind without turning it over to the Lord. I didn't submit myself to His will in the matter. I leaned on my own understanding. I could have saved myself all those months of torment had I just been humble to the Holy Spirit. Instead I obsessed over the entire thing and almost turned it into something it was never meant to be."

"Isn't it funny how the Lord works His will for our lives *despite* our interference?"

They both laughed as John gave his father a king-sized bear hug. "Thanks, Pop. I don't think I could have stood the waiting without God using you as His hands and feet. Your love and support have meant the world to me."

"I couldn't have done anything less. I'm so happy for you, Son. What a perfect answer to prayer!"

The adults stayed up late into the night with good food and stories each told about their first awareness of the two lovebirds.

"Remember the laundry room *accident*?" Daniel piped up. "When Alana told me what happened, I knew. Then all I had to do was watch John. Sorry, Dude, but you were pitiful. If you had *I love Alana* tattooed on your forehead, you couldn't have been more obvious!" This produced a big laugh and soon everyone was vying for who had the best story.

It was quickly decided: Daniel, Steve and Caleb

would all be in the wedding party with Steve as best man. Parson would preside over the ceremony; Lizzy and Megan would be the flower girls, and Sarah the maid of honor. The girls were so excited they clutched each other's hands and jumped up and down unable to contain themselves.

Despite John's vigorous protests, the wedding would not take place immediately. Alana convinced him she had to have at least one day to prepare, and reluctantly, he conceded defeat. Thus, the ceremony was set for not the next morning, but the morning after. The first thing Alana needed to do was to find a wedding dress. Although it was late in the season and most shops were closed, the Wallace's felt confident that, with a few well-placed phone calls, they'd find a shop owner willing to open for the special occasion.

Well past midnight, the group began heading off to bed. Sarah and Steve offered to take Lizzy back to John's room so he could say goodnight to Alana alone.

Sarah warned, "Remember you two, you have all sorts of wedding preparations to get to in the morning, so make it quick!" She gave them a wink as she and Steve turned to go down the hall with Lizzy in tow.

John and Alana held hands, swinging them back and forth as they headed toward Alana's room. John spoke first when they arrived at her door. "I don't want to let you go." He tenderly stroked her hair with both hands. "Lana, I can't believe it. I still can't believe you'll be my wife."

He leaned in to kiss her forehead.

He pulled back but caressed her face tenderly with his hands. "Enough of that kissing," he said affectionately. "You're not my wife yet... and it would be very easy to get carried away, right here, right in the hallway." He playfully began ravishing her neck while Alana squirmed trying to suppress her giggling.

Finally, he was merciful and stopped the tickle torture.

He smiled at her with so much devotion in his eyes, she wondered if she could ever be truly worthy of such a love.

"In about thirty two hours, you're going to be Mrs. Culver. And you're going to make me the happiest man in the world. As downright corny as that sounds, it's true."

Alana tried to say something, but stopped herself.

"What is it Lana?" John said suddenly serious. "Is this all going too fast? I'm not rushing you, am I? Listen, if you want to put the wedding off—"

"Shhhh, John, that's not it at all."

"Then what is it?"

"John, I have zero—z-e-r-o doubts. It's not going too fast for me at all. Well—truth be told—the arrangements for the actual wedding are, but not us. The *us* part of it is long overdue." She looked down and said, "I just don't know how to ask you this because I don't want you to take it the wrong way..."

"Ask me anything you want, anything at all." John clasped both her hands against his chest as he studied her face.

She took a deep breath then said quickly, "I thought we should somehow have the song *Angels Brought Me Here* played at the wedding. The words are so true of us, John, but I also want to pay a tribute to Mitch. If not for Mitch, we wouldn't be here today talking about our wedding. He was our angel, John. He's the first person who really made me realize how I felt about you." Tears stung her eyes.

"Of course—that's a great idea. But why were you afraid to tell me?"

"I didn't want you to think I still had feelings for him. I mean—I love him, John, but not in the way I feel about you. He'll always hold a special place in my heart because of my involvement in his conversion and then his—his death. It's all intertwined somehow... I can't explain it... do—do you know what I mean?"

"Alana, I understand. I only wish I had thought of it myself."

"Do you think he's looking down on us right now?"

John pulled her close to him, cradling her head against his chest. "He just may be doing that Lana, he just may be doing that."

They stayed in each other's arms for a few quiet moments.

John finally spoke. "Let me try to find the recording

tomorrow. You already have enough to do, all right? Listen, what do you want to do for your wedding march? We're probably going to be hard pressed for an orchestra."

She drew a slow breath, "Gee, I never thought of that. What about 'It Feels Like Redemption' by Michael English? Hardly a traditional song, but let's use that for so many obvious reasons. Mitch loved it so much. Besides…" She cast her eyes down, embarrassed. "It's not easy for me to express these things out loud, but I really feel that our love—my love for you, feels like a redemption of sorts."

When Alana brought her gaze back up, John's grin was so devastating; she almost lost her train of thought. "Alana, that is just about the sweetest thing anyone has ever said to me. For the longest time I felt that my love for you was wrong. You're right—it definitely feels like a type of redemption. I was actually thinking the same thing about that song. I'm pretty sure I have that cd in the truck!"

"John, another thing. What do you think happened to me when I was standing on the overlook?"

John turned pensive. "Honestly? The only thing I can think of is that you were attacked spiritually in the physical world, and the Lord protected you. It's the only feasible explanation, as hard as that is to wrap my mind around."

Alana considered what John said. "You know, I guess that makes sense. If something like what happened to me could ever make sense at all." She settled back into his arms comfortably.

"Well, I hate to say it, but I've got to leave. I don't want to, but I'm going to."

He kissed her on the forehead. "I love you, Lana."

"I love you too, John, more than I ever thought it was possible to love anyone." She blushed and looked down.

John tipped her chin upwards, "You really are shy about saying these things, aren't you?"

"Yeah, I guess so. I've never said these things to anyone. I'm just not an outwardly affectionate person, much less one to talk about it." She forced herself to look directly into his eyes. "But I want to change all that. I never really told Bianca I loved her, I mean... she knew and I did say it now and then, but I didn't express it nearly as much as I should have. I'll regret that for the rest of my life. I don't want any regrets between us, so I'm going to make a concerted effort to be obvious about my feelings for you. It's just going to take a little time for me to get used to it, that's all."

John dramatically heaved a sigh, rubbing the stubble on his chin thoughtfully. "Well, that *is* a concern, but I'm sure we'll find *some* way to express our feelings."

She couldn't help but laugh at his theatrics. He went on. "Seriously, you quite literally are a dream come true, and I could stay here and talk to you through the night, but—it's time to let you go." He began to back away. "You're not going to change your mind on me are you?"

Alana answered, "Just as long as you don't chicken

out!"

"Not a chance. Nothing but the Lord Himself could change my mind.

She blew him a kiss goodnight and turned the knob for her door, quite sure the smile lingering on her face would remain there long after she fell asleep.

CHAPTER 90

"Well, what have you to say for yourself WORM?" The voice reverberated throughout the oppressive dankness.

"I am not finished my Lord, great Master! We were overcome in the battle that is true, but I will not rest until I have accomplished what you commanded." The broken and tattered wing of the fiendish creature lay limp and useless by his side. Ink-black leathery feathers shed copiously as the beast moved.

The Master bellowed, "What good will you be to me wounded, you useless insect?"

"It has been very difficult my Lord, but... the... the Architect has sent many of his Messengers. I can and I *will* make her fearful my Lord. I will send one of my soldiers, they will frighten her. We will cripple her with fear. Let me prove myself Master. Allow me to break her down with fear and doubt!"

"My patience is at an end. This time, *DO NOT FAIL ME!*"

CHAPTER 91

That two people in love had chosen to get married on the island was nothing new—there were many weddings held on Mackinac Island. But the story of how John and Alana had come together seemed to captivate the Island residents. The tragic loss of Alana's sister and husband, fleeing the city and meeting John along the way, falling in love and losing Mitch, and miraculously surviving the fall from a cliff to finally proclaim love was an unparalleled tale of romance and grit that made the residents cheer and wish to be a part of it. They opened their hearts and Alana was stunned by their generosity.

A bakery donated the wedding cake and floral shops in town donated the flowers. The Wallace's provided all the food for the reception. When Alana and John protested, they graciously insisted that it had been some time since there had been any cause for celebration on Mac Island in the aftermath of the hailstorms—given such a special occasion, this was the least they could do.

After John placed a phone call giving his measurements, a suit of black gabardine with a white dress shirt arrived, compliments of a merchant in Mackinaw City who delivered it himself. Not to be outdone, a local shoe store messengered a pair of Italian leather cap-toed Oxfords to match. The local Veterans of Foreign Wars chapter had gotten wind that during the wedding ceremony there would be a tribute to a fallen soldier who had claimed Michigan as his home—and they offered to provide a color guard, which John and Alana humbly accepted.

As promised, after two calls to closed shops, Theresa had reached Mrs. Hempshire, proprietor of the dress shop, Sheer Elegance; she agreed to forestall closing for another day to help out the bride-to-be. After breakfast, Alana, Sarah, Megan and Lizzy took one of the horse drawn carriages into town to pick out her dress, the taxi dropping them off in front of a beautiful Victorian cottage.

Mrs. Hempshire, a buxom middle-aged woman sporting a coif of improbable red hair, met them at the door. They all bustled in with everyone talking at once. Originally from Georgia, Mrs. Hempshire greeted them with a genteel Southern drawl and inquired if they would like some tea and cookies. Having recently finished an ample breakfast, the girls declined and looked around.

Next to storefront windows trimmed in tea-stained lace, life-sized mannequins of a man and woman dressed in Victorian wedding attire stood facing each other. Dressmaker forms adorned with flowing white or ivory wedding dresses were stationed several feet apart. Ornate silver and gold-framed full-length mirrors stood on plush Wedgewood blue carpeting. Numerous rose and pink silk flower arrangements resided on small, damask covered side tables. Other tables held hand painted oil lamps that cast a warm glow. Gilt framed landscapes covered ivory-papered walls. The sun's amber rays that generously filtered through the storefront window gave the place a shimmering sense of antiquity. "Oh! This store is just a beautiful!" Alana said in awe.

Mrs. Hempshire immediately set about assisting their search for the perfect gown. She wheeled out a rack of some preselected gowns. "Now, the dressing rooms are to the left of our viewing area, *raht ovah theyuh.*" She pointed with a plump index finger.

The first three gowns were definitely stunning. The fourth one Mrs. Hempshire pulled off the rack elicited "oohs" and "ahhs" from all the girls.

As Alana went into the dressing room to try it on, Mrs. Hempshire cooed, "Oh, *Hone-eee,* I think this is gonna be the one for *yew.* This one is called *Mon Cheri Couture.* It is a simple sheath made almost *entie-uhly* of pure cream-colored silk. It has an empire waist with a drape cowl neckline in both the front and the back. There are sheer illusion insets and little teeny, tie-nah capped sleeves that are made with chiffon and Swarovski crystal beadin.' Your train has a fowuh foot sweep, and—" Her recitation ended abruptly when Alana stepped out of the dressing room and stood in front of the triptych mirror. She stepped up onto the platform and pirouetted. Everyone gasped audibly at the transformation. The girls squealed. She looked positively angelic. Lizzy cried out, "You look just like a princess!"

Sarah's eyes were wide with wonder. "Oh Baby, John isn't going to be able to say his vows. He'll be speechless."

Megan and Lizzy nodded enthusiastically, and then everyone began talking at once. Sarah raised her voice to be heard, "Honey, what do you think?"

Alana was examining herself in the mirror, taking in different angles. "I think I love it. You're right Sarah, what else could compare? It's just gorgeous. But I'm going to try on some others just to make sure."

Alana modeled several other dresses and while each was lovely in its own way, they all eventually agreed *Mon Cheri Couture* was *the* gown.

Once the question of the wedding gown had been settled, choosing the flower girl dresses came next. Alana took Mrs. Hempshire aside.

"Mrs. Hempshire, just how much is the *couture* gown?"

"Oh, your husband—I mean, your *fiancé* called to say that I should send the bill *dah-rectly* to Mission Point and that *mone-ay* was no object. I'm sellin' you the gown at cost, dearie, don't worry."

"Oh, how sweet of you, Mrs. Hempshire, but…"

"Just call me Mindy Sue, sweetie pie."

Alana paused for a heartbeat, not certain she could say the name 'Mindy Sue' with a straight face. Then she continued, "I'm still wondering what your cost is for the wedding gown."

"Why, it's only forty-seven hundred, darlin'!"

Alana blanched. "That's c—cost?"

"Oh my, my *yesss*! It's normal retail is almost *twahs* that! Oh! Believe me, *Hone-eee, yew* are gettin' a fabulous bargain!"

Alana become visibly upset. "I… I can't buy this. It doesn't even include the bridesmaid dress or the flower girl dresses… oh dear…"

Sarah rushed to Alana's side with Lizzy and Megan hot on her heels. "What's the matter?"

"Oh Sarah! This gown is way too expensive. I didn't expect it to cost so much and John said to send the bill to him… there is no way I'd spend this much…"

Sarah tried to calm her. "Alana. Alana, don't panic. Why don't you call him? Mrs. Hempshire?"

"Mindy Sue, please!"

"Ah—right, Mindy Sue. We need to call her fiancé.

Would you mind waiting a moment, please? Alana, can you get a phone signal out here?"

They both took out their phones, but neither had a good signal.

"Just use my phone, Darlin.'" Mindy Sue handed them the landline phone. Alana called John's room and was deeply relieved when he answered.

"John! Oh, thank heavens you're there!"

"What is it, Lana, what's wrong?"

She started talking so fast she began stringing all her words together. "Oh, John, I've been trying on dresses and we found one, but it's way too expensive and I needed to know how much I should spend, but like an idiot I forgot to ask before we came here and you told me not to bring my wallet and now we've found *the* dress... well... that was until I knew how much it would cost..."

All Alana heard was the sound of John laughing. "Oh, so *that's* the big emergency?" He kept laughing.

"John this isn't funny! You don't know how much this gown is!"

"It doesn't matter, Lana. Just get what you need and let me worry about the cost. Let's just say it's a gift from Mitch."

Alana held the phone at arm's length and looked at it as if it had just turned into a turnip. She put the phone back to her ear. "What are you talking about, John Joshua

Culver?"

John's roar of laughter through the phone was loud enough for everyone at Sheer Elegance to hear. "We're not even married yet and you're scolding me with my full name? I haven't heard that since I was a little boy!"

"Johnnn! Will you be serious for a second? This is important! The dress is over four thousand dollars!"

Infuriatingly, John said simply, "And?"

"*And*? Did you hear me? That's not including the bridesmaid dress and the flowers and—"

"Lana, listen to me. Do you trust me?"

"Trust you? Of course I trust you. I'm going to marry you, aren't I?"

Sarah tried to stifle her laughter.

"Listen, Mrs. Culver-to-be. Just trust me with this. Buy whatever it is you need and have them send the bill to me here at Mission Point. If they won't accept that, I gave Sarah my credit card and if you have any trouble with that, just call me. Don't worry. I promise all will be understood when you get back and I see you. I can't wait by the way. I... I miss you already..."

Alana blushed. Again? She was blushing *again*? She lowered her voice and murmured, "I miss you too." All of a sudden she said, "Hey. No fair! You're trying to sidetrack me!" The anxiety crept back into her voice. "You're sure about this? Are you really sure? I don't want you to think

I'm being extravagant or anything—I'll pay for this when I get back, but if you can't get me to a bank, I can pay you later. But if you don't think we should buy this dress, I'd rather get a less expensive—"

"Lana, Lana, shhhhh. Just get the gown and the bridesmaids dresses and anything else you need. I'll be ready for you to stop my heart when I see you on our wedding day."

She couldn't believe it, but she flushed deeper.

Sarah and Mindy Sue tried to pretend their necks weren't craning to hear every word.

"No heart stopping, John Culver, you better have it pumping when I get back…"

They both laughed and then, as if on cue, said at the same time, "I love you," causing further giddiness and still more flushing.

Alana's face was red-hot and her pulse was racing. Just hearing his voice was making her all a-flutter. She marveled at the fierceness of her emotions for him. Reluctantly, she hung up the phone. A faint smile lingered on her face.

Everyone was staring at her.

She blurted, "He said, just go ahead!"

Instantly Mrs. Hampshire's shop was filled with the hubbub of little girls choosing dresses and matching accouterments, and picking out a dress for Sarah. Alana decided no veil. She wanted to have her hair done, and finding a salon would be the next thing on her to-do list. After they returned to Mission Point she would place some phone calls to see if a salon could accommodate her.

The horse drawn taxi dropped them off in the front of Mission Point just before dinner. Alana got her wedding gown out of the back of the carriage, and even though it was protected by a garment bag, Lizzy and Megan treated it as if it would disintegrate if it even came close to the ground. Each seriously took a corner of the bag with one hand while holding her own tissue-papered bundle in the other.

Alana was laying the gown carefully on her bed when John came and stood in the doorway of her suite. He knocked on the doorsill. Lizzy screamed and ran to him. "Daddy, Daddy! You can't see her gown before the wedding!"

John immediately covered his eyes and, with a broad smile, allowed Lizzy and Megan to lead him into the living area of the suite where he sat down. Alana closed the bedroom door and went to join him.

Sarah gathered the girls. "Let's see if we can find Daddy and Caleb, then go to the big kitchen and get ourselves something to eat. Sound good?" She tossed over her shoulder, "Are you two going to join us?"

John teased, "I don't know if I can find my way with my eyes closed."

Alana jumped on his lap and pulled his hands away.

"We'll be right there!"

Sarah and the girls left and John growled playfully, "Danger, danger! You are *way* too close! Danger! Danger!"

"You goof!" Alana kissed him quickly and wrapped her arms around his neck, giving him a long hug before she asked, "Now. Tell me about this money-is-no-object thing and what Mitch has to do with all of it."

John told her about Mitch's will, how Mitch had approached him and Parson with the details and would not be dissuaded. Alana's mouth remained open the entire time it took him to tell her the story. He concluded with, "So, you're marrying a wealthy man, Alana Engles—thanks to Mitch Abbott, that is."

"Oh my gosh, John! I never thought about the cost of running the resort. How could I have been so stupid?"

"Dad and I said everyone's room and board would be paid by his labor, and we meant it. We just didn't anticipate how much of a drain it would be on our own personal resources. Who could have known? But, God certainly provided. Anyway, that doesn't matter now, Lana. We're good to go, for now. God willing. In the meantime—we'll figure out a way to make our own electricity and our own water treatment plant or something like it just in case it becomes necessary. But that's in the distant future. I want to talk about the *near* future."

"I can't believe he did that. Actually, I can believe it. What a special, amazing and wonderful man."

650

John stared off into the distance. "That he was. I sure wish he could be here—you know—for the wedding."

"Me too."

Alana kissed him again, then said, "You *do* realize I would have married you even if you didn't have a dime, don't you?"

"I kind of hoped that was the case."

"Well, it most definitely is." She paused and lowered her head, suddenly shy.

"What, Lana?"

She remained silent, rubbing her right thumb over the knuckles of her left hand. "Lana—tell me. You know you can tell me anything." He tipped her chin up so she was forced to meet his eyes.

"John, I've... I don't know how to say this... I've never been with a man before—you know, that way. Never. I am... woefully inexperienced. I won't know... I mean, I have an idea."

John couldn't help but laugh and then quickly tried to stifle it. "Oh! I see... well! In that case, deal's off! No wedding!" He feigned getting up.

Her fists balled at her sides. "John, I'm serious." She looked up at him worriedly.

"I'm sorry, Lana." He chuckled and settled back in the chair, letting her adjust herself snugly on his lap again. He gave her a squeeze.

"Now, listen to me. Listen carefully. I think it's wonderful, incredible that I'll be your first. That's a precious gift you'll give to me. I only wish I could give you the same gift." He focused on her lips, and then gave her a long, smoldering kiss. Alana instantly responded, exquisite sensations she never knew existed made her head swim and her breath quicken.

Abruptly, he pushed her off his lap and tried to stand. Bewildered, Alana protested as she scrambled to her feet. "Hey! Is this the kind of treatment I'm to expect as your wife?"

John held her at arm's length. "Listen, Lana—it's just best we keep it—uh—platonic, let's say—until the wedding. How 'bout we get to dinner where it's safe?"

Alana loved him so much. He was so impossibly good! How could she be more in love? As they walked out of her room to head to the kitchen, she put her arms around his waist and gave him such a hard squeeze, it made him grunt.

"What are you trying to do to me here?"

"Just trying to show you how happy I am." She gazed up at him adoringly.

They walked holding hands down the winding hallway to dinner, her feet barely touching the ground.

CHAPTER 92

Mission Point had an old bell tower that hadn't been used in years, and the Wallace's decided Alana and John's wedding day would be a good day to bring it out of retirement.

Early in the morning the bells in the tower were ringing, and their reverberating peals woke Alana up. For an instant she didn't know where she was. Then her mind thrilled with the realization—*this was her wedding day*!

Alana grabbed her phone to check the time. Seven am and no time to lose! The hairdresser was scheduled to arrive at nine.

The wedding was at eleven am. She needed to get a move on!

Later, Alana was standing in front of a heavy three-sided mirror, just like the type found in department store dressing rooms. The room given her for her bridal dressing room was the size of a normal hotel room, with a full view of the Mackinac straits beyond the French doors leading to the balcony. The king-sized bed had a white cotton duvet that covered a down comforter and a whitewashed headboard. Beside the French doors was an antique vanity with a floral petit point upholstered stool. The room had little else in it and only two doors: one leading to the bathroom and the other out to the hotel.

Alana examined her reflection with a keen eye. She was holding a small bouquet of pink and white sweetheart roses with steady hands. The ceremony was only forty-five minutes away.

She had always loved roses, especially pink. The bouquet was perfect, just as she had envisioned it with tiny sprays of baby's breath interspersed throughout the velvety petals. She glanced down at her three-inch open toed heels that were dyed to match the cream color of her gown. Parted on the side, her golden hair was smooth and glossy with perfect, looping curls on the ends. The hairdresser had styled her hair exactly as she had requested.

Theresa Wallace had given her a string of pearls—something borrowed. Sarah spent the last day making a garter out of light blue fabric and lace. That took care of something blue. Something old was next.

As she was going over her mental list of things to do

prior to the ceremony, Parson came to the door and barely above a whisper said, "Alana, may I talk to you?"

"Of course, Parson, come in."

He stood there a moment, quietly appraising her. "You are lovely Alana. You must know, you are going to make John the happiest man on earth this day."

Alana turned to him as tears once again wet her eyes. "Now, now, Alana, don't go crying or you'll have me blubbering too." Parson came to her and handed her a Kleenex along with a careful hug. "I guess I knew to bring this with me when we came up here." Parson was holding a black velvet jewelry box. "I hoped all of this would happen, you and John getting together and marrying, that is. It's what I prayed for." He opened the hinged box and revealed an exquisite diamond ring. "I want you to have this. *We* want you to have this. This was my wife's ring, and her mother's before her."

Parson held a platinum ring with a sparkling three-carat, emerald cut solitaire. All four sides contained pave set princess cut diamonds, as did the border around the center stone. Round, bezel set diamonds ran up and down the shank of it, making it look like a ring befitting a monarch.

All Alana could say was, "Parson!"

"John knows I'm going to give this to you. When he went to find your wedding bands, he said he was going to buy you a matching engagement ring, but I asked him if I could give this to you myself, you know, as something 'old.'"

Alana sat down on a bench near the mirror, still unable to say anything. He tenderly urged her, "Put it on and see if it fits."

Alana slipped it on her left ring finger. "Oh, my gosh, it fits, Parson. I just don't know what to say!"

"How about—*Dad*."

This time the tears spilled down her cheeks. "Oh, Parson... Dad!"

He bent down to hug her again.

"I... I'm not a big one for crying but it seems like I've been doing a lot of that lately." She dabbed at her tears with the Kleenex and moved in front of the vanity.

"Well, I guess this is a joyous occasion for us all, Alana. It's no surprise to see us all a little misty-eyed. I want you to know God couldn't have sent me a more perfect daughter-in-law."

Alana still couldn't speak, but tried, "Oh... Parson, Dad, thank you. Thank you so much. It's the most beautiful ring I've ever seen in all my life!"

Parson bent down and kissed her on the top of her head. "Wear it with my blessings and my prayers for many more blessings ahead. Well I'd better get going, it's almost time. I'll see you in a little bit."

Parson left as Alana slipped the ring off her left hand and placed it on her right. She would put it back once John placed her wedding band on her finger. She couldn't stop staring at her hand. She was so captivated by it she didn't hear Lizzy come into the room. "Miss Alana?"

Alana's face warmed when she saw Lizzy. She had already fallen in love with the child but now that she had given her heart to John unconditionally, she loved her even more. "Yes, Sweetheart, what is it? And by the way, when will you be dropping the 'Miss'?"

Lizzy's eyes turned to saucers, "Can I call you Mommy today?"

"I'd consider it an honor."

Lizzy bounced up and down. "Oh, goodie!"

The flower girl's dress they had chosen was a sleeveless, tea length, powder pink silk with a cream colored chiffon bow that tied in the back. Her light brown curls danced as she bopped excitedly. Alana knew Lizzy felt special all dressed up and was taking her part in the ceremony seriously.

"Oh! Daddy wanted me to bring you this." Lizzy held out a small jewelry box and white envelope. Alana took it from her eager little hands with a thank you and opened the box. Inside were beautiful matching Tahitian pearl and diamond earrings. Each earring held two round, perfectly white diamonds that glittered above a single large pearl. Smaller pearls dangled from the platinum setting.

"Daddy says they're something new."

The card read, *Just the beginning. I love you with all my*

heart, J.

She couldn't believe it. Alana wasn't the least bit superstitious, but John had seen to every single detail. She had something borrowed, something blue, something old, and now, something new. Perfect.

"Come here, let me give you a hug." Alana embraced Lizzy with more than just affection. She knew she was holding her new family in her arms and it made her heart swell.

"Now, I need you to find Sarah and Megan for me. Can you do that? And then I want all of you to come back here."

Lizzy ran off with an enthusiastic "Okay!" curls bouncing spritely around her shoulders.

In fifteen minutes, she was going to be married!

The girls arrived moments later. Soon they began making their way to Mission Point's Majestic Ballroom with its balcony and wall-to-wall, floor to ceiling windows overlooking the water.

John, Daniel, Steve and Parson were already there and looking up at the balcony for their arrival. John shifted nervously from foot to foot, occasionally worrying his perfectly knotted tie. "Hold on John, she'll be here, Sarah's got this under control," Steve chuckled.

John glanced at his watch. Had it stopped? Didn't it say that a few minutes ago? He wanted to pace.

The Wallace's sat in upholstered chairs facing the balcony. What small staff remained at Mission Point had all been invited, and they now stood in the back of the room, excited to have been included. Some townspeople and members of the local press had also been invited and sat in the beautifully upholstered and wooden chairs that lined the room. Even Mrs. Hempshire was in attendance.

Steve whispered, "John, if you twist your head one more time, it's going to twist *off*."

The signal was given for the music to begin and the opening chords to "It Feels Like Redemption" filtered through the inconspicuous speaker system. John's eyes shot up toward the balcony just in time to see Lizzy and Megan appear in their pink silk dresses, with rose-entwined headbands that matched their bouquets of ivory roses. He beamed at Lizzy with fatherly pride. Steve had trouble blinking back tears. The girls parted and each went down an opposite curved white staircase that had been decorated with fresh flowers, passing through sumptuous white satin bows at the foot.

Next Sarah appeared. John was moved by the open adoration on Steve's face as he looked up at his wife. She wore an elegant sheath of pastel pink silk that fit as if tailor made. She came down the right staircase to take her place opposite the men standing in front of Parson.

Just as the music began its crescendo toward the powerful chorus, Alana appeared. When she walked slowly toward the balcony, John's first sight of her did something to him he was unprepared for. He reacted body, mind, and soul and found himself holding his breath, willing this moment to live forever.

She was magnificent.

Backlit by the sun, she stood framed in a radiant light like royalty at the railing. She was incandescent, like an angel must look. Her honeyed curls descended over her shoulders. The engagement ring glittered brilliantly on her graceful right hand, her skin alabaster perfection. When she saw John, the smile that lit her face was dazzling. He was afraid his heart would burst.

Daniel uttered, "Woooo."

Alana took the stairs carefully and elegantly, her silk gown flowing over her like ripples of water. When she reached the bottom, she sought John's eyes and from that moment on, she was all he could see. She took her place beside him. John was almost unable to tear his gaze away from her to face his father.

The vows were simple. Exchanging rings, they promised to love, honor and cherish each other for as long as they both should live.

Just prior to pronouncing them man and wife, Parson stopped and turned to address those present.

"Normally, it isn't tradition to honor a fallen hero during a wedding ceremony. It is, however, the wish of John and Alana that today we remember the life of Mitch Abbott, a special young man taken from us too soon. Although we love him and we miss him, we rest assured that today he is with the Lord, having served His Father and his country well. Today it is our privilege to pay tribute to him. Please stand for the Posting of Colors by the Mackinaw City Veterans of Foreign Wars chapter."

The sound of a snare drum rolled for a few seconds then stopped. A sergeant followed by three soldiers in full dress uniform marched in from a door in the back of the room. The soldier positioned in the middle carried the American flag; the two flanking him carried rifles. When the soldiers reached the front of the room, the sergeant commanded, "Halt!"

In unison, they turned left to face the sergeant who now stood with his back to those seated. The sergeant commanded, "Post the colors!"

The soldier with the flag did an about face and placed the flag in the stand. He then executed another about face and returned to his place with the other two.

The sergeant then commanded, "Left face, column left, march!" The soldiers then marched in perfect formation out of the room.

John was usually able to keep his emotions in check, but following the Posting of Colors, tears flowed freely down his cheeks as he took Alana's hand to resume the wedding proceedings. He could see his father was struggling as well.

Parson adjusted his glasses, cleared his throat and

continued hoarsely, "Alana and John, the spirit of Mitch is with us today and we thank God for allowing us to know him in this life, no matter how briefly. We know that Mitch believed in the love you bear for each other, and we know he bears witness—with all the others in this room—to the joining of your hearts. And so, by the powers invested in me by the state of Michigan, I now pronounce you man and wife. In the name of the Father, the Son and the Holy Spirit. What God has joined together, let no man put asunder! Amen." He paused smiling with a gleam in his eye. "Go ahead, Son. You may kiss your bride!"

John pulled Alana to him as she threw her arms around his neck. He whispered, "I love you, Mrs. Culver."

She answered, "And I you, Mr. Culver!" Then they kissed their first kiss as man and wife.

The kiss was met with a roar of approval from everyone present. Many wiped away tears amid cheers and laughter.

Parson proclaimed over the sounds of celebration, "I introduce you to Mr. and Mrs. John Culver!"

More cheers erupted and then Parson added, "Mr. and Mrs. Culver would like to invite you all to their reception which will be held right here!"

Several pre-set buffet tables waiting in the wings were rolled out, and the staff began arranging the placement of them. John and Alana remained where they were as a receiving line began to form with guests wishing to offer congratulations.

Daniel was the first. Suddenly, he dropped to his knees before Alana. He put his head down and with his arms out in front of him in a display of mock worship intoned, "We are not worthy, we are not worthy, we are not worthy of such beauty!"

"Oh get up, you wild man!" Alana laughed and helped him to his feet. As soon as he brushed his pant legs back into place he said to John, "Dude, you got yourself an awesomely gorgeous babe! I don't envy you, you'll have to beat the world off with a bat!"

"I'm well aware of my wife's beauty, Danny, well aware!" John gave Alana's hand a squeeze.

Daniel turned his attention to Alana. "Seriously, John is a lucky guy, Alana. You're not only a knockout, you're a really, really sweet lady. I couldn't be happier for the both of you." He leaned over and gave her a hug. He put his face close to her ear and said, "I think Mitch would have been real proud."

Tears welled in Alana's eyes as she said, "I hope so Danny. I so wish he could have been here."

Daniel said in a choked voice, "Me too."

Then with a toss of his fuzzy, white-man's Afro he whooped, "On with the par-tay!"

CHAPTER 93

John and Alana were standing on the balcony that had once been John's room, now their honeymoon suite. The bed was adorned with fresh rose petals of every color. He had specifically requested that they be brought to the room during the reception so they would be at their freshest. When it appeared the reception was drawing to a close, house staff had performed the last piece of magic: now dozens of candles glowed warmly around the room. John stood behind Alana with his arms wrapped around her waist, his head resting on hers dreamily. Both were staring out over the glistening moonlit water. Alana tried to burn the view into her mind. She wanted to remember every single detail of this day.

The winds had picked up; a storm threatened to the southwest. To John and Alana, it only added to the whole wonderful atmosphere.

"I'm so happy, John. I'm just so happy… it's almost a little frightening."

"I know what you mean," came John's muffled reply, his lips resting against her hair.

"I wish Bianca could have been here."

John squeezed her tighter. "I wish she could have been too. I would have liked to have met her."

"Oh John, you would have loved her. And you and Dom would have been the best of friends…" She sighed sadly. "But that wasn't God's plan. Still, despite that— I've never been so happy, John… never."

"I plan on spending the rest of my life finding ways to make *all* of your days happy, Mrs. Culver."

He paused. "You know, I spent so much time crying out to God, asking Him to stop my feelings toward you that I never took the time to just listen. I was talking to Dad about that. I kept praying for the strength to put you out of my mind, but I didn't realize that maybe the Lord had something to show me." He paused in thought, then went on. "One thing I was reminded of was that even in the silent times, God is still there. The other thing I learned is that in my false pride, I had always been able to keep my emotions and feelings under complete control—that is, until I met you. I tried everything to get that control back—but all along, the Lord just wanted me to relinquish control to Him. Ironically, my Pop saw this and he tried to tell me, but I wouldn't listen."

"I'm sorry you struggled so much John. I never realized. I, on the other hand, didn't even turn to the Lord about my feelings for you. Oh sure, I said a few quick prayers, but I didn't truly turn to Him with a submissive heart. I just went along my way and that's when jealousy over Siena crept in, and confusion, and a whole host of other things. If only I had turned to Him sooner, I would have recognized my attraction and love for you, and you wouldn't have had to go through all that you did." Alana pulled tight against John's arms wrapped around her.

They were quiet a few moments. John began to gently nuzzle her neck, sending ripples of delightful goose bumps cascading down her arms.

"Well, as Dad said, isn't it amazing how God still works things according to His plan even when we get in His way?"

Alana seemed suddenly wary of too much happiness. She turned slightly to face him. "John? I'm worried about the future—our future together. I've been wondering if God will allow us to—well—to stay together. You know, with everything that's going on in the world."

The muscles in John's arms tensed as he held her

tighter. "Lana, we'll just have to take this day by day. No matter how long we have left on this earth, we have to remember that we are in it, not of it. So we'll take whatever time the Lord allows us—and I admit—I pray we have a long, long time. I don't believe I'll ever take a single day for granted again. You have awakened a part of me I thought had died. It's a tremendous blessing from the Lord, and I plan on never taking this gift—or you—for granted."

They remained silent then, watching the storm clouds slowly overtake the moon. John rocked her slowly in his arms. "You smell decidedly scrumptious."

Alana giggled.

Thunder rumbled as a shard of lightening sliced the sky in the distance.

"How about we go inside. Looks like the weather is taking a turn for the worse—and anyway, I want to talk to you about something, Mrs. Culver."

"Oh, it's talking you want to do, hmm?" Alana pretended reluctance as John dragged her by the hand to the French doors.

"Hey, I almost forgot!" John bent down and scooped Alana up into his arms. "I didn't do the traditional threshold thing! What was I thinking?"

Alana tossed her head back and squealed with laughter as he carried her through the doors and slammed them both shut with a backward kick of his foot.

The sound of her laughter filtered outside through the closed doors.

◊ ◊ ◊

On a rocky cliff high above Mission Point, three figures stood in silhouette, robes billowing in the wind. Their blood red eyes pierced the darkness.

END

The Watchers Book II coming soon...

GIVING THANKS

By God's grace, this story came to print but He also provided His vessels to assist along the way. Don Furr for taking on this project. Thank you for your help, patience and wisdom.

Allison Reker, thank you for such an insightful and detailed edit as well as your encouragement.

Sooz—what can I say? I am eternally grateful for the polish and panache dear friend that brought this story to life.

Trace – together we will take over the world. And when I grow up I want to be a smarty pants just like you.

For the Sister of my Heart – you are so adept at encouraging me to fix my eyes. Your prayers and constant support has been a lifeline. Bushels.

To all my grown children and their amazing spouses: You make me so proud. My love for you knows no bounds.

H.B. you will always be the greatest love of my life.

Jesus, you *are* my life.

www.ingramcontent.com/pod-product-compliance
Lightning Source LLC
Chambersburg PA
CBHW051926020726
47501CB00001B/5